Send Me Safe My Somebody

Send Me Safe My Somebody

Geri Bennett

iUniverse, Inc.
Bloomington

Send Me Safe My Somebody

iUniverse books may be ordered through booksellers or by contacting:

iUniverse
1663 Liberty Drive
Bloomington, IN 47403
www.iuniverse.com
1-800-Authors (1-800-288-4677)

ISBN: 978-1-4620-0077-7 (pbk)
ISBN: 978-1-4620-0078-4 (ebk)

Printed in the United States of America

iUniverse rev. date: 4/6/2011

For Mac and Mickie

"Frae ilka danger keep him free
And send me safe my Somebody"
Robert Burns

CHAPTER ONE

Paul Winslow frowned as he looked at the instrument panel in the A6 Intruder. The uneasy feeling he'd had since he climbed into the cockpit stayed with him. He and his bombardier/navigator, Don Jenkins, had launched only minutes before from an aircraft carrier off the coast of Vietnam on what was to be Paul's last flight before rotating home the following week. It was a night flight and they were alone in the sky, carrying eighteen five-hundred-pound bombs to be dropped on the bridge at Tranh Hoa.

A major highway and rail supply route for the North Vietnamese, the bridge had been a target of Rolling Thunder attacks for more than a year. American military legend said that the bridge provided a hinge, located beneath the ocean, that held the two hemispheres together. It had defied attempts to destroy it and the story claimed that if it were to fall, the world would fly apart. Paul Winslow had every intention of testing the theory by putting an end to the bridge, but he wasn't about to take any unnecessary chances. The increasingly more sophisticated radar of the North Vietnamese was making it difficult to sneak into their territory, but the A6 Intruder could fly low and alone through the darkness.

Paul ran a hand through his honey-colored hair, silently thanking God for his good fortune. Personal thoughts rarely intruded upon his concentration during a flight, as the plane became a world separate from all others once he climbed into the cockpit. It was a transition to another place in the universe and became the focus of his existence. In the early days of his training, he had found it hard to explain this apparent phenomenon and wondered if it was a quirk in his psyche. On the ground, he was a competent Navy officer, checking flight plans, fraternizing with friends, sometimes happy, sometimes not, but always part of the human community. In the air, the hum of the engine became the heartbeat in a womb, the instrument panel the breath that flowed through his body, the sky his pillow.

He had kept these feelings to himself until one night when he and his flight school buddy, Jack Schaefer, had been out on the town in San Diego, their first assignment following graduation. Jack was a Marine pilot, attached then to Miramar Naval Air Station, and Paul, a Navy pilot, was based at Coronado. A comparison of the Phantom jet used by Marines and the A6 Intruder of the Navy had developed into a discussion on the glory of flight, with each man confessing to the same feeling of detachment from the world as he soared high above the ground. In the months that followed, they discovered that it was not uncommon among pilots and accepted it as the norm.

Though Paul's missions had been uneventful for the most part, a few close calls and the never-to-be-forgotten sight of a wingman going down, Jack's luck had run out just weeks after his arrival at DaNang. He had been flying the Phantom on a mission aimed at Vinh, north of the demilitarized zone, when he was downed by 57mm anti-aircraft fire. Intelligence had reported a possible Surface to Air Missile installation in the area and Jack's squadron had gone up to check it out and destroy it if possible. Early in the war, dummy SAM batteries had been set up, then surrounded with camouflaged anti-aircraft guns waiting for a U.S. attack. Though the installation turned out to be a bonafide SAM site, it had not been operating that day. The guns were manned, however, and managed to get two of the Phantoms down.

Photographs had surfaced within a few weeks showing Jack, his head bandaged, as the object of derision in a Vietnamese village. At least he's alive, Paul thought. Or is he? That had been nearly a year ago with no further word regarding his whereabouts.

Now as he soared through the dark and lonely sky, Paul was unable to suppress thoughts of his impending leave, and of going home. He planned to spend a few days with his parents on the San Francisco peninsula before a ski trip to Europe. He was looking forward to sailing down the slopes of Switzerland – no more hot, humid jungles, just nice clean white snow, the cold wind in his face, and a hot buttered rum at the end of the run.

After a week on the slopes, he was going to look up his college buddy, John St. James, in Paris. John's father was an American sent to Paris by his business firm just before the outbreak of World War II. He had married a French girl and had been unable to escape with his pregnant wife as the German army approached. They had intended to move to the states after the war, but one year stretched into another as they became more and more involved in the operation of the small hotel owned by Monique's family. Before they knew it, one hotel had become three, John's father had left the American firm to assume more responsibility, and twenty years had passed. John, by that time of college age, was eager to attend an American school. He and Paul met in an American History class at Northwestern University and hit it off immediately. In fact, Paul had discovered that John knew more about American history than he did. As he flew this last mission over Vietnam, Paul wondered how John was doing as the head of the growing group of hotels he had inherited. It would be good to renew their friendship over some vintage French wine, he thought and smiled.

"Home," he murmured softly, "what a wonderful word."

"Did you say something, Skipper?" Don's voice came from the seat beside him, interrupting his brief daydreams.

"No, nothing, Don, just muttering to myself," he replied, his attention returning to the present. He gazed down at the terrain below.

Using radar echoes to pick out landmarks and avoid dangerous ridges, they were soon coming up on their target. Light from the moon combined with ground haze created a milky effect that made it difficult to distinguish between earth and sky. Just short of the bridge, Paul sighted the trail of burning propellant that indicated a surface-to-air missile heading toward them. Calling to Don to fire a flare to attract the heat-seeking missile, he checked his gyro and banked in a ten degree, left wingdown attitude. The flare also had the effect of lighting up the gun battery just ahead. They dropped half their load and headed for higher altitude, coming around again for one more pass and the chance to unload the rest of the bombs.

The plane shuddered briefly and began to lose altitude. Don screamed, "Jesus H. Christ! Look at the wing!" Paul turned his head to see the right wing riddled with holes, flames curling from beneath it.

"Heading out to the gulf," he announced tersely. "When I yell, count ten and eject!"

Their best chance of rescue lay in ejecting over the water. If they could get out of the parachutes and stay afloat long enough, the choppers might get to them before the locals did. "We'll never make it," Don shouted.

Seeing that Don was right, Paul called out, "Now!" He heard the hatch open and felt a rush of air as the earth came up to meet them.

He opened his eyes slowly, unable to recall where he was. "Ummm, what time is it?" he asked. Hearing no reply, he looked around at the lush greenery surrounding him and wondered why he was out of doors. A face peered down at him and a voice penetrated his consciousness with words he could not comprehend. As he struggled to clear his vision, the image began to come into focus. It was an Asian face, a man. Wrinkling his brow in concentration, Paul squeezed his eyes shut, then opened them again.

"Oh, shit," he said aloud, remembering. The man must be Vietnamese. Slowly flexing the fingers of each hand, he found them moveable and began to probe his upper body, searching for wounds. Discovering that his arms and upper torso seemed to be intact, he attempted to sit up. It was painful, but mostly bruises, he thought. The Vietnamese man nodded vehemently and supported Paul with one arm as he raised up on one elbow. Paul concentrated on his toes, wiggling those on his right foot gently and finding that they seemed mobile. Urged on by the man, he began to move those on his left foot. His effort resulted in a wave of pain. Nausea overwhelmed him as the shinbone of his left leg penetrated the skin before his eyes, and he sank into oblivion.

A cool dampness aroused him later as the long, dark hair of a woman fell into his face. Again, he struggled to open his eyes. Voices that were too high pitched to be men sounded as if they were coming through a tunnel. In a limited survey, he became aware of two women and a young girl in the room with him. Keeping his eyes mere slits, he expanded his examination of his surroundings and noted that the room was small, with a thatched roof overhead.

"Hello," he ventured quietly. The voices ceased, then began again more agitated than before. He tried again to sit up, gleaning a small measure of relief in the discovery that his leg was now in a makeshift splint. Apparently he was not in a Vietnamese prison camp, but a villager's hut. The owner of the long dark hair wiped his brow gently with a damp cloth and pushed him back down. Closing his eyes gratefully, he drifted into a more peaceful sleep.

He felt a curious sense of well being when he awoke for the third time. Lying still, he kept his eyes closed for several minutes to prolong the feeling. Finally, he opened one eye just far enough to see that he seemed to be alone. He sighed quietly and opened both eyes, realizing that he was lying on a platform about six inches off the dirt floor of the hut. Turning his head, he confirmed that he was indeed alone. He considered the situation.

"It would seem that I've been rescued by villagers," he said aloud. Startled by the sound of his own voice, he said silently to himself, "I wonder if by some miracle they're friendlies, or if they're just waiting for the soldiers to cart me off." Thoughts of escaping crossed his mind, but he determined quickly that his leg would not allow him to get beyond the pallet. Looking around the dimly lit room for some sign of Don, he saw none and wondered if he should call out. "Don?" he whispered once, then repeated a bit louder. There was no reply and he drifted off again, waking abruptly some time later as he found himself being transferred roughly to a stretcher by two North Vietnamese regulars.

One of the soldiers noticed that his eyes were open and held up a tattered piece of paper with a paragraph written on it in English. Paul strained to see what it said and found that it informed him that he was a captive of the North Vietnamese Army, and that any attempt to escape would cost him his life. Two more soldiers waited outside the hut, each taking a corner of the crudely made bamboo stretcher as they set off down a narrow trail.

A short time later they reached a highway where they dropped the stretcher in the sun and retreated a short distance to the shade beside the road. The soldiers settled against the trees, their guns cradled in their laps. One of the men leaned forward to draw a circle in the dry ground with the tip of the bayonet on his gun. Two of the others gathered small stones from the area around them, and the three men began to pitch the stones into the circle as the fourth man dozed.

After what seemed like hours to Paul, but was probably only thirty or forty minutes, a convoy of trucks appeared in the distance. The four men rose lazily and signaled to the lead truck to stop. Picking up the stretcher, they heaved it onto the rear of one of the trucks and climbed up. Paul cried out as he was unceremoniously dumped from the stretcher and pulled to a sitting position. The men laughed as they strapped him tightly to a fuel drum. Blood began to seep from the bindings around his leg as the convoy set off again, moving slowly in the darkening gloom.

Exhausted and hungry, he was nevertheless too uncomfortable to sleep, though his chin fell to his chest. There was no chance of rescue, he thought miserably. The bridge at Tranh Hoa was only seventy miles from Hanoi, and he had not been able to get very far south after they were hit. He calculated that the convoy was possibly on its way to Hanoi, though at the speed it was traveling, it would take several hours, if not all night. The drone of planes in the distance made him lift his eyes toward the sky as the trucks headed for the side of the road and switched off their headlights. Abandoning their positions, the soldiers jumped to the ground and moved quickly to the shelter of trees along the road, leaving Paul bound to the fuel drum.

He strained against the ropes in an effort to twist his head toward the sound of what he was sure must be friendly aircraft. "Give 'em hell," he mumbled, fervently wishing he could send up flares to mark the position of the convoy. "These bastards would just as soon be rid of me anyway," he muttered.

Four planes passed overhead, two of them breaking away to swoop down toward the convoy. Paul heard rather than saw the explosion at the head of the column of trucks, followed almost immediately by another explosion very nearby. Moving painfully as far to his right as he was able, he realized that the truck behind the one in which he was trapped was in flames. A gust of wind whipped pieces of burning metal toward the soldiers, catching one of them off guard. His cry became a scream of agony as his clothes turned him into a massive fireball.

"Right on!" Paul shouted, or at least he thought he shouted. No one seemed to hear him. There was a flurry of activity as the North Vietnamese soldiers scurried to the aid of injured comrades and tried to beat out the fires. A middle-aged officer, his face blackened with soot, lifted another man onto the truck beside Paul. His eyes widened at the sight of the American pilot. Rage swept through the man's body and he pulled a handgun from the holster on his hip, pointing it at Paul's head.

Their eyes met as mutual hatred bonded them together for a brief moment. In the instant that Paul knew would be his last, another soldier screamed at the officer, diverting his attention. He jumped from the truck, leaving the injured man lying beside Paul. Looking down, Paul was sickened at the sight of a gaping hole in the man's stomach, blood and tissue oozing out. Repulsed, his head jerked involuntarily to the side. Avoiding the man's body, Paul gazed into the face and was unable to stifle a gasp of horror. It was not a man at all, but a boy of no more that twelve or fourteen years. In that second, Paul understood the rage of the officer.

Eventually, the convoy moved on through the now dark night. The occasional moans of the injured blended with the sputtering of the engines as the trucks changed gears, and Paul slept in spite of himself. Waking as dawn began to creep over the horizon, he was certain from the stench that the boy beside him was dead. A guard appeared and heaved himself into the barely moving truck. Taking a filthy scarf from around his neck, he twisted it into a makeshift blindfold and pulled Paul's head forward roughly, covering his eyes. Sounds of a city coming to life filtered into the truck and a short time later they rolled to a stop and the engines were cut off.

The blindfold slid down allowing Paul to get his first glimpse of the yellow building with green shutters that was the old French prison known to the Americans as the Hanoi Hilton. Several soldiers approached the truck in which he was restrained with the young Vietnamese boy. Seeing that the boy no longer lived, their faces contorted in anger and they raised the rifles they carried, menacing the American flyer they held responsible for the death of a child. Two of the men clambered up to release the bond that pinned him to the fuel drum, shoving him with their boots to the edge where the others pulled him to the ground. Once again, Paul was sure that his life was about to end. He looked at the boy who now lay beside him, and a tear slipped unbidden down his cheek as a feeling of overwhelming sorrow for the boy, for himself, and for the world swept through him. This should not be happening, he thought.

Just then, a short, neatly dressed officer appeared in the entrance to the prison and barked an order to the men. The moment passed and Paul found himself in a sparsely furnished room, alone with the officer. Following a few questions, asked in English, the man realized that Paul would be incapable of answering until the delirium of fatigue and hunger had passed. In disgust, he ordered his prisoner taken to a cell where he was left on a cement floor with a bowl of watery soup.

Inching painfully to the bowl, Paul grasped it and held it to his lips, swallowing as quickly as possible, spilling some of it down the front of his flight suit, now filthy and crusted with blood. He laid back to examine the cell and found that it was barely wider than the wooden platform supported by heavy saw horses that served as a bunk. Stocks lay across one end of the bunk and a tiny window near the ceiling allowed the only light to filter in. A heavy wooden door prevented his exit.

For the first time, he realized that all of his personal belongings were missing – the watch he'd worn for many years was gone from his wrist and the pockets of his flight suit had been emptied. He pulled himself up onto the pallet, his bloody left leg now numb. Lying back against the cement wall, he let exhaustion sweep over him, almost wishing for death to relieve his suffering.

The dream began as he felt himself floating toward the ceiling. Looking down, he was astonished to see his body still slumped on the bunk, eyes closed. A soft, pale pink cloud enveloped him, carrying him beyond the confinement of the cell. How peaceful, how comforting it was. He tumbled gently among the pillow-like clouds and wondered, is this what death is like?

A light appeared in the distance, beckoning him. A feeling of ambivalence possessed him – it was so pleasant to bounce softly among the clouds and yet curiosity compelled him toward the light. Far away, somewhere in the light, he began to discern the outline of a woman's body. Though her face was blurred, he could see that she had smoky dark hair that fell to her shoulders in a tangle of curls. He had the feeling he knew her, but he was unable to remember her name. Her arm was extended, her hand reaching out to him, but he couldn't seem to get close enough to grasp it. Her image faded as an unseen force drew him back into the clouds. The light disappeared and he felt himself falling.

He awoke, startled, in the darkness of his cell at the Hanoi Hilton.

CHAPTER TWO

Daylight was fading in Sarah Fremont's living room as the sun slipped below the horizon, but she hardly noticed. She sat staring at the photograph in the newspaper. The face that gazed back at her from the page belonged to someone she knew was very dear, almost a part of her, but the name in the caption beneath the picture was as unfamiliar now as it had been from the start. Who was he? Though the photo was in black and white, she knew instinctively that his eyes were blue – deep, liquid blue. His jaw was finely defined, his mouth thin, but pliant and sensitive. It was a face that reflected the depths of his soul – at least it did to her.

She had no idea how old the picture might be, possibly several years, but the article that accompanied it said his name was Paul Winslow and that not only was he missing in action in Vietnam, his plane had been shot down more than a year earlier. The story went on to tell of his family, a mother and father, who lived nearby.

She read the article through again, and then another time. The ache in her chest increased with each paragraph until the pain was nearly unbearable. Putting the paper aside, she sat back and closed her eyes. Why this feeling of déjà vu, this absolute conviction that Paul Winslow was an important part of her life, perhaps more important than anyone had ever been? Her rational mind was saying 'don't be a fool, he's someone in trouble and you feel sorry for him, that's all.'

But her gut was screaming at her, telling her she must do something because if she didn't she would lose a precious part of herself. Her hand crept toward the photo, her fingers reaching out to trace the outlines of his face, to brush back the lock of hair that had sneaked out from beneath the helmet that covered his head. The lock stayed right where it was, however, and once again Sarah's rational side scoffed at the emotional chaos she was allowing herself to create. Her fingers closed around the edge of the folded newspaper. She picked it up and held it close, embracing the man whose face was so inexplicably precious. Her eyes closed and she felt the warmth of his arms as they enfolded her.

"No!" she exclaimed aloud. A rush of heat flooded her body, scorching her fingertips. Dropping the paper, she ran to the kitchen, turned on the cold water tap and plunged her hands under the water.

"Holy shit!" she cried, "This is insane!" She felt utterly ridiculous.

She switched on the kitchen light, then hurried through the rest of the apartment turning on lamps, breathing a sigh of relief as the evening shadows fled. Back in the kitchen, she reached into the cupboard that served as a liquor cabinet, pulled out a bottle of scotch and poured a hefty drink, berating herself for such puerile behavior. The ice cubes clinked hospitably as she paced.

She was, after all, a well educated, successful woman – certainly not one who was subject to fantasies of the mind. Unmarried and unencumbered by mortgage payments or children, she could afford to live in a luxury apartment complex that catered to an upwardly mobile clientele, and to furnish her home in what she thought of as an elegant, but comfortable style. She had a closet full of clothes – dark dresses and suits considered appropriate for her professional life, and the soft sweaters and tweedy skirts she preferred for leisure.

Though some of her Italian ancestors would no doubt consider her an old maid at the age of twenty-seven, her job as Convention Coordinator at one of the best hotels on the San Francisco peninsula was challenging and never dull. The varied lifestyles of the people she encountered each day kept her stimulated as well as busy. It might be conservative bankers who shuddered at the term 'creative financing,' or it might be big game hunters whose idea of a fine day included sweating profusely in an African jungle.

Sarah had never thought of herself as being beautiful in the traditional sense of the word. She knew she was attractive and had been told often that she was sensuous or sexy, mostly by men who wanted to get her into bed. Women sometimes exhibited a certain hostility toward her, threatened by a successful, single female, but Sarah knew that if she were safely married that kind of antagonism would probably fade. The trouble was, she just couldn't get enthusiastic about the idea of being tied down to one person for the rest of her life.

Returning to the photo of Paul Winslow that lay on the floor beside the sofa, the thought struck her that this man was the one with whom she would never be earthbound, never tied down to the ordinary. With him she would soar through realms she had yet to know even in dreams.

She had to know more about him. His parents...the article said they lived nearby. Pulling the phone book from a drawer, she turned the pages quickly to the W's where she found the name: Winslow, Col. Peter H.

"What on earth will I say?" she asked herself. "Hi there, you don't know me and I've never met your son, but I'm sure I know him? They'd think I was some sort of lunatic and hang up!"

There seemed no alternative, however, so she dialed the number. A gentle voice answered after the second ring.

"Mrs. Winslow? My name is Sarah Fremont and I've just read the article in the Times about your son. I wondered if there was anything I could do to help?" There, that wasn't so hard after all.

The gentle voice expressed her appreciation and went on to tell Sarah about the newly formed organization of family members of servicemen listed as prisoners or missing in Vietnam. It came as a shock to Sarah to learn that there were several hundred men on the lists and that the families had been urged by the government to keep quiet. Fed up with the lack of information about their loved ones, some of them had decided to publicize their plight in an effort to secure the release of those who might be sick or injured, despite government attitude. They'd had little idea how to go about doing it though, and providing information to the press on a local level had seemed a good way to begin.

"I know that U.S. participation in the war has escalated and that opposition to it is growing every day, but I had no idea that there were so many men captured or missing," Sarah admitted. "I just had to call you," she finished lamely. Mrs. Winslow invited her to come over for coffee the following afternoon and gave her directions to her home.

Sarah replaced the receiver and leaned against the kitchen counter. What am I doing, she wondered.

She moved slowly back into the living room, standing in the middle of the room, lost in a part of the world she did not understand. Without thinking, she went to the stereo and reached randomly for an album. Sliding the record onto the turntable, she curled up on the sofa and listened as the mellow tones of a song called 'My Foolish Heart' filled the room.

A place called Vietnam. So far away, so alien. How could an American, someone from her own community, have been flying a plane that someone who didn't even know him wanted to shoot down? And he was only one of many. But he was the only one who belonged with her, the one whose face filled her with longing, the one who should be here now, and not lost somewhere on the other side of the earth. He seemed to be watching her, beseeching her to find him. It would be so pleasant to just dream about him. After all, who would know?

A male voice - was it Perry Como? – was singing about the night being like a lovely tune and warning her foolish heart to beware. Sarah began to hum along with the music as the song cautioned against the folly of fascination, then ended with the claim that this time it wasn't fascination, this time it was love, my foolish heart.

The orchestra swelled in the finale and a happy little chill tickled her spine.

She dressed carefully the following day, fussing over her hair and at the same time repeating over and over to herself that this was ridiculous – you'd think she was meeting a lover's mother for the first time. Yet she couldn't shake her anxiety. As she parked in front of the Winslow home, she straightened her shoulders and took a deep breath, trembling with anticipation. The woman who answered the door had the same liquid eyes as those in the photo of her son. She was small, blonde and immaculately groomed. Her smile was as soft as her eyes and her voice, and Sarah was drawn to her immediately.

They went into a room that was warm and inviting, decorated in shades of blue with a Mediterranean flavor. In the next hour, Sarah learned that the family had lived in many parts of the world, but was especially fond of the south of France. In his career as an Army officer, Paul's father had been transferred more times than Merrie Winslow could remember.

"Would you like to see the den?" Merrie asked. "That's where I've put all the things that were sent back to us by the Navy after Paul was reported missing," she explained.

Sarah's heart was in her mouth as she entered the room that held the personal belongings of the man to whom she was so drawn. There were filmy curtains covering the windows and a huge tree just outside created mysterious shadows that fluttered on the walls and carpet as its branches swayed. As though someone were out there trying to get in, she thought. Sure that Merrie would notice her ragged breathing, she inhaled deeply, letting the air out slowly through her mouth.

The room was suddenly illuminated as Merrie switched on a three-way lamp that sat on a leather-topped desk. The treasures that Paul had collected came to life. Some exotic musical instruments, a bronze horse. His mother began to point out photographs of Paul with his friends.

"This one has always been my favorite," she said. "Paul was so proud of that car. The boy with him is John St. James, his best friend at Northwestern University."

Sarah took the framed photo that Merrie held out to her. The two young men were standing beside a two-tone brown fifty-seven Chevy, Paul about to get into the car on the driver's side and John looking over the top from the passenger side. Paul's posture was casual and unstudied, his tawny hair slightly ruffled by the wind, his eyelids lowered just a little, giving him the appearance of a honey-colored jungle cat. Wishing she dared ask for a copy of the photo, Sarah examined it for a few moments, then put it back on the table reluctantly. She hardly heard Merrie's explanations of the rest of the room as her eyes were drawn again and again to the picture of the man she wanted so desperately.

Merrie's attention was diverted suddenly by sounds that came from the garage. Pete Winslow came through the door into the kitchen accompanied by two energetic hounds, home from a day of duck hunting. Surprised to find a stranger with his wife, he was somewhat reticent as he clattered around, hanging up his plaid jacket, then feeding the exuberant dogs. Once the dogs had been safely confined in the garage, he adjusted his wire rimmed glasses and approached the two women hesitantly, asking if they'd like to join him in a martini, smiling shyly as Sarah agreed.

He warmed appreciably when she expressed her pleasure at the taste of the vodka martini he presented - his specialty - and the three of them sipped companionably as the sun sank and shadows lengthened. In the course of conversation, Sarah came to a better understanding of the conflict in Vietnam. She gave voice to her surprise that the American government had urged the families of missing servicemen to keep quiet, ostensibly in the interests of national security.

"Why is it such a secret?" she asked.

"Probably because they don't want the public to know just how involved we obviously are," Pete answered. "The demonstrations in this country are increasing every day and I guess they don't want it noised about just how many Americans are being killed or captured over there. As a retired military officer myself, I don't feel that I can speak out publicly, but I agree with Merrie and the others who are frustrated by the lack of information we've been given. It seems that nearly everything is classified, right down to whether the men are in fact prisoners, or missing, or known dead."

Merrie's face crumpled a bit at the word 'dead,' and Sarah asked, "What can I do to help?"

"Well, we're not sure what direction to take," Merrie said thoughtfully, "but any kind of awareness we can bring about would be a start. There's a woman down in Sunnyvale who is starting a local group of family members and concerned citizens, sort of an arm of the one that began in San Diego not too long ago. Would you like to meet her and help us get it going?"

Assuring the Winslows that she'd be happy to help in any way she could, Sarah left. It was so easy to be with them. It wasn't until she turned into her driveway that she realized she had told them very little about herself. She sat in the car for several minutes, musing at how they had seemed to believe in her sincerity without questioning her motives. It was not only easy to be with them, it was easy to feel a strong commitment as well. Where was this leading her, she wondered.

The only child of prominent financier William Alexander Fremont, Sarah had enjoyed comfort and security as she grew up. That had ended when she was a senior in high school. Bill and Suzanne Fremont had been traveling in a small plane on their way to another of many important meetings, when the plane crashed in a storm, killing them both. Bill's sister, Charlotte, who lived an Auntie Mame existence in New York, had assumed responsibility for Sarah's well being until her graduation from college, but now that they resided on opposite coasts, they rarely saw each other and kept in touch with occasional phone calls. Sarah's grandparents on both sides were deceased and what little family was left on her mother's side had either gone back to or never left Italy.

The story of how her parents met was one of Sarah's favorite memories. Bill Fremont had been with a group of friends at a Chicago speakeasy during Prohibition when he noticed a shy and obviously frightened girl at the next table. Charmed by her innocence, he was determined to meet her, and eventually succeeded in convincing her to dance. The youngest of a very traditional Italian family that would rather see her dead than in jail, Suzanne Vincennes had been terrified of a raid. Bill had seen her home in a taxi and married her a few months later.

Sarah got her dark, tousled look from her mother's side of the family and her green eyes from the Fremont side.

With a sigh, she got out of the car and unlocked the back door to her apartment. Reluctant to let go of the mood, the comradery, and the sense of belonging with these people, she fixed herself a vodka martini. A quick search of the refrigerator failed to yield any lemons, however, so hers lacked the zest of Pete's specialty. Carrying the drink into the living room, she absentmindedly switched on the stereo without changing the record that was still on the turntable.

"The night is like a lovely tune,

Beware, my foolish heart..."

Were the words prophetic? Was it fascination, a dream that would fade and fall apart? Or was Paul Winslow someone that she knew on some higher plane of consciousness, one that superseded reality? If she tried very hard, could she communicate with him somehow? Could he be trying to communicate with her?

Leaving the record to finish and turn off automatically, she went down the hall to her bedroom. She turned on the water to fill the bathtub, undressed slowly and slipped into the tub to soak luxuriously as she dreamed.

She began to float amid fleecy pink clouds that carried her weight even though they had no substance when her fingers touched them. A figure appeared, coming toward her through the puffy clouds and a hand reached out to her. She knew that it was Paul Winslow and drifted into his arms. Words were unnecessary as they tumbled gently, their eyes locked. She stroked his face, feeling the texture of his skin, the contours of his cheeks, the softness of his hair. She felt his fingers in her tangled hair, his hands sliding down her body. All too soon, he began to draw away, disappearing into the haze. She woke abruptly, grasping vainly at the bubbles in the tub.

CHAPTER THREE

The next few weeks passed quickly. Sarah met with Merrie Winslow and others in the area who were forming groups of family members and concerned citizens. She learned more about the many Americans who had been prisoners not just months, but in some cases, years. Her friendship with the Winslows deepened as her involvement increased and she began to feel a natural part of their family. The strangeness of her attraction to Paul Winslow ebbed away as she began to think of herself, however subconsciously, as having known him as well as his parents for a very long time. Now and then she found herself staring at her hands, remembering the feel of his skin as she stroked his face in the dream, but she rejoiced in the memory rather than allowing it to frighten her. She came to believe that fate had somehow intervened, bringing her another family to replace the one she had lost.

Petitions to be sent to the Vietnamese delegation at the Paris peace talks had been prepared for signatures, and on one Saturday morning, Sarah was sitting at a card table outside the local supermarket speaking with passersby, telling them that the Vietnamese had signed the Geneva Convention Accords which guaranteed prisoners of war the right to humane treatment and regular visits from the International Red Cross.

She spoke with dozens of people and was surprised as well as gratified by the overwhelmingly favorable response from most of them. No one had refused to sign the petition, and most confessed to being as ignorant as she had been a short time before. Around noon she gathered up the stack of papers from the table she had brought from home and carried them to her car. Stowing them carefully on the front seat, she moved the car to the curb in front of the store, folded the table and chair, and lifted them into the trunk. Pleased that she had been useful and had accomplished something worthwhile, she anticipated an afternoon beside the pool, swimming laps and conversing with friends.

Later in the afternoon when the sun had strayed toward the horizon, she returned to her apartment tired, but contented. Dropping her beach towel on the floor by the door, to be retrieved later, she collapsed on the sofa to rest for a few minutes before heading for the shower. Across the room, her cabinet grand piano seemed to beckon, reminding her that she had not played it for quite some time - an old friend that had been neglected. She smiled at it fondly, then rose and went to run her fingers over the keys.

Sitting down, she played a few warm-up exercises, then selected a Brahms concerto from the stack of music that lay on top of the instrument. She began slowly, then felt the intensity of the heavy chords that began in the lower register of the keyboard and rose to dramatic crescendos. Imagining a full orchestra behind her, she could almost hear the stringed instruments as she lost herself in the music. The drums rolled in her ears, signaling the start of another run of chords, and the sweet sound of a horn lent an air of momentary melancholy to the piece. The sonorous broken chords and cross rhythms inspired rich emotions, and her fingers flew over the keys, building to the finale. As the last notes faded into silence, she sat back, her eyes closed, her heart full.

Sifting through the sheet music in search of something in a lighter mood, she came upon a copy of 'My Foolish Heart,' that she had forgotten she had. On the cover, Dana Andrews and Susan Hayward smiled happily, their arms around each other. Why did that particular piece of music keep reappearing? Sarah paused for a moment, then opened it and began to play, hesitantly at first, then with gathering confidence as the notes came naturally. Shadows lengthened on the wall as daylight faded into dusk.

Suddenly the hair at the back of her neck tingled as she sensed someone standing behind her. Her hands froze on the keys and she whispered, "Who's there?"

Resisting the impulse to whirl around, she turned slowly. A figure seemed to be retreating into the shadows, disappearing as she struggled to see it. She rose from the piano and followed it as it disappeared into the wall, putting out her hand, running it along the wall, searching for some indication of the presence that eluded her. Switching on a lamp, she found herself alone in the room. The newspaper photo of Paul Winslow stared up at her from the lamp table.

Thinking that perhaps the song might be the key to the elusive entity, she went back to the piano and played it again. Peeking around peripherally as she played, she willed Paul to appear, but he did not and she was filled with an unbearable sadness. Crossing her arms against the piano, she put her head down and began to cry.

Powerless to control her sorrow, she cried for all those who suffered. She cried for those who loved and for those who had never loved; she cried for those who wept with loneliness and those who had no tears. She cried for every wrong ever done to mankind and for every joyful moment in the universe. She cried for no reason at all. And when she could weep no more, she staggered down the hall to her room, clutching at the walls for support. Crawling beneath the covers on her bed, she fell asleep, exhausted, and drifted easily into the dream.

He was standing just outside the window, entreating her to follow him. She smiled and rose, feeling curiously content. He took her hand in his as she floated obediently into a pale pink fog, and they moved together through the mist.

Her eyes glistened as she gazed into his, telling him without the need for words that she had been waiting for him to come. He gathered her into his arms, stroking her hair, kissing her forehead, her eyelids, her earlobes, her neck. She was Sarah and yet she was not. He was Paul and yet he was not.

It was so natural to be together that they stood in the now colorless void, each taking in the other's features as the void metamorphosed into a wooded mountain. The sound of temple bells mixed gently with the notes from a wind instrument being played by an elderly monk seated on a log beside the path where the lovers found themselves. Neither of them noticed the transition as they became Ikkyu and Yoshiko, lovers of an era long past.

Crossing the short wooden bridge that spanned a small pond, they walked hand in hand through an arched torii and down the path that led into the temple grounds. Unseen through the tall trees, the sound of a waterfall was barely audible, adding to the tranquility of the peaceful setting.

Yoshiko wore a pale rose-colored kimono with a burgundy obi and flowing sleeves. Her shiny black hair was done in an elaborate style, swept up and held in place with a series of large pins, and adorned with glittering combs. The samurai beside her carried a sword at his side.

Adjusting the sword, he guided her along the path to the flat round stones that led up to a tiered pagoda. She folded her arms inside the full sleeves of her kimono and bowed her head demurely. They walked silently for a time as each eased into the roles they had once played in life.

Noticing a small tear in Ikkyu's robe, Yoshiko touched his arm saying, "You must let me repair your robe, Ikkyu. Your garments must reflect your strength and orderliness so that your enemies will know you are someone of importance."

"Ah, Yoshiko, sometimes I wonder if I am very important. My master has been gone for more than a year now, and I have yet to pledge myself to another one. Am I to roam the roads a ronin until death comes to claim my body?"

"An honorable master is not always easy to locate, my brave lord, and you must settle only for the best."

"You are my salvation, my solace. When I am discouraged, I need only come to your arms and my hopes are restored. What should I do without you?" Ikkyu's voice was tender.

Small birds chirped in the trees and a leaf fell slowly from a branch above, swaying to and fro in the breeze before it came to rest on Yoshiko's sleeve.

"Come, Ikkyu. The leaf is telling us it is time to rest. We will go home now and I will fix your tea."

Yoshiko's home was a simple house secluded among the trees. A tearoom had been added to the original building and it was there that Ikkyu enjoyed spending time in meditation with tea served by his love. He sat on the hand-hewn bench at the rear of the house preparing his spirit for the tea as Yoshiko went inside and removed the elaborate kimono, exchanging it for one that was plain and of a neutral color that would not disturb the harmony of the tearoom. She entered through the anteroom to prepare the water in an iron kettle, washing the utensils carefully and setting out the tea bowl and cups.

Ikkyu waited until he heard the sound of a tiny bell from inside, then walked silently down the roji, the garden path, breaking his connection with the outside world in the first stage of meditation. He removed his outer robe and his sword, leaving them outside as he crouched low and entered the tearoom through the small door provided so that all who entered might accept their humility.

The water was singing in the kettle, producing a sound not unlike that of the sea breaking among the rocks or the wind whistling among the tall pines. This was accomplished through the use of strategically placed pieces of iron in the bottom of the kettle. Bowing to the tokonama in acknowledgement of the flower arrangement there, he seated himself on the cushion beside the low table. Yoshiko entered from the anteroom and poured Ikkyu's tea. Handing him his cup, she waited for him to finish before preparing her own.

They sat quietly for a time, then Ikkyu left the room the same way he had entered, and came around to the door into the main portion of the house. She greeted him, took his robe to be mended later and urged him to be comfortable while she started the evening meal. They spoke very little throughout the meal, each content in their companionship and the tranquility of the night, anticipating the lovemaking that was to come. When the remnants of the meal had been cleared away, they spread futons on the floor and extinguished all but one candle. Yoshiko sighed joyfully as her lover's arms encircled her.

She began with his toes. Gently massaging each foot, she took the little toe of his left foot in her mouth, pulling on it ever so slightly, her tongue making feathery little circles on the tip. Repeating the movement on each toe, she went on to his right foot. Then she kissed each foot lightly on the instep as her fingernails caressed his arches. Moving oh so slowly, she worked her way up each leg, the tips of her fingers and her fingernails stroking one leg as her tongue moved up the other to the little hollows at the backs of his knees.

Approaching his crotch, she pushed him gently onto his stomach and parted the crease between his buttocks. Distracting his attention with her fingernails, she slowly inserted a small string of pearls into his anus, leaving just enough protruding to grasp later. Then she knelt over his back, once again depositing feathery kisses in the hollow near his waist. Her fingers reached for the hair at the nape of his neck as she positioned herself astride him. Letting the tuft of her golden triangle barely touch the small of his back, she began to undulate, running her fingers through the hair on his head and using the heels of her hands to massage the back of his neck.

He began to moan softly and turned over onto his back again instinctively as Yoshiko moved aside. Resting for just a moment to ensure that he would not reach climax prematurely, she began to nibble at his neck, her hands kneading his chest. Playfully, she tickled his sides as her lips moved down to his stomach. Taking a little of the peach fuzz that grew there between her teeth, she pulled on it very slightly, then feathered the skin beneath it with her tongue. Finally, she reached for his swollen penis, taking it in her mouth and sucking gently, then harder, then releasing it to run her tongue slowly around the tip.

Unable to wait any longer, he rose and moved her under him, parting her legs and entering her roughly. Her legs encircled his back as she moved to his rhythm. Reaching around to his buttocks, she grasped the end of the string of pearls and began to pull them one at a time, very slowly, as he shouted in ecstasy. As the last of the pearls came out, he rose up, pulling her with him, then fell back to the softness of the futon, exhausted. He panted heavily, perspiration covering his body.

She disentangled herself with soft cooing noises and reached for a nearby towel. Beginning with his forehead, she carefully wiped the sweat from his skin. By the time she reached his legs, he was snoring softly.

"I will love you through eternity, my love," she whispered.

CHAPTER FOUR

A bell was ringing. Was it the phone? No, the alarm clock. No, not that either. It must be the doorbell. Someone was pounding. Who could be doing that? Sarah woke in confusion. Feeling fuzzy and unable to focus, she sat up and swung her legs over the side of the bed, tangling them in the sheet so that when she tried to stand, she fell to the floor. Pushing herself to her knees with her hands, she kicked at the covers until they finally fell away and she was able to stand. She stumbled down the hall toward the noise that was making her head pound.

"All right, all right, I'm coming!"

The chain on the door stuck as her fingers fumbled to open it. Finally, she wrenched the door open to find her secretary, Ellen, standing outside speaking words that made no sense. She leaned back against the wall, putting up one hand to stop the questions, and massaging her temples with the other.

"What *is* it?"

"Are you all right? Are you sick? What's the matter with you? We've been trying to call you since yesterday morning! Where've you been?" Ellen's questions ran on until she stopped for breath.

"Slow down, *stop*! I've been right here. What's the emergency?"

"Emergency? We thought maybe *you* had one! You didn't come in yesterday, you didn't phone, you didn't answer *your* phone. What in God's name is wrong? If you hadn't answered this door, I was prepared to break it down!"

"What are you talking about? It's Sunday. I almost never work on Sunday."

"Sunday? Sunday?" Ellen repeated, her voice rising. "It's Tuesday! What did you do, tie one on and sleep for two days?" Her concern was turning to annoyance.

"Tuesday?" Sarah asked dumbly. "It can't be Tuesday."

"Well it is, and you've obviously been out of it for the past two days or so. What the hell happened?"

"I don't know. Come in and sit down. Better yet, make some coffee while I take a shower and get the cobwebs out of my head." Sarah waved vaguely toward the kitchen and headed back down the hall to her bedroom.

"Are you sure you'll be okay in the shower? I'm almost afraid to leave you alone even for a minute," Ellen said dubiously.

"I'll be fine. I just have to get the fuzzies out of my head and figure out how I managed to sleep through two days." Closing the door to her room, Sarah stood gazing at the bed. The vision of a tiny house surrounded by tall pines flashed through her mind, vanishing as quickly as it had appeared. Rubbing her temples, she staggered to the bathroom and turned on the shower. When the water was steaming, she stepped in and plunged under the showerhead, letting the warmth wash away her agitation.

The dream began to come back, sending a chill up her spine. I was in Japan, she thought. And Paul was there...no, it was Ikkyu, and my name was Yoshiko. I was wearing a rose colored kimono. It was more than three hundred years ago! It was a dream, it *had* to have been a dream, but it seemed so real.

She could almost feel the silk of the kimono on her skin. She remembered Ikkyu's strong arms around her, his face near hers, Paul Winslow's face. She began to tremble as she struggled to understand what had happened. Could it be that this strange attachment to Paul was because she *had* known him in some previous life? Since she'd never been to Japan in this lifetime, how could she have seen it so clearly unless she'd been there in another lifetime? A previous incarnation?

She shivered, recalling that she had stepped into the dream with Paul. If she could bring him into her reality, then go back with him to another lifetime as Ikkyu and Yoshiko, could that mean that he still lives as Paul Winslow? If Paul is dead, she thought, wouldn't his soul, or spirit, or whatever it was that made humans immortal, have gone on to another plane, no longer caring, perhaps even unaware, that their physical connection had been broken once again?

Stepping hastily from the shower, she toweled herself quickly, then wrapped another towel around her head. Had she really been sleeping for two days? Or had her soul visited another plane of consciousness? No, it was just too bizarre. But how else could she explain the loss of two days?

The smell of fresh coffee wafted down the hall as she pulled on a terry-cloth robe and went toward the kitchen, her mind racing. She must tell Pete and Merrie that Paul had to be alive! That thought was followed immediately by the realization that she couldn't tell anyone. No one would believe her. They'd think she'd lost her mind. And maybe they'd be right. It had to have been a dream, the desperate hope that he was alive manifesting itself in this strange way. It just couldn't be anything else.

She paused midway down the hall, thinking, Holy shit! I can't possibly be taking this seriously! Maybe there is some supernatural kind of connection, but I'm a rational person. I live in a today kind of world! And if I'm going to keep on living in a today kind of world, I'd better get it together.

"I'm really embarrassed," she said as Ellen handed her a cup of the freshly brewed coffee. "I sat at the shopping center with petitions Saturday morning, then swam and sat by the pool all afternoon. Must have had too much sun or something." She hoped her impromptu explanation would satisfy Ellen's concerns.

"Are you sure you shouldn't see a doctor?" Ellen wondered.

'No, I'll be fine, Ellen. But would you tell the boss man that I'm just stressed out and need a little rest? I'll be in tomorrow bright and early."

Ravenous after two days without food, Sarah went to the refrigerator and considered its contents. Since she often ate at the hotel, there wasn't always much to be had at home, but she usually tried to keep cold cuts and salad makings around. She had just taken the first bite of a cold roast beef sandwich when the phone rang. It was Merrie Winslow on the other end, apologizing for disturbing her if she was busy.

"No, I'm not busy, just feeding my face. I meant to call you Sunday, but apparently I had a little too much sun and slept my way through Monday. I decided if I was that tired, I needed an extra day off today."

"Pete and I were wondering if you'd be free to stop by for cocktails this evening," Merrie said, "or do you feel up to it?"

"I'd love to, Merrie. The response to the petition was even better than we'd hoped it would be. People were so nice and I discovered that I'm not the only one who didn't know about the missing and prisoners over there."

She agreed to bring the petitions with her when she came over that evening, and replaced the phone pensively. Details of the dream were fading, and everyday things like making plans to go out made her feel a little silly for overreacting to the dream in the first place.

She looked forward to the time she spent with Pete and Merrie. Most of the conversation over their vodka martinis centered around proposed publicity, but personal tidbits that friends share with one another often entered into the easy comradery they enjoyed, and Sarah felt sure that the Winslow's genuinely liked her aside from the issue that had drawn them together.

Merrie had discovered that their suburban San Francisco town had adopted an entire military airborne division, and that local residents were being encouraged to send letters to servicemen in that division. The discovery brought forth the idea that the city council might be willing to adopt Paul as well, with residents encouraged to write government representatives and sign petitions on behalf of the Americans listed as missing or prisoner in Vietnam. They had applied for permission to speak at the next council meeting, but had yet to decide who would do the speaking.

"I'd never be able to get through it!" Merrie exclaimed.

"And it wouldn't be appropriate for either of us to speak, Sarah," Pete added. "We can provide pertinent information and maybe photos for handouts, but someone other than a family member should do the talking. Would you do it?"

"It's such a big responsibility," Sarah protested. "Don't you know someone with public speaking experience?"

"You deal with the public every day, Sarah. And you handle large groups of people at the hotel. This would be pretty much the same – you'd just be talking on behalf of a person instead of a building," Merrie said earnestly.

Sarah had no choice but to agree, and by the time the scheduled day arrived, she was in a frenzy of nervous tension. Questions scurried around in her head like ants in a honey pot. *How did I get into this? What if I blow it completely? It isn't fair to the Winslows, or for that matter, any of the families, for me to be doing this if my motives aren't the right ones. Is it just some strange attraction to Paul? Is it a romantic notion that has gotten out of control? Oh, God, I can't do it, I just can't do it! But what if there really is a connection between Paul and me? Some master plan in the universe? I'd have a duty to follow through, wouldn't I? If I do it well and the council agrees to adopt Paul, at least the Americans in Vietnam would have a voice speaking on their behalf. I* have *to do it.*

She began her remarks that evening by thanking the council for the opportunity to speak and went on to tell them a little about Paul and his family. Then she listed the ways in which the community might help.

"Letters to congressmen, senators and ambassadors, urging them to use their influence to obtain the names and physical conditions of those who are prisoners, to secure the release of those who are sick or wounded, to ensure the flow of mail, and most of all to require impartial inspection of prisoner facilities as set forth at the Geneva Convention, are just one way in which concerned citizens can help. Church and community organization support is another. Tables with information and petitions at shopping centers are a third way," she told them. Urging the adoption of the resolution, she concluded her speech.

"Gentlemen, when Americans are killed in the service of their country, we bury them. When they are wounded, we heal them. When they are prisoners of war or missing in action, can we just forget them? They cannot speak for themselves. You with a voice must use it. Please help take the 'missing' out of missing in action. Thank you."

Returning to her seat in the audience, she asked, "Was it okay?"

"It was wonderful," Merrie assured her, grasping her hand and squeezing it. Pete leaned forward to smile warmly across his wife as one of the council members moved to adopt the resolution. Another seconded the motion and a unanimous vote followed.

When the meeting concluded, the three of them returned jubilantly to the Winslow's living room to toast their success.

"Now we're really committed," Sarah commented. "Where do we go from here?"

"How about some sort of kick-off event?" Merrie asked. "We could invite the council members, the mayor, and as many prominent citizens as we can find, along with other family members from the area and a few military types who might be able to fill in the information gaps."

"That's a great idea, Merrie!" Sarah responded. "It would give us an excuse to call people and ask them to volunteer to help on a committee, give them something constructive to do and something to look forward to as well!" Still euphoric from her successful speech, Sarah's enthusiasm was growing.

"Great idea, yes, but who's going to pay for all this?" Pete inquired practically.

"Right, I hadn't thought about that. We don't even have money for the postage to send out invitations unless we pay for it ourselves," Merrie said gloomily.

"Well, what is this committee all about anyway?" Sarah asked. "We'll get businesses to donate services. They can write it off, and we'll get the publicity we need to raise public awareness. How about a dinner? I'm sure the hotel will cooperate. Hey! Maybe one of the car dealers in the area would give us a car to raffle!"

"Good ideas, Sarah, but maybe a little ambitious," Pete commented. "We'd have to sell tickets, but we can add the miscellaneous expenses to the cost of them."

Their already high spirits rose even higher as they planned what must be done and made lists of contacts to be generated. Merrie was eager to begin with the sources from her growing files and Sarah promised to appeal to the general manager at the hotel the first thing in the morning.

Sarah's head was spinning with ideas as she undressed for bed. She turned out the lights in the rest of the apartment and settled back against the pillows on the bed, notebook and pen in hand. Half an hour later, the notebook slipped from her hand as her eyes began to close. A shadow appeared in the doorway and she smiled sleepily at it, feeling light and happy.

She began to float upward toward the ceiling as the shadow reached for her hand and they drifted together. Looking down at the bed, she was surprised but unafraid as she saw her body lying there asleep. Though she couldn't see him clearly, she knew that the shadow was Paul. They moved gently through the air until they found themselves on the back of a great, white swan, climbing into the night sky. The swan's feathers were soft and warm, his wings shielding them as they dipped and soared, higher and higher. Sarah threw her head back and laughed with pure joy.

It wasn't long before the swan landed in front of a sumptuous castle high above the earth. They rolled off the splendid bird and ran gaily toward the heavy wooden doors, throwing them open to race through the rooms. Double doors at the back of the castle opened onto a field resplendent with brilliantly colored flowers. Hand in hand, they romped, weightless, through the field, unable to contain their joy. They tumbled in ecstasy, falling amid the multitude of blooms that extended beyond the horizon. Finally, they lay exhausted on the warm earth. Sarah reached for Paul's hand. His blue eyes were filled with love as his arms reached out to her.

As she moved into them, he seemed to withdraw, receding further and further as she tried to grasp his outstretched hands, finally fading into the nothingness at the edge of the world. She called his name, then began to cry as she found herself alone in the meadow. The swan appeared beside her and she struggled up onto his back, clinging to the downy feathers that were wet with her tears.

Gliding gently, down, down, down, she saw her own form once again, lying on the bed, still sleeping, and slid soundlessly back inside.

Sarah awoke in the morning feeling a mixture of melancholy and joy, but oddly at peace, the memory of her flight to the castle with Paul remaining clear in her mind. Her pillow was still damp with the tears that fallen as he receded into the mist.

"Holy shit," she said aloud. It had seemed more like an out-of-body experience than a dream, she thought in amazement. It might have been frightening had she not returned so easily to her own body. Did this mean that Paul was alive or did it mean that he was beyond her reach? Her conviction that he was alive and somehow connected to her filled her with hope. She *must* do something to help bring him back. On the other hand, she couldn't allow her judgment to be clouded if her credibility were to remain intact. People would think she was downright nuts.

CHAPTER FIVE

I t took Paul Winslow longer than usual to awaken as the gong rang in the courtyard. He was deep in another dream of the woman with the smoky, dark hair. Her hands had been cool as they caressed his face and she had called him by name, or had she? He closed his eyes again, frowning as he tried to piece together the parts of the dream. A small house, the rooms sparsely furnished and serene. His clothes – he had been wearing robes and carrying a sword such as he'd seen in pictures of Japanese samurai! She had been wearing a rose colored kimono. It had seemed so real, but it couldn't be. His feet were still firmly encased in the stocks. Images of trees and a wooden bench appeared briefly, then were gone.

His thoughts were interrupted as static came from the loudspeaker in his cell and the Voice of Vietnam began its daily diatribe of news. Paul sighed and mentally tuned out the sound from the radio, stretching out to the best of his ability within the constraints of the leg irons. A guard would appear soon to unlock them and escort him down to the wash area where he was allowed to empty his waste bucket and splash a little water over himself in an effort to clean up as best he could. Taken one prisoner at a time, the process was not concluded until nearly min-morning when the usual meal of watery soup with a bit of bread was placed on the floor of his cell.

The bone in his leg had finally repaired itself to some degree with a little help in the form of a sloppy cast put on days after his capture and removed too early when he was too slow in moving to suit his captors. He had changed cells several times as the North Vietnamese sorted out the prisoners in an attempt to isolate the ones they feared might be troublemakers and those they hoped to break.

Using the alphabet code made up of five lines, five letters to a line, he tapped on the wall tentatively twice, then three times indicating line two, third letter – "H" – then twice and four times for the letter "I." As usual, there was no reply. He had managed to contact only one other man in the months that he'd been there, an Air Force pilot named Sanders.

A guard he secretly called Porky appeared at the door to the cell. Porky had a round face with fat cheeks and small ears. His eyes were coal black and piercing, a characteristic on which he capitalized often in an effort to intimidate his American prisoner. Porky raised the cover on the peephole into Paul's cell, ascertaining that he was still confined in the leg irons. He flipped the bar that controlled the irons from the hall, releasing them. The door was unlocked and Porky's menacing bulk appeared, eyes flashing and arms waving as he gestured for Paul to get up.

Paul's control snapped suddenly and he began waving his own arms, yelling in an imitation of the guard's behavior.

"I'm sick to death of you and your bullying," Paul screamed. "How does it feel to be on the receiving end of the maniacal attitude?" He opened his eyes wide, adopting the look of a man gone insane.

Porky's reaction was one of stunned disbelief. He remained absolutely still for an instant, then backed slowly from the cell. The shock Paul felt at his own actions equaled that of the guard. Now I've done it, he thought. As though silence would somehow render him invisible, he sat down very slowly, staying perfectly still until he realized that he'd stopped breathing. Inhaling softly, he listened as the voices outside the cell grew louder and progressively more agitated. Anticipating the worst, he waited apprehensively.

Several hours later, he was still waiting. He considered the situation. Since his capture, he'd been subjected to varying degrees of torture, depending upon what his captors were after. He'd been suspended upside down from the ceiling. He had had his arms tied behind him and pulled upward until they nearly came out of their sockets. Always it had ended with a form of compromise in that he admitted to a lesser 'crime' than they were after, but they had nevertheless achieved a modicum of success in that they had a 'confession.'

It was an endless game that he was afraid they might be winning. The fear that one day they would go too far and he would die led him to confess, but the guilt he felt following his confession was beginning to break down his spirit. His resistance was faltering. Would he one day be unable to keep from making the ultimate confession? He would be disgraced, his military career over.

Late in the day, Porky reappeared with a superior officer who spoke English. None of the guards wore insignias of rank, but it was not difficult to discern the leaders.

"You have made a grave error. You do not seem to realize that you are beaten," the officer began. "The people of Vietnam do not have to beat you; you defeat yourselves on the streets and college campuses of America. Your own people do not care what happens to you." The man's voice was flat and unemotional. He motioned for Paul to gather his few belongings, the mosquito net, his blanket and cup, and prepare to move once again.

Porky forced his arms behind him and fastened handcuffs securely around his wrists. He was blindfolded and led from the cell. The night air felt good as he was taken outside and pushed roughly into a jeep. They drove for what Paul estimated to be about forty minutes, leaving the city sounds behind. When the jeep came to a halt, he was pulled out and forced to the ground. A few minutes later many hands moved him into what he could tell was a bamboo cage. The blindfold and handcuffs were left on, but his feet were unshackled. Emotionally and physically spent, he slept.

At dawn an unfamiliar guard opened the cage and removed the cuffs and blindfold. Squinting to adjust his eyes to the light, Paul saw that he was surrounded by foliage. The guard indicated that he should follow him to a nearby stream where he gestured for Paul to strip and clean himself in the water. He was given clean black pajamas, the type worn by Vietnamese guerrillas, then led up a path toward a windowless shed where he was given a bowl of rice and some bread. He was allowed to sit outside the shed to eat, but was then locked inside and left in semi-darkness. Oh, God, he prayed silently, help me to accept this without giving in. I'm so tired of the pain and loneliness, so tired of being alone. It would be so much easier to just stop living.

He began to think of home, his mother and father. He visualized his mother in the kitchen fixing dinner. Let's see, he mused, it's about eight in the morning here, so it must be about five o'clock yesterday afternoon for them. Maybe they were sitting in the living room sipping his father's famous vodka martinis. Maybe they had company. Who would it be? The image of the dark haired woman sprung to his mind and he mentally placed her in the room with his parents. Abruptly, the images he had created became so painful to watch that he nearly cried as he longed to join them. He wished for oblivion, temporary or permanent.

Suddenly it dawned on him that this was just what the Vietnamese wanted. They knew that Christian doctrine made its followers more malleable under the stress of guilt. New resolve strengthened him as he made a silent commitment.

I WILL NOT DIE HERE ALONE, BURIED IN A HOLE. I WILL SURVIVE. I MUST ESCAPE.

A few days later, Paul lifted his face toward the gentle rain that fell as he splashed in the narrow river. The water was cold in the morning. The guards always took him there for his bath, such as it was, in the hour just after daybreak. At first they had made great sport of laughing at him as he shivered, stumbling on the uneven rocks, pushing him back into the water with indications that he was not yet clean, enjoying his misery. As time passed, however, they had grown tired of the sport and more or less ignored him for this brief period of time.

He began to look forward to these moments of tranquility and relative comfort. His small hut was hot, humid and wretched. He was left there alone, chained to a heavy log, for most of the time. Though he tried to keep track of how long he had been held here in the jungle camp, he knew there were days that he had lost following torture sessions. One of their favorites was to tie his hands behind his back and suspend him by his feet from a tree until he lost consciousness. This, they knew, was all the more excruciating because of his injured leg and caused him to limp for days afterward. Occasionally, they tied a bag over his head and left him in the shed, feeding him sporadically until he was no longer sure how much time had passed or whether it was light or dark outside.

He spent as much time as he could on a physical reconditioning program, massaging his skin and muscles, stretching to the best of his ability. The water in the river gave him the best opportunity for exercise, providing resistance against any vigorous movement.

A plan began to form in his mind. If the guards could be lulled into believing that he was too weak to attempt an escape, he might be able to get away some morning. He looked back toward the shore and studied the lone guard who sat, his back against a tree, near Paul's small pile of clothes. I'd have to be able to overpower him, he thought, and that doesn't seem likely. That night as he lay on his straw bed, it came to him. I'll have to hide extra clothes somewhere and wait until a guard dozes off. But what if that never happens?

The following morning he began to venture a little farther away from the shore, until the guard called harshly for him to come back, raising his rifle menacingly. Paul returned docily with a shrug and bowed penitently. They seemed to feel more important when he bowed, considering it a sign of respect.

The guards here in the jungle were all smaller and much thinner than the guards in Hanoi, a fact Paul attributed to the more stringent life they led. From what he'd been able to see, their diet wasn't much better than his, though they did get an occasional chicken or a small pig to roast. Their attitude toward him was somewhat different as well. Where the guards in Hanoi were dictatorial and just plain mean, the ones here made a point of showing him their camaraderie, making sure that he understood that they shared everything they had. Where the ones in Hanoi were obsessed with their power over him, the ones here seemed to have a genuine ideology in mind. Paul began to contemplate how he might be able to use this to his advantage. If they thought he was beginning to see things their way, he might even be able to generate some form of laxity from them.

Thus far, he'd been unable to determine whether or not there might be any other Americans in the camp. He'd caught glimpses of men leaving the camp in a group, apparently to work in nearby rice fields, but he'd been unable to distinguish any individual faces or features. One day he thought he saw a man with a beard and knew that the Vietnamese rarely grew facial hair. He wasn't sure why he wasn't being put to work in the fields, but assumed that his solitary lifestyle was punishment for his actions in Hanoi. They considered him a troublemaker and had no intention of allowing him to become an instigator among any other Americans who might be there.

One morning as he was being led to the river, Paul pretended to stumble over a fallen branch and hurt his foot. As he sat on the ground, he seized a prickly leaf and surreptitiously scratched the foot, drawing a small amount of blood. Pointing to the blood, he convinced the guard that he wanted to wear his rubber sandals into the water and limped to prove that the foot was indeed injured. At first reluctant to let him wear the sandals, the guard finally shrugged and relented.

A short time later, Paul ventured toward the shore some distance downstream and slipped the straps of the sandals over a branch before the guard noticed him and motioned for him to come back. Returning to a more visible spot, he began to splash and grasp for the 'lost' sandals, indicating in sign language that they had come off and were headed downstream. Disgusted, the guard motioned angrily for him to come back, that the bath was over for the day. He was given another pair of sandals to wear and as he lay on his pallet that night, he contemplated how he was going to be able to hide an extra pair of the black pajamas and perhaps a blanket. He sighed, realizing what an impossible task he'd undertaken.

Despondency crept over him. Did anyone know he was here? Did anyone even know if he was alive? Was anyone looking for him? Probably not. He was sure that the Vietnamese had not released the names of many of their prisoners and since his plane had crashed, the Navy may well have assumed that he and Don had been killed. He wondered again whether Don had managed to survive the ordeal, and if so, where he was. The isolation strategy practiced by his captors served them well as prisoners believed that they were alone in their despair.

His head dropped to his hands. Pressing his palms against his temples, he felt the mats that had developed in his hair. It was long and shaggy now, dulled by the lack of care. His nails were ragged and dirty and a scraggly beard covered his chin. He drew his legs into a fetal position and closed his eyes, hoping that sleep, and perhaps dreams of the dark haired woman who had become his only companion, would be possible in the steamy night.

He began to ascend into the night sky, gliding gently away from the jungle below. His outstretched hand grasped the smaller one that reached toward him and the silhouette of his beloved companion appeared before him. Together, they climbed aboard the great white swan that waited nearby and began to soar through the blackness, leaving the earth far behind. He heard her laugh in delight as they rose higher and higher.

His arms held her tightly, reveling in the softness of her body. He buried his face in the tousled curls that cascaded over her shoulders, inhaling the heady fragrance that enveloped them. The giant bird deposited them in front of a gleaming castle and they ran joyfully through its rooms, then into a field of riotous blooms. His body was whole once again, unfettered by the injuries that had been so painful and he followed her in ecstasy as she bounded through the meadow. They fell, lying exhausted on the earth. She turned to him, her green eyes aglow. His heart was so full of love for her that he thought it might shatter as he extended his arms. She moved toward him but he was suddenly weak and unable to hold her. He began to fall, down through the inky sky, plummeting toward the earth.

He woke in terror, his body bathed in sweat, back again in the hovel that was his prison. He began to cry softly.

CHAPTER SIX

The headline in the paper read, "Ho Chi Minh, Vietnamese Chief, Dies." The article went on to say that U.S. officials said that Ho's death and the change in leadership would probably not alter the course of the war in South Vietnam or affect the peace talks in Paris. Apparently, it would be war as usual. Scientists could put a man on the moon, Janis Joplin could warble at Woodstock, and thousands might protest throughout America, but it would be war as usual. Unknown numbers of young men from farms in Wisconsin, machine shops in New Jersey and beaches in California would sacrifice arms, legs and even their lives, but to the bureaucrats they were not faces, only numbers.

The end of summer was near and in the face of global degeneration, flights of fancy aboard a mythical swan took on the appearance of a total denial of reality. Sarah could not believe that an educated, urbane hotel executive could be entertaining thoughts of floating weightlessly through fields of flowers with someone she had met only in dreams.

She sat at her desk torn between the desire to close her eyes and flee permanently into that illusionary cosmos, and the knowledge that to do so would invalidate any prospect of solving the mystery of her increasingly undeniable obsession with Paul Winslow.

If only I had someone in whom to confide, she thought. Everything's easier to cope with when you can talk about it without fear or ridicule. But even if she could think of someone she trusted, it was hard to imagine anyone, at least anyone not confined to a padded room, who wouldn't tell her it was just a fascination that had grown into an obsession. So why bother to look for anyone?

Sarah sighed and folded the newspaper, tossing it onto the credenza behind her desk. She rose and went to the table across the room that held the hotel's catering book, the bible of coming events. Turning the pages to the first two weeks in November, she saw that the third Saturday night was open, no meetings or dinners on the agenda. She penciled in the letters, "POW/MIA."

She'd have to speak to Van Carducci, the General Manager, about sponsorship by the hotel, then consult with the chef and the food and beverage manager about prices. It would be essential to the sale of tickets to keep the price affordable if they expected to have a good turnout. Some celebrity support wouldn't hurt either. Van had pictures on the wall of his office of himself with a number of famous people. Maybe he could find somebody whose name would be a good draw.

After some initial reticence, Van proved to be an ally and Sarah returned to her office in a jubilant mood. The phone was ringing as she opened the door. Ellen was not at her desk, so Sarah dropped her files and picked it up.

"Catering Office, Sarah Fremont," she said abruptly.

Merrie Winslow's voice came on the line. "Sarah? It sounds like you're really busy. Am I interrupting?"

"I'm never too busy to talk to you, Merrie. You really don't have to apologize for calling. As a matter of fact, I just got back from Van's office. He's the G.M. here and he's agreed to help out in any way he can, which means that we can go ahead with plans for a kick-off dinner here at the hotel. I'd have called you if you hadn't called first."

"Oh, Sarah, what can I say? You give us reason to hope." Merrie's voice cracked a little. There was the briefest of silences before she went on to say, "I know this is short notice, but would you be free to have dinner tonight? Pete has a meeting of our neighborhood association, so he can't make it, but I've just spoken with a woman who moved up to the Bay Area a couple of weeks ago from San Diego. Her husband was a friend of Paul's in flight school. It's a sad story...Jack was shot down very shortly after he arrived in Vietnam. Julie didn't know she was pregnant when he left and he doesn't know he has a baby daughter now." Merrie was breathless from hurrying through the story in an effort to be brief.

"I take it you mean that Julie would be joining us, Merrie," Sarah chuckled.

"Oh, I'm sorry. Yes, I thought you might like to meet her. I've never met her either, but Paul used to talk about them, and I've seen pictures of their wedding. Paul was best man."

"I think I can get away from the office fairly early today. There isn't much going on, just one small meeting that doesn't need anything in the way of set-up and certainly doesn't require that I be around."

"Wonderful! What time would be good?" Merrie asked.

"How about six thirty at the Coachman?"

"That would be fine, dear. We'll see you then."

Julia Summerhill Schaefer, daughter of a San Francisco surgeon, was born to a life of country club dances, golf, tennis and swimming. She was never what would be called a great student, but managed to get by with a minimum of studying and took an active part in school leadership. She took her popularity for granted, considering it a right rather than a privilege, if she considered it at all. It wasn't that she was selfish or conceited, it was just that in her world privilege *was* a right.

Julie bordered on being tall, with brown eyes and golden brown hair that she had always worn in simple styles over the years, claiming that curls tended to distract one's attention from the overall product. She had a finely developed fashion sense at an early age, being one of those girls who could wear nearly anything from satin to burlap and look terrific.

Her habit of saying just what was on her mind had attracted Jack Schaefer the moment they were introduced. She had turned to the friend who made the introduction and said, "I like him!"

She was waiting with Merrie in the lounge when Sarah arrived at the restaurant. Merrie waved and as Sarah approached the table, Julie stood up and extended her hand, saying, "Hi, I'm Julie Schaefer. Merrie's told me a little about you and I can't tell you how much it means to me and to all of us in this miserable predicament to have your support!"

"Well, I'm just sorry that I was so unaware of it until now. It's about time someone does something and about time the American public knows what's going on over there. I think most people believe, as I did, that it isn't a real war. I certainly never thought that American servicemen were prisoners of the Vietnamese," Sarah responded.

"We're both anxious to hear about your meeting with the hotel manager, Sarah. Sit down! What would you like to drink?" Merrie asked.

Ordering a scotch and water, Sarah began eagerly. "I went over the catering book before I went to see Van, looking for a date that seemed good for the hotel and would give us enough time to get it all together. I came up with several alternatives," she explained. "I figured we probably couldn't put it together in less than about three months, but that much beyond that and we've lost too much time."

Both Merrie and Julie nodded in agreement.

"Van was a little reticent at first, but when I gave him more of the facts, he was as surprised as I had been at how uninformed we all are. He agreed that not only was it a good cause, but that the hotel should get behind the effort a hundred percent. What the hotel might lose in revenue would be more than compensated by the publicity anyway, not that that's a reason for doing it. He even volunteered to get in touch with a few of the celebrities he's come in contact with over the years to get them to lend their names to the program. Of course, if any of them come, we may have to foot the bill for their meal, but ticket sales and contributions should make up for it in the long run."

"What do you think we're talking about in terms of the number of people attending?" Julie asked.

"Hold onto your hats," Sarah said jubilantly. "Would you believe between three to five hundred?"

Merrie's eyes widened. "How can we get so many?"

"Well, if you figure about a hundred of them will be family members, volunteers, dignitaries and assorted celebrities, we should be able to sell tickets to several hundred more, at say twenty-five dollars each. *And* you haven't heard it all yet! I sneaked out for an hour or so this afternoon and called on Bill Bellini, the owner of the Ford dealership in Burlingame. He agreed to give us a new Ford Maverick to raffle!" Sarah sat back in her chair, held up her glass and grinned.

"I'm overwhelmed, Sarah! When you do something, you sure do take off like a steamroller!" Julie chortled, adding, "Merrie, where did you find this dynamo?"

"The best part of it is that she actually found me," Merrie replied.

Sarah blushed a little and thought to herself that this was one commitment she really had no choice about, and that it wasn't really as self-sacrificing as it seemed to these women. They discussed the plans for committees over dinner and were in a flurry of enthusiasm by the time they left the restaurant. Julie got into her car and waved goodbye, promising to keep in close touch, and Sarah drove Merrie home. They sat in the car for a few minutes, enjoying each other's company.

"Why did Julie move up here from San Diego," Sarah wanted to know. "We were so busy discussing the plans that I really didn't get a chance to find out."

"As I told you on the phone earlier, her husband, Jack, was shot down very soon after he arrived in Vietnam. He didn't know Julie was pregnant and doesn't know that little Sandy was born months ago. There were pictures of Jack after he went down, with bandages around his head, being poked and prodded by Vietnamese villagers, so at least Julie knows he was alive then. It's been well over a year since then, however, and most of the friends they had in San Diego have been transferred somewhere else, so she decided to move back to the Bay Area to be closer to her own family," Merrie explained.

She went on to say, "As I understand it, she and her mother don't get along very well, but she's close to her father...when he has the time," Merrie sighed. "Sometimes it's hard to know what the right thing to do might be. Pete was gone a lot of the time and I was always wondering if I should wait until he got home to have the children's teeth fixed or something. Paul's sister, Sheila, was always getting banged up knees or measles or was in some sort of scrape. I don't know what I would have done if Pete had been a prisoner of war." She shook her head slowly.

"I've never thought much about things like that," Sarah said sympathetically. "I've had only myself to worry about for so long. It puts things in a different perspective, doesn't it?"

CHAPTER SEVEN

Sheila Winslow Koslowsky Donnelly thrust the letter she was holding onto the table in front of her. How could her mother possibly expect her to be in San Francisco over Thanksgiving? She *knows* that it's the beginning of the holiday season and that the calendar is always full at that time of the year. If I miss any of the parties, I might be dropped from the guest lists and wouldn't some of those North Shore snobs love to do that!

She felt a twinge of guilt as she picked up the letter and reread it. Well, the dinner *was* scheduled for the weekend *before* Thanksgiving, some sort of kick-off thing on her brother's behalf, and she could come back to Chicago right away. But there'll be so many people traveling that week, she moaned. She sighed and grudgingly admitted that she probably should make the effort to be there.

Sheila lived opulently in an apartment on Chicago's Lake Shore Drive, the result of a generous settlement from her second husband, a wealthy industrialist who was grateful to resume a well ordered suburban life following a stormy marriage to the tempestuous Sheila. She rarely saw her parents unless she happened to be passing through San Francisco on one of her erratic journeys. She knew she was something of a cross for them to bear, having run off with the highschool football hero who had been her first husband, however briefly. Then, fascinated by the older man who introduced her to a life of glittering parties and exotic vacations, she had entered into a second marriage which, though it lasted longer, also ended in divorce.

Sheila had the confident mannerisms that children of military men frequently have, the result of life in a variety of countries and cultures. She also had a strong defiant streak. As soon as she was told she couldn't do something, she set out to do it anyway. That attitude had gotten her into her first marriage, though she wouldn't have believed it at the time.

She and Bob Koslowsky had been the most popular couple in their senior class in high school, he the football hero, she the exuberant cheerleader. When her parents suggested that it was a pleasant fairy tale, not the stuff from which lasting relationships are formed, she had sworn in a tearful rage that it was nothing short of true love and that she intended to live happily ever after, in poverty if necessary.

Pete and Merrie Winslow had known that poverty was a romantic notion in their daughter's mind and that once faced with the actuality of it, she would turn and run. Bob was a nice enough fellow, but his prospects of providing Sheila with the kind of life she anticipated were remote. His greatest ambition in life was to become a foreman at the local brewery, live in a tract house and consume some of the beer he was responsible for making during weekend football games.

The marriage hadn't lasted through their first tiny apartment over a grocery store. When other friends had gone off to college, Sheila and Bob were left with each other and a few of their friends who either had no interest in college or insufficient funds to go. They found that they had nothing to say to each other and Sheila soon tired of the small black and white television for entertainment. When the routine arguments became raging quarrels, she bailed out.

Ashamed to admit that her parents had been right, she went into Chicago to stay with a girlfriend until she could get a job. Unprepared and untrained, she relied on her good looks and her supreme confidence, and eventually landed a job as a receptionist on the executive floor of one of Chicago's premier banks. It wasn't long before Quinn Donnelly came into her life. Forty, good looking, charming, and the heir to a family business that he was converting from the manufacturing of radio parts into the still relatively new field of electronic computer chips, Quinn was entranced by the bright and beautiful Sheila. He had been too busy to think about marriage until then, and was as supremely confidant of his judgement as Sheila was of hers. Sure that this was a perfect alliance, they were married following a three-month courtship during which Sheila was showered with gifts, flowers and candy.

Their first year together passed quickly in a haze of cocktail parties, dinner parties, the opera, the symphony, and for Sheila, a non-stop round of shopping. The trouble began when Quinn suggested that they stay home more, refusing at least some of the invitations, and if that wasn't enough, he'd had the effrontery to suggest that perhaps Sheila had enough clothes and might curtail her spending somewhat. Astounded, Sheila had acquiesced initially, then begun to pout when her efforts to entice him from his comfortable den failed more and more frequently. She managed to lure him on a lengthy cruise to Tahiti and one to Europe as well, but eventually Quinn tired of being on the move and insisted that they settle down.

Once again, Sheila discovered that she was married to a man with whom she had nothing in common. Their conversations were limited to whatever gossipy tidbits Sheila had picked up or what to have for dinner. In desperation, Quinn had finally told Sheila that she could keep the large apartment in town, but that he intended to move back to the suburbs for some peace and quiet.

Divorced again, Sheila found that this time it suited her very well to be alone. She still went to parties, she had a beautiful apartment, and best of all, she had the money to live well. It still had not occurred to her that there might be something more to life than continuous amusement. Though some of Quinn's friends had dropped her, the prestigious Donnelly name kept her on the society merry-go-round, and she lacked the maturity to realize that it had nothing to do with her personality.

Sheila wanted her parents to be proud of her. Her father had always been so sure of himself, so sure of what was right, and her mother was always every inch the lady, the perfect officer's wife. Sheila was sure they had never made a mistake any more serious than forgetting something on the grocery list. Her brother, Paul, never seemed to make mistakes either, at least until he went to Vietnam. Sometimes when feelings of uselessness crept into her somewhat vacuous mind, she wondered if maybe someone had switched babies on Pete and Merrie – except that she looked too much like Merrie, only taller, for that to be a possibility. Why couldn't I have been just a little more like Paul, she mused as she considered her mother's letter, and why should someone like him be missing somewhere that I can't even find on a map?

Torn by her own self-centered desires and her love and respect for her parents and her brother, she sat for a few moments staring at the paper in her hand, then sighed again and said aloud, "What the hell, I'll go."

John St. James watched the lights above his seat on the jumbo jet, waiting for the 'Fasten Seat Belt' sign to go off. He was enroute from Paris to San Francisco at the request and expense of a San Francisco based hotel chain that had asked him to serve in the capacity of consultant for their new European style hotel project.

John's family-owned company had grown measurably in the years since he had taken charge. What had begun nearly a century before as a single wayside inn had become a chain of the finest small hotels in most of the major cities of Europe. The combination of European attention to detail and his American education had led to a reputation for excellence without the formality that scared off many American tourists.

As the sign went off, he unbuckled his seat belt and unfolded his long legs to stretch in the aisle. He hated long flights and this one would be many hours, with a nine hour difference in time, making it nearly the same time in San Francisco when he arrived as it had been in Paris when he left. The cabin attendants pushed a cart up the aisle in preparation for beverage service and John took his seat again, picking up the paperback book he had brought along. His mind began to wander, however, as he thought back to the days when he and Paul Winslow had been friends on the shores of Lake Michigan as students at Northwestern University.

Since he'd grown up in France rather than Illinois, John had no friends nearby and his slight French accent made him shy around the boisterous American students who used so many slang terms that he was often in the dark as to what they were talking about. In spite of his American father and French mother, he didn't seem to belong to either nationality.

Paul Winslow seemed to have more friends than anyone in their history class and John had been pleasantly surprised when Paul waited for him one day, asking if he'd like to stop by the local pub for a beer. In conversation as they shared a pitcher, John learned that Paul's easy manner and good looks made him popular with other students, but that the frequent moves by his military family had awarded him few lasting friendships. Paul had told John that the year they'd spent in France had given his family many happy memories, and that he was glad to make a new friend from that country.

The two young men had kept in touch for several years after John returned to Paris, and Paul's eventual transfers in his military career were a continuation of the pattern formed in his early life. When an unusually long period of time went by without a letter, John had written to the Winslows and was shocked to discover that his friend was missing in action in Vietnam.

As he flew high above the earth toward San Francisco, John wondered what he'd say to Paul's parents. He didn't know them well, having met them only a few times. He remembered Merrie as a small, blonde woman with a soft smile and quiet voice. Pete had been dressed in an American Army uniform and seemed somewhat intimidating to John, though Paul had assured him it was just the posture and that Colonel Winslow was probably as much at a loss as to what to say as John was.

His current travel plans were indefinite. He thought that a week would be enough to go over the plans for the hotels and he hoped to stop off in Chicago on his way back to Paris. He smiled, remembering the fifty-seven Chevy that Paul had loved so much, and that the two of them had spent so many hours washing and polishing before dates. He still carried a photo in his wallet of the two of them standing beside it.

A representative of the hotel met him at the airport and after a brief chat with one of the executives, he was shown to his room overlooking the City. Aware of possible jet lag, his hosts had not scheduled meetings to begin until the following day. He was just about to doze off when the phone rang. Who could that be, he wondered. Picking it up, he was surprised to hear Merrie Winslow's voice on the other end.

"Hello, Mrs. Winslow! How did you know that I was here already?"

"Well, I didn't know for sure, but your letter said you'd be in today, so I just took a chance. I hope I'm not disturbing you?"

"Not at all. They've allowed me a night's reprieve before the first meeting, thank goodness. I'm sure I wouldn't be particularly brilliant at the moment."

"I did want to catch you as soon as possible so that we can be sure to get together while you're here," Merrie told him. "Do you think you might be able to join us for dinner Thursday evening? There are a couple of people I'd like you to meet, just good friends and a quiet evening. And if you'll be here over the weekend, there's another dinner scheduled that Pete and I would like to invite you to."

"Let me check on things tomorrow and let you know, but I imagine my hosts will be glad to get rid of me by then," John chuckled.

"Wonderful! We'll arrange the details tomorrow then, and both Pete and I will look forward to seeing you soon!"

CHAPTER EIGHT

On the Saturday before Thanksgiving, the day of the big dinner, Sarah sat at her desk in the hotel trying to calm the butterflies in her stomach. Papers from a folder in front of her were scattered across the desk – the hotel catering sheets with instructions, the guest lists, the committee lists, and a sheaf of last minute notes. How on earth had she gotten herself into this, she wondered rhetorically. Because of her unreasonable fascination with Paul Winslow, not only was she risking the possibility of making a complete fool of herself, she could be risking her career as well if this event were to be a disaster.

She pushed her chair back and got up to check on the arrangements in the ballroom one more time. Crossing the lobby, she went up the wide staircase to the second floor where the set-up crew was putting cloths on the tables that surrounded the small dance floor in front of the orchestra platform. David, the florist, saw her in the doorway and rushed up, calling out as he approached, "Miss Fremont! When will these Neanderthals be finished setting up the tables? I *must* begin the arrangements!"

"I'm sure they'll be ready soon, David. Why don't you and I go down to the coffee shop, have a quiet cup of coffee and go over things while we wait?" Sarah replied in her most soothing professional voice, repressing the urge to scream.

An hour later the tables were ready and David was bustling back and forth from his worktable in a room adjoining the ballroom. Things seemed to be taking shape. Sarah went back to her office to go over the lists for what she hoped would be the last time before she went home to relax for awhile before she had to get ready for the evening. She hoped no one would notice her shaking knees.

John St. James was to pick her up at six o'clock. He had insisted, despite her protests, that she must be at the hotel at least an hour before the guests arrived, in case of any last-minute problems. She had enjoyed the evening that Merrie arranged on Thursday, and John had opted to remain over the weekend to attend the dinner. They had discovered that they had much in common – he had the same taste in music as she did, though he professed that the Russian composers she liked were too loud and discordant for him. He was pleased that she had more than a nodding acquaintance with the French language, and flattered her considerably with admiring glances.

In addition to her worries concerning the plans for dinner, Sarah was a bit apprehensive about meeting Paul's sister, Sheila. Merrie had hoped she might be in town by Thursday for the dinner with John, but she had not arrived until Friday, so Sarah had yet to meet her. Julie Schaefer was to join Pete, Merrie and Sheila at the Winslow's home and they would all be at the hotel a little early as well. Concluding that there was nothing more she could do for the moment, Sarah left to go home.

Opening her closet door sometime later, Sarah reached for the new emerald green dress she'd bought for the occasion. She felt guilty about the amount of money she'd spent on it, but as she looked at it, she decided it was worth every penny. Holding it up in front of her, she surveyed her image in the mirror. The green made her eyes look far greener than they really were, and the low cut, tight fitting bodice and long slim skirt would show off her figure to its best advantage.

She hung the dress on the closet door, collapsed on the chaise lounge in her bedroom and sighed. Reviewing the preparations for the evening, she couldn't think of a thing that hadn't been done, probably twice. Closing her eyes, she dozed off, dreaming of a samurai warrior, his sword at his side. Just before she awoke, she watched him get into a fifty-seven Chevy, waving as he drove away. She smiled at the fantasy and rose to dress.

Always inclined to be early rather than rushed, Sarah was ready when the doorbell rang and was met with an appreciative whistle from John as she opened the door. "You look spectacular!" he exclaimed. "I should have hired a limousine to escort such a beautiful woman to the ball!"

"You look pretty terrific yourself," she retorted, noting the formal attire he wore. "Where did you find such an elegant tux on such short notice?"

"Since I never know where I'll be called upon to go, I always pack one when I travel," he admitted sheepishly.

"Well no wonder it fits you so well! You really do look very dashing."

"Thank you, my dear. We shall undoubtedly be the most striking couple at the ball. Shall we go?" He offered his arm gallantly and grinned at the sparkle in her eyes.

They arrived at the hotel in plenty of time to go over everything one more time with the banquet manager, and picked up drinks from the bartender as Sarah checked to make sure he was well stocked. She placed 'reserved' signs on the now beautifully decorated tables near the orchestra for dignitaries and special guests, holding one large table for the Winslows, Julie, Sheila, the mayor and his wife, and herself and John. She circled the room again and came to the entrance just in time to greet Pete, Merrie, Julie, and an extraordinarily beautiful blonde that she assumed must be Sheila.

Pete made the introductions, saying, "Sheila, I want you to meet our 'other' daughter, Sarah Fremont." The look that Sheila gave her father was not lost on Sarah as she extended her hand.

"I'm so glad you were able to be here, Sheila," she said quickly. "It wouldn't have been complete without you." At that moment, several of the other committee members and family members arrived, saving Sarah from further conversation with Sheila. She pointed out tables to those who were not greeting guests and confirmed the order in which those who were should stand.

The piano player and two violinists she had engaged for the cocktail hour began to play and the evening was underway. By nine o'clock, dinner had been served, welcoming speeches had been given, the celebrities had been introduced and those who had something to say had said it. Sarah returned to her seat at the table where the rest of her little group were enjoying the party. Merrie was glowing.

"It's going *beautifully!*" Merrie exclaimed. "The room is just gorgeous, the flowers are wonderful, and I'm sure everyone is having a marvelous time!"

"Even the speeches weren't too long," Pete observed dryly.

"Too bad Paul can't be here to have a ball with the rest of you," Sheila remarked caustically. "Quite a gala party for such an unhappy cause."

Merrie flushed as Pete looked angrily at his daughter. "I'm sure no one has forgotten why they're here," he said quietly, "but the best way to get attention, not to mention raise money, is to give people an excuse to dress up and let all their friends know what good Samaritans they are. Please don't spoil the evening. Your mother and Sarah and Julie have worked very hard on this. I haven't seen any activity on your part to help your brother."

It was Sheila's turn to flush as she mumbled, "Sorry. I guess you're right."

"It's okay, Sheila. We all wish there was a happier reason for this dinner party and maybe everybody feels a little guilty deep down inside," Sarah said graciously. The orchestra began to play and John extended his hand to her as he stood to escort her onto the dance floor.

It was soon time to draw the winning raffle ticket and Sarah approached the podium again. She spoke into the microphone, requesting everyone's attention. "Where is Bill Bellini? Would you come up here please? And I'd like to introduce the general manager of the hotel, Van Carducci and his lovely wife, Sabrina, who will draw the winning ticket." She waited, smiling, as they made their way to the platform from various places in the room.

The drum containing the raffle tickets was spun several times and Sabrina Carducci reached in to pull out the winning stub. She squinted at the name on it and laughed. "It must be a doctor," she said, "because

I can't read it!" Together, they finally deciphered the name and Sabrina announced, "Michael Buchanan!"

A young man whooped and leapt toward them from the edge of the crowd, calling out, "I'm not a doctor yet, but I will be next year!" Everyone laughed as Bill Bellini, the Ford dealer, handed over the keys to a new car to the future Dr. Buchanan.

Sarah resumed the microphone. "All of us who worked on this dinner would like to thank you from the bottom of our hearts for coming and for lending your support to the families of American servicemen who are prisoners or missing in Southeast Asia. As you probably noticed on your way in here, there are petitions out on tables to be signed and as much literature as we have on the issue. Bracelets will be available soon, inscribed with the names of the men, along with the date on which they were captured or shot down. The idea is that you pledge to wear the bracelet until the man whose name is on it is either accounted for or has returned home. You'll be hearing from us again, but in the meantime, please enjoy the rest of the evening. Once again, thank you." Applause rang out as she made her way back to the table.

The orchestra resumed playing and Sarah found herself in John's arms. "You really are a special lady," he whispered in her ear. "I wish I didn't live so far away from you."

"Thank you. You're rather special yourself." His arm tightened around her waist as he pulled her closer to him. She relaxed against him, lifting her chin slightly toward his face.

The tune ended and they stood swaying gently on the floor, waiting for another to begin. The orchestra leader raised his arm and the strains of 'My Foolish Heart' wafted through the room. Sarah hummed along for a moment, then began to sing softly, unaware that she was doing so.

"The night is like a lovely tune, beware my foolish heart. How white the ever constant moon, take care my foolish heart." John's arm tightened around her and he raised her hand to his chest, holding it firmly. She whispered his name and was stunned when he released her abruptly. Startled, she asked, "What is it? What's the matter?"

"You just called me Paul," John said sharply. "I was under the impression you had never met Paul Winslow. Is there another Paul in your life?"

Sarah's shoulders slumped visibly. She stood still, her head down, unable to look into John's eyes. "It's that song," she whispered. "It does strange things to me, evokes memories of a romance that never was. I'm sorry."

"How could you have memories of a romance that never was? A memory is by definition the recognition of a previous experience, something that happened in the past. Don't tell me that a woman as bright as you are has allowed herself to become infatuated with a man she's never met," John's tone was incredulous.

Sarah winced, feeling the scorn that must be behind the incredulity. She turned to run from the room, but his hand held her back.

"Is there somewhere we can go to talk?" he asked.

"Yes, my office downstairs, but are you sure you want to talk about it? This may sound like an excuse, but it really isn't just your everyday, garden variety hero worship."

John led her from the ballroom and down the staircase, holding her hand gently. Unlocking the door to her office, they went past Ellen's desk to the privacy of the office beyond.

"Wait here," John ordered and left the room to return a short time later carrying two snifters of brandy. "Now, tell me why I shouldn't take the first plane back to Paris and forget I ever met a beautiful lady whose lovely green eyes seem to see only my best friend?" The words were said kindly.

She told him how drawn she'd been to the photo in the paper and how strongly she felt that she knew Paul Winslow. Pausing as she tried to make up her mind whether or not to go on, she heard John say, "There's more to it than that, isn't there, Sarah?"

"Yes," she admitted. "I had a dream that was as real as we are right now in this room. I've tried to push it out of my mind, told myself the same thing you must think, that it's just some sort of fantasy, but it's as though I've known Paul in some previous life, as two other people. As though we have a connection that hasn't ended."

"What was the dream about?"

"My name was Yoshiko and Paul was a samurai named Ikkyu. It

was in the early seventeenth century and we were lovers." She blushed recalling their lovemaking on the futons.

"Well, perhaps you did know each other in another lifetime. Lots of people believe in reincarnation and there's certainly no way to prove it either way."

"John! Something just occurred to me! I slept through two days while I 'dreamed' of that life in Japan. What if Ellen hadn't come to my apartment to see if I was all right? Would I have stayed in Japan with Ikkyu? Been stuck in some sort of time warp? Would the person that I am now have died?"

"Surely not, Sarah. Maybe you were overly tired and that's what brought on such a deep sleep. You may never have another dream, and I should think you might be better off to look at it as objectively as possible. Otherwise you could be opening yourself up to unnecessary mental anguish. I find you very attractive and would rather you didn't have a 'soul' connection with anyone else, particularly my best friend!"

They sipped their brandy quietly for a time. Sarah felt somewhat comforted knowing that John found her attractive and hadn't dismissed her as being a lunatic. Eventually they went back upstairs to say goodnight to the others and left the hotel.

She was about to ask him in for a nightcap when he put a finger to her lips, silencing the request.

"I won't come in tonight, Sarah, but I will be back one day soon. I like you very much, but I want you to be sure that it's me you want to be with and not Paul."

He kissed her tenderly and left.

CHAPTER NINE

Sarah listened as the engine turned over, then as the car accelerated away from the curb. What a special person he is, she thought. I'm sure there's no doubt in his mind that I have an overactive imagination, but he didn't seem to think I'm completely mad. He's everything I could want in a man – good looking, educated, well to do, likes the things I like, and even has the same business interests as I do.

Overall, it had been a splendid evening and Sarah smiled happily as she slipped out of the green dress and into bed, switching on the radio that was pre-set on a classical music station. One of her favorite Vivaldi concertos was playing. She closed her eyes. Drowsy and content, she let the violins nourish her soul.

She was drifting off as a weight settled on the edge of the bed and someone took her hand. A soft baritone voice said, "Marguerite, come with me."

"My name is Sarah," she murmured, unable to open her eyes to see who was there. "Who is Marguerite?"

"*You* are Marguerite, my love. At least to me," he whispered. "Come, you'll remember soon. We must be there to greet our guests when they arrive."

"Paul? Is that you?"

The man sighed patiently and said, "I am Antonio and you are Marguerite. We really must go now."

She rose to follow him, her fingers entwined in his and together they moved through a familiar rosy mist, back in time to eighteenth century Italy.

Marguerite stood at the window gazing out at the gathering gloom of the evening. The faint pink glow from the fading sun was gradually turning grey as the clouds above began to shed moisture in the form of a light rain. The cobblestones on the street below glistened as they reflected the light in growing puddles.

"Where is Berthe?" she inquired peevishly. "It's time the fire was started. Gianni and Prudence will be here any minute now."

At that moment, she heard Berthe's tread on the narrow staircase as she struggled to carry an armload of wood up the steps. The plump girl that entered the room was disheveled and smudged with dirt. Dropping the wood beside the large fireplace, she gasped, "Sorry, mum, I didn't know it was so late."

"All right, Berthe, just get the fire started and for heaven's sake, clean yourself up before my guests arrive. You look a fright! Is the food ready?"

"Almost, mum," Berthe replied.

The embers began to glow as the wood warmed and small flames grew into larger ones, giving the room a rosy light. Antonio crossed the room to the grand piano that stood in one corner. Setting his brandy glass down, he ran his fingers up and down the keys as a tune formed in his head. He gazed up at the high ceiling as chords took shape and the tune developed.

"Tonio, my precious, you aren't going to get wrapped up in a new piece now, are you?" Marguerite asked. "I know you don't care much for Prudence, for that matter neither do I, she's a silly fool, but Gianni is taken with her and we must be polite."

"Yes, yes I know. Just let me put down the notes before I forget them." Antonio searched among the clutter of music on the piano for a sheet of paper on which to record the notes. In desperation, he began to scribble on the bottom of an already crowded sheet of music, the words of a song sprinkled among them.

"Oh, Tonio, that's my new song! What am I to do with you?" Marguerite rolled her eyes. Just then they heard the sound of the door chime signaling the arrival of Gianni and Prudence. Marguerite tucked a stray wisp of hair into the chignon at the back of her head and went to the railing at the top of the stairs to greet her guests.

Located on a narrow street in the heart of Milano, Marguerite's home was not far from the opera house where she was one of the lead singers. Though not a large house, it was a pleasant one. The ground floor held an ample kitchen and quarters for Berthe, the frowsy blonde English maid who was Marguerite's only servant. The girl was often slow and untidy, but she managed to keep the house itself in decent order.

The tall, narrow windows of the roomy salon on the second floor looked out on the cobbled street. Comfortable chairs that had been shipped from England were grouped cozily by the fireside. Marguerite considered the elegant, but stiff Italian furniture available in Milano as unsuitable to her informal lifestyle. A large dining salon filled the back portion of the second floor. Although able to seat twelve persons for formal dining, the room was seldom used, as Marguerite preferred the intimacy of the front room.

Above the rooms used for entertaining was a bedroom that contained a massive four-poster bed covered by a downy white comforter and several down-filled pillows. An equally soft and inviting chaise lounge occupied the space alongside the fireplace, and two smaller rooms in the rear were used as a study and fitting room. Shutters covered all the windows of the house, allowing light to spill in when open, keeping it out on days following performances when the darkness let Marguerite sleep. She loved the house.

She was taller than average, with thick dark hair that she wore severely drawn back into a chignon at the nape of her neck. She tended to wear dark conservative dresses that gave her an air of supreme dignity, though she loved the colorful costumes she was called upon to wear in performances of the opera. Outwardly calm and composed, she rarely lost her temper. But those who knew her well were careful not to aggravate her unnecessarily, as she could be a formidable opponent. She was always carefully prepared at rehearsals, but only a very few of her friends and associates knew how strictly she had to discipline herself to keep her penchant for daydreaming from distracting her.

On this particular evening, she and Antonio, her married lover, were entertaining the opera company's tenor and his newest light of love on the eve of their departure for a holiday in London. "Where does he *find* these creatures?" Antonio had asked incredulously on several occasions.

Antonio lived in a large country house with his frail and petulant wife. He rarely saw her, however, as he kept a small studio near the opera house and spent much of his time with Marguerite. Their friends suspected that their relationship was more than platonic, but few would have dared speak of it openly.

Following a supper of prosciutto, creamy cheese, black olives and fresh fruit, washed down with wine and brandy, Gianni and Prudence took their leave, promising to travel cautiously and be in touch when they returned.

Antonio and Marguerite climbed the stairs slowly. Removing his coat and cravat, Antonio lowered himself onto the chaise and watched as Marguerite undressed. Aware of his sensuous temperament, she undid the buttons down the front of her jacket one at a time, allowing her fingers to caress her breasts gently, almost unobtrusively, as each button was released. The jacket slid from her shoulders and fell to the floor as she reached behind her back to undo the fasteners on her skirt, which billowed gently as it floated to the floor. Removing the rest of her apparel, she stretched languorously. Years of voice and theatrical training had given her the ability to control her body well and she moved slowly toward Tonio, watching as he began to stir. Lowering herself over him, she removed the remainder of his clothing one piece at a time, massaging his bare skin gently.

They rose as one and crossed leisurely to the huge bed. Time stood still as each sought out the secret places on the other's body, knowing as only longtime lovers know, how to bring their passion to a mutual climax. They slept soundly and dreamlessly until just before dawn. Waking her with soft kisses, Tonio spoke her name.

"Sarah, my beloved, we must continue on our journey now. We have far to go before we can be together for all time."

Dazed, she rose from the bed, following him to the window where the pink glow of the sun was creeping over the horizon.

"Sarah?" she repeated, stunned to discover herself in a room that she knew was not her room near San Francisco, but was more than familiar. She pulled the comforter from the bed to hide her nakedness, but he drew it from her fingers, saying, "Don't be afraid, my love, you won't need it."

"Paul?" she whispered hoarsely, "how did you get here? How did *we* get here?"

Holding his index finger to his lips, he opened the shutters on the long window and pushed the panes outward. Reassuringly, he put his arm around her shoulders, drawing her close. The pale fog crept in through the open window, enveloping them. Very slowly, they moved through it to another space in another time and another dimension.

The horse drawn carriage moved rapidly down a long drive toward the big house at the end.

"Ah, Tonio, it's good to be home," Marguerite sighed. "The opening was wonderful, the orchestra was superb, and our friends are such fun, but I am too old for so much excitement."

"I, too, am too old for all the frivolity. I have always loved this house and the countryside around it, but since you have joined me here as my wife, it seems so full of love and joy that I want only to spend my days here at the piano."

"Don't tell me that you already have another melody running through that head of yours! Is there some fountain inside of you that cannot be stilled?"

"The only fountain around is the one in the courtyard, my love. And my days of creating music seem to be dwindling, but a small melody remains in my heart and sings to you alone."

"Tonio, my precious, you are such a romantic soul. Tomorrow we must walk in the garden as we used to do," Marguerite smiled.

"Do you still miss your little house in Milano, my dearest?" Tonio asked.

"Sometimes," she answered, "but the years we have spent here together have been such happy ones, years I never thought I'd have with you, that I feel I have been blessed twice over. Once in having found you at all, and then again when we were finally able to marry and let the world know of our love."

"But you must miss your performances and the recognition you were so accustomed to receiving," Tonio persisted.

"No, not really. It was good to leave it while the audiences still wanted me. And singing the melodies for your operas has been more than satisfactory. I am still part of the world of music without the endless rehearsals, the fittings for costumes, the aggravations that come with temperamental people. I could not ask for more than I have been fortunate to have been given."

"I am glad. You are the gem of my life. I always thought that the constant illnesses Maria suffered were mostly in her head and that I was doomed to a life unfulfilled. Sometimes I feel a little guilty that I neglected her so much. Perhaps the illnesses began as an attempt to get attention and became real as they continued. But this house that was once so gloomy now seems filled with light."

Marguerite reached up to caress his face as he helped her from the carriage. They went through the front door and Tonio hung his hat on the hall tree as Marguerite lifted her veil and removed the pins from the small black hat she wore. Crossing the foyer, he went through the large salon to the French doors that led to a courtyard beyond. Throwing them open, he inhaled deeply and gazed up at the cloudless blue sky.

"Tonio," Marguerite called, "remember how much we used to love those little suppers in my salon? Let's ask cook to fix one for us now! We can eat outside on the terrace and watch the sunset."

A little while later they did just that. Once again, they sipped wine with prosciutto, cheese, olives and fruit. They moved inside as dusk turned into night, finding that a fire had been laid in the fireplace.

Antonio got out the cognac and two glasses and they sat companionably in the overstuffed chairs that had been brought from Marguerite's house in the city. Enjoying the firelight, they did not light the lamps, content with each other in silence until Marguerite rose.

"I must get ready for bed, Tonio, before I am too tired to move from this chair. Would you bring the cognac up for one last little sip when you come?"

As she climbed the stairs, Marguerite ran her hand over the dark wood of the railing, smooth from years of rubbing and cool to the touch. Nearing the top, she experienced a small pain in her chest, then a sharper one that took her breath away. She sat down on the top step for a moment, then pulled herself up by clutching the banister and went on to the bedroom. Still breathless, she lowered herself onto the chaise that had also been brought from her little house, and began to take the pins from her hair.

It was there that Tonio found her when he came into the room several minutes later, carrying the glasses of cognac. Her eyes were open and she was smiling a small and tender smile. He did not realize until he set the glasses down and took her hand that her eyes were lifeless. Closing them gently, he stroked her hair and wept.

Sarah watched as Tonio held Marguerite's hand to his cheek, his face wet with tears. Though she had been in Marguerite's body only moments ago as she climbed the stairs, and had felt her pain, she was now strangely detached. A shadow emerged from Tonio's form, calling to her.

"Sarah? Have you left Marguerite's body? You must, you know."

"I'm so tired," she replied, her voice barely audible. "I want to go home." The fog enveloped her instantly and as it began to dissipate, she found herself safe in her own bed in her own apartment, once again Sarah Fremont. Awake and cognizant, she grasped the covers on the bed, then reached out to stroke the wood on the bed table, assuring herself that they were real. This time she knew she had left Sarah's body to become Marguerite. It still seemed too bizarre to understand, but she believed that it had happened. She remembered it all. The way it felt when Tonio touched her, when Ikkyu had touched her. Even now, the tips of her fingers tingled with desire as she recalled wiping the perspiration from Ikkyu's sleeping form, remembered the course and curly hair of Tonio's chest as she massaged it.

How many more lives were there in which she had loved Paul Winslow? Would there be more experiences in another dimension? If they were really soulmates, why had they not met in this lifetime? That must be it, she thought. That must be why he had come to her now. They had not yet fulfilled their destiny together. But if he could come to her, did that mean he was already dead and waiting for her to join him? Must she die to know him again, to love him again?

Reluctant to relinquish what remained of her other world, she turned over, closed her eyes and hugged the pillow that lay beside her, falling into a deep and undisturbed sleep.

CHAPTER TEN

Sunday morning brought the dawn of a magnificent day in the San Francisco Bay Area. It was one of those days when motorists on the Golden Gate Bridge could almost see into living rooms in Berkeley on the other side of the bay. The sun shone in a cloudless sky and the air was crisp and clean. Summer fog and autumn heat were but memories and the drizzles that accompanied the winter season were yet to come.

Sarah awoke feeling inexplicably joyful. She rose briefly to open the draperies and let in the sunlight, then ducked back under the covers to savor a feeling of absolute contentment. When she closed her eyes, she could still see Tonio at the piano or reclining on the chaise in their bedroom, Sarah's own bedroom in that life. When she opened her eyes, the green dress that hung on her closet door reminded her of John's arms around her as they danced just the night before. Any sane person would regard the two instances as contradictory, she thought, but she reveled in the memory of each instance and delighted in the knowledge that she was loved and appreciated.

Feeling a sudden need to look at the photos Merrie had given her of Paul, she threw off the covers and went quickly to her den down the hall. Would she be able to see Ikkyu or Antonio in Paul's eyes? Of the three likenesses she had, only the one of him wearing his flight helmet showed his eyes clearly, but the spark was there.

Carrying the photo with her, she went to the door to retrieve the heavy Sunday issue of the San Francisco Chronicle that lay outside. She lifted her face to the sunlight, breathing deeply before bending to pick it up. Dropping it on the dining room table, she hurried to pull the sections apart in search of the one that might contain an account of the previous night's party. Turning the pages in anticipation, she was delighted to discover a fine article on the second page of the suburban section.

Friends who had either attended the dinner or read about it already in the paper began to phone to offer congratulations and support. Merrie phoned to thank her and to say what a wonderful time both she and Pete had had, and John called from the airport to tell her that he'd meant what he said about her being special to him and that he would be back soon.

Late in the afternoon, Julie Schaefer called. "I've been trying to call you all day," she complained. "Your line has been busy each time. Is the phone permanently attached to your ear by this time?"

Sarah laughed, "Yes, it has been busy. I think practically everyone I know in the area has called today. And each one has been so great, volunteering, asking for literature, etcetera. I could go into this full time if I didn't already have a job!"

"Are you doing anything exciting this evening or could you come over for a light supper and some girl talk?"

"As a matter of fact, I'd love to come over. There's something I'd like to talk to you about," Sarah said, thinking that perhaps she could confide in Julie.

"Oh? Sounds serious. Did the handsome Frenchman ask you to fly away to his chateau with him?" Julie was only half joking.

"No, not yet anyway. He is awfully nice though and I would like to see him again."

"Well, come on over anytime and tell me all about it. You know how to get here?"

"Oh, yeah. I'll be there in a little while."

A short time later she was driving up El Camino Real through

Burlingame. She made a left turn and checked the numbers of the apartment buildings in the first block, concluding that Julie must be up two or three blocks. She soon found it and parked in front.

"What a wonderful apartment," she said, turning around appreciatively as Julie hung her jacket in the hall closet. "It's a townhouse, isn't it? I've often thought it might be nice to have the bedrooms upstairs, but then I admit I'm too lazy to want to climb stairs."

"I do like having the baby away from the living room," Julie responded, "though I'm afraid I may have trouble with her falling downstairs when she starts to move around more. As a matter of fact, I'm having a gate installed next week."

"It must be hard on you, knowing that Sandy's father doesn't even know he has a child," Sarah commented. "I know your parents live in the Bay Area, but I thought they were up in Marin County. How did you happen to choose Burlingame?"

"Well, I had to move from San Diego. Most of the people I knew there had been transferred and I was taking up quarters that they wanted to give to replacement officers, so I decided I should be near enough to my parents to see them now and then, but not so near that my mother could interfere too much in my life. It was a big decision to move so far from where Jack would expect me to be if he suddenly came home, but after the months dragged on, it got easier. I think if Jack knew about Sandy, he'd want me to be near family. My father is a doctor, you know."

"Yes, Merrie told me."

"Isn't Merrie the dearest person you'd ever hope to meet? I'm so glad I got her number from the woman who started the action group in San Diego. That was another reason I chose the San Mateo Peninsula. I figured being involved in some kind of activity on Jack's behalf would keep my mind occupied and most of the military personnel around here are either in Sunnyvale or Alameda. Since the East Bay is *two* bridges away from my parents, I decided Burlingame was the logical place to be.

"I'm glad you came to all of those conclusions," Sarah said, smiling at her new friend.

"Merrie said you called her after you saw the picture of Paul in the paper. What made you want to help us?" Julie asked curiously.

"That's partly what I wanted to talk to you about," Sarah said tentatively. She paused to organize her thoughts, then continued, "When I saw the picture, it was like he was someone I knew very well. Someone I not only knew, but loved. Does that sound incredibly foolish?"

"Whooo…," Julie's eyebrows went up as her breath escaped from her mouth. "Kind of strong stuff, but not necessarily foolish. You haven't met him, have you? Somewhere other than here? Are you sure you aren't just romanticizing him a little? The fallen hero?"

"No, I know I haven't met him, but when Merrie took me into the den where she has all of his stuff and I saw the picture of him with John, I was sure she'd notice my knees shaking. And it is romantic, but not in the way you think. Some really strange things have happened since I first saw the newspaper story. I'm not even sure I should tell you – it sounds so bizarre when I put it into words."

"Oh, come on. I haven't lived in a vacuum all my life. I doubt if you could shock me too much."

Sarah related the story she'd told John just the night before, this time adding a little of the more intimate moments as well as the episode with Antonio and Marguerite. "I'm sure that Paul was both Ikkyu and Antonio. Do you believe in reincarnation, Julie? Or out of body experiences?"

Julie shrugged. "I don't know. I've never thought much about either one. I don't think anyone could say positively that there is no such thing, but on the other hand, it's a little hard to assimilate into my WASPy background."

"Merrie said that Paul was best man in your wedding. What's he like?" Sarah asked a bit wistfully.

"Jack knew him much better than I did, of course. They were in flight school together and then they were both sent to the San Diego area. Jack was flying out of Miramar and Paul was assigned to a carrier out of Coronado, so they stayed in touch. I met Jack at a party, but Paul was gone so much that we didn't see much of him until the wedding. I was so crazy about Jack that I didn't pay a lot of attention to anyone else, but I do remember that Paul always looked so at ease, no matter where he was or what he was wearing. He looked great in the dress uniform that he wore for the ceremony. He's one of those rare men who are comfortable in anything. My wedding album is right here. I'll show you." Julie went to a bookshelf to get the album and handed it to Sarah.

Looking through the pages, Sarah paused at the ones of Paul with Jack, and at several of the entire wedding party, experiencing small pangs of jealousy at one in which the maid of honor, a pretty blonde, was smiling up into Paul's eyes. He does look at ease, she thought. Why couldn't that have been me?

Aloud she said, "I've never given any thought to reincarnation before this either. Do you think it's really possible that I *have* known Paul in more than one previous life? Or is this just some romantic obsession? Am I crazy?"

"You don't seem to be the least bit crazy to me," Julie assured her. "As for obsession, I couldn't say. Why don't you do some research on it at the library? Remember that Bridey Murphy thing a few years ago? Some housewife was hypnotized and remembered being an Irish peasant?"

"Yeah, but I also remember that everybody thought she was either making it all up or was nuts. What about the feeling that I've had that Paul has been right there in the room with me? Or when I was sure we were soaring through the sky on a swan? Now *that* does sound crazy! One song, 'My Foolish Heart,' seems to trigger something in me. I was dancing with John last night when the orchestra played it and all of a sudden I felt that I was dancing with Paul. I even said his name!"

"That must have been a shock to John. He likes you a lot – he hardly took his eyes off you all evening. How did you explain using Paul's name?"

"We went down to my office for awhile and I told him some of it, but the part about Antonio and Marguerite hadn't happened yet. He didn't seem to think I was crazy either, but he did say he wanted me to be sure that it was him I wanted to be with and not Paul Winslow." Sarah sighed.

"This may not be an entirely palatable idea, but you don't suppose that Paul is really dead and that his spirit is visiting you, do you?" Julie grimaced at the thought.

"I did think about that after last night's dreams, or whatever, but I just can't accept that theory. No, I feel very strongly that Paul is alive and that he's trying to contact me to let me know. Oh, God, nobody'd *ever* believe this, would they?"

"Well, I guess the best way to start is to get some reading material and find out whether or not there's any credible evidence of the paranormal. Unless you don't really want to know. It might be easier to just wait and see what happens next," Julie said pensively. "What about John? How does he figure in this relationship?"

"That's another strange thing," Sarah said, looking away. "I don't seem to have a real problem accepting the fact that I have feelings for both men. That could change, I suppose, if I were to begin an intimate relationship with John. The lovemaking with Ikkyu and Tonio was perfection even if it was, strictly speaking, not really happening, at least not in this time and space, so I suppose there is the possibility of comparisons. It's a little like living two entirely separate existences, one as the person you know as Sarah Fremont and one as the soulmate, if you will, of Paul Winslow. Oh, God! I can't believe I'm saying that and actually believing it!"

At home later, Sarah was torn by conflicting feelings once again. Now two other people knew and though neither had scorned her, she knew that neither of them really believed in the reality of her experiences. They might acknowledge the possibility of the paranormal, the metaphysical, but they didn't really accept it as more than a romantic notion. And in the telling, she feared her credibility was being stretched, perhaps beyond repair.

She wandered from room to room, touching the furniture, the things she had so lovingly gathered to furnish her home: her piano, the paintings, the books. The feeling of warmth and joy that these rooms created crept into her heart as she surveyed her personal domain, and she whispered, "If you're here, Paul, or if you can hear me, don't give up. I *will* find you and we *will* be together again."

CHAPTER ELEVEN

P aul stared dejectedly at the scratches he'd made on the dirt floor of his hut. Allowing for the days he knew he'd lost track of during the torture sessions of his early days in the camp, he figured that the scratches added up to nearly a year. This time, combined with the months he had spent in Hanoi, indicated that it must be nearly Christmas, 1970.

His captors had apparently decided they were not going to get any significant information from him and had announced harshly one day that he must earn his keep by working in the rice paddies beyond the camp. At first he'd been overjoyed, believing that at last he might make contact with other prisoners, but that had not come about. He was kept carefully separated from the other men and told that if he'd cooperate with the guards as others had, giving relevant information, he'd be allowed to socialize as a reward. He was sure they were bluffing in the attempt to make him believe that others had cooperated, but depression threatened to consume him on occasion.

His escape plan had proven to be even more difficult than he'd originally thought it would be. He had managed to add a black pajama top to the little pile of supplies beside the river, but so much time had passed that he feared the sandals and the top were probably rotted by jungle growth and would be useless anyway.

He made constant attempts to occupy his mind, one of which was to recall plots of movies he'd seen, replaying each film in his head. During one of these entertainment sessions, he'd been 'watching' John Wayne movies when he remembered that the duke had an imaginary companion he called 'Baby' in a movie with Lauren Bacall called 'Blood Alley.' He began to think of the woman with the dark hair as his own 'Baby,' confiding in her quietly at times when he was alone in the darkness of his hut. She had become his salvation, his reason for living, often seeming to be with him, though what was left of his rational mind told reminded him she was imaginary.

He told her about his fifty-seven Chevy and his friendship with John St. James, and played scenes with her in which they were seated in front of a fireplace discussing their favorite foods, music and places. In dreams he saw her clearly, once holding her in his arms as they danced to a tune he could not identify. She had been wearing an emerald green gown and had whispered his name as her fingers played with the hair at the nape of his neck, her eyes glittering like precious gems. Recently he'd watched her as she undid the buttons of a black silk jacket one at a time, caressing her breasts sensuously, letting the jacket fall to the floor followed by the long, billowing skirt she wore. He had felt her hands as they stroked his chest, pulling gently, teasingly, on his chest hair.

He thought he'd heard her crying once, and had tried to comfort her, had spoken with her, but the images sometimes ran together in his mind until he was no longer sure what he had made up and what he had dreamed. She often seemed more real to him than the guards in the camp, and he began to fear that he might be losing his sanity.

Gazing at the scratches in the dirt, he spoke to her again, asking wistfully, "What will we be doing for Christmas this year?"

"Your parents are expecting us to be at their house," she replied, smiling.

"Ah, yes. That would be great. I hope Mom will have a turkey *and* a ham, or maybe even a goose. And stuffing with everything but the kitchen sink in it. There won't be any snow in San Francisco, but we'll listen to Bing Crosby singing 'White Christmas' on the stereo."

He stroked his matted beard and lay back on the straw that was his bed.

Sarah stood at the window in her office staring out at the rain. It had been grey and dreary for more than a week and the hotel parking lot was a mass of tiny puddles, each one exploding like shattered crystal as new drops of moisture fell into them. The door opened and Ellen came in to tell her that Van Carducci wanted to see her if she was free. She closed her eyes for a moment, then straightened her shoulders and took a deep breath. The holiday season was over and the rain intensified the inevitable letdown that came when the decorations were removed.

She had spent Christmas Day with the Winslows. Though it had been only the three of them, Merrie had been determined to make it a cheerful occasion and had prepared a feast of both turkey and ham.

Sheila had returned to Chicago as quickly as possible after the kick-off dinner, claiming she simply could not miss the house party to which she'd been invited for the holiday, so would be unable to return. It had been a disappointment to both Pete and Merrie that their daughter cared more for parties and friends who probably would not have invited her had it not been for the Donnelly name and money. Merrie was falsely cheerful and Pete said more by his silence than if he'd reacted angrily.

Sarah was inclined to believe that Sheila's apparent indifference stemmed from a hidden insecurity on her part, and that she found it easier to lead a superficial existence that face a reality she knew in her heart would hurt.

Julie Schaefer had dropped by in the evening, having spent a frustrating day with her parents. Her mother had invited a young doctor, new to the staff of the hospital where Dr. Summerhill was Chief Surgeon, to join them for Christmas dinner, an obvious attempt to introduce him to Julie. There had been a very awkward moment when the poor man had asked Julie if she was divorced. She had stared at him in amazement, at a loss for words, as she realized that he had no idea that her husband was a prisoner of war in Vietnam. She felt sorry for him in his acute embarrassment, and apologized for her mother's lack of communication. A terrible argument that left Julie angry and in tears had followed his departure and only her father's somewhat harried intervention had saved them from total estrangement.

"It wouldn't hurt you to be nice to him," her mother had said. "After all, you might be glad to have him around one of these days."

Sarah turned away from the gloom outside the window and made her way down the hall to Van's office. Nancy, his secretary, greeted her warmly and asked about her holidays.

"Quiet, but pleasant," Sarah told her. "How about yours?"

"Pretty much the same. I'm not sure whether that's good or bad. You'd think one of us might have had a little excitement. Go on in – he's waiting for you."

Sarah went through the door into Van's office and found him frowning over the papers that lay in front of him on his desk.

"What's up?" she asked. "A problem I'm not aware of?"

"No, no. This is just the estimate for replacing the cooling unit in the walk-in refrigerator. Higher than I thought it would be, but then what else is new?" He waved a hand toward the chair in front of the desk, indicating that she should sit down.

He leaned back in his chair, formed a pyramid with his hands, and looked at her. "Are you free for lunch?" he asked.

"I don't even have to check my calendar. There's hardly anything going on in the whole hotel. Post-holiday blues, I guess. Why? Are you buying?"

"No, not me. Dick Beaumont from the Chicago office is in town and would like you to meet him in the City. I'm not sure just what's up, but I think he might be planning to make you an offer."

"What kind of offer? Business or pleasure?" Sarah asked mischievously.

"You wish!" Van shot back. "Seriously, he only phoned me as a courtesy. He came in late last night and then left to go into the City before I got here this morning. Something's up, but I'm pretty much in the dark myself. You're to meet him at one o'clock at the Buena Vista Café. The implication was that unless you're entertaining the President, or maybe the Pope, he'd expect you at one o'clock."

The Buena Vista Café, one of the oldest restaurants in the City of

San Francisco and home of the original Irish coffee in America, was located at the foot of the Hyde Street cable car. Its windows looked out on the cable car turnaround and the Golden Gate Bridge. Most of the customers on a rainy day in January were the regulars who often met there to exchange business tips and gossip as well as partake of the good, hearty breakfasts that were served all day. Probably, Sarah thought as she entered, because many of them were out until the wee hours and didn't get up again until late morning or even late afternoon.

She had met Dick Beaumont, Vice President of the Davidson Hotel Group, once or twice and saw him sitting by a window halfway between the front and back doors. A man of seemingly boundless energy, he was one of those men whose age is impossible to determine. He turned from the window, saw her approaching, and rose to greet her.

"I love this place," he said after the mandatory pleasantries had been exchanged. "I lived in San Francisco for several months after college and before I took the job with Davidson hotels. You never know who you might see in here. Did you know that Herb Caen, the Chronicle columnist, comes in here a lot? He probably gets most of his ideas here – not hard to see why!"

Over the next hour, Sarah learned that she was being offered the position of Director of Public Relations for the entire Davidson Group, with a substantial increase in salary and an office in downtown San Francisco. It had been decided that since two of the hotel properties were in California, it would be to the company's advantage to have someone on the West Coast to coordinate the overall image, promoting all four hotels to business travelers as well as vacationers.

Dick Beaumont had been approving the brochure updates that had been presented by the individual hotels, but his schedule left little time to do the job properly. He had already selected an office in the financial district that had a small reception area, a comfortable office for Sarah and an adequate conference space. She would move into it as soon as a replacement could be found for her present job.

The rain had abated somewhat, but pools of water remained on the streets as darkness fell and motorists turned on their headlights.

Sarah turned into the driveway that led to her parking space behind her apartment and sighed gratefully as she switched off the ignition. Unlocking her back door, she stepped into the entry and reached for the light switch on the wall just inside.

She felt slightly soggy, having run from doorway to doorway in a vain attempt to avoid the rain in San Francisco. The meeting with Dick Beaumont had been congenial and her head was still spinning at the opportunity she had been offered. The salary that went along with the title, Director of Public Relations, was considerably higher than the one she currently earned. The job would involve a good deal of traveling as she would be expected to attend functions held at the hotels in the group as well as make personal calls on some of the major clients who used the properties frequently. She'd be highly visible as an executive of the Davidson Hotel Group.

The apartment was cloaked in a shadowy chill that caused her to shiver involuntarily. She hurried through the entry hall to the living room where she switched on lamps and closed the drapes to shut out the dreary weather. A pleasant glow filled the room as she lit the gas jet in the fireplace and the only evidence that remained of the gloom outside was the muted sound of the rain.

Sarah had never possessed a proclivity toward introspection, having drifted through childhood surrounded by an aura of love and affection that enabled her to assume, if somewhat unwittingly, that if she simply did her best at whatever task was at hand, life would move on in a natural and comfortable manner. The deaths of her parents had been a terrible shock initially, as they had been her source of security, a sense of which had never been challenged and that she took for granted. But along with the assumption of self-worth had come an eagerness to meet life head-on and experience it to its fullest. She had gone off to college only months after the funerals and been quickly absorbed in new activities that dimmed her loss and directed her attention toward the future.

The enormity of the responsibility that came with her new position suddenly dawned on her as she stood rubbing her hands together in front of the flickering fireplace. An admittedly small, but important company was depending upon her to enhance their public image. They had entrusted her with a duty that was vital to the wellbeing of the business. She had never questioned her ability to earn her paycheck each month, but then she had always considered herself remarkably lucky to be in a job where she planned meetings or parties and actually got paid to do it. A minor slip now and then would be forgiven if it were even noticed. But the loss of a major account, or a failure to satisfy the requirements of a potential client could result in a loss that might be disastrous to Davidson Hotels.

She felt an immediate need to see her face in a mirror – to examine the image that she presented to the world. Her hand went to her face, stroking its contours, feeling the skin that covered what lay hidden beneath. Though she looked at that face each morning as she applied her makeup, she rarely saw anything beyond the shadows and highlights that made the overall picture appealing. She realized suddenly that her attention to detail in her makeup and clothes was directed toward confirmation of her personal perception of what she *should* look like, and had little to do with the person that lived underneath. Was it that image that had achieved this success? Was she in reality an enormous hoax, about to be discovered if she wasn't very careful to hide the real person lurking beneath the surface? She approached the mirror in her dressing room in trepidation.

The woman who looked back at her from across the bathroom sink was someone she knew, but not someone who seemed truly familiar. The dark hair was tousled from exposure to the elements outside, but that only made it look friendlier. The mouth was full, with lips that seemed to invite intimacy without being obvious. The nose was in just the right place in the oval face, not too big, not too small. The eyebrows curved distinctly above eyes that stared back at her with an intensity that was almost frightening. She leaned toward the woman facing her in an effort to see into the depths of those eyes.

They were green eyes, but flecked with other hues that made the observer unsure of what might appear as her expression altered. There were tiny gold highlights that appeared and disappeared as the light changed; there was even a hint of lavender that fled when pursued.

Sarah stared into the eyes in the mirror, aware of how little she really knew of herself. Her entire life had consisted of assumptions, the validity of which had never been challenged. Who was this person who functioned more than just successfully within the confines of society, but lived with the belief that she was somehow connected to a man she had never met, yet knew better than she knew herself? Who was this woman who was attracted to a handsome and accomplished man in what was perceived to be real life, but dedicated to another man who dwelt on an elusive plane that existed only in her mind?

How long would her new job last if she were found out? What would they think of their new Director of Public Relations if they knew what lurked beneath the façade that she presented to the world? She backed away from the mirror, retreating from the stranger who had entered her life as suddenly as had Paul Winslow, John St. James, Pete and Merrie, and Julie Schaefer. Who were all these people? How had they crept into her life and assumed such importance without her invitation? And the dreams that seemed so real. The experiences in which she was sure she had left her body and ascended to another plane – what would Dick Beaumont and the corporate office think of their choice of representatives if they were aware of these things? How deep was her own belief in their reality? She must be very careful, tread softly, lest she be consumed by forces over which she seemed to have little or no control.

Sarah hastened back to the warmth and security promised by the fireplace, fleeing the demons that threatened her safe and comfortable existence. Reassured by the feel of familiar fabric as she ran her hand over the chairs, the gleaming wood of her dining room table, the appliances that waited patiently on the kitchen counter, she reached into the cupboard for the bottle of expensive scotch that represented success and achievement, the familiar.

This was not the time to drift into the shadows of her mind, this was a time to celebrate life – this life. A time to share her good fortune with good friends, to enjoy her accomplishments. Maybe she'd even telephone John in Paris…

CHAPTER TWELVE

The days slipped into weeks, then more than a month had passed as Sarah became engrossed in her work. The task of familiarizing herself with her new responsibilities was monumental. Fortunately, the first months of the year were generally the slowest in the hotel business as people recovered from the holiday season. This allowed time to pore over a multitude of files on corporate accounts, media blitzes, preparations for weekend savings brochures to be distributed to travel agencies and expansion plans that were on the drawing board.

There was to be a convention of tour operators from all over the country in New York in April that would be the first major function at which Sarah would officially represent Davidson Hotels. In attendance would be travel agents who specialized in affinity groups, airline representatives, and other companies who put together packaged itineraries – all potential clients. The competition among destination areas and representative hotels would be fierce. This would be Sarah's opportunity to find out just what the tour operators were looking for and how the Davidson Group might meet their needs.

European interests would be represented as well and Sarah wondered if John St. James would be there. She had not phoned him with the news of her promotion after all, and was quite sure that he was unaware of her good fortune. He had written several short notes, but she had put off answering them, intending to sit down to write a thoughtful letter when time permitted. The time had never seemed to materialize, however, so she assumed that even if her schedule allowed for any personal activities, it might be difficult to locate him at the convention.

She had spoken with both Merrie and Julie often by phone, but had seen them only a few times since the holidays as she was usually in her office until late in the evening and on weekends as well. The bracelets made of either copper or silver and inscribed with servicemen's names had arrived and she now wore one that carried Paul Winslow's name and the date on which he was shot down. She had been too exhausted when she got home at night to dwell on the dreams of past lives with him, and had come to accept the probability that it had been a subconscious desire, a romantic fantasy on her part. Immersing herself in the pursuit of corporate profit, she had little time to dwell on psychic dreams and out-of-body experiences.

She did, however, rub the bracelet on her arm gently each night as she turned out the light, seeking to send whatever warmth and concern that might travel through the cosmos to give comfort and solace – just in case.

The dark wood paneling that covered the walls in the lobby of the Davidson Hotel in New York glowed from years of polishing. It was the oldest of the Davidson properties and was the habitat of many writers and theatre people who looked upon it as a second home. Much of the furniture in the lobby cocktail lounge had been recovered rather than replaced over the years and antique cabinets along the far wall still held mementos of days gone by. There was an air of stability to the room, reassuring the visitor that the Davidson could be relied upon.

Sarah found fresh flowers in her suite when she checked in, a touch she appreciated. Though she had visited New York many times over the years, she had never stayed at the Davidson as Aunt Charlotte's bohemian apartment had always been an amusing home away from home. She sincerely hoped to find at least a couple of hours to spend there again, but had not given Charlotte advance notice of her stay in New York in the event that it didn't work out.

She had a dinner date with Bob Mattheson, the New York Sales Manager, in a couple of hours, leaving her just time to unpack and change clothes, and briefly review the advance program for the convention. The exhibits were scheduled to open at noon on the following day. Many were suppliers to the industry who hoped to sell their products to the airlines, hotels and cruise lines represented, and many of the more popular destination areas such as the Caribbean and Hawaiian Islands would be setting up elaborate displays of posters and native delicacies to offer convention goers.

The Davidson Group had arranged for a smaller space that would be set up to look like an intimate lobby area with a miniature front desk on one side that held brochures on the four different properties. It would be manned by the Sales Manager's staff from New York on an alternating basis, as well as white gloved banquet personnel serving coffee and tea.

Descending in the elevator for her dinner date, Sarah checked her appearance one last time in the mirror and stepped off as the doors opened. Crossing the lobby to the dining room where she was to meet Bob Mattheson, she was surprised to see a short, stocky man stand to greet her as the maitre d' showed her to the table. He extended his hand, laughing jovially, and said, "I know, I know. You were expecting a suave, sophisticated man-about-town and you get me instead." His expression told her that he was accustomed to the reaction and she smiled in return.

She discovered during the course of the evening that Bob was not only knowledgeable when it came to marketing the New York Davidson, but a witty conversationalist as well. He outlined her schedule for the next few days, giving her a brief rundown on the appointments that had been arranged for her with area executives whose personnel used the West Coast hotels. She found that she would have very little time to spare if she were to accomplish everything she hoped to do.

As they finished dinner, Bob signaled the waiter to bring cognac and coffee, then cleared his throat and said, "There's one more person you might want to meet."

"The way you say that, it sounds like you're not sure," she responded.

"Well, she's not a client, just the reverse in fact. Maggie Davidson is in town from Chicago. She's Michael Davidson's daughter and heir to the family fortune. She's only about twenty one years old, and graduated last year from a private women's college in Missouri. I don't know the whole story, but apparently the Davidsons were unhappy with the young man she fell in love with, and managed to convince him that it wouldn't work out. Maggie is still pretty bitter about it from what I hear."

"What was wrong with the young man?" Sarah asked.

"He's Japanese," Bob answered tersely.

"Oh. I met the Davidsons a couple of years ago when they were in San Francisco, but I guess Maggie must have been in school at the time. I didn't really get to know them, but I can see where Michael Davidson probably has pretty definite ideas about the kind of man his daughter should marry," Sarah commented. "Why is she in New York? Is she here for the convention?"

"Ostensibly she's here to see some shows and do some shopping. She's staying at the hotel, but apparently has college chums who live in the area. I think her father timed it so that she'd be here while all the excitement was going on in the hope that she might develop some interest in the hotel business and get her mind off the unhappy love affair, so to speak. He didn't actually suggest that you take her under your wing or anything, but I gather he's hoping that meeting a woman as successful and glamorous as you are might be a good influence on Maggie," Bob said tentatively.

"Glamorous and successful!" Sarah laughed. "I've never thought of myself in those terms!"

"Well, you are, you know. I guess I can admit that some of us were a little intimidated at the thought of you. We were afraid you'd be some sort of no-nonsense career type that might start throwing her weight around. Now that I've met you, I can see why you were chosen to head up the Public Relations Department. I should have known you'd be easy to be with, because that's what's required in this kind of job."

"Thank you. It's hard to believe anyone could have considered me threatening in any way, shape or form. I can admit now that I was somewhat apprehensive about meeting you and the New York staff as well. As you said earlier, the suave, sophisticated man-about-town image. When can we squeeze Maggie into the schedule? I don't know what I can do, but I would like to meet her."

"How about lunch tomorrow? I left it open on purpose, thinking maybe Maggie might enjoy a stop at the exhibit hall with you afterward," Bob suggested.

"That's fine. Why don't you give me her room number and I'll leave a message for her tonight and then call her in the morning to confirm? By the way, I'd also like to check to see if a friend of mine is here from Paris. I think if he *is* in town for the convention, he might like to join us for some of the events."

"Sure. We can stop by the front desk when we leave here and get both room numbers." Bob signaled the waiter again and signed the check that was brought.

The next morning Sarah gave careful consideration to what she would wear that day. She didn't want to be too severe, nor did she want to appear to be a suburban housewife. It's a good thing I packed more than I thought I'd need, she thought, selecting a soft peach colored suit and creamy white blouse. Her reflection in the mirror satisfied her that she looked tailored, but feminine. She reached for the phone just as it jangled to indicate that someone was calling her.

She picked it up and was surprised to hear John St. James' voice on the other end. "They told me last night that you weren't registered here, so I didn't know if you planned to be in New York or not!" she exclaimed.

"I am staying here, but the reservation wasn't in my name, it was under the company name," he told her.

"Of course. I should have thought of that. You are here for the convention then?"

"Yes, and I was hoping to find you here as well. I've been in London for the past few days and didn't have time to check with my office for messages before my plane left. I assumed you'd be here, though, in your new capacity as head of public relations. How's it going?"

"Then you do know about my fantastic good luck – how did the news get all the way to Paris? It must have been Merrie. I'm sure it couldn't be important enough to be included in the hotel hotline."

"Don't sell yourself short! It may not be headlines, but the Davidson

Group has a fine reputation worldwide, and their executives are always news. But you're right. Merrie did spread the word first. Are you happy with the change?"

"So far it's been mostly drudgery, getting to know the ropes by reviewing more files than any one company should be allowed to have. I haven't really gotten my feet wet yet. The New York Sales Manager, Bob Mattheson, took me to dinner last night, and I'm meeting Michael Davidson's daughter for lunch today, or at least I think I am. I was just about to call her."

"When can I see you?" John asked. She explained that she had a full schedule, but that she was sure she could see him even if it had to be later in the evening. They agreed that if they didn't run into each other sooner, they'd meet in the lobby cocktail lounge at ten o'clock that night. Sarah dialed Maggie Davidson's room fearing that she might hear a sullen and angry young woman on the line. She was pleasantly surprised to find that Maggie was cheerful and polite, as well as eager to meet her for lunch.

CHAPTER THIRTEEN

I t was a little before ten that evening when Sarah looked around the lobby lounge for John. Her day had been hectic and she wondered if she might have time to go up to her suite to splash a little water on her face and change her clothes. She was about to turn toward the elevator when she saw John's tall frame approaching. In the moments before he reached her, she was startled by the pleasure she felt at the sight of him. His stride was that of a man whose confidence was undisputed, and heads turned as other patrons watched his progress, then stared openly as they saw him greet the darkly beautiful woman who stood waiting for him.

"There you are at last," he exclaimed. "I feel as though I've spent an eternity in this room, but I guess it just seems that way."

"Have you been here that long?" Sarah asked, checking her watch. "I thought I was early and you probably weren't even here yet."

"I've been here for about half an hour, hoping you might be early," he replied. "I'll take it as a promising sign that you were at least a little bit ahead of schedule."

He led her back to the table and gazed at her appreciatively as they sat down. She had to laugh at the foolish grin on his face as he told her how glad he was to see her.

"I must seem like a teenager with his first crush," he commented, "but it seems like an eternity since I last saw you."

"It does seem longer than a few months, doesn't it? I've been so busy with this job that I haven't had time for much of anything but work. Sometimes I think I may have bitten off more than I can chew, and that I'll be found out and banished in disgrace."

"If anyone can do it, you can," John said. "Tell me what's been happening. How do you like being part of the corporate structure?"

"I think I love it, but I haven't really evaluated everything yet. Most of my time the past three months has been spent in reviewing client files and familiarizing myself with advertising and promotion, not to mention the other properties in the group. I still haven't seen the Davidson Chicagoan, or the one in San Diego. That's next on the agenda."

"Did you get over to the exhibits today? I had another appointment, so I haven't seen them yet."

"As a matter of fact I did spend a couple of hours there. I had lunch with Maggie Davidson and then took her over for a look. She turned out to be a very nice girl. I can't help but feel sorry for her," Sarah reflected, going on to tell John about Maggie's unhappy romance.

She had found the young woman to be remarkably philosophical and mature for her age. While still depressed over her loss, she was able to understand and forgive her parents for their rigid viewpoint. The thing that had caused her the greatest amount of sadness was the fact that until that time she had seen her father as unfalteringly fair and just, and was unprepared to realize that he could be fallible.

"I've always thought he was perfect in every way," Maggie had said. "It was a shock to find that his values seem to be double sided. He accepts anyone at face value in business or social situations, but when it comes to his daughter, the coin flipped and his darker side surfaced."

"She was so forthright and honest, totally unpretentious about it," Sarah went on. "I felt a little as though I was peeking through their windows and that perhaps I shouldn't be privy to so much of their personal lives. It just goes to show, you never know what people are like deep down inside. What they present on the surface isn't the whole picture." She stared pensively at a distant point near the ceiling for a moment, then turned to look into John's eyes, slightly embarrassed by her own apparent naiveté. He smiled tenderly, silent for a time as he rejoiced in her nearness.

"Have you resolved any of your feelings toward Paul?" he asked apprehensively.

"I don't know, John. I think so, but I've been so busy lately that I haven't had time to do any research on the idea of reincarnation or psychic experiences. I can accept the possibility of previous lives, but I think I have to live in this time and this life if I'm to stay sane. You remember Julie Schaefer, don't you? I told her about it and she didn't seem to think I was crazy either."

She held up her arm, showing him the copper bracelet. "I admit that I do rub the bracelet now and then as though that might satisfy some unknown responsibility toward Paul."

"Have there been any more episodes like the one with the samurai?" John inquired.

"Well yes, as a matter of fact there was another one the night of the party, but there hasn't been one since then. Are you sure you want to hear about this?"

"Everything about you interests me, Sarah. I've never been as drawn to a woman as I am to you. Maybe it's all part of the scenario intended in the overall scheme of things that Paul should have been my best friend, and that you have a powerful connection to him as well. I've never given any thought to past lives or anything more spiritual than my mother's devotion to Catholicism. I went to church like a dutiful son when I was young, but I've fallen away from it completely as an adult. My father was agnostic at best, so religion was sort of background security. My mother prayed for our souls and my father and I went on our way. There was always a priest or two around at family gatherings on my mother's side, upholding the family respectability, but no one ever suggested that I consider the church as a career."

"I know what you mean," Sarah responded. "My mother was Italian Catholic in much the same way that yours was French Catholic. She was very sheltered as a young girl, but when she married my father her life changed considerably. They traveled a lot and she became far more sophisticated over the years. Religion sort of took a back seat after awhile."

"Tell me about the second dream, or whatever it was," John said, leaning back in his chair expectantly.

"It does seem more like a dream now," she began. "You know how you look forward to a trip or a vacation, then the time comes and you go to some unfamiliar place, have a great time, and then six months later it all seems a little unreal?"

John nodded, smiling in agreement. She went on to tell him about Marguerite and Antonio, leaving out some of the specifics and falling silent as she finished the story.

"Is the memory of it painful?" John wanted to know.

"Yes and no," she answered, considering. "I had pushed it so far back in my mind that I thought it really was just a dream. But talking about it again brought it back. I can remember the texture of the dress I wore and I can feel the fabric on the chair, taste the cheese. I can even feel the pain I felt as I went up the stairs, which must have been a heart attack. The last thing I thought before I 'died' was how sad I was to leave Tonio, how sorry I was to cause him pain. Then I seemed to be detached somehow, watching. A voice asked me if I had left Marguerite's body, and all I could think of was how tired I was. Then I was back in my own bed again."

"I have to admit that I'm a bit ambivalent about this connection with Paul. Had you not been drawn to his picture, you and I would not have met. I wonder if there is some kind of destiny in it. It may sound self-serving, but maybe there's something in our karma that made it necessary for you to meet the Winslows and thereby meet me. A little far fetched, though." John's voice trailed off as he realized how preposterous his explanation sounded even to his own ears.

"I hadn't thought of it that way. I guess it could be possible." Sarah reached for John's hand, saying, "Oh, John, I feel so silly putting you through all this."

"Sarah, call it fate, call it anything you like, but I feel that I've been waiting for you all my life. It may sound a little bizarre, but my feelings for you grow stronger each day and if you feel even a little as I do, why don't we take it from there and let it happen?"

They were interrupted by a discreet cough from the waiter who stood beside the table. Startled, they realized that they were the only people left in the lounge and that the lights had been dimmed in anticipation of closing. John signed the check and they headed for the elevator. As the doors closed behind them, he took her hand, pulling her to him. She looked up into his eyes and let herself relax in his arms. There was no question but that he would follow her into the room as they reached her door.

The room was still dim as daylight began to creep around the edges of the drapes on the window. John opened his eyes briefly to check the time on the luminous dial of his watch, then settled back into the pillows on the bed, reveling in his contentment. He dozed off, waking again a short time later and smiled as he looked at the mass of dark curls on the pillow beside his.

He turned carefully, propping his head on one hand as the other reached out to touch the strands of hair that fanned out around Sarah's head, partially covering her face. Gazing at the contours of her face, he willed himself to remember every detail. Her forehead, her nose, her cheekbones, the mouth he had so recently kissed, the eyes that hid beneath her lashes. She stirred slightly and he held his breath hoping she would not wake, allowing him to cherish this first experience of waking up beside her. The first of many, he hoped.

He took the end of a curl between his fingers, playing with it gently as he reviewed their conversation of the previous evening. A strange beginning, he thought. Is she mine or will she be forever Paul's? How can I compete with the mystery, the intrigue, of the man who was my best friend? Am I getting into a relationship that can only bring me pain? Am I starting to believe in her dreams myself? I've always been so practical, so careful to be fair, but nothing seems to matter more than being with her on whatever terms necessary. How can I hope to convince her when there's an ocean and a continent separating us? She isn't going to leave her home and her career, and run off to Paris to be with me, and I can't drop everything to hang around San Francisco.

He signed deeply and she opened her eyes, startled at first to find John beside her. She stretched, smiling lazily, and asked, "Is it morning already?"

"Yes, I'm afraid it is, my love," he said tenderly. "I wish we could stay right here forever, but we both have busy schedules and if I don't leave here soon, the hallways are going to be filling up with people on their way to breakfast. God knows who I might run into. I wouldn't want to start any gossip about the Davidson Hotels newest executive."

"I guess you're right," she admitted, "though I think everyone around here is pretty broadminded. Maggie Davidson is the only one I'd be concerned about, not that she'd care, but it might get back to her father."

They compared notes on their respective schedules for the day, determining that once again it would be after dinner before they could be together. Promising to leave messages for one another if there was any change, they clung together briefly and John left for his own room.

They spent each night together after that, talking for hours, making love, then talking some more. They told each other childhood stories, shared feelings that each swore they had never told anyone else, explored each other's bodies and discovered a world of intimacy neither had known until then. Reluctant to say goodbye, John had accompanied Sarah to the airport, insisting that he meant to see her until she had vanished into the plane and he was sure it had left New York.

As the plane roared down the runway in preparation for take-off, Sarah leaned back in her seat and closed her eyes. She was terribly tired, but her mind was filled with pictures of the places, the people and the events of the past few days. The dozens of business cards she had collected were tucked into both her handbag and her briefcase, most of them with notes scrawled on the back that should be transcribed before her memory faded and she forgot who had said what.

Closing her eyes, she relived the warmth of John's arms around her as he bid her goodbye just a short time earlier. She felt such a sense of wellbeing and security when he was nearby. Perhaps not the excitement, the passion that Paul inspired, but happiness and yes, love. The memories of Paul that she thought she had come to terms with began to flood into the recesses of her mind, making him as real to her at that moment as John was.

In telling John of the dream about Antonio and Marguerite, she had recalled the texture of fabric and wood, the emotions that she felt in leaving Tonio. Now as she thought of Paul, she remembered just as clearly the contours of his face as she stroked it, the sensation of his lips as they kissed her forehead, her eyelids, her neck. She knew without doubt that they had been together, but she also knew that it was simply not possible. Unless…could one move through time and space without the need for a physical body?

They had left Paul and Sarah behind to become Ikkyu and Yoshiko. Had they really been those people in a time that no longer existed, or was time somehow eternal and unlimited? Could it be that the limitations are only in the human mind?

The Japanese lovers had strolled together through temple grounds, then made love on soft futons. Sarah's flesh flamed at the memory of their passion. Her fingers moved involuntarily, her nails caressing the hollows behind his knees. Oh yes, he had been flesh and blood. She was sure of that.

And yet he could not be flesh and blood. But she had clung to him as they soared above the clouds on the back of a glorious swan. She had seen his eyes, filled with love, as he reached out to her amid the flowers. No, it could not be. Tears slid down her face. She knew she would love him throughout eternity and yet, she also loved the man whose arms had so recently held her.

She jumped as a hand touched her shoulder and the flight attendant spoke words that she couldn't make out. The girl repeated them. "Are you all right?"

"Oh..oh, yes. I'll be fine," Sarah assured her. But would she ever be fine again? How easy it would be to slip away from reality. To retreat into a world where Paul became her Heathcliff and she his Kathy. But Kathy had married someone else when Heathcliff disappeared, hadn't she? Yet in the end, they were together, lovers through eternity. Perhaps that was how it was meant to be. Sarah would marry John, the man who promised her so much tenderness and security, while Paul remained in her heart, the soulmate she would have to wait another lifetime to meet again. Eventually, like Heathcliff and his Kathy, they would be together for eternity.

"Get a grip," she whispered to herself.

CHAPTER FOURTEEN

The parking lot was crowded with cars as Pete Winslow maneuvered into a space. Enthusiastic sports fans were filling the stadium and it was clear that fans of the San Francisco Giants anticipated victory to be theirs in the game with the New York Mets. Sarah and Julie clambered out of the back seat and joined Pete as he unloaded picnic supplies from the trunk of the car. They planned to buy hot dogs in the stadium to go with the bags of goodies they carried with them. A ballgame wouldn't be a ballgame without hot dogs, they reasoned.

It was a bright sunny day and the four of them were in the mood to have a good time. Walking toward the entrance, Pete commented jovially that he would be the envy of every man there with the three most beautiful women in San Francisco on his arm. Merrie retorted that it was more likely people would think it took three of them to keep him in line. The banality of their humor served to remind them that this was a day strictly for pleasure.

Detouring to a souvenir stand, they chose pennants, pompoms and a hat for Pete, then went on to the food concession. Each balancing an armload of what they considered ballgame basics, they made their way to the seats located between home plate and third base for which Julie had tickets.

"These are terrific seats, Julie!" Pete exclaimed. "How did you manage to come up with the best seats in the house?"

"My father gets them," she responded. "People are always giving him tickets to one thing or another. Maybe they think he'll try harder to make them well, or be more careful with the knife if they need operations. I think he passed them on to me as sort of a bribe as well, so that I'll feel guilty and maybe bring their grandchild up to see them more often."

A vendor came around selling beer and Pete bought large sized cups for each of them over protestations that the women would be unlikely to finish them. They ate companionably, chatting with newcomers as they arrived. A young couple came in, taking seats behind Sarah and Julie.

"Looks like you folks are setting up housekeeping," the young man joked.

Turning toward them, Pete held out a bag of potato chips, offering them to both the man and the plump girl with him. They both refused politely, then laughingly accepted pretzels as Pete continued to hold up one bag of treats after another, urging them to determine their preference. The ice broken, they began the usual small talk about the weather and moving on to discuss the probably outcome of the game.

The two teams appeared on the field and the announcer's voice on the public address system announced it was time for the national anthem. The crowd rose to their feet as silence fell and the stadium organ began to play.

As a career military officer, Pete stood straight and proud. Sarah had always found the music very moving and began to sing along with the crowd. Her voice faltered as tears burned in her eyes. Embarrassed, she brushed them away with her hand, saying aside to Julie, "I'm such a goose over that song. I always cry." Seeing that Julie's head was bowed, her shoulders shaking almost imperceptibly, Sarah put an arm around her, knowing that her friend was similarly moved.

The song swelled to its conclusion." 'O'er the land of the free and the home of the brave.' Applause and shouts of 'Play ball' filled the stadium in anticipation of the start of the game. All four of them noticed at the same time that the couple behind them had not stood for the national anthem. Sarah leaned toward them to ask if something was wrong.

"Oh, we're all right," said the man, "we just think it's hypocritical to pretend to support a government we think is very wrong."

Pete, Merrie, Julie and Sarah all stood staring at them for a few moments before Merrie found her voice and asked, "What do you mean?"

"We believe that the U.S. involvement in Vietnam is totally wrong and that American soldiers are killing innocent people who didn't want them there in the first place. It would be hypocritical of us to stand up and pretend we're patriotic citizens when we're wholly against what our government stands for," said the chubby blonde as calmly as though she were reciting a bus schedule.

Julie's eyes widened and her hand went up to slap the girl's face soundly. Time was momentarily suspended as nearby spectators paused to gape. The silence was broken as the man sprang to his feet, his body throbbing with the hatred that spewed from his mouth as he grabbed Julie's arms and shook her violently.

"You mother fuckin' bitch! What are you? One of those warmongering cunts that gets high dropping bombs on babies?"

Several men joined Pete in pulling the man away from Julie. She fell backward, saved from tumbling into the rows in front by Sarah's hand in the small of her back. An usher raced toward them, joined by security officers who materialized from the crowd. The young man's arms were quickly pinned behind him by one of the officers and he was dragged to the exit, followed by the blond girl, both screaming profanities.

Everyone sat down, the incident forgotten quickly by most of the onlookers as the game started and the stadium was filled with the cacophony of sounds that mount as fans become more frenzied in support of their temporary heroes. Julie was trembling visibly, and Sarah and Merrie each put an arm around her shoulders while Pete lowered his head to his hands, unable to assimilate such hatred. They sat, unable to respond to the action around them; the outing that had begun amid such jubilance now spoiled. They tried for a time to concentrate on the plays, but as the third inning began they looked at each other and agreed without speaking that they preferred to leave. Gathering up the remnants of their picnic, they avoided looking directly at anyone and made their way out of the ballpark.

Pete pulled into the driveway in front of the Winslow's home and turned off the engine. Opening the car door, he said, "Come on in. I think we could all use one of my vodka martinis."

Sarah was the first to speak. "I didn't know anyone could harbor so much hatred. America is so much more than just the war. It's the space program, education, the right to live where we choose, the freedom to do what those people did. By refusing to stand, they were denying all those things as well. Don't they understand that?"

"I shouldn't have slapped that girl," Julie said dully. "That's what started the whole thing. It was a reflex action."

"You only did what any of us might have done had we been standing in your shoes, Julie," Merrie said. "Actually, I'd love to have pulled her hair out by its dark roots! You just beat me to it." The others looked at her in amazement, then saw the twinkle in her eyes. The mental picture of meticulously groomed, diminutive Merrie in combat with the chunky blue jean clad girl made them all laugh and the tension was relieved.

The mood, though less taut, remained serious as they discussed the anti-war attitude that was so prevalent on college campuses. Pete expressed his astonishment at the notion of avoiding the draft by going to Canada and speculated that altruistic patriotism was a relic from the past. Questioning the authority of the government would have been heresy in his day.

Merrie sighed. "I've been wondering lately whether we *are* doing the right thing by violating the silence we were told to keep. We're ignoring the traditions of the military by begging for help from the American public. Will the men come home one day and resent us for degrading them? On the other hand, will they come home at all if we do nothing? Will their anger or disappointment be justified by the possibility of saving their lives? Am I thinking of Paul, or only of myself?"

No one had an answer for her.

"Some days I feel so lonely and abandoned," Julie began, "and some days I feel nothing but anger, that I *must* do *something* even if it's the wrong thing. I'm not even sure who I'm angry with, whether it's Jack for leaving me here to cope with everything or the government for sending him over there, or the Vietnamese for shooting him down."

"I know what you mean," Merrie said, nodding. "I used to get so frustrated when Pete was gone. One time the vet said the dog needed surgery and I was mad at Pete for not being with me to decide what to do. I was *really* worried more about him and whether he was all right or not, but I directed my anger at him for not being there. It seems silly when you talk about it later, but each crisis seems bigger than it is when you're worried or have to make a decision."

"You never told me any of this," Pete said, his surprise evident on his face. "I always thought you were such a rock. I used to tell the other guys in the outfit that you might look fragile, but you were more solid than the Rock of Gibraltar."

"I know, my darling," Merrie said soothingly. "I knew your problems were much bigger than mine and that you counted on me to take care of things at home. Once the crisis was over, it didn't seem so terrible anyway."

"Funny, the things you worry about, never tell anyone, and then find that they weren't important," Pete mused.

"What did you worry about?" Merrie asked.

"I used to wonder if I'd measure up to your expectations. I was afraid I'd look into your eyes some day and see disappointment there. I don't think I could bear that," he admitted.

"You could never disappoint me, Pete. The only reason you might not succeed at something would be because it wasn't right for you in the first place. And if it wasn't right for you, it wouldn't be right for me either." Merrie reached out to take Pete's hand. His eyes clouded and he removed his glasses to rub them, swallowing the lump in his throat. Embarrassed, he rose to check for empty glasses and went to the kitchen to refill their drinks.

Julie stared into the glass she was holding. "You know, I've spent my whole life trying to please the people around me. My dad is so successful and my mother is so demanding that I never felt I could measure up to their expectations. Maybe that's why I love Jack so much. He's such a rebel himself that he gave me a way to be a little rebellious too. Now he's in some God-forsaken place that I can't even picture in my mind. He might be dead, but he might be alive and suffering, needing help that I can't give. I'm completely helpless. And then we run into people like that couple at the game. Of all the seats in that stadium, why did they have to sit behind us?"

Sarah listened as they shared emotions that military families face with each separation and the threat of danger. The discovery that they were not alone in their fears, their anger and frustration, was a welcome relief, a sort of absolution. She was the outsider. She longed to tell them how she felt about Paul, how close she felt to him, how much she loved him. She couldn't, of course, as their fears were steeped in reality while hers were unsubstantiated fantasy.

The moment passed and in an effort to restore the genial mood that had started the outing, Julie brought up Sarah's trip to New York, wondering whether or not John St. James had been in attendance.

"As a matter of fact he was there, and we had a wonderful time together," Sarah told them.

"And when do you leave for Paris?" Julie asked slyly.

Sarah laughed. "Even if I wanted to go to Paris, I have too many responsibilities right here. But I have to admit, he is a marvelous person and great fun to be with."

In the car on the way home, Julie turned to Sarah. "I know you didn't want to get into it in front of Pete and Merrie, but just how serious is it between you and John?"

"We did get pretty close. In fact, I care a great deal about him. We talked for hours about everything and before you have to ask, yes, we did spend the night together every night that we were there. I could love him very much if things were different. It scares me."

"Why? You're perfect for each other. You're even in the same business. You can take over public relations for his hotels once you're married!"

"We haven't discussed marriage and it's much too soon to think about it." Sarah paused, staring out the window. "He's still concerned about my feelings for Paul."

"Did you talk about Paul?"

"Only the first night. After that we were both caught up in the excitement of the convention, not to mention getting to know each other." Sarah stopped abruptly, recalling her thoughts on the plane back to San Francisco. "I probably shouldn't tell you this, but I found myself comparing them as lovers. I thought I had accepted the fact that the experiences with Ikkyu and Antonio were only dreams, but talking about it with John brought it all back again. I *feel* as though I've made love to Paul. It even occurred to me that we were like Heathcliff and Kathy in Wuthering Heights. They were star-crossed lovers, too." She looked down, embarrassed by the comparison.

"Have you checked the library yet? It isn't really a new idea that people who've died can contact the living. I've always thought that seances and mediums were a hoax, but there must be some kind of legitimate research into it. It would be a start at least. In fact, if you're too busy, I'll do it myself. I'm not working fifty or sixty hours a week like you are. Besides, I'm curious."

They were silent for a moment or two before Julie changed the subject. "Did Merrie seem a little more frail than usual?"

"She's so small anyway that it's hard to tell. Why?"

"I don't know exactly. I think she's torn between trying to do whatever she can to bring Paul back, and coming to terms with the possibility that he might well be dead. It would be easier to get on with life if they both accepted it."

"No! It's too soon for that!" Sarah's reaction was immediate and powerful.

Julie sighed heavily. "I know. But sometimes the limbo that we're all in wears us down. Even though Jack is actually listed as a prisoner, I have no proof, no letters, nothing tangible. There are days when I get so depressed, I wonder if maybe my mother could be right after all. And Pete and Merrie haven't even got what little I have to hang onto."

"Wouldn't Pete know if the strain was getting to be too much for Merrie?"

"I don't think he'd notice. He sees her every day and we don't, so we might sense a change. It's almost imperceptible, the kind of thing a woman would see before a man does anyway."

"I've been so busy for the past few months that I haven't seen as much of them as I'd like. I'll look more closely next time we're together," Sarah promised.

CHAPTER FIFTEEN

Sheila Donnelly hurried out the Wabash Avenue exit of Marshall Field's and turned toward Michigan Avenue, intending to catch a taxi home. She was running late as usual and the blast of hot air that hit her as she left the air-conditioned store served to increase her impatience. Intent upon her own thoughts, she failed to notice the crowd of demonstrators that lined Michigan Avenue, spilling out into the street. Before she knew what was happening, she was swept along with the crowd. Attempting to resist, she pushed her way toward the curb and suddenly lost her balance. Had it not been for the arm that went around her waist, nearly lifting her off her feet, she would have fallen.

Her unknown benefactor led her gradually toward the safety of a doorway as she struggled to regain her footing. He released his grasp, stepped back and studied her face, then said brusquely, "You should be more careful where you walk. You could get into a lot of trouble." His dark eyes were expressionless as he surveyed her expensive clothes and well-coifed head.

"Who *are* these people?" Sheila demanded. "What right have they to obstruct the sidewalk this way?"

"They are exercising their right to freedom of expression," the man said dispassionately.

"What the hell are they expressing?" Sheila yelped.

"Their objection to the war in Vietnam," he responded, his voice flat.

"Their objection to the war in Vietnam," Sheila screeched. "And that's why I've been manhandled, pushed around and can't get to a taxi?'

"This may come as a big surprise to you, but some people don't consider your need for a taxi a matter of paramount importance," the man said.

"I don't believe this is happening." Sheila shook her head in amazement. Suddenly realizing that the man had saved her from possible injury, she took a closer look, brushed herself off and said grudgingly, "Thanks for getting me out of that mess. Are you one of them?"

"More or less, yes," he answered. "A lot of them are just letting off steam. They don't really know what it is to be a revolutionary…"

"Revolutionary? Revolutionary?" Sheila's voice rose again as she repeated the word in astonishment. "They're protesting the war, right? What the hell does that have to do with being a revolutionary?"

"You wouldn't understand," he replied sarcastically.

"Try me," Sheila sneered back.

The man stepped back slightly, looking her over deliberately, his expression clearing showing his disdain. "You were in a pretty big hurry a little while ago," he commented. "Are you sure you have time to listen to anyone but your rich friends?"

"What makes you so sure my friends are rich?" She inquired.

Looking her up and down again, he made an exaggerated sweep of her obviously expensive attire, shrugged his shoulders, and said caustically, "I can't imagine."

"Just because I dress well doesn't mean anything other than that I have good taste," Sheila said defensively.

He gazed at her a moment longer, then sighed and said, "Okay, come on, you can buy me a cup of coffee.' He peered cautiously from the doorway, then led her out, hugging the walls of buildings as they made their way down the street to a coffee shop. Sheila deliberated briefly whether she should try again to find a taxi. She was due at a cocktail party in an hour and still had to get home to change. Besides, she really shouldn't be allowing this scruffy stranger to lead her down the street. Oh, what the hell, she thought, this might be interesting.

They ordered coffee, then studied each other openly. "I've never met anyone like you before," Sheila began.

"Well, I've seen a lot of your type from a distance, but I can't say I've ever shared a table with one before either," he replied. He slumped against the back wall of the booth, one leg bent at the knee as he put a foot up on the seat. His unruly dark hair fell casually over his forehead, lending an air of intensity to the sharp eyes that peered out from behind horn-rimmed glasses. He was very tall and thin. Put a cape on him and he could be Count Dracula, Sheila thought.

"What were you doing in the middle of that crowd?" he asked.

"It was purely accidental, I assure you. I was trying to get across Michigan Avenue to get a taxi going north. I was running a bit late and didn't know I'd be in danger of being killed by revolutionaries in downtown Chicago! So sue me!"

"Then what are you doing in here now, slumming? Checking out how the other half lives? No, you couldn't care less how the other half lives, could you? A story to tell your friends, maybe?"

"I'm not sure what I'm doing here," she retorted angrily. "I was scared when that mob pushed me around, but I can see that I made a mistake by coming in here with you." She started to rise. He raised one hand airily to stop her and mumbled, "Okay, okay, sit down. I'll try to dredge up a little sympathy."

"Don't do me any favors," Sheila responded.

"I already did you a favor. I got you out of the crowd with hardly a hair out of place," he said drolly.

"What did you say you were? A revolutionary? Is it written somewhere that all revolutionaries must have bad manners?"

"Knowing which fork to use doesn't put food on the table, hard work does. And while you and your rich friends sip martinis and discuss your latest ski trip to Switzerland, figuring out how you can take more from the poor to support your expensive habits, there are people starving all over the world."

"Oh, please, I heard all about the starving children in China when I was a little girl and had to clean my plate! Manners and money don't make people uncaring. What's with you?" The stereotypical view as well as the banal statement annoyed Sheila. At the same time, she was perplexed by the obviously antagonistic attitude of the man.

"I told you. I'm a revolutionary in the truest form. Actually, I'm a Maoist. I'm committed to cooperative labor and the power of the people. If people like you were forced to live alongside dirt farmers in the south, you might have a different attitude toward the poor in the world. What we need to do is educate the masses and increase the purchasing power of the peasant population."

"The 'peasant' population?" Sheila scoffed. "I didn't know there was such a thing in this country."

"Figure of speech," he replied blithely. "This country must stop its aggression and baby killing in Vietnam and begin to concentrate on the poor and hungry right here at home!"

"My brother is missing in action in Vietnam," Sheila said evenly. "Are you calling him a baby killer? He doesn't even kill spiders."

"Anyone who willingly supports U.S. aggression in Vietnam is responsible for the deaths of thousands of innocent people. They are war criminals and the response to war criminals should be what was done to those at Nuremberg. They should be locked up or executed. The warmongers in Washington think they have free reign to commit genocide against the people of Vietnam."

"That's ridiculous. Our government sent my brother there and now no one knows where he is or even whether he's alive or dead. I thought he was there to save the South Vietnamese from communist aggression, not from the United States."

"South Vietnam doesn't need to be saved from communism, nor does it want to be. The Viet Cong are the resistance fighters that this country admired so much in France in World War II. Don't you see that? The sooner true Americans see to it that we get out of there, the sooner your brother and all the American servicemen will be home. Then we can begin the re-education process and the world can live in harmony."

"Who *are* you anyway? I don't even know your name, or should I just call you 'comrade?'"

"I'd be proud to be called 'Comrade,' but I don't think you'd mean it as a compliment. Let me introduce myself. My name is Dave Marshall. What's yours?"

"Sheila Donnelly. Do you have a job or do you just hang around with other revolutionaries?"

"I do have a job. I'm an assistant professor at the University of Chicago. I teach creative writing." He pulled his glasses down his nose, looking at Sheila over the top with a wry smile that made her laugh in spite of herself.

"I'll just bet you're creative!" she exclaimed.

"What do you say we get out of here and go have a beer someplace? I'll buy this time, but my budget doesn't extend to martinis at the Ritz."

"Well, I…"

"You'd rather go to your cocktail party, right? Well, some other time maybe," Dave said a bit defensively, rising from his seat in the booth.

Making a spontaneous decision, Sheila said, "I'd like to have a beer. I won't pretend I'm not a little apprehensive, but you did save me from an angry mob, so to speak, and I'd like to know more about you and the way you think."

She allowed him to lead her to a nearby bus stop, protesting that she'd pay for a taxi when she realized that he expected her to get on a southbound bus. Smiling, but firm, he pushed her onto the bus, telling her she could take a taxi home later. They rode for several minutes in silence before she asked just how far south he planned to go.

Assuring her they weren't far from their destination, he leaned over to peer out the window, then pulled the cord to stop the bus at the next corner. He took her hand and led her another two blocks down a side street, his long strides making it difficult for her to keep up as her apprehension grew.

"Almost there," he said cheerfully, steering her toward a doorway that led down a flight of stairs to a cellar. Sheila looked around her, panic beginning to surface. She really knew nothing about this man, she thought, and she could be getting into something dangerous. Oh come on, she reasoned, you've done dumber things in your life, you'll be fine. She was prepared to bolt back up the stairs, however, as he held the door open and she found herself in a German style bratskellar, the sound of laughter emanating from its shadowy interior.

As her eyes adjusted to the gloom, Sheila saw that Dave was leading her toward a table already occupied by several people. Three men and a young woman lounged in chairs, making caustic comments regarding her appearance as they approached. Realizing that she was rather obviously overdressed for the casual setting, Sheila flushed, embarrassed. None of the men stood or offered to pull out her chair, so she sat down in the only unoccupied chair while Dave brought another from an adjoining table. Dave made perfunctory introductions, then told the others he had brought her there to be re-educated. The young woman, whose name Sheila had not understood, was openly hostile.

"She looks like a hard case to me, Dave. In fact, she looks like window dressing at Saks Fifth Avenue. What did you do, take her on approval?" the girl snickered.

"Don't be so hard on her, Sally, she just doesn't know any better yet," Dave replied. Sheila wasn't sure whether to be angry or scared, and made herself as small as possible in her chair.

Dave went on to explain how they met and the conversation turned to plans for a meeting scheduled by the group for the following week. Sheila heard words that were whispered if used at all in her circles: proletariat, bourgeois, class struggle, manifesto, and a few she was sure she'd never heard before. She listened quietly, hoping to remember the words she meant to look up at home later.

She had begun to think they'd forgotten she was there when Dave turned to her and asked, "Getting anything out of this or are you just bored?"

"I don't understand much of it," she admitted, "and I don't see what it has to do with me or for that matter, the rest of the world."

"The rest of *your* world, you mean," Dave corrected. The others snickered as he continued, "Your world is comprised of a very small percentage of the overall population. Do you know anything at all about the class struggles that are going on in Asia?"

Sheila shrugged her shoulders and mumbled, "Not much, I guess."

"You must understand the concepts of morality and duty," he

emphasized the word 'must,' then paused and said, "maybe you don't really understand even that."

"Of course I understand it," Sheila countered indignantly. "Morality is doing the right thing and duty is fulfilling your obligations."

Sally snorted, saying, "You're fighting a losing battle with this one, Dave."

Motioning for her to be still, Dave went on patiently. "Morality is a matter of what's right and what's wrong. But one must move beyond this to the level of social ethics. Duty exists only as a social responsibility and membership in the community is the individual's highest duty. The state is the manifestation of the general will, which is the highest expression of the ethical spirit. Are you with me so far?" Sheila nodded hesitantly and he continued, "Would you agree that the community exists for the good of everyone in it?"

"I guess so," Sheila said. "I've never given it much thought."

"Obviously," said Sally sarcastically. The other men grinned in agreement, but appeared to be slightly more sympathetic toward Sheila's discomfort.

"Most of Asia has been ruled for years by emperors, czars and landlords who lived opulent lives that resulted from the labor of the masses," Dave continued. "What we believe in, simplified, is the redistribution of the land, the obliteration of the landlord class, fair taxes or no taxes, and representative community government. Cooperative effort on the part of the entire community."

"How does all of that make my brother a baby killer?" Sheila asked, confused and defensive.

"Was your brother a pilot?" one of the men inquired.

"Yes, he was shot down about two years ago and we still don't know whether he went down with the plane or parachuted out and is alive," she answered.

"Don't you see that he was dropping bombs on innocent people that had no faces for him, but who had brothers and sisters just like you? And wives and children as well?"

"But he was there to protect the people of South Vietnam from the communists in the north!" Sheila exclaimed. "And you are all sitting here telling me you believe in communism!"

"No, Sheila, we're not communists, we're Maoists."

"He's a communist, isn't he? What's the difference?"

Everyone looked at Dave as he attempted to explain their position. "Russian communism is based on sharing through industrialization. Mao is giving the peasants a better life and self-reliance through cooperative agriculture and community effort. He is integrating the intellectuals with the workers as an economic and social strategy."

It sounded so reasonable as Dave explained it, but Sheila frowned in troubled confusion, unable to integrate these theories into her concept of life. Checking her watch, she realized it must be well after dark and that she was far from home in strange territory. Dave noticed her discomfort and decided she'd had enough for one day. He accompanied her outside, putting her into a taxi.

"Why don't you come down to the meeting next week?" he asked, giving her the specifics on where it was to be held, then waving as the cab drove away.

Returning to the table in the pub, he was contemplative. The others stared at him, their eyes questioning his silence. Finally, Sally spoke up.

"What's with you and that broad? Your hormones acting up or something?"

"I don't know. There's something about her, an innocence…" Dave's voice trailed off.

"Aw jeez, why don't you lay her and get it out of your system? Or better yet, just forget her," Sally said disgustedly.

"I probably should…" he replied. Somehow the others knew that he probably wouldn't.

Sheila had missed the cocktail party, but she didn't seem to care. She, too, was quiet as the cab took her back to the north side of Chicago and the safety of her own home. Despite the hostility of the people she had encountered, she felt slightly exhilarated. Here were ideas that were as foreign to her as any alien planet, spoken of in words that she feared she might not be able to spell, much less find in the dictionary. Was this what she had missed by not going to college? Did everyone who had acquired higher education know these things or were these people beyond even that?

Part of her wanted to forget the whole day, remaining protected in her familiar realm, but a kernel had begun to germinate in her mind. What if Dave and his friends were right, and what if she became a part of a movement that ended the war in Vietnam and brought Paul back? Wouldn't her daddy be proud of her then!

CHAPTER SIXTEEN

Paul lay on his pallet, feverish, but feeling better than he had in many days. His guards were becoming friendlier, even showing some sympathy for him in his illness. He knew he'd had bouts of delirium, slipping into them intermittently when the fever and chills were too much for his body to bear.

Months had gone by and his isolation was increasingly difficult. He had begun to talk to 'Baby' more frequently, visualizing her in greater detail. Her companionship eased the loneliness and he was becoming adept at transporting himself into another time and space with his fantasies. He had fallen in love with Baby, delighting in the texture of her hair, enraptured by her eyes – eyes that shimmered with colors that came and went as they gazed into his. He had considered the possibility that he was losing his mind, but then determined that if he was lucid enough to wonder about it and still able to admit that Baby was imaginary, he must be all right. Besides, what harm could it do?

He closed his eyes, willing her to appear. The faint sound of a melody came from far away. He strained to make out the tune, and as it increased in volume, he began to hum along, then remembered the words.

"The night is like a lovely tune, beware my foolish heart. How white the ever constant moon, take care my foolish heart." The music swelled to a conclusion, so real that he fought the urge to search the corners of the hut for its source. Then he saw her. She was seated at a piano, her fingers flying over the keys. Moving slowly toward her, he reached out to caress the dark curls that tumbled to her shoulders. The song ended and without turning, she raised one hand to cover his, drawing it to her cheek in a loving gesture. Suddenly she was all the women of his dreams, the reticent girl in the rose colored kimono, the beautiful woman in the black dress and the radiant companion in an emerald green gown who had danced with him. Afraid to move lest she vanish, he stood silently, savoring her nearness. He knew at that moment that she had been and would always be a part of him and he whispered her name, "Sarah…"

He woke clutching the thin blanket that covered the straw on his pallet, calling her name again, "Sarah!" As she faded from view, he rolled over, throwing one arm across his face, alone again.

Sarah sat staring at the keys on the piano. She had not played it for months. It was an old friend, waiting for her touch. Her fingers hesitated, then began tentatively, one at a time as her right hand picked out a melody. The notes came naturally and her left had joined in, adding the bass. Softly, building to a crescendo as she neared the end of the song, she poured her heart into the music and whispered the last line, "It's love, this time it's love my foolish heart."

Sensing his presence, she raised one hand to her shoulder to grasp the hand that caressed her hair, surrendering herself to the warmth of his touch. She sat very still, her eyes closed, rejoicing in the texture of his skin, longing to be with him again, anywhere, anytime, hearing his voice as he called her name, "Sarah!" And then he was gone and she was alone.

She turned away from the piano and looked at the pile of books that Julie had delivered earlier. It seemed that there had been more written about reincarnation and dreams than either of them had thought. In finding one book, others were discovered in bibliographies and each produced a little more insight. Julie had obtained a few from the library and had found more in used bookstores.

It seemed that though most of the scientific community wanted tangible proof of any theory, there were an increasing number of psychologists, psychiatrists, and religious leaders who were making use of hypnosis on subjects who claimed to recall other lifetimes. Terms such as 'lucid dreams,' and 'astral projection' might not be part of the average person's terminology, but the concepts had apparently occurred to and been considered seriously by individuals in respected academic positions.

Sarah picked up the book that lay on top of the stack and glanced at the title, Edgar Cayce on Reincarnation. Opening it at random, she was startled by the title of a chapter: 'If We Have Lived Before, Why Don't We Remember?' It compared the soul to a deep sea diver to whom reality becomes the bottom of the sea until weariness, claustrophobia and defeat overwhelms him and he is hauled back aboard his boat. In the period of time it takes him to recover, the memory of the sea becomes a vague dream and the deck of the ship becomes reality once again.

It went on to add that a professional actor often becomes the person he is playing on stage and that character becomes reality to the actor, eliminating the real person for a period of time. The character might be a thoroughly bad person, but that does not mean that the actor is a bad person, and the actor is not affected by the misdeeds of the character. It asked, what if we were allowed voluntary access to our previous lives, and one day we discovered by chance that we had been some sort of monster at one time? How would we deal with that? Cayce believed that we are not called upon to settle old debts owed to fellow souls until we have reached a sufficiently mature level to make such compensation possible and practical. "For the Lord does not tempt any soul beyond that which it is able to bear."

Cayce further analyzed, "When a soul enters a new body, a door is opened, leading to an opportunity for building the soul's destiny. Everything which has been previously built, both good and bad, is contained in that opportunity." The conclusion was obvious: we are fortunate that we cannot recall previous lives until we are sufficiently evolved in our enlightenment. Additionally, Christian doctrine does not allow for the possibility of such theory.

Thumbing through the book, Sarah came across a quote that seemed to leap off the page: "None of us can now remember his earliest years.

But any psychologist will stress their importance and the effect they had upon us."

Stimulated and eager to see what may lie ahead in the other books, she laid the one aside and picked up the next: 'Astral Projection, A record of Out-of-Body-Experiences' by Oliver Fox. Turning it over, she read the blurb on the back:

"The Astral Body is the double or ethereal counterpart of the physical body, which it resembles and with which it normally coincides. Each of us has one… Out-of-the-body experiences are *facts* no matter how each of us explains them to himself."

Turning to the table of contents, she read through it quickly and went immediately to a chapter that promised to tell her the ways that might be employed in the effort to get out of the body. The first and easiest was through dreams, and the second by way of self-induced trance. Obviously, one would have to do some programming in advance and be able to remember the dreams, if one were to rely upon that method. Though perhaps more dangerous to anyone inexperienced in doing it, the self-induced trance seemed more reliable and ultimately more dependable if one had a particular destination in mind. She read on:

"There is one thing that is sure to trouble the student sooner or later in his out-of-body excursions: he will lose his time-sense more or less completely. He will be quite aware of his identity and have a perfect memory of the events of the day up to the time of making his experiment; he will know well enough that his physical body is at home in bed; but he will *not* know how long he has been out, how long the experiment really lasted."

A chill went up her spine. That must be what happened when she first met Paul on an interim plane and traveled with him to another lifetime of long ago. That was why she had supposedly slept through two days. Could it be possible to leave one's body at will, moving through time? She thought back to what had happened just before the journey to seventeenth century Japan. She had first been drawn to the photograph of Paul, then had been in the room in his parents' home with objects that he had once held. Maybe if she had some object that had been his, something on which to concentrate. Suddenly she remembered the music, the feeling that it was somehow prophetic.

"For this time it isn't fascination,
Or a dream that will fade and fall apart.
It's love, this time it's love
My foolish heart."

The first experience had been momentary, following her first visit to the Winslow's. The second, the journey through time, had been after the morning when she sought signatures on the petitions. The feeling that it was Paul she was dancing with at the dinner, using his name as John's arms encircled her…all three times it had been the same song that brought on the occurrences. It had even occurred to her before the dream of Marguerite and Antonio that she might be able to bring back Yoshiko and Ikkyu with that song. How could she have forgotten about it? It must have been fear of the unknown, or fear of ridicule that caused her mind to bury the idea.

But now she felt vindicated, exhilarated! The dreams, the out-of-body experiences had been validated. There were others who believed it was possible to leave the body and the idea of unlimited, unconditional and unending love was an acceptable one. A love that supersedes lifetimes – soulmates.

She frowned. But what role did John St. James play in this drama? He cared so deeply for her and she cared for him as well. She could not hurt him with the knowledge that Paul would forever occupy her heart. If she continued the relationship with John, which of the two men would she be betraying? Must her love for Paul be a wound that never heals, hiding far beneath the surface?

The words on the last page of the book that lay in her lap jumped out at her:

"Then in silence, after the seeking, the tilling, the sowing, after the watching, the sorrowing, the hoping, into the fields of Harvest shall we go hand in hand."

She closed the volume, holding it tightly to her breast and began to plan her next journey into the past with Paul. If it was the music, she would begin with that. Where would she find herself? Could she find a way to be with him throughout eternity if such a thing was predestined?

Would that mean leaving this life or could it be that he was waiting for her to find him in this life, going on together? Would the understanding and acceptance of their destiny be the key that unlocked the gateway to the future? Or was it, as so many people thought, merely fantasy?

CHAPTER SEVENTEEN

J ulia Schaefer stood at her kitchen window. She spread the fingers of
her left hand and placed them on the small of her back, kneading
the area around her spine. Rolling her shoulders, she heard the
crackling sound of tension throughout her neck and leaned against the
sink gazing out the window.

What a weekend, she thought. First those people at the game, then a
day with my mother on Sunday. Bowing to pressure from her parents to
bring Sandy up to see them, she had decided to let the little girl spend a
few days there. Her mother couldn't understand why Julie wouldn't stay
as well, but she had claimed to be planning a thorough cleaning job and
catching up on correspondence while Sandy wasn't there to interrupt.

The little yellow daisy-like flowers that sprouted from the big green
plant outside the window made her smile briefly. Turning from the
window, she felt rather than heard the silence that surrounded her.
Walking slowly from the kitchen through the dining room to the
living room, she wondered if she really should get busy and do some
housecleaning. She glanced around for a place to start and noticed the
dust that had gathered on the elaborate stereo system that Jack had
loved so much.

She ran her fingers over the albums that stood in a row on the shelf, waiting for someone to bring them to life, then selected an old Benny Goodman record and put it on the turntable.

She sat listening to the music and thinking about the events of the weekend, getting more depressed with each thought. So much hatred, she mused. It had been more than a year since the students were killed at Kent State and the anti-war demonstrations were getting bigger and bigger. Just recently nearly 500,000 people had converged on Washington, D.C., and at least 150,000 protesters had marched in San Francisco. What effect is all of that having on the Vietnamese, she wondered.

She had written dozens of letters to senators and congressmen and had received a reply from one of them the previous week. Her letter had been most disturbing, he wrote, and he had made inquiries of the Department of Defense. Unfortunately, the news was not favorable. He had been reassured that every effort was being made to obtain information on our men who have been captured, but very little was available. He went on to say that he had reason to hope that with the troop withdrawals in progress would come more cooperation from the Vietnamese. Members of Congress were discussing a separation of issues, he said, compartmenting the questions of release of prisoners versus the question of application of the Geneva Convention guidelines toward treatment of prisoners.

What a crock of shit, Julie thought. The peace talks didn't seem to be getting anywhere either. Would she ever see Jack again? She let her mind wander, recalling the day they were married.

The wedding had been romantic, with just the right touch of glamour. The many guests drank great quantities of champagne and ate equally great quantities of delicious canapés. Julie had thought that Jack was the handsomest Marine in the country in his dress uniform, the creases in his pants razor sharp. And he was just as sure that Julie was the most beautiful bride ever. They were to spend the night at a cozy little inn on the coast, not telling anyone where it was.

Unwilling to relinquish the romantic ambiance of the day, Julie had suggested a walk in the moonlight along the beach. The sky was bright under an almost full moon, creating the impression of a home in which the lights had been turned on to welcome a visitor.

Looking up, Jack had said gruffly, "Look honey, God's at home. He's turned on the lights."

"Makes it seem like He's on our side, doesn't it? We'll be the two luckiest people on earth!" Julie had replied, her eyes shining.

"Did you ever doubt it?"

"Not for a minute!"

"Whatever happened to all our luck, Jack?" Julie asked of the empty room. Just then the doorbell rang. Checking her watch, she knew it must be the postman's signal that her mail had been delivered. She opened the front door, waving to him as he retreated down the walk toward the next building.

Extracting the pile of envelopes and magazines from the black metal box, she leafed through them absentmindedly. A small, greyish envelope with the address written on it in pencil, then crossed off and forwarded, fluttered to the stoop. She glanced at it briefly, sure that it was probably meant for a neighbor's teenager. Then the familiar scrawl that was Jack's handwriting registered in her mind and her head jerked back. She staggered, nearly falling against the doorframe.

Staring at the face of the envelope, she searched for some sign of where it had come from. There were stamps on it that said 'Vietnam' but no postmark or return address. Julie's fingers trembled as she slit the envelope open carefully. The rough paper inside contained only a few lines, dated three months earlier.

> My Precious Cinderella,
> I'm alive and being taken care of adequately. I
> miss you more than I can tell you. Try not to worry too
> much. We'll all be home as soon as possible.
> Your faithful prince,
> Jack

Julie clutched the paper to her chest, too numb to move or even consider what to do next. Jack had called her his Cinderella since they first met, his tone always jovial, his eyes telling her that he considered theirs to be a storybook romance, the Colorado Cowboy and the San Francisco Lady. She moved in a trance into the apartment and sank down on a chair. Her fingers caressed the paper, knowing that Jack had actually touched the same page and was alive – at least he was alive recently.

An overwhelming exuberance began to replace the numbness. She sprang from the chair and reached for the wall phone in the kitchen, dialing Sarah's number so rapidly that she made a mistake and had to begin again. Be there, be there, she repeated to herself as it rang. Six rings later, she realized that of course Sarah wouldn't be there, she'd be at the office. Replacing the receiver on its hook, she searched for the business card that she knew should be by the phone. Unable to find it in her excitement, she pulled open the cupboard door under the counter to get out the phone book. After several frustrating moments of flipping pages, she finally found the number and forced herself to dial it slowly. The receptionist answered after only two rings and routed the call to Sarah's office.

By the time she told Ellen who was calling and got through to Sarah, Julie was near hysteria. "I got a letter! I got a letter," she yelled, emphasizing the word 'letter' the first time and the word 'got' as she repeated the sentence more slowly a second time.

"From who? About Jack?" Sarah asked, startled.

"*From* Jack!" Julie shouted.

"Oh, my God, Julie, from where? What does it say?"

"It's written in pencil and the date is blurred, but I think it was about three months ago. The envelope has stamps on it that say Vietnam and it isn't very long, but it's a letter!" Julie's voice trembled as she read the letter aloud to Sarah.

They talked on for several minutes discussing the possible significance of the wording in the letter. Julie felt that Jack would not have used the word 'adequately' if he was being well treated, and they agreed that the use of 'we' instead of 'I' meant that he was being held with other Americans.

"Look Julie, I can get away from the office soon. I'll stop and get some deli sandwiches. You pick up some champagne and meet me at my place in about an hour. We'll celebrate, okay?"

After a brief phone call to her casualty assistance officer in Washington, Julie danced her way through the apartment to her car and hummed happily as she made her way down El Camino, remembering the last time she had seen Jack, envisioning the joy that would be theirs when they were reunited.

She had driven him to the base where his Phantom jet was waiting. His squadron was to meet the aircraft carrier in the Pacific as it headed toward Asian territory. She had given him a silver cigarette lighter engraved with two lines from a Robert Burns poem, "For the Sake 'O Somebody." On one side it read, 'From each danger keep him free,' and on the other, 'And send me safe my Somebody.' Jack's eyes had clouded as he kissed her and said he'd left something in the car for her.

She had watched the sky until long after his plane had disappeared. Walking back to the parking lot, she had noted how quickly everyone had disappeared and felt more lonely and lost than she had anticipated. Opening the car door, she had discovered one red rose on the seat along with half of a photograph of the two of them. He had kept the half with her in it and left the half that showed himself. The inscription on the back of her half read, 'All my love until we're together again.'

In conjuring up an image of his return, she knew that she would not be watching for the Phantom to appear in the sky, but perhaps a Marine transport plane. He might be weak or injured, but even if he appeared on crutches, he'd be able to hold her in his arms and everything would be okay again.

Julie's exuberance was contagious as Sarah poured champagne into her best crystal goblets and they prepared to toast Jack's health, his early return, love, and life in general.

"Oh what a beautiful morning, oh what a beautiful day," Julie sang joyfully.

"I've got a beautiful feeling, everything's going your way!" Sarah finished.

"You know, before I met Jack, I used to think that the girls in my dorm at school were crazy to go steady, get pinned or get engaged. I wondered how they could be so sure when there were so many men they hadn't met yet. But somehow, deep down inside, I was longing for someone who really cared about me. It sounds kind of trite, but Jack really did give meaning to my life. He was so strong, so honest and so funny. He made me laugh like I never had before."

"Here's to laughter, past, present and most of all future!" Sarah toasted, lifting her glass again.

"Right on!" Julie responded. The letter seemed such a positive sign that it was easy for the two young women to be euphoric in their celebration. Though she refrained from saying it, the seeds of hope began to germinate in Sarah's heart. This could be the sign she had been searching for – that Paul, too, was alive and would be coming home.

A light rain had fallen during the evening and as Julie headed up El Camino on her way home, the stars joined the streetlights in creating a magical aura that was reflected in the shimmering roadway. Her eyes shone with pleasure of the promise of kismet that lay ahead.

The neon sign that announced the Coachman restaurant and lounge loomed just ahead. Making a spontaneous decision, Julie swung into the parking lot. It was still nearly full and seeing an empty space along the side of the building, she accelerated toward it just as a black Mercedes came around the corner from the other direction. The two cars reached the spot at nearly the same moment, but the Mercedes won the space. A minor setback, she thought and went on around the building in the direction from which the Mercedes had come. As she rounded the corner to the entrance, another car backed from a space in front. This is surely my lucky day, Julie thought, pulling into the slot.

The lounge was cool and dark. Julie stood to one side of the door searching the room for someone she might know, but seeing no one, she made her way to the bar. The bartender smiled cheerfully as he brought her the brandy she ordered. She sipped on it for a few minutes before she began to think perhaps she had made a mistake by coming in. She really should go home.

Just then, the bartender came over, asking, "What's a pretty lady like you doing all alone tonight?"

"I've been doing a little celebrating and just didn't feel like going home yet," Julie answered.

"What's the occasion?'

Unsure of how to explain, she kept it simple. "My husband has been a prisoner of war in Vietnam for three years and I finally got a letter from him today."

"You mean you haven't heard anything at all? In all that time?" the bartender's voice indicated his surprise.

Resigned to the lack of information available regarding Americans captured in Southeast Asia, Julie told him that even though there had been photos of Jack, he was still listed as missing in action rather than a prisoner because he had not been reported as a prisoner by the Vietnamese, and the American government had no knowledge of where he might be being held.

"Could I buy you a drink for a toast?" she asked.

A tall, husky man with dark curly hair, greying at the temples, was seated a few stools away. "What are you celebrating?" he inquired, smiling.

Julie grinned. "A letter from my husband," she told him, realizing how trivial it must sound to a stranger who knew nothing of the background.

"Lucky man to have a wife who celebrates just getting a letter from him," the man said appreciatively. "Let me buy you both a drink."

The bartender filled their glasses and asked, "What's his name.?"

"Jack."

"To Jack," he toasted, lifting his glass. He looked questioningly at Julie. "And…what's your name?"

"Julie," she said.

"And to Julie," both men said at once. Called away to the cocktail waitress's station, the bartender left Julie and the other man alone.

"What makes you so happy to hear from an obviously absent husband?" the man asked, moving closer to where Julie sat.

"He's a prisoner of war in Vietnam and I haven't heard from him in nearly three years," she explained again.

"Oh, sorry." He looked into his drink, then back at Julie with renewed interest. "You've been all alone, waiting for him to come home?"

"Of course. Though I'm not really 'all alone.' I have a daughter who was born after Jack left, and parents, and lots of good friends. As a matter of fact, I was celebrating the letter with one of them tonight.

I was on my way home when I stopped in here. Just didn't want to let go of the moment, I guess."

"Well, Julie, my name's Sam and I'm mighty glad you decided to stop in. I'm new in these parts, just transferred from the East Coast, Virginia actually. Came out early to look around for someplace for the family to live."

They chatted congenially over another drink, watching the dancers on the small dance floor.

"I'm not the world's best dancer," Sam said, "but how about a getting-acquainted turn around the floor?" Julie consented and was pleasantly surprised by his firm grip and quiet confidence as they danced.

How nice it was to feel someone's arms around her again, she thought. How safe and warm. Sam's arm tightened as she missed a step, the effects of the champagne and subsequent brandy beginning to show. His hand caressed her back, his head bending slightly to put his cheek next to hers. The music ended and they stood alone on the dance floor, each aware of the other but reluctant to make eye contact. Taking her hand, Sam led Julie back to the bar.

Music and brandy made close friends of strangers and their conversation began to take a more intimate turn as the hour grew later. Sam encouraged Julie to confide in him, brushing a strand of hair from her face as she told him of the loneliness and uncertainty that tormented her days and nights. Grateful for his sympathetic ear, she didn't pull away when his fingers touched hers, tentatively at first, then holding her hand gently. They danced, barely moving as their bodies swayed to the rhythm of the small combo.

"Let's get out of here," he said brusquely. He left money on the bar for their drinks and led her to the door. Neither of them heard the bartender's observance as he muttered to himself, "I hope she's not sorry in the morning."

"Leave your car here, I'll drive you home," Sam instructed Julie, leading her around the corner to where his Mercedes was parked in the space she had missed out on when she arrived.

"So it was you that aced me out of the space," she teased, lowering herself giddily into the front seat as he held the door open.

Sam got into the car on the driver's side and put the key in the ignition, then turned to look at the woman beside him. Julie's longing for Jack gave way to desire as Sam's arms went around her and his lips met hers. She was unaware of the minutes that passed before he straightened and asked directions to her home. It seemed like hours and yet only moments before they were in her driveway. Julie was trembling as she fumbled with her keys and unlocked the door, leading him into the living room. Resisting only momentarily, she gave in to the longing and they fell together on the sofa.

His hands pulled her jacket down her arms, then his fingers reached for the button at the opening of her slacks. The zipper came down easily and she felt the fabric slipping over her thighs. No longer in control of her responses, Julie's hands reached under his shirt, then sought out the hard bulge in his trousers. Her hips began to move up and down in a frenzy of desire as she moaned, "Oh, God, hurry, hurry!"

Several hours later, Julie opened her eyes. Her head was throbbing and she wondered what she was doing sleeping on the sofa in the living room. She looked around blearily, saw her slacks and panties on the floor beside her and realized that she was naked from the waist down, covered only by the small crocheted blanket she kept on the back of the sofa. She was alone in the room.

Despair swept over her as she began to remember. Grabbing for the items on the floor, she ran up the stairs to her bedroom where she stripped off her remaining clothes and headed for the shower. The cold water that stung her flesh at first gradually turned to hot water and she slumped against the shower wall. Putting her head under the water, she soaped herself frantically in an effort to cleanse away the filth she was sure covered her body.

Toweling herself roughly, she put on a heavy terrycloth robe and collapsed on the bed. Tears of regret and shame consumed her. How could I have done that, she moaned, on the day that began as such a happy one with everything to hope for ahead? Sobs racked her body until exhaustion took over. I wish I was dead, she thought.

Pushing herself up heavily, she stumbled into the bathroom and opened the medicine cabinet, blindly pulling bottles from the shelves until she found the Valium she knew was there. The image of her tiny daughter appeared in her mind. I'm not fit to be a mother or a wife, she thought, her judgement still clouded from the alcohol. Reaching for the glass at the side of the sink, she turned on the cold water tap and filled it. Opening the bottle of pills, she poured them into her hand, swallowing them a few at a time until they were gone.

I wonder how long it will take, she thought as she stumbled back to the bed she had shared with Jack. Carefully folding back the spread, she turned down the covers and crept in, making herself as small as possible. She reached for the pillow on Jack's side, holding it close, imagining his scent. As she closed her eyes, a tiny tear slid down her cheek, dissolving on the pillow.

Thoughts of Pete and Merrie, and Sarah tumbled around in her head as the pills began to take effect. I should really say goodbye to them, she thought. I'll call Sarah and she can tell Merrie that I'm sorry I won't be here to help anymore. Drowsily, she reached for the phone on the bed table. Her first attempt to dial the number failed as her vision began to blur. She started over, dialing each digit very slowly, finally hearing it ring.

"Hi, Sarah, it's me, Julie," she said, her words slurring. "I just called to say goodbye and ask you to tell Merrie that I'm sorry…" The receiver fell from her hand as she lost consciousness.

CHAPTER EIGHTEEN

Sarah was sound asleep when the phone began to ring. She struggled to reach for it to still its intrusion and managed to tangle herself in the covers. Groggily, she choked out, "Hello?"

She was startled to hear Julie's voice on the other end of the line, sounding as though she was a very long distance away, though Sarah knew she couldn't be. Her words jarred Sarah into wakefulness, then sent a chill up her spine as the line seemed to go dead.

"Julie? Julie, are you there? Julie, what's wrong?" she yelled into the receiver. "Julie? Answer me! Are you all right?" She pressed the lever to disconnect the line, released it again and dialed Julie's number. The line was busy, indicating that she had not hung up, but for some reason had ceased to speak. At first unsure of what to do, Sarah considered calling the police or fire department for help, then thought, no maybe she's just been celebrating too much and passed out. It wouldn't do for her to find the police at her door. It was obvious, however, that something was wrong. Why would she say goodbye and ask me to tell Merrie that she was sorry?

"I hope it isn't what is sounds like," Sarah said aloud. She threw on a pair of jeans and a shirt and raced out the door. There was almost no traffic on El Camino as she sped up the street. Hoping to see a patrol car and thus get the help she feared she might need, she drove far in excess of the speed limit, pausing, but not coming to a complete stop at red lights.

There was no sign of life inside Julie's apartment as Sarah pounded on the front door, calling out. No one answered and Sarah sped around to the back, hoping it might be unlocked. She considered finding a building manager, then decided to break the glass on the back door and let herself in. Every minute might count, she reasoned. Her fear turned to panic when she saw Julie lying on the bed, the phone beside her on the floor.

Pulling her up, Sarah shook her vehemently, but got no response. Water, she thought and dashed into the bathroom. Her eyes widened in shock as she saw the scattered bottles on the floor and the empty Valium bottle on the sink. Dousing the still form on the bed with the water, she grabbed the phone to call for help. As she waited for an ambulance, she tried again to get Julie up, to get her to walk, but could not support her weight.

"Oh my God, Julie, what have you done? And why?" she cried.

The image of the revolving red light on the police car burned in Sarah's mind as she sat slumped on a plastic chair in the hospital emergency room. The firemen had done the best they could to revive Julie, but had offered little hope when they were unable to wake her. The fact that she was breathing at all was apparently something of a miracle.

A harried doctor came through the swinging double doors from the interior area. He headed toward Sarah, looking grim. In response to his questions, she could only shake her head negatively, unable to shed any light on how many pills there might have been in the bottle of Valium.

"She had a fairly large amount of alcohol in her blood when they brought her in," the doctor indicated, "which means she must have consumed quite a lot before she decided to take the pills. Would she have any reason to attempt suicide?"

"No, no, no! She just got a letter from her husband," Sarah cried, "why would she want to die when she'd just been given the best reason in the world to live?" She explained the situation to the doctor, who stood with his arms folded across his chest, staring down at the floor. "It must have been an accident!" Sarah finished miserably.

"Well, we've done all we can do for the time being. All we can do now is wait. I suggest you go home and if there's anyone who should be notified, you'd better do it soon." He nodded abruptly as he accepted her phone number and disappeared again through the swinging doors.

"What on earth do I tell your parents?" Sarah asked aloud of no one in particular.

The night of the meeting on the University of Chicago campus found Sheila sitting at her dressing table in a state of anxious anticipation. She was determined to attend, but was more than a little afraid of what she might discover in a world with which she was totally unfamiliar. Three things concerned her: would she make a fool of herself with these people whose ideas were so foreign to her; could she keep her dangerous liaison a secret from her friends; and most immediately, what does one wear to a gathering of revolutionaries? Well, she'd lived through more trying times than this, hadn't she? She could always hop into a taxi and come back to the safety of her own world and no one need be the wiser.

But it certainly would be gratifying to be seen as someone who was politically savvy rather than as a bit of fluff that looks good at a party. She really couldn't abide those do-gooder families that her parents were so involved with, and Sarah Fremont, the ultimate goody-two-shoes they were so fond of, well, she'd learn that Sheila was to be respected, too. Maybe Dave Marshall and his friends could show her the way. Besides, he intrigued her. She let herself imagine his long fingers touching her skin, moving up her thighs…maybe tonight.

But first things first. She searched her closet for something that would make her look as though she belonged and came up with a pair of faded designer blue jeans. They'd just have to do, she thought and went through her blouses and sweaters to find something simple. Pulling her blonde curls into a ponytail, she tied a scarf around her head, got out her raincoat and tied the belt that went with it. She surveyed her image in the mirror and decided she might pass if she kept quiet and slouched a little.

Expecting to find the meeting in an auditorium of some sort, Sheila was surprised to find it was being held in a rather small room that was crowded with chairs, most of which were already occupied when she arrived. She huddled just inside the door, looking for Dave and caught sight of him in a group of people who were listening intently to a short, greying man. In a sudden burst of timidity, she thought maybe she shouldn't be here after all. She looked around for an out-of-the-way place to sit and found a chair against the wall not too far from the door, reasoning that she could sneak out before anyone knew she was there if things got too uncomfortable.

The speaker for the evening turned out to be the short, greying man Dave had been with when she came in. Much of what he said sounded like a foreign language as he used words like existentialism, phenomenology and dialectically, and criticized just about everything Sheila thought was sacred. Even what she understood didn't really make sense to her.

"What is rational is real and what is real is rational," he said, and Sheila wondered what he considered real or rational.

After the talk, there were announcements regarding scheduled peace rallies and when no one seemed to take any particular notice of her, Sheila's courage began to return. She hovered in the hallway when the meeting adjourned, waiting for Dave to come out. When he did, he was surprised to see her and expressed his belief that he hadn't thought she'd have the nerve to come.

"Who *are* all these people?" she asked him.

"This is the Hegelian Society," he replied, "followers of George Wilhelm Friedrich Hegel."

"Who's he?"

"A German philosopher who lived about a hundred and fifty years ago," Dave told her. "His ideas are partly the basis of Marxism today. Come on, some of the group are coming over to my place for a beer or coffee. Maybe you'll learn something if you listen carefully."

Sheila regarded him skeptically, her courage ebbing. "Where do you live?" she asked.

"Just a few blocks from here. Did you take a cab or do you have a car? Never mind, it isn't important. I'll see to it that you get back to your car if you have one, but we have to hurry if we're going to get there before the rest of them do." He took her arm, leading her out of the building and down the street.

Dave's apartment was in a four-story brick building, one of many that lined the dimly lighted street. It had a small living room that seemed even smaller than it was because of the large, overstuffed furniture that filled it. French doors separated the living room from another small room that served as a bedroom and a narrow hallway led to the bathroom and the antiquated kitchen. There was very little space in which to move around as the others began to arrive.

Apparently they had all been there before as they made themselves at home, getting beer from the refrigerator and conversing jovially. Sheila noticed Sally arrive and tried to remain as inconspicuous as possible. It was some time before Sally saw her and said, "Well if it isn't Miss Rich Bitch!"

"Aw, give her a break, Sally," Dave urged. "She just wants to learn about things she's never been exposed to before. You've got to give her credit for that."

"Okay, okay, maybe I should be more charitable," Sally grumbled. "I doubt we'll ever be friends, but let's call a truce for now." She extended her hand to Sheila, smiling grudgingly.

The group enjoyed a camaraderie such as Sheila hadn't known even in her cheerleader days. They were completely at ease with each other, sometimes joking, sometimes discussing such mundane things as the weather, occasionally even referring to their families. Somehow she had expected them to be far more intense, and had not anticipated understanding more than a smattering of the conversation. She hovered in the tiny hallway, moving between the kitchen and the living room, staying out of the way as people made trips to the refrigerator for beer. Now and then someone stopped to introduce himself, welcoming her to the group, though not yet to their inner circle. As time passed, she began to wonder if she should leave before her presence caused Dave any embarrassment, but thought she would bring more attention to herself if he insisted on seeing her to a taxi. Besides, she had no idea where she might find a taxi on the dark street in this unfamiliar part of town.

Eventually the others began to leave and Dave draped one arm around her, casually possessive, as he said goodnight. Sheila was warmed by his attention and relaxed against him. When everyone had gone, she moved to get her coat and handbag, preparing to depart as well.

"What's your hurry?" Dave asked, dropping onto the sofa and patting the cushion alongside of him, indicating that she should sit down too. She did and was soon enveloped in his arms as he kissed her tentatively, then with increasing ardor.

"No," she protested, pushing him away.

"Why not?" he inquired. "Isn't that what you wanted when you came down here tonight?"

"No! That is, I thought about it a little, but I came because I really do want to know more about your kind of people. I've never met anyone like you before." She stopped, confused and afraid she'd said the wrong thing.

"Actually, we're all pretty normal sort of people," he said. "Did you expect us to be making bombs in a basement or something?" Dave smiled tolerantly at her and went on, "You thought because I was there at that protest march that I was one of the real radicals, didn't you?"

"Well, you call yourself a 'Maoist' and have meetings with speakers who talk about things I've never heard of, not that I've been overly educated, but my ex-husband was very well educated, as are most of his friends, and I've never heard any of them talk the way you do," Sheila retorted.

"They're too busy protecting their money from the laborers who earn it for them. They don't want to see the poverty that surrounds them."

"The people who work in Quinn's plant are very well paid and very well treated. They get Christmas bonus' and he even gives every single employee a turkey for Thanksgiving," Sheila cried, growing more agitated.

"Just like the benevolent plantation owner who sees to it that all his slaves get an extra ration of food on Sundays, right? God forbid they should ever have the temerity to set foot in the manor house though!" Dave was sarcastic.

"It's not like that at all! I'm sure they're not unhappy! And they certainly aren't communists!"

Dave sighed and said, "I can see you need a great deal of re-educating, but let's leave that for another day." He pulled her to him once again, kissing her gently and stroking her hair as she leaned her head on his shoulder. She wasn't sure whether she really wanted to pursue this relationship and had no idea where it might be leading her. It would so much easier to go home and forget all about Dave Marshall, but his arms felt good. It had been too long since she'd been in the arms of such an exciting man. She began to respond to his touch. She'd think it over tomorrow, she decided, and lifted her face toward his, her lips parted, inviting his kisses. She hardly even noticed when they moved together through the French doors to the bedroom as she gave in to desire and let passion dictate.

They were cautious with each other in the morning. Unsure of their feelings, each treated the other with an uneasy courtesy as they dressed and Dave led her up the street to a taxi stand at the corner. Sheila was sure the driver smirked knowingly though she could see only the back of his head as she hurriedly wrote her phone number on a matchbook and handed it out the window to Dave. Promising to call her soon, he stood watching as the taxi moved away from the curb.

Sheila huddled in a corner of the seat, enormously thankful when she was finally able to see her apartment building ahead. She kept her head lowered as she hurried through the mirrored lobby and into the elevator. I must be loony tunes to have done that, she thought. But she was unable to forget his touch as she soaked leisurely in a bath. How soon would he call? Would he call at all? A small part of her hoped he wouldn't, but mostly she hoped desperately that he would.

CHAPTER NINETEEN

The pale, early light that preceded dawn was growing brighter and the sun peered through the trees as Sarah made the return trip down El Camino Real. Strange, she thought, how events and the state of a person's mind can alter perception. In the dark on the way up to Julie's, she had been absorbed in the effort to get there as quickly as possible, but now the early morning stillness was comforting. She drove slowly, aware of commuters who were beginning to back out of driveways, but feeling detached from their everyday world.

The immediate emergency had been handled and she had managed to cope with the phone call that had to be made to Julie's parents. She had looked up Dr. Summerhill's office number in the phone book, hoping he would break the news to Mrs. Summerhill, but his service had told her he was at the hospital in preparation for an early surgery and could not be immediately located. The call to Mrs. Summerhill at home had been difficult. She had been distraught and unable to make decisions, never having had to handle emergencies by herself. Sarah had been afraid she might have to drive up to Marin to get her, but Dr. Summerhill had received the urgent message and called back. At a loss as to what to tell him, Sarah had said she was sure it was an accident, that they had celebrated together and Julie must have taken the Valium when she was too excited to sleep. That explanation had satisfied him temporarily, but Sarah knew that he would have questions she could not answer when he was told how much Valium and alcohol were in his daughter's system. Julie remained comatose and there was seemingly nothing anyone could do to help her, an idea that was unacceptable to her medically trained father.

Exhausted, Sarah stripped off the jeans she had worn and fell back into bed. Though she slept for several hours, it was not a restful sleep as she tossed and turned. Upon awakening, she phoned the office to say she wouldn't be in and made coffee that she sipped absentmindedly. She knew that Merrie would want to know about Julie, but rather than tell her on the phone, Sarah decided to go over to the Winslow's home.

She was shocked to find Merrie in a bathrobe in the afternoon, looking pale and wan. Pete was away for the day on one of his fishing expeditions and in his absence, Merrie had given in to her feelings of desperation and hopelessness.

"At first I was sure that we'd hear something any day as to where Paul was, or that he'd been found and was on his way home. Then the days turned into months and the months have turned into years, and still we know no more than we did in the beginning," Merrie said. "We get little tidbits of information every now and then, mostly just to appease us temporarily, make us keep quiet a little longer. I've tried to believe that he's alive and that he'll be coming home, but some days my heart feels like lead. I haven't let Pete see how I feel, but I know that he does the same thing without letting me see it either," she finished.

Sarah longed to confide in Paul's mother, to tell her of her conviction that Paul was alive, that she shared a destiny with him that wouldn't let him die. But her fear of losing touch with his family entirely if they thought she was hallucinating over their son kept her from speaking. Besides, she had come to tell Merrie about Julie. She broke the news as gently as possible and cried along with Merrie as they both allowed themselves to give in to despair, if only for a moment.

After a time, Merrie stood up and said, "Well, enough of the self-pity for one day. I have to get cleaned up before Pete comes home and finds me like this."

She truly is a remarkable woman, Sarah reflected later as she stood by the window in her own home. It was very still outside, unnaturally still. Almost as though the world had been evacuated and no one had told her. It occurred to her that she often felt alone these days, as though everyone else had left for another planet without letting her know. She moved through her days, making business decisions, talking to people, handling situations, but it was as though the real Sarah was somehow an observer rather than a participant.

It seemed such a short time ago that she had assumed she would meet the right man, get married, have children and a home with a white picket fence next door to June Allyson and Van Johnson. This time of evening would find her in the kitchen preparing dinner, the children watching television or doing homework. Her husband would come home and they'd discuss the day over cocktails and she'd be loved and secure. Until that time, she had her job, her apartment, nice friends and a decent social life. It seemed so impossible now, though if she married John she'd have the love and security if not the house with the picket fence. And an exciting life of international travel and adventure. She sighed.

The phone rang. "Miss Fremont? This is Dr. Morrison. I thought you'd want to know that Mrs. Schaefer has begun to come around."

"Oh my God! She's conscious?"

"Not exactly, but she has opened her eyes several times and tried to speak, but we don't know yet whether or not she is aware of her surroundings or even if she will ever be aware of them. It's just too soon. I've tried to phone her parents in Marin, but there's no answer at their home. I thought you might know where they are, or be able to get in touch with them. I'd like to stick close to Julie's room rather than spend my time on the phone."

"Yes, I mean no, I mean yes, I understand, and no, I'm not sure where Dr. and Mrs. Summerhill are, but I think they're probably just out for dinner and will be back at the hospital soon. Dr. Morrison, you have to help Julie."

"I'll try, Miss Fremont, I'll try."

The next few days were difficult for everyone. Julie drifted in and out and finally regained consciousness. At first she simply stared straight ahead and then as she began to remember, she turned away from anyone who spoke to her, refusing to communicate. Doctors were unable to explain her physical recovery, saying only that there must be some higher being that had determined her life on earth was not yet finished. The amount of alcohol combined with the pills had been more than enough to end her life and there was still some doubt as to whether or not she would make a full recovery.

Unwilling to admit that their daughter may have suffered irreparable damage due to what they were still convinced was an accident, the Summerhills refused to consider psychiatric help for her until it became evident that she was not responding to any of the efforts being made on her behalf by the medical staff. Mrs. Summerhill insisted that Dr. Summerhill use any and all of the influence he had to call in the best in their field, regardless of time, distance or money, confessing to Sarah one afternoon that not only would Julie be getting the best help available, but that it would save embarrassment later when the whole nasty business was behind them. None of her husband's local colleagues would ever know there had been any mental problem.

The psychiatrist imported from the East Coast in place, Dr. Summerhill went back to his surgical practice and Mrs. Summerhill returned to her comfortable home, her housekeeper and little Sandy, both relieved that they had done the best they could and that what would follow was out of their hands. Sarah assured them that she would keep an eye on Julie's apartment and take care of the mail.

Soon after that, Sarah let herself into the apartment and gathered up the pile of correspondence that had accumulated in the mailbox. Thumbing through it, she was surprised to see an official looking envelope from the police department. Reluctant to pry into Julie's privacy, she decided that Julie would probably rather she opened it than her parents and tore open the flap. As she examined it, she realized it was a notice that Julie's car had been towed and could be retrieved from a garage in San Bruno. Good grief, she thought, I assumed Julie's car was in her garage. Had it been on the street and been towed for street cleaning? She checked further and noted that the address from which it had been towed was on El Camino in San Mateo. Maybe this would shed some light on where Julie might have gone before she took the pills.

She tucked the envelope into her purse and drove down El Camino, checking street numbers until she reached the Coachman Restaurant and Lounge. Had Julie stopped there on her way home? It was still too early for the happy hour crowd and there were few cars in the parking lot. Sarah pulled in by the entrance and went in. She asked to see the manager and introduced herself to the dark haired man who came from the rear of the dining room.

"My friend is in the hospital," she explained, "and this notice came in the mail for her. Can you tell me why the car was towed from here?"

He frowned, then recalled, "Oh yes. It was parked right in front for two or three days before we called the police. I don't know anything myself, but I think John, our bartender, might be able to tell you." He led her into the cocktail lounge, then left them after a brief explanation.

John was silent for a moment before asking, "what does your friend look like?" Sarah described Julie and John sighed heavily. "I was afraid that's who the car belonged to," he said.

"Afraid? Why do you say that?"

"I remember thinking when they left that I hoped she wouldn't be sorry in the morning," he replied ruefully. "I could tell she'd had a few drinks when she first came in here, but then she told me about the letter she got from her husband. I didn't know much about servicemen missing in Vietnam, and she told me he'd been gone a couple of years and she just got this letter and wanted to celebrate. There was a guy sitting a few stools away who overheard some of the conversation and he bought drinks for a toast. They got to talking, had a few more drinks, danced a few dances and looked like they were getting pretty close when they left together. That's about it," he finished.

"What time did they leave?" Sarah asked.

"It must have been around midnight, I guess, maybe a little after that," John answered.

"And the car stayed here until it was towed, right?"

"Right."

It was beginning to make a little more sense now, Sarah thought. She just hoped it wasn't what she suspected. She thanked John for his help and left the restaurant. Sitting in her car, she considered what to do next, then started the engine and headed for home. She phoned

Dr. Morrison and was told that Julie's condition had not changed. Explaining that she had learned a little more about the night before Julie had been brought to the hospital, she asked again about Julie's chances for recovery.

"At the moment, Miss Fremont, she doesn't seem to want to recover. Perhaps you should talk to the man her parents brought in from New York. He could probably give you a more educated idea of her symptoms, along with more of a prognosis." He finished by telling her he would leave a message for the psychiatrist to call her. She hung up and stood silently by the phone.

Oh, Julie, did you do what I'm thinking you did? Is that what made you so desperate that you wanted to die? Should I tell that psychiatrist or talk to you myself? I know you wouldn't want your parents to know and I'm not sure you'd even want the doctor to know. I wish there was someone I could trust to help me with this.

Her mind was churning as she sought a solution to the problem. If this is all part of some master plan in the universe, it's a shitty plan. Why me? She fixed herself a drink and went into the den to turn on the television, hoping that the diversion of the evening news might help clear her mind, but she was unable to concentrate on it.

If only John were closer. Dear, rational, reasonable John. He'd know what to do. She looked at her watch, considering what time it was in Paris and realized it must be the middle of the night there. She knew he wouldn't mind her calling at any hour, but decided maybe she'd phone him in the morning.

She awoke early the following day. Determined to see Julie and then decide whether or not to talk to her about what she was now convinced was a suicide attempt, she called her office to say she'd be in later if possible. She stopped at Julie's apartment to look for the letter from Jack, thinking that it might shock Julie into reality, forcing her to confront the fact that he might very well come home one day. It wouldn't be fair to him to find that the wife he loved had destroyed herself, leaving their small daughter without a mother. Sarah felt sure that even if Jack knew that she had given in to loneliness and frustration, he would not want to lose her forever.

She unlocked the front door and looked around the living room.

Noticing the rumpled blanket on the sofa for the first time, she picked it up and refolded it carefully. She climbed the stairs to the bedroom and found the pile of clothes that had been discarded on the floor in a heap.

Gathering them up, she hung the black pants suit as far back in the closet as she could. She made the bed and took the lingerie back downstairs where she put it in a bag and then in the trashcan outside the back door, sure that Julie would not want to see it again. She went from room to room doing a final check for any further evidence of that night, then found the letter on the kitchen table and left for the hospital.

The nurse on duty at the nurse's station told Sarah that the psychiatrist had not yet received the message as he had not called in or been to see Julie that day. Sarah walked slowly down the hall to Julie's room, knocked gently and went through the door. Julie's eyes were open, but she didn't turn as Sarah entered, continuing to stare at the ceiling.

"Julie? Julie, it's me, Sarah. I see that you're awake. Please look at me." There was no response, so she went on, "Julie? I stopped by your apartment and brought the letter from Jack for you."

Still no response though Sarah thought she detected a change in the expression in her friend's eyes. She went to the bed and leaned over to smooth the hair from Julie's face. Gazing at her for a few moments, she let down the rail on the side of the bed and sat down on the edge.

"Julie, I think I know what happened that night. It might help if you could talk to someone about it," Sarah began hesitantly. "I told your mom and dad that I'd take care of your mail and stuff, and when I went over there yesterday there was a notice from the police department that your car had been towed. None of us had thought to look for your car, so I was surprised that it had been towed. When I saw the address it had been taken from, I went down there to see where you'd been. It was the Coachman, Julie, so I went in and talked to the bartender there." She paused and looked away, unsure whether to go on or not.

"It isn't so terrible, Julie," she continued. "You think it is now, but it really isn't. After all this time, it was an emotional shock to get the letter and you needed to share your feelings. Maybe if you'd stayed at my house instead of going home, this wouldn't have happened. Oh

God, Julie, please come back to us. Merrie loves you, I love you and I know that Jack loves you. You may not think so, but I know he'd want you here when he comes home. And Sandy needs you. You can't just abandon everyone who loves you like this. Please Julie…," Sarah's voice broke as tears welled in her eyes.

The small sound that came from the still form on the bed began as a whimper, like that of a wounded animal. It grew slowly as Julie began to release the agony that had devoured her. Her chest heaved as a high pitched wail came from the depths of her soul, tapering off into a guttural sound that came from the depths of her body. She began to tremble as the tears came, turning into sobs that wracked her from head to toe.

Sarah reached out to the miserable creature beside her, gathering her in her arms, holding tightly as they cried together, one in shame, one with compassion and understanding. They clung to each other as the healing began.

CHAPTER TWENTY

Paul Winslow sat on the ground outside the hut that he had called home for more than a year. He had more or less recovered from the bout with jungle fever, but he knew it could recur at any time and that he would eventually succumb to it as his system grew weaker. His plan to hide extra clothing for an escape during his morning bath in the river had not worked out, and he knew that time was no longer on his side. He must escape soon if he were to escape at all.

He finished his evening bowl of watery rice and vegetables as darkness fell on the camp. There had been an unusual amount of activity in the camp that day as his Vietnamese guards bustled around in what appeared to be an effort to clean the compound. They must be expecting visitors, he thought. Could it by some miracle be that the Red Cross or maybe representatives of a neutral nation were being allowed in? More than likely it was just some high-ranking officer. He sighed deeply as one of the guards came over to him, indicating that it was time for him to be chained to his pallet for the night. He heaved himself up and entered the hut, submitting meekly to the chains that the guard secured around his ankles.

Lying on the rough wooden planks, he thought about Sarah and the time she had spent with him. He was still not sure how to interpret his conviction that he knew her and occasionally rationalized that he must have been hallucinating, real as it may have seemed at the time. His heart told him that he had known her through eternity while his rational mind tried to convince him that this was not possible. The variety of clothing he had seen her wear prompted him to consider the idea that he had known her in some previous life, a hypothesis he found difficult to accept. The kimono she'd worn, the black silk he'd watched her remove, the emerald green evening gown that made her eyes so luminous – all had been from distinctly different eras in time. He whispered to her now, calling her name, willing her to appear.

"Sarah?" he called softly. Closing his eyes, he visualized her thick dark hair, her green eyes, her softness. His skin began to tingle at the remembrance of lovemaking he no longer even attempted to separate from reality, though he was unable to come up with a reason that would explain why he could not seem to call her to him at will. The experience he'd had when he suddenly knew her name, grasped her hand, caressed her cheek, had not been repeated and he struggled to understand. If their destinies had been preordained, why could he not call upon her for comfort now when he needed her? Perhaps it was all a trick of his mind, a way of entertaining himself in an effort to retain his sanity. Should he allow it to take its course or should he reject it before he crossed a line into total illusion? His heart and mind seemed to be at war.

The next day it was apparent that someone of importance was to visit the camp. Following his morning bath in the river, Paul was issued a clean pair of the black pajamas. Instead of being led to the isolated spot in the fields where he worked alone, he was chained outside his hut and left to wonder who might be coming.

As the sun rose higher in the sky, a small convoy of jeeps drove into the camp. The guards in the area rushed to meet the men who climbed out of the jeeps, saluting as smartly as they were able and leading the group toward the thatched roof building that served as camp headquarters. A short time later, two of the visiting officers came out, accompanied by the camp commander, striding importantly toward Paul's hut.

"So! You are the American pilot who drops bombs from his plane, killing our innocent people and then returning to his comfortable ship for steak dinners!" The man's English was excellent and Paul wondered whether he might have attended an American college.

Two of the guards pulled Paul roughly to his feet, forcing him to stand straight with a blow between his shoulder blades. "Paul Winslow, Lt. Commander, U.S. Navy," he began.

"I know your name," the officer interrupted. "I also know that you would like to be back in San Francisco with your family. Your father, Peter Winslow, is a retired Army officer, another imperialist warmonger. Why don't you tell us about the ship you came from and then we might be inclined to help you get back to California?"

"Paul Winslow, Lt. Commander, U.S. Navy," Paul repeated. One of the guards raised his rifle, hitting Paul in the shoulder with the butt, knocking him to the ground. Instinctively, he raised his arms to protect his head. He heard the sound of a pistol being cocked and thought, this is it, it's all over.

"Get up, you're not worth a bullet," the officer said disdainfully. "You will wish you had cooperated with us. Or you may wish I had fired the gun. Take him away!"

The two guards beside him dragged him to his feet, pulling him by his arms. He stumbled and fell several times as they half carried him to the edge of the camp where another guard waited with a shovel. Motioning for him to dig, the guard threw the shovel at his feet. He picked it up and began to dig, fighting the urge to throw the dirt in the faces of the guards. It wasn't long before he realized that the space he was digging was approximately six feet long and three feet wide. The size of a grave.

When they decided it was big enough, they produced leg irons and shackled his feet with only a few inches of chain between the irons. Pushing him roughly into the grave, they covered the hole with logs and piled rocks on either end, leaving only slits for ventilation.

As night fell once again, Paul shivered in the damp earth, cold, hungry and wishing the Vietnamese officer had pulled the trigger. Over the next few days, the guards came three times a day to feed him a few spoonfuls of rice, removing only one of the logs far enough for him to sit up. He had lost track of time when they finally came to let him out, stepping on his hands as he attempted to push himself up far enough to climb from the hole.

Again they half dragged him, half carried him, this time to the river. Pushing him into the water, they motioned for him to remove his now filthy black pajamas and clean himself. The shock of the water combined with the effects of the bright sunlight after days of darkness nearly made him pass out. The bath finished, he was given another pair of black pajamas and marched to the camp command post.

A new officer, again English speaking, greeted him saying apologetically, "You see how well you have been treated in this camp? We have been very remiss in letting you get used to such comfort. It is time now for you to tell us what we want to know and then we can let you go back to your comfortable hut, perhaps even kill a chicken so that you can have some meat. Would you like that?"

Paul did not answer, unable to lift his head from his chest. The officer reacted angrily. "Tell me the name of your ship!"

"Paul Winslow, Lt. Commander, U.S. Navy…"

"How many planes come from that ship?"

"Paul Winslow, Lt. Commander, U.S. Navy…"

Paul's voice was barely audible as he mumbled his name and rank. The officer grew more and more agitated. In a moment of lucidity, Paul realized that the pressure must be on to get information from him and if they failed, there would be trouble ahead. They're going to let me die anyway, he reasoned. I hope the bastards suffer for it. Once again he mumbled only his name and rank, the serial number no longer important. Red faced, the officer shouted, "Take him back to his hole!"

Shoved forcibly back into the 'grave' in which he had been living for the past week, it was some time before Paul realized that the guards had forgotten to check the lock on his ankle chains. Reaching up, he tested the logs above him and was elated to discover that while heavy and anchored with rocks, they would move slightly. He sat back, considering the possibility of escape. Forcing himself to breathe deeply, he felt his arms and legs to check for sore and painful spots. I'll have to wait until dark, he reasoned, and which direction do I go?

It was around mid-day. He'd need all the strength he could muster, so he'd better try to sleep. The ground had warmed and the temperature in his tiny prison had risen noticeably, but for the first time since his capture, he felt that this time there was really hope. He slept for several hours, dreaming of his love, his Sarah.

The daylight was fading when he woke. Stretching in the cramped space, he massaged the parts of his body that he could reach in an effort to stimulate his circulation. Pushing his fingers through the cracks between the logs, he began to move the rocks a little at a time, just enough so that the guard would not notice when his evening spoonfuls of rice were brought. He continued to work on moving the rocks, listening for approaching footsteps. No one appeared with food and he came to the conclusion that they were going to let him starve, at least for today. Inch by inch, he pushed the rocks to one side, using his shoulder for leverage to tip the logs when he could no longer reach the rocks. Finally, the log on the outermost edge moved far enough for him to get his arm and shoulder through. Cautiously, he raised his head through the opening, moving slowly, checking each direction for a sign of the guards. What if it's a trap, he wondered. Well, he couldn't be any worse off and he'd rather be dead than live through this hell any longer, he decided.

He waited until there was no sign of activity in the camp, then gave the log a final push and stood up. Not daring to move at first, he inched his way out, lying flat on the ground until he was sure that there was no one nearby. He began to crawl toward the relative safety of the trees around the perimeter of the camp. He had gone only a few feet when he realized that he'd left the log out of place. Scrambling back, he replaced it over the grave and hastily rearranged the rocks to conceal his escape until morning. Once again, he headed for the trees.

Resisting the temptation to run wildly, he moved slowly away from the camp. Circling part way around the camp, he reached the river and crept in. Summoning all he could remember of astronomy, he looked up at the sky, scanning it for the North Star. At first unable to decide which star was the one he sought, he settled on the one he thought most likely and headed away from it, hoping he was going south.

CHAPTER TWENTY ONE

Pete Winslow was a thoughtful man, a careful man. These qualities were more or less responsible for his position in life. He didn't take chances and he didn't rock the boat. He considered his options when a choice had to be made and selected the one that appealed to his common sense without disturbing things too much, discarding the ones that were not based solidly on fact. The result was that his professional career as an Army officer had been methodical and predictable. His promotions were not meteoric, but he rose in rank at a steady rate.

Pete had spent most of his years in the Army building roads that went where they were supposed to go and held up well in all kinds of weather, and bridges that inspired confidence in their durability. He could look back on his years of service with pride as he remembered duty stations in many parts of the world where those roads and bridges still stood, a silent tribute to American ingenuity.

He enjoyed the camaraderie of his fellow officers, but rarely saw the rowdiness that occurred as parties progressed into the wee hours of the morning. His sense of duty and his respect for Merrie made it imperative that he follow his own rules of decorum and leave before anything happened that might cause later regret. His sense of humor was subtle and the twinkle in his eye made those around him feel that each had a rapport with him that was singular in nature. Those who tended to be loud or boisterous were sure that Pete understood and appreciated their jokes and those who were annoyed by what they considered inappropriate behavior were equally sure that Pete Winslow felt as they did, but was too diplomatic to say so.

In short, Pete Winslow was the consummate man for all seasons without even being aware of it. He was dependable, a gentleman. In his retirement, he enjoyed the solitude that came with fishing and duck hunting, though he didn't often bring home the fish or ducks. He would never admit it, but there were many times when he deliberately missed as shot or pulled in his line to avoid killing a creature he admired.

Occasionally, he wondered if Merrie was as content with their marriage as he was, but he didn't spend a lot of time worrying about it. Their sex life had been tender rather than passionate and their attitude toward each other was one of affection. He assumed that Merrie was satisfied with their relationship.

The only thing that didn't fit into Pete's otherwise well ordered life was his daughter, Sheila. She was so unlike either Pete or Merrie in temperament that he wondered what long gone relative she might resemble. It might be interesting to look into the family tree someday to see if there had been a rebel great grandmother around. He loved Sheila and had thought her the most beautiful little girl in the world as she grew up, but he didn't understand her. Every now and then he thought it might be his fault, but he was at a loss as to what to do about it.

Pete's greatest pride came in the form of his son, Paul. From the moment of his birth, Paul had been a source of joy and amazement to his father. The perfect little boy with the tousled hair and deep, liquid eyes had seemed a miracle. As a child Paul had listened carefully to his father's explanations as they worked together on various projects, and developed an insatiable curiosity about how things worked. More mechanically minded than Pete, the boy couldn't wait to get an automobile and had spent hours as a teenager with his head buried under the hood of the family car. He had saved his money and managed to buy an old convertible in his senior year in highschool, but the fifty-seven Chevy he acquired in college had been his pride and joy.

The development of jet airplanes had turned Paul's thoughts toward the sky. The idea of soaring above the clouds was irresistible and the engines that made it possible went beyond those that kept the adventurous boy on the ground. Realizing that his best chance of achieving his dream lay with the military, Paul began taking aviation courses as well as flying lessons, applied for officer training with the Navy and received his commission shortly after graduation from Northwestern. Pete could not have been more proud than he was when his son, wearing his new uniform, saluted his father.

Pete drove more slowly than his usual moderate pace as he returned home from his duck-hunting trip. The weather was getting colder and he'd decided that this would be his last hunt for this year. As so often happened, his thoughts turned to Paul and the slight nausea that appeared deep inside whenever he thought about where his son was began to surface. Alone, he could let the pain show in his eyes, something he tried not to allow otherwise. As the months became years with still no word on Paul's whereabouts, he found himself needing solitude more frequently as his despair became harder to hide. He tried to keep up an optimistic front for Merrie's sake, but he could see that she was losing hope and he was powerless to help her. He knew that she tried to remain cheerful for his sake just as he did for hers, but he was finding it more and more difficult to look into her eyes, knowing that her grief was as intense as his.

At first, the activity of the families of missing men had been reassuring, Something positive was being done. There was a bond between them, unspoken except as they shared a new idea or some new tidbit of information, some tiny hint of progress. But eyes that once gleamed with hope were becoming dull and hard even as lips smiled.

One of the brightest spots in Pete's life was a visit from Sarah Fremont. He had begun to think of her as another daughter and had gone so far as to introduce her that way now and then. He looked forward to seeing her though he knew that her added responsibilities with the Davidson Hotels took more of her time. He was glad that she seemed to be very fond of Paul's friend, John St. James, but he couldn't help the twinge of resentment that he kept hidden, ashamed, as he thought how much he'd like to have her for a daughter-in-law when

Paul came home. He was glad, too, that Sarah and Merrie were such good friends and that Merrie had Julie Schaefer as well. But sometimes he felt that he was the only one who was alone in his grief, a thought that he brushed away as being unworthy and selfish.

Nearing his home, Pete decided to ask Merrie to call Sarah. They hadn't seen her for quite some time and it would be a real shot in the arm to have her over for cocktails. He squared his shoulders and smiled. The house seemed inordinately quiet as he entered the kitchen from the garage. Funny, he thought, usually Merrie was right there.

He called out, "Merrie? Merrie, I'm home!" Dropping his jacket and hat on a kitchen chair, he went into the living room, looking around expectantly, finding no one. He couldn't remember a time when Merrie hadn't been there to welcome the hunter home from the hill and, though not yet alarmed, he was apprehensive.

The mail was lying on the dining room table unopened. Pete picked it up, leafing through it disinterestedly, though compelled by years of strict organization to sort it into two separate piles, one to review later, the other most likely junk mail. He paused, considering whether or not to be concerned as to Merrie's whereabouts, then decided she was probably at a neighbor's house. After all, it wasn't as though she *had* to be there. It was just that he was accustomed to finding her there.

He climbed the stairs to their bedroom, intending to shower and clean up before mixing the vodka martinis. As he entered the bedroom, he was startled to discover that the drapes were closed, the room in gloomy darkness. He glanced around, impatient for his eyes to adjust. He caught his breath as a stab of fear clutched his chest, seeing the small form lying so still on the bed.

"Merrie? Merrie, are you all right?" he exclaimed, hurrying to her side. Relief swept over him as she stirred, then opened her eyes and smiled at him.

"Pete? Haven't you left yet?" she asked.

"Left yet?" Pete was bewildered. "I'm back. It's five o'clock in the afternoon! Did you sleep all day? Are you sick?"

"Oh, my goodness, are you sure?" Merrie was appalled at the thought that she had spent the whole day sleeping. "I was a little tired this morning and thought I'd just sleep a little longer!" She struggled to sit up, throwing off the covers, but sank back against the pillows as quickly as she had risen, dizzy and disoriented.

"What is it?" Pete's voice rose as his concern increased.

"I can't imagine," Merrie answered. "I just can't seem to get up. Why is it so dark in here?"

"Because it's getting dark outside and the drapes haven't been opened all day," Pete replied. Turning on a lamp, he went on, "Why don't I call the doctor?"

"No, no," she protested. "I'll be fine. Just give me a few minutes to wake up. Were you headed for the shower? Go on, by the time you're out, I'll be up." She smiled reassuringly and waved him toward the bathroom. Reluctantly, though encouraged by her cheerfulness, Pete turned to leave her.

Merrie lay back for a few moments, considering how she could have slept the entire day. I haven't been eating well and I've let myself get depressed too often, she told herself. Resolving to regain her strength, she sat up, putting her feet on the floor, then standing tentatively. Finding her legs wobbly, she moved carefully to put on a dressing gown and brush her hair. Some orange juice, toast and coffee – that would do the trick. Holding tightly to the stair rail, she made her way to the kitchen, determined to present a healthy image to Pete when he came down.

Pete stood for several minutes under the shower, letting the hot water run over his shoulders. I've neglected her too often. I've left her to carry her own burdens, assuming she could cope alone. We should talk about it more, he concluded. But how to begin? Always sure of his reasoning when faced with a problem during his career, he was at a loss when it came to his wife, the one person who had been by his side throughout the years. He dressed slowly, torn between the desire to make sure that Merrie was all right and his utter helplessness in finding a way to share the sorrow that had engulfed them. Could it be something that was strictly physical that was wrong with Merrie? Or was it the result of the years of concern and frustration, the uncertainty of not knowing their son's fate? Pete wasn't sure which he'd prefer it to be. If it was a physical illness, he had it within his power to do something about it, but if Merrie was truly ill, he wasn't sure he could cope. On the other hand, if the problem was emotional, he hadn't the slightest idea how to help her.

His step was heavy as he descended the stairs to find Merrie in the kitchen, smiling brightly as she sipped freshly brewed coffee.

"Feeling better?" he inquired tentatively.

"Much," she assured him. "I haven't been eating well lately and I'm sure it just caught up with me, Pete. I'm sorry if I gave you a scare."

He realized that she was giving him the opportunity to disregard his earlier concern, letting him off the hook so to speak. "Merrie?" he began.

"It's all right, Pete. I'll be fine," she said gently.

He lowered himself onto a chair at the table, avoiding her eyes as he considered what to say next. "Merrie," he began again, "I know that the past few years have been difficult for you and that I haven't been much support. At first, it seemed like something that would be resolved soon and we'd all get on with our lives. Then when the months turned into years, it got harder to talk about it other than at meetings or as a basis for conversation with strangers, or as an excuse for some activity."

"Pete…"

"Please, Merrie, don't interrupt. I may never have the courage to go on and we both need to talk about it. You've been the foundation for my life, my source of strength, everything that gave meaning to life. I want you to know that. I want to say it at least once. I guess it's something I've never given much thought to, just taken for granted. But without you, there would be no purpose to anything for me. The children completed the picture, gave me stability, a sense of being needed, but it's you that is the center of my universe. Somehow I've let Paul's disappearance overshadow everything else, but I want you to know how very important you are to me."

Merrie reached for his hand, unable to speak. It was the first time he'd ever put his feelings into words other than the many times he'd simply said, "I love you." She had always known how much he cared, but hearing him say it moved her immeasurably. The lump in her throat rendered it impossible for her to respond other than to take his hand in hers. The pressure he returned as he squeezed her hand was painful, but gave her greater joy than she could have imagined.

It was several moments before he asked, his voice trembling, "Do you want to talk about Paul, Merrie?"

"I don't think we can, Pete. We each know how the other feels and that there are some things that defy expression. At this moment, my heart is so full of love for you that I think it might burst." Tears began to roll down her cheeks as he looked up. He stood, pulling her up and enfolding her in his arms. They clung to each other, allowing the tears to mingle as they shared their sorrow, their love, and their joy in one another.

Merrie's spirits rose appreciably in the days that followed, though she still seemed to be tired most of the time. Attributing it to the fact that she had not been getting proper nourishment, she made it a point to eat balanced means though her appetite had diminished greatly and she was unable to eat very much of any one thing. In addition to her resolve to regain her health, Merrie was determined to restore her emotional well being. Sure that liking what she saw in the mirror would be a good start, she visited the hairdresser, then headed for the mall to find something cheerful to wear. Tired, but in a happier frame of mind than she'd been for several months, she decided to call Sarah Fremont.

CHAPTER TWENTY TWO

S arah watched nervously as the illuminated numbers above the elevator door descended slowly. The meeting with a workaholic client had run longer than anticipated and she was running late. She glanced at her watch hoping it might tell her that time had not passed as quickly as she knew it had. She wished there was time for a quick drink to calm her nerves before she tackled the streets of Los Angeles. Each week that went by made it harder to function in her two separate worlds, to keep her life together.

She was to meet Merrie at the Ambassador Hotel for the conference being sponsored by a student organization at U.C.L.A. that was supporting the cause of American servicemen in Vietnam. The scheduled speakers for the afternoon were to be a Midwestern senator and a California congressman giving their views on the issue.

The elevator reached the lobby. Sarah's heels clacked noisily on the tile floor as she hurried to the street. It was a Saturday and Wilshire Boulevard was quiet compared to the usual hustle and bustle of weekdays. The parking lot where she'd left her rented car was nearly two blocks away and she wished briefly that she could somehow spirit herself to it without actually covering the distance physically. Like I'm really having any success with *that* kind of thing.

She had tried repeatedly to achieve another out-of-body experience or to find her way back to the lives of either Yoshiko or Marguerite, but to no avail. The excitement she'd felt at the discovery of documentation on what she had thought was pure fantasy had been corroded by her failure to move into those realms on her own.

She had tried everything she could think of to find the path that would lead her to Paul Winslow. She had set the scene with soft lights and candles, then concentrated on her goal as she played the piano. She had recorded the music and played it in her bedroom in the dark. She had recreated the settings that preceded the previous experiences, carefully recalling details even to the clothing she'd worn. But it seemed that Paul had simply vanished from whatever subconscious part of her mind that had been able to communicate in the past.

Each failure served to distress her further. Had something happened to Paul? She'd been so sure that he was alive and being held captive. Could his physical condition have deteriorated to the point where he no longer lived? Unable to accept that possibility, she had turned to the liquor cabinet as she struggled to find answers.

Telling herself that compared to what most people drink, she wasn't really drinking that much, she justified first one drink, then two, then sometimes three at a time until she finally decided to stop counting. So far it hadn't affected her ability to do her job – no one knew what she did in the privacy of her own home, and what the hell, it wasn't as if she was a lush or falling down drunk. Besides, once the war ended, Paul would either come home or he wouldn't, and it would all be resolved. She wouldn't need to drink.

Hurrying down the street, her eyes were drawn to a stone figure in the window of an antique shop. The serenity reflected in the face of the beautiful Kuan Yin seemed to call out to her and she stopped involuntarily to stare at it. In spite of her tardiness, she felt compelled to go into the shop and at least inquire about the price of the statue. It was surprisingly reasonable and without much debate, she bought it, stowing it carefully in the trunk of the car when she finally reached it.

Tapping her fingernails on the steering wheel, she waited impatiently for traffic lights to change as she drove toward the hotel. She had spent the previous few days in San Diego at the Davidson Hotel there and called on a couple of valuable clients in the Lost Angeles area prior to taking the weekend off to attend the conference. She breathed a sigh of relief as the last few lights turned agreeably green.

She checked in quickly, leaving instructions for the bellman to leave her luggage in her room, and strode down the corridor to the conference room where the meeting was already in progress. Pausing at the registration table outside the door to pick up the packet of materials and a badge with her name on it, Sarah slipped in and took a seat in the rear of the room.

The Midwestern senator was just finishing his remarks. "We have been facing a skillful propaganda campaign," he said, "and fixing a firm withdrawal date would only lead to more demands. The communists have duped the American public and they are still using the POW's and MIA's as pawns."

He sat down amid enthusiastic applause from most of the audience and the congressman from the West Coast rose to present his views. The issue under discussion had become an emotional one, with family members divided. It was tied to proposed legislation calling for total withdrawal of American troops from Vietnam within six months of the date of enactment, the only condition being the release of Americans held captive. Those family members whose loved ones were known to be prisoners favored the legislation, while many others were afraid that the fate of those missing in action would never be determined if the United States agreed to total withdrawal.

The congressman was urging negotiation of proportional repatriation linked to troop withdrawal on both sides. He indicated that he had discussed the issue with communist negotiators in Paris and asserted that under present policy, the U.S. must maintain a considerable nucleus force in South Vietnam even when total victory was beyond the rooftops. He concluded by saying, "We must negotiate today from strength. Vietnamization is not a solution to the POW problem."

His comments were met with some enthusiastic applause, some polite applause, and more than a few jeers. A question and answer period was to follow the talks and a woman's hand shot into the air immediately.

"Congressman, over fifty million letters have been sent to Hanoi and to the peace talks in Paris by organizations from all over the country including the Jaycees, churches, school children and the American public in general. This has resulted in a slight increase in letters from a few prisoners, but to date all we get from our own government representatives are more promises that we should know something in two or three months. There are now more prisoners who have been held for a longer period of time than in any war in the history of the United States, some going into their seventh year in captivity. When will the rhetoric stop and the action begin?"

"I would suggest that setting an unequivocal withdrawal date would go a long way toward getting the information that you seek," the congressman replied.

"What about the men whose names aren't on any of the 'official' lists? What would prevent the Vietnamese from just eliminating them?" shouted another voice from the audience.

"Excuse me, Congressman," the senator interrupted, "I do not question your intentions, but the subtleties of the Vietnamese language very often make it impossible to interpret their meanings. When they say 'total' withdrawal, do they mean to include every piece of machinery that may have a bolt made in the U.S.? Could a farm tractor be considered in contention in determining the ratio? Do they include disarmament of the South Vietnamese as part of the deal? All of these things could affect the outcome of any prisoner release and must be clarified prior to any agreement on unequivocal withdrawal!"

Another hand went up in the audience, this time that of a distinguished looking older gentleman. "I direct this to both the senator and the congressman," he said. "The United States ratified the Geneva Convention in 1956, thereby making it law. Is it not the duty of each and every member of the current congress to uphold the law? We call upon you to take whatever measures are necessary to see to it that the Red Cross or some other impartial agency is allowed into the Vietnamese prison camps, and we demand an accurate accounting of all Americans held by any and all arms of the enemy, North Vietnam, the Viet Cong, Laos, and even China!"

The rhetorical question was met with cheers and a standing ovation, bringing the session to a close. Sarah searched the room for some sign of Merrie, but was unable to see her as the crowd began to move toward the doors. Hoping to intercept her as she came out, she took up a post beside the registration table outside.

"Sarah! There you are!" Hearing Merrie's voice, Sarah turned to greet her friend. They embraced and Sarah was happy to see that Merrie looked terrific. She told her as much, adding, "You *are* feeling better, aren't you?"

"Yes, dear, I just get discouraged now and then, but being surrounded by all these people who have the same problem and seeing the courage and activity is a real shot in the arm."

"I was hoping that Julie might have felt up to joining us here. Have you seen her this week?"

"I didn't have a chance to get over there, but I did speak with her on the phone," Merrie said. "She admitted that she still feels as though she has a sign over her head telling people what she did or that the words 'Bad Person' are stenciled on her forehead, even though she knows it isn't so. It will take a little more time, but she seems to be mending." Merrie turned away, a heavy sigh escaping before she could stop it.

"What is it, Merrie? Has something else happened?" Sarah could see that Merrie was troubled.

"Let's sit down and have a drink in the bar," Merrie suggested. "Jane Forbes asked us up to her room to get together with some of the others, but I could use a few minutes to clear my head a bit."

Thinking of her earlier wish that she had time for a drink, Sarah agreed gratefully and the two women found a secluded table against the wall of the dimly lit lounge.

"What is it, Merrie? Sarah repeated. "I can see that something is troubling you. Is it Julie or are you not feeling as well as you look after all?"

"It isn't Julie, though her problems are part of it," Merrie began. "This whole thing seems to have taken on a life of its own. Sometimes I think maybe we made a mistake and I wish I could erase it like chalk on a blackboard." She paused, staring into her drink. Sarah was still, waiting apprehensively.

"Remember when you found me in my bathrobe the day Julie went into the hospital? Well, Pete went duck hunting one day after that and found me still in bed when he came home. I've never done anything like that in my life, but that day I felt as though my body was made of stone and I just couldn't seem to move. It scared him half to death and I vowed I'd never let it happen again. But our lives haven't been the same since we started this campaign to get information about Paul and the others over there. At first it was a great relief to be doing something, anything that might be productive. But now it seems to be consuming us, with each day bringing some little tidbit, a carrot dangling before our noses, none of it really encouraging. It's like there's some evil plot that we don't recognize."

Sarah was startled by the words she was hearing. Though she had not thought of it as an evil plot, she knew that her own life and well being were threatened by her conviction that Merrie's son was somehow a part of her as surely as anyone could be. Could the dedication to this cause bring about the destruction of them all? It was frightening.

"Have you talked to Pete about how you feel?" she inquired tentatively.

"We talked as much as we could that day and Pete said more than would normally be possible for him, but it's hard for him to share his feelings. His way of dealing with pain is to hide it far away inside, away from his window to the world. His training, his career, his very life have been dedicated to the appearance of strength as a military officer, always in command of the situation. But this is one situation he can't control and he doesn't know how to cope with it.

"The role of dutiful wife came with the marriage vows for me. I accepted that when I became an officer's wife and it has been a happy life for the most part. Our roles were pretty clearly defined and we each knew what was expected of us. We weren't prepared for this. Some days bring hope, but as the months go by, we keep up a façade that we don't really feel inside. At first just doing *something* gave us a sense of being useful, but now I think if we had accepted the loss of our son, we could have gone through the pain and gotten on with our lives. We've gone too far now to quit, so we're stuck with daily reminders of the pain with no end in sight."

Sarah had no idea what to say. She wanted desperately to confide in Merrie, to tell her how strongly she felt that she had known Paul, indeed had even communicated with him over the past year. She also knew that telling Merrie would only add to her torment. If she believed it, she'd have to accept that Paul may be alive and that belief would make it impossible to give up the activities on his behalf that were tearing her apart. If she didn't believe it, the relationship that had come to mean so much to Sarah would be irreparably damaged and Merrie wouldn't be any better off anyway. She could think of no words that would help, so she kept still.

Merrie didn't seem to notice the silence as she stared into the murky shadows of the room, then continued, "Pete and I aren't the only ones who've been adversely affected by this crusade. If it hadn't been for the increase in letters, Julie might never have gotten one from Jack and that whole terrible thing wouldn't have happened. And we've dragged you into our circle of despair, too, Sarah. You've given us so much of your time, your energy and your caring. We depend on you so selfishly."

Tears filled Sarah's eyes as she reached across the table to grasp Merrie's hand. "Please don't say that. I've come to think of you and Pete as family. If there's any selfishness involved here, it's on my part. Paul means a great deal to me, too. I feel as though I know him as well as I know you. For me there's more than despair; there's the joy I've found in knowing you. I just can't bear seeing you so miserable."

"Well, there isn't any use in wallowing in it, I guess. We should go on up to Jane's room. I told her we'd be there. Are you all checked into your room?"

Sarah confessed that she'd had her luggage sent on up, but that she had yet to see the room or unpack. Admitting that she'd like to change from the business suit she was wearing, she suggested that they stop there together. Merrie smiled, saying she'd go on up to Jane's alone so that Sarah could take her time and join them when she was ready.

"Are you sure you'll be okay? I hate to leave you alone."

"I'll be fine, my dear. Thank you for letting me pour out my troubles to you. I hadn't realized it, but I needed to talk about it to someone and thought I had no one to turn to. Everyone here has a loved one of their own in the same predicament, so having someone around who can be less subjective is a godsend."

Sarah opened her suitcase and pulled out the clothes she'd brought, absentmindedly hanging them in the closet. How ironic that she should be considered less subjective, she thought. If Merrie only knew what a shambles her life was because of Paul. Taking the pins from her hair, she shook her head and reached for a hairbrush. The bristles felt good against her scalp and she let her shoulders relax as she brushed slowly. Glad to be rid of the confinements of the suit, she changed into dark green pants with a soft sweater.

The group that had assembled in Jane Forbes' room included two wives, another mother and one sister. When everyone had been introduced and Sarah had accepted a glass of wine, Jane assured her that she hadn't missed anything and said they were about to hear about Barbara's recent trip to Paris.

"Did you feel that it was successful, Barbara?"

Barbara laughed shortly. "That depends on what you consider successful," she said. "It was mostly frustrating, but we did get to meet with the press secretary for the National Liberation Front for over an hour on the last day we were there. The senator was right when he said that the subtleties of the Vietnamese language make it impossible to interpret their meanings. They're masters at evasion. He had a little black book full of things said by family members. He quoted some concerning U.S. aggression and how the U.S. was prolonging the war. It makes great propaganda for them so we should all be very careful what we say in public about our government!"

"Did he or anyone else ever say they'd actually release prisoners if the U.S. agreed to a withdrawal date?" Merrie asked.

"That's the key," Barbara replied. "They never really say they will release anyone, just that they will *discuss* the release of all prisoners. I think we're all so eager to hear good news that we fail to hear what they're really saying."

The woman who had begun the questioning earlier at the general session asked, "Did you all hear the results of the poll that was taken in California regarding the question of setting a withdrawal date?' She looked around the room as each of the others shook their heads negatively.

"We sent out 250 questionnaires and got 93 of them back. The vote was one third in favor of setting a date and two thirds against it. I know that upsets some of the families who know that their man is a prisoner, but I think it shows that most of us don't trust the Vietnamese to actually release the men."

Someone else told of a letter she had received from one of the peace organizations that said, 'every day of delay in acceptance of the Vietnamese terms is another day of needless separation, of continued killing and destruction of homes and land.'

"How cruel," Sarah murmured.

"There's such an emotional connotation to the word 'peace' that I wonder if the American public cares more about the prisoners or the war," Merrie commented. "We can't win no matter what we say. If we use the word 'peace' we're siding with the peaceniks and if we resist 'peace at any cost' we're warmongers. It's really disturbing, isn't it?"

"We've become an embarrassment to the government," said Jane. "I've been getting little hints again that maybe I should keep my mouth shut. Stay low key is how they put it. I wonder if it will ever be over?"

There was a silence in the room as each woman wondered the same thing.

The years from 1968 through 1971 had a profound effect on so many American lives. Prior to 1968, the undeclared war in Vietnam had been escalating in American participation to the point where United States military strength was at 486,000 troops. As awareness of offensive air strikes into North Vietnam grew and the general public became aware of the number of servicemen killed, taken prisoner or missing in action, bitterness and division of opinion prevailed.

Not only were many American servicemen losing their lives halfway around the world, those who came home were treated as little short of criminals. Young men were moving to Canada to escape the draft, demonstrations in the streets set college students against law enforcement agents, and political conservatives and liberals became hawks or doves. Richard Nixon was elected president of the United States in November, 1968, promising a gradual troop withdrawal from Vietnam as troop strength reached more than 536,000. Formal troop negotiations began in Paris in January, 1969, moving agonizingly slowly as the war continued. By the end of 1971, troop strength had been reduced, but American planes carried out the most extensive air operations against the communists since 1968 in reaction to a North Vietnamese build-up. Vietnam had become an embarrassment to the U.S. government, but no one seemed able to stop it.

CHAPTER TWENTY THREE

Following the conference in Los Angeles, Sarah was forced into an even more tormented re-evaluation of her life. She had a promising career, a comfortable home and a bright future, but she had to admit that her work was suffering even if no one else had noticed. Her mind was continually diverted toward issues that seemed infinitely more consequential than the image of a hotel chain and her emotions threatened to overwhelm her. She wrestled with herself daily in the effort to maintain a balance she knew was vital, clinging to reality, but unable to ignore the certainty in her heart.

Like Merrie, part of her longed to forget all about Vietnam and part of her was forced to confront the agony it had caused. She buried her obsession as far down inside as she could and began to try to focus on her relationship with John. She knew that he loved her and believed in her, and on the rare occasions when she was able to think only of him, she believed in her love for him as well.

During her visit to the Davidson Hotel in San Diego, she had been unable to concentrate on the ideas presented by the staff there. That property was as different in attitude as it could possibly be from the New York Davidson. Where New York considered itself a civilized refuge for a literary clientele, San Diego catered to health conscious people who demanded exercise machines, jogging trails and tennis courts.

Returning to her office in San Francisco, she found herself hard pressed to care about either one of them.

She wished she could turn to religion for solace, but could find no foundation upon which to draw. It seemed that organized religion only provided different pathways for different people according to their specific needs and cultures, giving them an outline to follow when in doubt about proscribed behavior. Christian churches had no problem accepting the idea of life after death, but were unable to comprehend a life before birth. She was bereft of guidance.

Wrestling with herself on a continuing basis, she often nursed one drink after another until she fell into bed when her eyes refused to stay open. She slept soundly for a few hours, then fretfully for the rest of the night, rising each morning to drag herself to the office. She realized that she was becoming introverted and introspective, avoiding contact with co-workers by claiming mounds of paperwork that required her to spend the day alone in her office, the door shut, the demons of the night a secret. Finding herself staring out the window or into space, she would square her shoulders and vow to get herself under control. It was a dangerous game to play with her career and her life, but she was powerless to stop herself.

She stopped the attempts at transporting herself to lifetimes of a past spent with Paul in an effort to reconcile the reality of the present. But when her determination failed to bring about the desired results, she decided to try one more time to reach him on the intermediate plane where they had spoken before. If this final attempt did not succeed, she would acknowledge that for whatever reason, he was no longer an actuality in her life.

She set the scene as she had before, with the orchestral arrangement of 'My Foolish Heart' on the cassette player and candles on her dresser. Lying quietly on the bed, she began to breathe deeply, relaxing more with each breath, her eyes closed. She concentrated on Paul's image, willing him to appear, if only for a moment.

Several minutes passed and Sarah's heart grew heavy. She began to get drowsy and was having trouble concentrating. Her mind drifted into the void that marked the approach of sleep just as the cotton candy cloud surrounded her. She tumbled serenely and effortlessly, the smile that appeared on her lips becoming a joyous bubble of laughter. She was still bouncing merrily when a white light appeared in the distance. A dark and tattered figure came toward her. She shielded her eyes from the brightness in an effort to see who it was.

The figure stumbled, then fell, reaching out to her in what seemed to be a desperate attempt to leave the light and join her in the pink mist.

"Paul!" she cried. "I thought I'd lost you!" She ran to him, her arms outstretched. His face was shrouded in pain as he answered her and she realized that he was terribly ill. Her legs turned to jelly as some unseen force seemed to be pulling him back into the light. He rose and began to turn away, moving into the light. Suddenly she knew that if he gave up and walked willingly into the light, he would be lost to her forever.

Summoning all her energy, she screamed, "No! Don't go!"

She woke bathed in sweat, still screaming and sat bolt upright. Her whole body shook with the sobs she couldn't control as she cried over and over, "No, no, no! Come back, Paul, come back!"

Throwing off the covers, she leapt from the bed and began pacing. "Something is terribly wrong," she said aloud. "He was so very ill, so tattered and dirty. What could have happened?"

Still shaking, she went down the hall to the kitchen where she poured a hefty amount of scotch into a tumbler and gulped several swallows before adding ice cubes to what was left. "Why couldn't I have left well enough alone?" she berated herself. "I had to make one last fucking try! Did I think some rosy picture of love in bloom or that cottage with the white picket fence was going to show up?"

Calmer, she sat down in the dining room, still clutching the glass. Taking a deep breath, she forced herself to remember the dream. Was it a dream? Had she wanted to see him so badly or had she somehow wanted to eliminate him from her personal reality? What made her change her mind, calling out so desperately to him to come back? Why was he in such frightening condition?

She closed her eyes, willing the image to reappear and as it did she realized that she had seen no bars, no prison, only the blinding light and his battered figure. She recalled having read or heard that people who were near death or had died and come back told of going into that kind of light. Was Paul near death? The thought that she may have saved him by calling him back struck her with the force of a blow to her stomach. "Oh my God," she wept, "either that's what happened or I've gone over the edge if I let myself believe it!" If it wasn't just a dream, how could she dismiss it as one? But if it was just a dream, believing it to be something more could lead to her destruction.

What about her lovely cotton candy cloud? Did her joy as she frolicked represent the joy of life, while the white light beyond it led to death's portals? She huddled in the chair, sipping at the whiskey in the glass until there was none left. Though physically exhausted, she was afraid to go back to bed. Well, that's silly, she thought. This is the first time it's worked and I've actually been able to find him. Surely there won't be a repeat performance tonight.

Leaving the glass on the kitchen counter, she returned to the bedroom. She turned on the lamp on her bed table and blew out the candles that still burned on the dresser. The tape had run out and stopped some time ago, so there were no reminders of her recent journey to another plane. The bed felt so good. Lulled by the warmth of the whiskey, she fell into a dreamless sleep.

Paul lay beside the river under a tropical shrub, delirious with fever. In occasional periods of lucidity, he found he was too weak to get up. He had no idea how long he'd been in the jungle since his escape. His strength ebbed as fever and malnutrition sucked the life from his body.

Opening his eyes, he squinted into the bright sunlight. He was terribly thirsty, his mouth dry and parched. Lifting his head a little, he saw that his feet were very nearly in the water. If he could just move enough to get to the water, he could get a drink. Attempting to rise up on one elbow, he fell back before he could get his arm into position. This must be the end, he thought, and closed his eyes in resignation.

Visions of the girl in the kimono and the woman in the black dress mingled with those of his beloved Sarah. He saw her laughing joyfully as she bounded among the rosy clouds that had the texture of cotton candy. He reached out to her. She ran toward him, her arms outstretched to envelop him, but something was pulling him away. He turned his head to see what it was that was keeping him from her and heard her scream his name. It was such a desperate scream that it frightened him and his eyes flew open.

The branches on the tree above him took on the appearance of human forms and he struggled to see who they might be. He tried to call out, but his throat was too dry and the words wouldn't form. Dark clouds had gathered and the humidity in the air turned to rain that fell softly at first, then became a torrent. His parched lips welcomed the water that soothed his swollen tongue. The sudden storm ended as quickly as it had begun and the sun created a rainbow of colors that flickered through the branches.

A shadow fell over him. He reached out to push it away, his hand brushing the fabric of the robe worn by the monk who stood beside him. He passed out again and was unaware of the silent figures that made a stretcher from bamboo poles and a shawl. He did not feel the bumps and jolts as they carried him many miles along the river and was unaware of the cart in which he rode many more miles to the monastery in Southeastern China, several miles beyond the Vietnamese border.

In the weeks that followed, he did not hear the sound of his voice as he called out to the faces that swam in his mind, separate, then merging into one image, that of Sarah Fremont. When he finally emerged from his semi-comatose state, he had no idea who he was, where he was, or why he was there. Still weak from the effects of the fever, he was unable to rise from the cot on which he lay.

The monks who brought small bowls of soup to him several times a day nodded reassuringly, but silently. As his strength began to return, his diet was expanded to include a little rice and then steamed vegetables. Eventually he was able to walk short distances and was led outside to a bench made from a felled tree trunk. Communication with his benefactors was limited to smiles, nods and gestures very basic in nature. Occasionally, he thought of venturing away from what had become his home, but since he didn't know where he'd be going and wouldn't be able to get far in his physical condition, he dismissed the idea and let the muted sounds of temple bells and wind instruments soothe his tattered soul.

CHAPTER TWENTY FOUR

arah huddled miserably at her desk, waiting for the double strength aspirin to take effect. Michael Davidson, founder and Chairman of the Davidson Hotel Group, and the top executives from each of the four Davidson properties were gathered in the conference room next door to discuss future promotional ideas. Since most of the existing files had been transferred to her office, Sarah was hosting the meeting. Her throbbing head convinced her that she could no longer pretend that her solitary drinking did not affect her work and she groaned aloud, pleading with God to be merciful. The pain began to subside and she stood, straightened her shoulders, took a deep breath and moved resolutely toward the door.

Michael leaned casually against the wall at the rear of the conference room, watching the others as they mingled casually. Each was distinctive and each knew the property they administered better than they knew their own homes. An outsider might think they had little in common, but Michael was well aware of the combined expertise they brought to his hotels.

Bob Mattheson, representing New York, stood at the window absorbing the limited view of downtown San Francisco. Van Carducci, Sarah's former boss, was chatting with the tall, blonde and leggy Allison Jennings, Michael's administrative assistant from the corporate office in Chicago. Tanned to a shade of gleaming walnut by the San Diego sunshine, Parker Torrance was stirring cream into the coffee he had just poured for himself and looking thoughtful as he listened to Buzz Craddock, General Manager at the Davidson Chicagoan.

Burly Buzz, as Michael thought of him privately, was a bear of a man, broad shouldered, barrel chested, and wearing a tan suit that appeared to be in danger of splitting a seam. His chin jutted out and his eyebrows met above piercing dark eyes as he looked up at the elegantly dressed Parker Torrance.

Sarah Fremont entered the room followed by her secretary, Ellen Ferguson, who carried a stack of files and a steno pad. Michael cleared his throat and moved toward the chair at the far end of the table, a signal for the rest of them to take seats. Allison claimed the one on his right and Buzz Craddock headed toward the one on his left, both clearly stating their affinity with the Chairman of the Board. Bob Mattheson and Parker Torrance took non-combative positions across from each other as Van held the chair opposite Michael for Sarah. Ellen took the remaining seat to Sarah's left, across from Van.

Until now, each of the four hotels had been run pretty much independently, reporting to Michael as occupancy rose or fell, or decisions were required. Since each was vastly different from the others, it had never seemed necessary to coordinate their images. But communication would soon become instant and computer technology would be adding sophistication to even the most naïve traveler's itinerary. It was becoming apparent that there was a need for some sort of adhesive that would encourage loyalty to Davidson properties.

"Let's begin with a brief rundown on each property," Michael said. "Bob, why don't you start us off?"

"I think the New York Davidson is the oldest of the four hotels – that is, it's been a hotel longer than any of the others, though not originally a Davidson. Many of our clientele have been coming there for more years than some of us have been alive and some even live year-round in their suites. There are 'reserved' signs on many of the tables in the lobby area at cocktail time, and the regulars consider this their privilege.

"For the most part, they're well educated and witty and the tourists who do stay with us come there on purpose because of the reputation of the hotel, that of being a civilized haven in a world gone slightly mad. Even the personnel remains fairly stable.'"

"What would you say the average age and income are?" asked Michael.

"Except for the younger ones who hope to meet some literary personality or agent, I'd say over forty and upper middle class. They respond well to me because I'm non-threatening, I think," Bob finished with a chuckle, making fun of his short stature.

Turning toward Parker Torrance, Michael gestured without speaking for him to describe the Southern California hotel that was his domain.

"The Davidson San Diego is as far to the opposite pole as one could get from what Bob has just told you. Though we have about the same number of rooms, two hundred and seventy five, rather than being stacked on top of each other in a high-rise, we're spread out over twenty-five acres. Our clientele is mostly of the rising young executive variety, under forty years old. Though we have excellent meeting facilities, they're used mostly by local groups for banquets or weddings rather than conventions. The room guests are families there on vacation who enjoy the variety of sports available – the pool, the beach, the tennis courts, the putting greens and the hiking trail."

Though each member of the group was already aware of the general differences between the hotels, they raised eyebrows and smiled as each wondered where they might find a common denominator that would be useful.

"How about San Francisco, Van?"

Sarah's former boss laughed. "Our airport location lends itself to business travelers and conventions. The only thing we seem to have in common with the others is the number of rooms – there are two hundred and ninety. Actually, I think we have more meeting and banquet rooms than the other properties and since we're only twenty minutes from downtown San Francisco and have courtesy airport service, we solicit most of our business from major industry executives who want the convenience of the airport combined with the glamour of San Francisco."

Buzz Craddock shifted in his chair and began, "I guess that brings us to the Davidson Chicagoan. If there are any comparisons to be made, it would be between us and New York. We have somewhat fewer rooms, only two hundred and fifty, but they're larger and newer than those in New York. Our location on the Near North side of Chicago makes us the place where the 'elite meet to eat' and our clientele are upper income people who look for prestige and luxury, many of them repeat visitors. Our banquet and meeting rooms are used mostly by Chicagoans for executive entertaining or society weddings."

There was a brief silence in the room, with only Michael Davidson looking around the table. The others looked down at the yellow pads in front of them, unwilling to be the first called upon for ideas.

"Okay, everyone. I know nobody wants to stick his neck out, but let's start with a list of common denominators," Michael said. "We know that all four properties are about the same size. What can we do with that?"

Sarah spoke up. "Not too big and not too small. We're large enough to provide all the amenities, but not so large that a visitor is lost or neglected."

"Good, good," said Michael.

"Each hotel provides above average accommodations and an atmosphere that represents a sort of 'hometown' elegance, something unique that may not otherwise be available," Parker Torrance remarked. "For instance, vacation in San Diego and enjoy the theatre in New York. Be pampered after a day of shopping on Michigan Avenue in Chicago, and inspire your company executives by meeting in San Francisco."

"No matter what your requirements are, we have something special to offer," Van said, nodding pensively. "A symbiotic sort of relationship – dissimilar, but mutually beneficial."

"Find what you're looking for at a Davidson Hotel," Sarah agreed. "Can we put together a brochure that conveys the idea, and if so, do we emphasize each individual property or do we project the overall idea?"

Allison Jennings looked directly at Michael and expressed her concern regarding the marketing of the idea. "Should there be only one brochure or should each hotel have its own? Maybe people who are only interested in New York don't want to carry around a bunch of stuff on San Diego. And how do we distribute the brochures so that they're cost effective?"

"It would seem that we should put together a profile from each property and incorporate the information into an overall profile. For instance, if we make up a list of corporate accounts and then look at the size of the companies, maybe the type of products they represent, the geographical areas they cover, etcetera, we can research similar organizations and put together a viable mailing list that will target the audience we want with the least amount of expense," Sarah said, speaking aloud as she thought.

"How does that get business for San Diego?" Parker wanted to know.

"Well, I'm just formulating this as I go along," Sarah responded, "but maybe we can plant a suggestion in the minds of corporate travelers that they'll get the same service at the Davidson San Diego when they take the family on a vacation..."

The meeting that each of them had approached from individual perspectives had begun to take on an air of accomplishment as one idea led to another. Michael Davidson's mouth turned up slightly in pleasure as the leadership qualities of the personnel he had chosen to represent his company were confirmed. He sat back in his chair and watched as the others grew more and more animated in their discussion. Time passed quickly and it wasn't until the office receptionist knocked timidly and entered the room that they checked their watches and realized that it was past lunchtime.

The receptionist leaned over and spoke quietly into Sarah's ear. "You had a call over an hour ago from Colonel Winslow," she reported. "He sounded upset and said to ask you to call him at the hospital as soon as possible."

"The hospital!" Sarah exclaimed. "Why didn't you tell me before this?"

"He said not to interrupt your meeting, but that whenever you took a break you should call the emergency room. When it got to be past lunchtime, I decided you should know about the call."

Sarah hurried from the conference room to her office and dialed the number that the receptionist had noted for her. The nurse who answered in the emergency room was expecting her call and Pete was on the line almost immediately. His agitation was evident as he explained that Merrie had collapsed and been unable to get up.

"Did you know that there was something really wrong with her, Sarah? I knew she was tired, but she seemed to be all right most of the time."

"I knew she was depressed, Pete, but I thought she was coping with it. She promised me when we were in Los Angeles that she'd take better care of herself and eat well. She covered it so well that I didn't realize how serious it was. Do the doctors have any idea what the problem might be?"

"Nobody seems to know anything! Can you come over here? Maybe she'll talk to you, tell you more than she's telling the doctors."

Sarah promised that she'd get there as quickly as possible, then sat back in her chair wondering how she was going to tell Michael Davidson that she had to leave. The key people in his organization had flown across the country to meet in her office and he wasn't going to be pleased if she left him high and dry. Well, it couldn't be helped, she thought. I'll just have to hope he understands.

She hurried to the hospital, the same one in which she had spent those first critical hours with Julie the previous year. As Pete had said, the emergency room doctor was at a loss to determine what was wrong with Merrie. Her vital signs were weak, but there was no indication of any specific cause for her collapse.

"This may sound unprofessional, but she seems to be simply wasting away," he said, apparently mystified.

"That's impossible," Pete cried. "Get someone in here who can find out what it is and *do* something for her!"

"I know this is difficult for you, Mr. Winslow, but is there some reason why your wife may have lost the will to live?" the doctor's tone was gentle.

Pete's shoulders sagged as he lowered his head miserably. "Our son, Paul, has been missing in action in Vietnam for nearly three years," he said softly.

"I don't understand," the doctor said, puzzled.

"That's just it, no one does. She's worked so hard to get some sort of support from the American people and still no one seems to realize what's happened over there. All they know is what they read in the papers about student demonstrations on college campuses and general opposition to the war. She hears our son called a 'war monger' and a 'baby killer,' and it breaks her heart."

"I'm sorry, Mr. Winslow. I knew there were American pilots who had been shot down over there, but I guess I didn't relate it to anyone who might live next door to me, so to speak."

"I came home from a hunting trip one day a couple of months ago and found her in bed. She *never* stayed in bed all day and I worried at first, but she kept saying she was fine, so I ignored it. It's my fault. I should have insisted she see a doctor," Pete finished wretchedly.

"Pete..." Sarah put her hand on his shoulder consolingly, "you didn't know. She didn't want you to know because she knew you were as devastated as she was about Paul and she didn't want to add to your burden."

Pete's head jerked up. "You'll help her, won't you? She *will* be all right again?"

"I think perhaps the first thing we should do is get some nutritional supplements into her," the doctor mused. "Sometimes the human body lets us know when it can't take anymore, and we are forced to listen to it. Once she's aware she doesn't have to put up a front for anyone and gets some additional nourishment, both physical and mental, she may rally."

"You have to make her well again, doctor. I don't think I can live without her," Pete said brokenly.

"I think she may know that, Mr. Winslow," the doctor said softly.

Merrie was moved into a private room, but was too drugged to speak to anyone. She squeezed Pete's hand comfortingly and smiled a tiny smile before lapsing into a deep sleep. Sarah left Pete sitting beside her to make a call to Julie, telling her that she didn't think they should leave Pete alone. Julie agreed immediately, adding that Merrie wouldn't want him to be alone either. They decided that Julie would go to the Winslow's home and be there when Sarah and Pete arrived.

Later Pete sat disconsolately in his favorite chair, allowing Sarah and Julie to take charge. At first he refused the vodka martini Sarah offered him, accepting it only after she reassured him that Merrie would want him to carry on as normally as possible.

"How could I have been so blind?" Pete wondered.

"Maybe I should have told you that I was concerned, Pete, but Merrie was so adamant about not worrying you and she kept saying she was fine," Sarah told him, hoping to assuage his guilt. "What about Sheila? Do you want to call her?"

"Sheila?" Pete looked up in surprise.

"Yes, Pete, do you want to let her know that Merrie is in the hospital?"

"No, not just yet anyway," Pete replied wearily. "She's never been around through any other family crisis and she probably isn't home anyway. No one ever knows where she is or what she's doing."

Sarah and Julie exchanged glances in silent agreement. They would cross that bridge when they came to it, but for now they'd prefer not to have to contend with Sheila's irritating presence either.

Merrie seemed to rally slightly the following day, reiterating her assurances that she'd be fine, that she just needed a little rest. Then she began having trouble breathing. That evening the doctor told Pete that she had developed pneumonia. She was moved into an intensive care unit and hooked up to an ominous assortment of tubes and machinery. It was nearly midnight when Pete phoned Sarah at home to tell her that Merrie was gone.

The man who had been a pillar of strength, in command of every emergency, was a broken human being. Once again, Sarah raced up El Camino toward Julie's home to pick her up and get to the hospital to be with Pete. From somewhere in the back of her mind, the thought arose that the terrible war in Vietnam had caused so much suffering. Those who actively protested it in the streets and on the campus' of America did not begin to know the consequences that had come about, creeping unbidden into the homes and hearts of average Americans who were baffled by the changes in their lives. Will it ever end, she asked herself.

CHAPTER TWENTY FIVE

S heila stirred slightly, then pulled the covers up over her head as the shrill ringing of the telephone penetrated the fuzz that clouded her brain. Maybe it'll stop, she hoped. When it didn't, she raised her head slowly, checked the bedside clock and saw that it was five o'clock in the morning. Whoever this is will live to regret this day, she promised silently.

"Hello?" she muttered into the receiver.

"Sheila? I know it's the crack of dawn there, but this is important," said a female voice.

"Who is this?"

"Julia Schaefer in San Francisco, Sheila. We met a year ago last November when you were out here. Sheila, are you awake enough to hear me?"

"Yes, yes. What is it? Are you in Chicago?"

"No, Sheila, I'm in San Francisco. You need to talk to your dad. I'm afraid he has some very bad news for you." Julie tried to be gentle, breaking the news slowly. She didn't want to be the one to tell Sheila, but Pete had seemed unable to make the call. She held the receiver out to him now, her eyes filled with sorrow as she willed him the strength to speak to his daughter.

Sarah sat in the wing chair beside the window. Somehow the three of them had made it back to the Winslow's home, Pete riding with Sarah and Julie driving his car. Every ounce of energy seemed to have evaporated from Sarah's body once they crossed the threshold and she had dropped into the chair, unable to speak or move. It was Julie who took charge, making a pot of coffee and pouring each of them a cup.

She had found Merrie's address book beside the phone and looked under 'S' for Sheila's name, reasoning that people tended to list those closest to them under their first names. Finding it as expected, she had dialed the number and when Pete finally took the receiver from her outstretched hand, she joined Sarah in the living room.

They both looked up when he finished his conversation with his daughter though neither of them spoke, waiting for him to share whatever he wished when he was ready. He stood for a moment, his eyes scanning the room as though unfamiliar with it.

"Did Sheila say when she might arrive?" Sarah asked, breaking the silence.

"She said she'd call back in awhile," Pete replied. "She's like a stranger to me," he went on, "my own daughter and she's someone I don't know. She sounded angry," he concluded.

"That might not be an altogether unusual reaction, Pete," Julie said. "Sometimes when people don't know what to say or are suddenly shocked, they respond by being angry."

"Maybe I neglected her too much. God knows, I was gone enough and when I was home I spent most of my time with Paul. I didn't know what to say to Sheila even when she was a little girl. She was always so rebellious! If I said black, she said white. If I said she couldn't do something, she did it anyway. Now here we are, two strangers, the only ones left of the family." Pete's chin dropped to his chest and tears drizzled down his cheeks as he sobbed silently.

"Why? Why Merrie? Why Paul? Why not me?" he cried, his shoulders heaving.

Sarah stared at the ceiling, her eyes burning as she fought the urge to break down. Julie turned to stare out the window into the darkness outside. There was nothing to say that would ease his pain. All they could do was be there with him.

Gathering himself together a few minutes later, Pete decided that they should all have a little brandy in their coffee and went to the kitchen to get some. He returned carrying not only the brandy, but a small package that was gift-wrapped. He handed it to Sarah.

"Merrie wanted you to have this," he said. "I'd forgotten about it until I saw it there on the table."

Sarah took the flat box from him and pulled off the card that was attached. 'Not really a gift, just something I thought you might like to have. Love, Merrie' it read. Sarah pulled the ribbon from the package and slid the top from the box, amazed to find the photograph of John and Paul beside the beloved Chevy in a silver frame.

"Oh, Pete, I couldn't take this from you! It's too precious!" she exclaimed.

"Merrie had it copied for you. She said since you were seeing John and you had been so dear to us, she wanted you to have it."

"I'll treasure it, Pete. I can't tell you how much it means to me that she wanted me to have it," Sarah said softly, her eyes burning with tears she tried to blink away. Glancing toward Julie, she saw that tears were flowing down her face as well. Unable to hold them back, Sarah let her own misery take over and the three of them cried together.

Once again, the dawn was breaking as Sarah drove Julie home. They had left Pete reluctantly only after he insisted he would try to get some sleep, and that since the night was over, it wouldn't be quite so lonely.

"Julie," Sarah began slowly, "I feel very strongly that Paul is alive. I was trying to contact him by setting the scene as it had been when I had the first dreams about him. I don't really know for sure whether it was another dream, or if I managed to move to that other plane again, but I saw him. He was coming toward me, reaching for me, and as I ran to him, he stumbled and turned away. There was a brilliant white light behind him and I knew that if he walked back into it, he'd be dead. I screamed at him, and then I woke up."

Julie shook her head. Shrugging her shoulders in a gesture of helplessness, she didn't reply.

"Maybe I should have told Merrie about all my crazy feelings. Maybe it might have helped her to carry on, knowing that someone else believed Paul was still alive."

It was a moment before Julie responded, saying, "Sarah, don't torture yourself so. You know in your heart that Merrie probably would have thought you *were* crazy, so it wouldn't have done any good. You've been there for all of us when we needed it. Now let's just be there for each other."

CHAPTER TWENTY SIX

Sheila stared moodily out the window of the plane that was carrying her to California. Why couldn't her life ever go the way she wanted it to go? Just when she thought she had everything under control, there was some new crisis. Her mother's death had come as a terrible blow to her. The one person who had been on her side at least some of the time was gone and she had only her rigid, uptight military father left. She'd been unable to face the thought of being alone with her father, or worse, having that good-two-shoes, Sarah Fremont, looking at her accusingly and had begged Dave to accompany her to San Francisco. He sat beside her, brooding.

He had flatly refused at first, but she wore him down with tears and cajoling until at last he agreed on the condition that they stay in a hotel and he was not obligated to spend any more time with her father than absolutely necessary.

Sheila's relationship with Dave was a peculiar one. She suspected that he was as fascinated by the luxury in which she lived as she was by the people with whom he associated. He would never admit to such heresy, of course, but they were spending more and more time at her apartment lately. His comments were nearly always caustic as he criticized the decadence of her lifestyle, asking things like, "Do you realize how many Chinese families could live in the space that you occupy alone?"

She noticed that he had no trouble swallowing the equally decadent meals that she served him with wine and candlelight. So far she had resisted the urge to suggest that he move to China and share his quarters with a hundred Chinese if that was what he thought would make him happy, mostly because she was afraid if she did say such a thing, he might leave her forever, and that terrified her.

She was sure that given enough time, Dave would see that her continued presence in his life was what they both needed. She visualized an academic atmosphere with a home in which he sat by the fireside, an Irish setter beside him, the room lined with bookshelves on which books she would never read stood gathering dust. He would be smoking a pipe, wearing a tweed jacket and have the rapt attention of students who were dazzled by the scholarly pearls of wisdom he dropped into their worshipful minds.

Sheila was still struggling to understand the political ideology that he espoused, but noble as it sounded when she listened to speeches, she had a vague notion that there was something wrong with it. She tended to hope that time would either help her to become one of the group with a vital cause of her own, or convert Dave to her way of life. Besides, he was the most incredible lover she'd ever had. When the lights went out, she became his slave. She began to think about the touch of his hands as she sat beside him on the plane. The mere thought caused the muscles of her vagina to twitch. She glanced sideways at his hands, the long fingers twined around the book he held, and wondered if there was some way he could get those fingers under her skirt without anyone noticing.

As the stewardess passed, Sheila motioned to her and asked sweetly, "I wonder if you could get me a blanket?"

Dave put aside his book to help her arrange the blanket, surprised when she spread it across his legs as well as her own. Silencing him by putting her index finger to her lips conspiratorially, she turned so that one shoulder snuggled under his, her arm linked in his, and grasped his other hand with her free hand. Pulling him toward her and guiding his hand to her thigh, she giggled as his eyes widened in amazement.

She pushed firmly on his fingers, forcing them to begin to knead the flesh between her legs, then lowered her head to conceal the fact that her mouth was open and her breath coming in short gasps. She began to tremble slightly as his hand reached the silky fabric of her panties. Her buttocks moved in response as he pushed aside the crotch of the panties, touching the dampness beneath, one finger searching out the opening there. Suddenly her back arched involuntarily, she shuddered and slumped, her breath expelled in a whoosh. She slept peacefully the rest of the way to San Francisco.

Julie drove toward the Winslow's San Mateo home in silence, Sheila beside her in front, the tall, dark man who had accompanied her looking uncomfortable in the back seat. Julie had volunteered to meet Sheila's plane when it appeared that Pete was too distraught to be trusted on the freeway. She had been astonished to see Sheila clinging to Dave Marshall as they exited the plane. Sheila had introduced him somewhat perfunctorily and demanded to know why her father wasn't there to meet her. Julie had tried to explain that Pete was understandably upset by Merrie's death and that she hoped Sheila wouldn't mind too much that Julie was there instead.

"Does he think I'm not upset?" Sheila asked petulantly.

"I'm sure that's not the case, Sheila. We just wanted to make it easier on him and perhaps on you by saving you from a public reunion at such an unhappy time," Julie said gently.

Turning onto their street, Julie wondered how Pete was going to react to this silent and inscrutable man that Sheila had brought with her. So far, Julie knew nothing more than his name. Well, there was nothing she could do about it anyway.

Though taken aback by the sight of a stranger, Pete's reaction was admirable. He hugged Sheila tightly, then stretched out his hand to Dave, saying, "I'm sorry we have to meet under such difficult circumstances."

Sarah hovered in the kitchen, reluctant to interrupt their reunion, but finally had to greet Pete's daughter. Sheila's annoyance was evident in her eyes and her manner. Showing his first sign of animation, Dave stepped forward to greet her just in time to stop Sheila from asking,

"What's *she* doing here?" He could see the hostility in Sheila's body language, and resigned himself to remaining at the Winslow home instead of the safe haven of a hotel room.

Sarah was immediately aware of Sheila's hostility and was at a loss to explain it. After the first few minutes she gave up trying, deciding it just wasn't worth the effort. Her own grief over Merrie's death was too intense for her to play roles and Pete didn't seem to notice much of anything. Sarah knew that he had his own problems when it came to dealing with Sheila. She wasn't sure, but she thought that Pete was glad to have her and Julie there to ease the situation.

The next few days were difficult. Sheila took over in the kitchen, asking cheerily of anyone who entered the room what it was that she could get for them. Sarah and Julie resigned themselves to keeping Pete company when they were there and tried to be as tactful as possible. The tension grew in spite of their efforts.

The memorial service was small, held at the chapel on the Presidio at the south end of the Golden Gate Bridge. Their little group returned to the Winslow's afterward. A few neighbors dropped in but didn't stay long and then they were alone again.

Sheila's annoyance at Sarah's presence had turned to outright hatred and after a few minutes of small talk, she burst out, "Well, Sarah, do you plan to move in with Dad before Mother's body is even in the grave? Or do you plan to take over as the dutiful daughter that I've never been?"

No one said anything as each of them turned to stare, their mouths open in shock. Pete was the first to respond.

"Sheila! How could you say such a thing?"

"Well, she certainly seems right at home, doesn't she, Dad?"

"Sarah has been a dear friend to both your mother and me, Sheila, and yes, we have come to think of her as another daughter. You'll note that I said *another* daughter. Additionally, what you are forgetting is that she has been seeing Paul's best friend, John St. James. You may recall that he was here for the kick-off dinner when we first began the public awareness campaign. You have been surly ever since you arrived, Sheila, and I want it to stop. This is not the time for one of your tantrums."

He turned apologetically toward Sarah. She shook her head at him, waggling her fingers in an effort to indicate that it was all right, but she couldn't stop the tears that slid down her cheeks. Sheila sat silently, obviously seething.

Pete turned back to his daughter, his face purple with rage. "Apologize!" he shouted.

Sheila winced and again he shouted, *"Apologize!* Or get out of this house! Your mother would be furious with you if she were here!"

Sheila began to cry as she said, "Mother was the only one who was ever on my side! She was the only one who loved me. You never had time to bother with me," she gulped. Rising, she teetered unsteadily for a moment, then turned and ran up the stairs. Everyone winced as the bedroom door slammed.

"I think it's martini time," Pete said through clenched teeth. He rose and went into the kitchen.

Dave didn't move, wondering to himself how he had let Sheila talk him into the whole journey. He should be in Chicago, not in San Francisco, suffering through the squabbles of the All-American family. He looked up when he heard Julie ask, "What is it that you do in Chicago, Dave? I'm afraid we haven't paid very much attention to you."

"I teach creative writing at the University of Chicago," he replied, glad that at least someone had eased the tension in the room. Just then Pete came back carrying a tray of martinis.

"A teacher?" he asked.

"Yes, at the University of Chicago," Dave repeated. "I'm an assistant professor."

"How did you happen to meet my daughter?"

"I saved her from getting trampled by a crowd of anti-war demonstrators."

Pete's antenna went up. "Anti-war demonstrators? What was Sheila doing at an anti-war demonstration?"

"She wasn't part of it, Colonel, she was trying to get a taxi and didn't realize that the crowd was so thick."

"Were you part of that crowd, young man?" Pete asked.

"Sort of…that is, I was, but I'm not part of the student group that organized it," Dave answered.

"Were they university students? Were they some of your students and were you there in support of the demonstration?"

"Some of them were in my class, sir and if you're asking whether or not I'm against the war, the answer is yes. I am one hundred percent against the war in Vietnam." Well, here it comes, he thought. I'm in for it now.

"You seem to know Sheila rather well, so apparently this demonstration wasn't a recent one. Is Sheila involved with an anti-war group, too?" Pete was trying to keep his voice level.

"I wouldn't say she's involved with an anti-war group, but she has come to a few meetings of the Hegelian Society that I belong to."

"What the hell is a Hegelian Society?"

Dave sighed. "It's named for George Hegel, a German philosopher who was responsible for developing the dialectic methods that support the dictatorship of the proletariat that's the foundation for Marxism today," he explained.

"You mean you're a goddanmed *Communist?*" Pete yelled.

"I'm really a Maoist," Dave began, "and I believe that membership in the community is the individual's highest duty. Where Russian communism is based on sharing through industrialization, Chairman Mao has instituted a plan whereby the intellectuals are being integrated with the workers as an economic and social strategy. The peasants enjoy a better life and the intellectuals understand what it means to work with their hands for the common good."

"And I suppose you've been filling my daughter's head with this garbage? Tell me, are you aware that her brother is missing in action in Vietnam?"

"Yes, she told me that the day I met her. To be truthful, she didn't like me very much at first. I don't think she really understands much about Vietnam at all, but I think she's learning. She had never heard *both* sides of the story."

Julie and Sarah looked at each other, aghast, as Pete got up from his chair and walked purposefully to the foot of the stairs where he yelled, "Sheila? Sheila, you come down here right now!"

No one spoke as they listened to the sound of the door opening upstairs and watched as Sheila descended to face her father.

"Sheila," Pete said, keeping his voice low and controlled, "were you aware that this man is a communist and that it is the communists of Vietnam who shot down your brother's plane?"

"He's a Maoist, Daddy," Sheila said tentatively.

"Are you so ignorant that you don't know that Mao is a communist, just Chinese instead of Russian?"

"I'm learning, Daddy," she replied defensively. "And if you'd ever bother to listen to anyone else, maybe you'd learn something, too."

Pete's face turned several shades of purple as he struggled for control. "On the day of your mother's funeral, you have insulted one of our dearest friends and you have dared to bring a goddamned, fucking communist into our home!"

"Maybe 'fucking' is the operative word here, Daddy," Sheila interrupted. "And he fucks real good," she shouted defiantly. "Or have you forgotten how a good fuck feels?"

"Get out! Get out now before I kill you both," Pete shouted back at her. "You're no daughter of mine and you'll never set foot in this home again!"

Dave got up and crossed to where Sheila stood, unable to move, as Pete stalked into the kitchen. Sheila began to cry hysterically and Dave guided her up the stairs to pack. Neither Julie nor Sarah moved, in shock as they watched the disintegration of a family.

In what seemed like hours, but was only a few minutes, a taxi pulled up in front and Dave hurried the still slightly hysterical Sheila out the door. Pete came back into the living room and apologized. "I'm so sorry you had to witness that."

Sheila huddled in a corner of the taxi and was still whimpering when they arrived at the motor hotel just south of the airport. Dave was annoyed with her, but couldn't help feeling sorry for the distraught woman. After all, it wasn't her fault that she had such bourgeois values. How could she help but suffer from political myopia, having been brought up in a cultural stupor by an aggressive, war-mongering father and a submissive, male-dominated mother?

He left her sitting with their luggage while he checked in at the front desk, returning briefly to get her credit card when told he either had to pay cash for the room or put it on a card. They found their room and he urged her to take a long, hot shower while he arranged for room service to send up some food and a bottle of brandy.

Somewhat calmer after a shower, Sheila still burst into tears every few minutes, wailing, "I've never been able to live up to their standards! Why doesn't Daddy love me? I can't help what I am and they've never been happy with *anything* I do!"

"Get hold of yourself, Sheila. I'd say it's going to be a long time before you have to worry about what your father thinks of you, so you'd better get used to the idea of going it alone."

How had he gotten mixed up with this fruitcake, he wondered. She was a sexy broad and he'd thought maybe he could educate her, but even the great food she served him wasn't worth all this aggravation. He'd have to make that clear to her as soon as they got back to Chicago.

Almost as though she'd sensed his attitude, she cried, "You won't leave me, will you? I love you so much and I need you so. More now than ever! Promise you won't leave me!"

"Now Sheila, control yourself. I'm here," Dave responded patiently. He went to the phone to call the airline and change their reservations back to Chicago, hoping to get a flight as early as possible in the morning.

CHAPTER TWENTY SEVEN

Sarah stole furtively into her apartment, devastated by the pain of Sheila's attack. Every part of her body seemed useless, a burden to be dragged pitilessly along through the mire of grief. The shock of Merrie's death had been tolerable as long as she could be useful and comforting to Pete, but how could she comfort him when her own anguish was too much to bear?

She had tried to make excuses for Sheila, knowing that the girl felt herself an outsider in her father's home, but reason failed as the ache in Sarah's heart intensified. Her throat hurt with tears she had yet to shed; her eyes burned from those that had already fallen. She was teetering on the edge of a precipice, sinking into the bog of destruction. A part of her longed to lose herself in the chasm and only a slender thread connected her to the Sarah that once was.

Desperate to cling to that thread, the familiar furnishings of her home, possessions gathered over the years with loving care, became her womb. She moved through the rooms, stroking the fabric of the cabbage rose chintz sofa that had taken so long to be delivered, gazing at the jumble of colors in the painting above the fireplace, the lamp made from an antique vase, the books she had rescued from a country barn, the piano she loved. She went slowly down the hallway to her bedroom.

A little water splashed on her face might clear away some of the webs that seemed to envelope her. The faucet stuck, then turned suddenly as she exerted pressure. Her hand slipped, knocking the little crystal drinking glass into the sink where it shattered. It was too much. Tears streamed from her eyes, mixing with the water from the faucet which mingled with the blood that stained her fingers as the skin was torn by shards of glass.

She reached toward the face in the mirror, the vibrant red blood on her hand smearing the image and the room began to swim in a collage of color. Her vision blurred. Red became purple, then blue, green and orange, taking on a tissue paper texture that turned into chiffon floating in a breeze. The face was no longer that of Sarah Fremont and as she slid to the floor a masculine voice called out, "Rosella? Rosella! Where are you, you lazy witch? Not up yet? Come, come, my new student will be here at any moment and you are not even out of bed!"

"Yes, yes, I'm coming," she answered, stretching lazily. Pushing aside the sheer curtain that surrounded a soft and lumpy bed, she rose and crossed the room to a cracked mirror on the wall beyond. Peering at the image, she grasped the mane of dark hair that fell carelessly below her shoulders and without benefit of comb or brush, braided it loosely at the bottom to keep it out of her face. Tying it with a bright ribbon, she strolled languidly into the adjoining room where a tall, slender man waited.

"Have you no shame at all, Rosella? Put some clothes on," he ordered disgustedly.

Rosella looked down at her naked body, shrugged and went back into the bedroom, returning a few moments later in a long, filmy skirt, long sleeved peasant blouse and a dark weskit that she buttoned casually. It was apparent that she wore nothing under these few items of clothing.

The man looked up from the easel that stood in front of him, rolled his eyes and returned his attention to the painting on the easel. A well-trimmed dark beard that came to a point a few inches below his chin covered his long, finely boned face.

"I thought you liked to look at my naked body, Emile," Rosella said sardonically. "You do it often enough."

"I do it when I'm painting you, Rosella, or when we are alone in our bed. My new student might find it distracting if it's the first thing he sees when he comes through the door, however," Emile retorted.

"What difference does it make whether he sees it now or when he begins to paint it?" Rosella queried, not really expecting an answer. She lowered herself indolently onto a chair, picked up a peach from a bowl on the table beside her and took a large, slurpy bite. The juice dribbled slowly down her chin. Through the open door that led to a lattice-framed terrace, she watched as a young man approached. He moved gracefully with the ease of a cat. His deep, sad eyes fascinated her as he peered through the open door, hesitated, then said, "I have come for instruction."

Rosella watched as he came closer, the fruit in her hand dripping unnoticed and forgotten. "Paul?" she whispered. Rosella and Sarah were one. Her cheek resting on the cold tile floor of the bathroom, Rosella became Sarah Fremont once again as the images of the two men faded into illusion. Grasping the edge of the tub, Sarah pushed herself to a sitting position, then opened her mouth to scream. The sound that emerged was a thin wail that dissolved into a torrent of sobs over which she had no control.

"No, no, no…" she moaned. "No more…I can't take any more. Go away, go away!" She pressed her hands against her head as a cacophony of sound filled her ears: the singing kettle in Yoshiko's little house, the tinkling of piano keys in Marguerite's cozy salon, the bubble of the fountain in the courtyard of the home Marguerite shared with Tonio, the whisper of the trees that swayed beyond the terrace as Rosella watched the approach of the young man that Sarah knew was another incarnation of Paul Winslow.

Trembling from head to toe, she staggered from the bathroom and down the hall to the kitchen, her hands leaving bloody prints on the wall as she fought to remain on her feet. Too distraught to consider amenities, she drank directly and deeply from the whiskey bottle, then coughed violently as the liquid burned her throat and set her stomach aflame.

"Help me, help me," she cried aloud. "I need help. Isn't there anyone who can help me?" The cacophony ceased as suddenly as it had begun and the rooms of her home were silent and unresponsive. She took another swig from the bottle and crept from room to room, switching on lamps in a frenzy to frighten away the demons that pursued her. Still clutching the bottle, she huddled on the sofa, sipping at the whiskey as she struggled to restore order to her mind.

There was no one who could help. Pete had lost his son, his wife, and now his daughter. Julie was still fragile from her own battle to regain some sense of self-worth. Sarah's business associates were already questioning her stability as she spent more and more time away from the office and she had lost touch with the few friends who had been hardly more than acquaintances anyway. A doctor? How does one find a doctor that would even listen to such a bizarre story?

The phone rang. It was several moments before Sarah realized it. There was no one she wanted to talk to. She tried to ignore it, but whoever it was on the other end seemed determined to reach her as the ringing continued. She sighed and went to stop the noise.

"Sarah? Are you all right? I just spoke with Pete Winslow and he seemed to think you might want to hear from me, so I took a chance that it wasn't too late to call." John St. James was the one person Sarah had not thought of and hope surged through her at the sound of his voice. Words tumbled from her mouth as she tried to explain her desperation.

"Are you saying that you need me, Sarah?" he asked.

"Oh, yes, John, yes! More than I can tell you!"

"Then I'll be there today. That is, tomorrow for you. Can you go to bed now and get some sleep?"

"I'll try, John. And John…thanks."

Sarah replaced the receiver on its hook and inhaled deeply, releasing the breath in a whoosh as she looked around and gave silent thanks for the call that had brought her back from the darkness. She put the whiskey bottle back in the cupboard, pushing it as far out of sight as it would go, and headed back toward the bedroom.

The sight of the bloody handprints on the walls was appalling. She hurried to get cold water and a sponge. Rubbing each spot furiously, she was gratified that since they had not dried, they came out quickly, leaving only slight shadows to remind her that she had given in to hysteria.

The bathroom looked worse than it really was, with most of the damage confined to the sink. She picked up the pieces of glass carefully, carrying them to the kitchen where she disposed of them. All remnants of the vibrant colors that had apparently triggered the emergence of Rosella had vanished. It had been such a brief appearance that the memory of it had already faded and Sarah was left with only a vague impression.

It must have been the combination of shock and grief at Merrie's death and Sheila's attack that had caused her to lose control. Sleep, I must sleep. Very soon trauma and exhaustion joined forces with the whiskey to transport her to the deep valley that was the home of Somnus, God of Sleep, where dusky twilight wraps all things in shadows.

She awoke in the morning as the telephone beside her jangled urgently, and was delighted to hear John's voice informing her that he was in New York and would be with her very soon.

She fought the urge to stay safely in bed, luxuriating in the warmth and softness that sheltered her there, and rose to dress for the office. Neglected profiles of the four Davidson Hotels awaited her review. She would be unable to focus her attention on them as she should, but if she didn't put in an appearance and at least look them over, the project that was important to Michael Davidson would be delayed and her frequent absences would be even more apparent. Buzz Craddock at the Chicagoan had already phoned, leaving messages that were increasingly impatient.

A few hours later, Sarah hovered at a window in the corridor near the gate where John's plane was due to arrive, watching as one plane after another landed and taxied down the runway. She scanned the sky for a sign of the one carrying John to San Francisco. Conflicting emotions threatened her eagerness to see him. Was it fair to have asked him to come all the way from Paris when she wasn't sure of her feelings for him? Would he assume that she was ready to make a commitment? Was that what she wanted to do? Could he make her forget the torment that had become such a debilitating part of her life?

Then the jumbo jet was there, being directed to the gate by a ramp agent with signal lights. The passenger ramp was put into place and the doors opened to disgorge the travelers aboard. Two or three people emerged and then he was walking toward her. She went to him, her arms outstretched, overjoyed at the sight of the handsome face that brought back happy memories of their nights together in New York.

"How did you manage to get out so quickly?" she asked.

"It helps when you fly first class," he answered. "They make everyone else wait for you to deplane." He put his arms around her, enveloping her. She rested her cheek against his chest for a moment, savoring the safety of his arms, then raised her face to his for a kiss.

"Oh, Sarah, how good it is to hold you again. You can't know how much I've wanted to see you, to hold you, to keep you near me!" John's voice trembled as he spoke, unaware that his words were the very ones that she needed to hear.

They walked slowly to the baggage claim area, their arms around each other. Sarah leaned her head against his shoulder, letting him guide the way to the carousels where John looked for a sign that would tell him which one might spill his luggage from its depths. Seeing other passengers from his flight gathered around one of them, they went toward it.

"How is Pete holding up?" John asked as they waited.

"I haven't spoken to him today, but yesterday couldn't have been worse," Sarah told him. "Sheila was so vicious and that man with her was so obviously the antithesis of Pete, it's hard to believe she could even have anything to do with him. But maybe that's part of the problem."

"Problem?"

"I think Sheila is so sure that her father disapproves of her that she might be subconsciously choosing someone who is his opposite and therefore might give her the approval she needs."

"Possibly. But from the sound of things, it's a little academic anyway, isn't it? If Pete threw her out of the house, it's pretty obvious he doesn't approve of her."

"Well, it was Sheila's attack on me that started the whole thing. She began by asking if I planned to move in with Pete before her mother's body was even in the grave and then altered that to making me the dutiful daughter she hadn't been. Pete was furious and ordered her to apologize, and then Dave, the fellow Sheila brought with her, told Pete that he was a 'Maoist,' whatever that means, and things went from bad to really bad.

"Poor Pete. It's hard to believe the bad luck that family has had. Merrie's death was so sudden. How did it happen so quickly?"

Sarah was still for a moment before she replied. "I don't really know. She just seemed to waste away. She confided in me a little when we were in Los Angeles and we all knew that she was depressed, but she kept assuring everyone that she'd be fine."

"It isn't just Merrie's death that has you so troubled, is it Sarah? There's more to it than that."

The baggage carousel began to move and John's attention was diverted as he turned to watch for his bags. Sarah turned away, grateful that he would not see the tears that welled up despite her efforts to stop them. Loading the luggage into the car and then the drive south on the freeway postponed any serious discussion, but once they were inside Sarah's apartment their eyes met and the composure she'd tried so hard to maintain dissolved. He held her tightly, stroking her hair and whispering gentle reassurances.

An hour passed and then another as John listened while Sarah recounted the experiences that had brought her to the point of despair. He already knew of the dreams, or what he'd thought of as dreams, of Yoshiko and Marguerite, but was surprised by the vision Sarah had had of seeing Paul disappearing into the white light and knowing that it was the pathway to death. That she had communicated with someone on another plane in the universe was not easy to accept. And the idea that she had made a deliberate attempt to reach Paul seemed to indicate that she was convinced that it was a possibility.

It disturbed him, too, that she had continued to pour one drink after another, though there was no visible effect, no slurring of words, no loss of coordination. That she was using whiskey as a crutch to see her through this darkness gave credence to her pain. The alcohol gave her courage, preparing her for the ordeal ahead as she related the events that led to her call for help.

"I don't think I can take any more," she told him now. "I want all of it to go away. I can't go on living in two worlds, one real and the other just as real in my mind. I've accepted the idea that Paul and I are inextricably connected, but to continue these journeys into another realm will destroy my life here. I need to let go of everything that reminds me of Paul, including the Vietnam effort.

"But how can I desert Pete now, when he's lost everyone who is important to him? How can I desert Julie when she's so fragile and clinging to the hope that has been raised by our efforts? How long can it go on? Will it all end in despair anyway?"

"I don't know, Sarah. I have no answers for you except to tell you how much I love you, and ask you to marry me. Come with me to Paris and we'll start a new life there together. You wouldn't be deserting them, you'd just be moving on with me."

Her eyes met his and his heart cracked a little at the combination of suffering and hope that were reflected in them.

"Oh John, can I do that? I couldn't marry you unless I was sure that my love for you was strong enough to break the ties with the past that haunt me. It wouldn't be fair to you."

"But you do love me, don't you, Sarah? Don't you see? I'm the one you turned to when you needed help." He took her hand in his, turning it gently, and they both stared at the cuts that remained as evidence of the previous night's ordeal.

"Who do you suppose Rosella was?" she asked rhetorically. "She must have been some sort of artist's model. It's pretty vague now, but I remember lots of color and a tall man standing at an easel."

"It doesn't matter, Sarah. Whoever she was, she wasn't strong enough to keep you in her existence very long. Maybe that means you won't see her again, or that you're resisting the past now and you'll be able to find your way into a future with me."

He pulled her closer to him, sheltering her, comforting her as she nestled willingly in his arms. Her eyelids began to droop. He held her for a time, then carried her to the bedroom and laid her gently on the bed.

"Don't go," she whispered. "Stay with me. Hold me, please."

"Yes, my darling. I'm here, for now and for as long as you want me."

CHAPTER TWENTY EIGHT

S arah appeared to have dozed off and John was slipping into the nether world that lies beneath the tangible when he felt his body rising from the bed. Startled, he held tightly to the woman beside him, then realized that they were moving together into a mist that had surrounded them without warning.

Seized by a terrible sense of foreboding, he flailed against the force that carried him relentlessly onward. Sarah's hand slipped from his as her face began to change and he knew that he was being drawn into Rosella's world. He called out to Sarah as the mist cleared, but he was no longer John St. James; he was Emile, the artist from another time and place.

"Where is your mind, Rosella? You're losing your pose! How can Lucien paint you if you keep moving?"

Rosella stretched indolently. It was difficult to concentrate with the eyes of the new student examining every curve, every muscle, every strand of her hair. She had never before been shy. In fact, she usually reveled in the certainty that her body was a thing of beauty. But this man was different somehow. When she allowed herself to look directly at him, she was seized by desire. When he looked directly at her through half closed, liquid blue eyes, he took away the power that had always been hers, assuming it for himself.

Emile had been her lover for more than a year. His dark, handsome face had seemed a little sinister at first, fascinating her with the promise of danger. He was a forceful and demanding lover, sure of himself in a way that no previous lover had been. They suited each other. Emile was a noted artist and her body, combined with a lack of prudery, was useful to him as she modeled for his students. She usually delighted in provoking lascivious glances from his drooling students, turning away in disdain just as they had begun to hope that she might be available for more than the distant study of her soft limbs.

Lucien took no notice of her, however, discussing her face, her arms, her legs, with Emile as though she were no more than a vase of flowers. The only time he communicated with her was as he left the hillside house in which she resided with Emile. Then his eyes would look into hers as he thanked her for posing and she knew that he could see far into her soul, could read what was in her mind as surely as if it were printed on her forehead. She was careful to conceal her feelings from Emile, fearful of giving him cause for jealousy, viewing his volatile nature with some anxiety.

She was becoming increasingly more detached as Emile made love to her, fantasies of Lucien growing as she imagined his hands caressing her, his arms encircling her. Emile seemed unaware of her detachment, however, sure of his claim on her sybaritic attentions. As time went by, her soul seemed to separate from her body and she found a private place of her own where love became more than a word used by poets.

It was not long before Lucien's paintings began to be noticed by members of the Paris art colony and the sale of his first painting combined with an honorable mention at a showing were occasion for a party on the rooftop of his apartment building. Emile, his teacher, and Rosella, his model, were honored guests. The partygoers were exuberant as they drank the hearty red wine, sang bawdy songs and danced to the music of the variety of musicians in attendance.

Emile was dashing in a silk shirt with full sleeves and ruffles at the cuffs, and Rosella had chosen a skirt with layers of colorful chiffon that clung sensuously when she stood, drifting lightly with the breeze. A bright red shawl covered her shoulders and flowers twined gaily in the unruly mass of hair atop her head. The effect was stunning.

A violin played slowly, weaving a tune that was melancholy, even mournful. Another violin joined the first, and Rosella began to sway in time to the music, moving to the gentle beat, soon lost in the mood as the strings harmonized, then competed for the melody. She raised her wineglass, examining the color of the liquid, watching the flecks of light that changed its essence, fascinated by the images that were distorted into curious shapes through the wine in the glass. She moved the glass from hand to hand, up and down, then set it on a table, playing to it as to a lover. She moved from side to side, her shoulders and arms undulating, her hips shifting the layers in her skirt, creating a rainbow of sensuality. The flowers in her hair fell one at a time as the pins that held her dark curls came loose.

Little by little, the revelers ceased speaking, enthralled as the music swelled and Rosella's movements grew more exaggerated, then almost frenzied. Emile, seated at a table some distance away, watched the watchers. He was not unfamiliar with Rosella's occasional departure from the lethargic attitude that was the norm for her, into passionate excesses. He considered her a lazy slut for the most part, useful as a vessel for his physical satisfaction, an energetic bed partner, or an object to be captured on canvas. As the others stared, entranced by her fervor, he began to feel slight pangs of jealousy and fought the urge to claim her as he might a child that was showing off.

The several instruments that had joined together to develop the meandering tune ceased playing one by one until a single violin continued the wistful, brooding melody of the spontaneous piece. Rosella's movements slowed as her breath came in short gulps. She stumbled and would have fallen had it not been for Lucien, who caught her in his arms. She rested there for the briefest moment, then raised her face to look into his eyes, deep and molten, filled now with desire. The noisy party was still for an instant, suspended as everyone waited for the conclusion of the drama that had unfolded, primitive and animalistic, as Rosella danced. She shook her head exultantly and laughed. Lucien pulled her to him, holding her firmly until she gasped for breath, then kissed her. Released from their suspension in time, the others laughed too, and resumed their merrymaking.

Rosella gave in to the overwhelming pleasure that filled her being, whispering his name, her fingers twined in his hair.

Time fast-forwarded a few months. Rosella and Lucien sat companionably under a tree on the bank of the Seine. Emile was at the atelier, busy working on a newly commissioned painting. The commission was an important one and the painting was to be one of massive proportions. Emile was absorbed in the sketches for the work, focusing all his attention on the inflections of each flow of light on the forms that tumbled over each other in the painting. He had no need for Rosella, giving her the freedom to meet with Lucien without fear of discovery.

For the first time in her life, Rosella was very much in love. Since the rooftop party, she had spent every moment possible with Lucien, escaping the hillside house with the flimsiest of excuses, often sure that Emile would know by looking into her eyes that she was unfaithful. She had never before felt the need to conceal her feelings, but then she had never before experienced the kind of feeling she had for Lucien. She went from the thrill of anticipation to the torment of despair at the thought of not seeing Lucien. When he touched her, made love to her, she reached a pinnacle of happiness. When he had gone and she had returned to Emile, she lived in terror that he might one day leave her for good.

Lucien wanted to go to America. Rosella had never been more than fifty miles from Paris. She had no clothes, she had no education, she spoke only French and even her French vocabulary was poor, but if Lucien left Paris, she would go with him or die. But what if he was ashamed of her? What would she do? It was terrifying to consider, but she would follow him anyway.

She would be a little sad to leave Emile. After all, he had been good to her in his way. But she knew that Emile did not love her in the way that a husband loves a wife. He thought of her as a possession, like his canvasses or his brushes. He would be angry with her if she left, but he'd get over that quickly, or at least she thought he would.

Rosella turned to gaze at Lucien. There was no one nearby to see, and she put her hands on his face, running her fingers over his eyebrows, his nose, his chin, then reached up to stroke the unruly hair that fell where it chose. Rising, she stood above him, slowly undoing the buttons that went down the front of her cotton blouse. Allowing her own tousled hair to fall over her face, she studied her breasts as the fabric fell away, caressing the skin gently. With the tips of her fingers, she pushed the straps of her camisole down slowly, massaging her shoulder blades, then her upper arms, reaching over her shoulders to knead the flesh on her upper back. She rolled her head languorously, enjoying her amour-propre as her hair swung from side to side.

Shrugging out of the blouse, she let it fall to the ground and reached for the fasteners on her skirt. Stepping from the circle it made on the ground, she let the camisole drop and very slowly began to lower the pantaloons she wore beneath the skirt. The soft mound of her stomach crept into view and she paused, using her finger tips again to stroke the flesh, her thumbs making circular movements as her hands formed a vee that reached her generous thatch of pubic hair.

She gyrated slowly, her hips moving forward as her buttocks responded. Her hands continued to push the pantaloons down inch by inch, over her hips, down her thighs, until they lay in a heap at her feet. Stepping out of them, she stretched, aware of the rapt expression on Lucien's face. Her hands went back to her breasts, pushing them forward as she massaged their sides with the palms of her hands. Flicking her fingertips over the nipples, her shoulders rolling as the centers hardened, she caught her breath in a gasp of pleasure. She squeezed the muscles in her buttocks as her vagina began to throb. Engrossed in her own enjoyment, her hand moved from her breasts downward, caressing her hips, reaching behind to grasp her undulating bottom.

Lucien watched, beguiled, as her head swung from side to side, reveling in the intense physical pleasure that came so naturally to Rosella. He felt himself harden, pushing against the cloth of his trousers, desperate for release. Rosella's fingers had crept between her legs, stroking lightly at first, becoming more agitated as her arousal increased. She rubbed harder, her knees bending involuntarily until, with a cry of exultation, she fell toward him, pulling at his trousers, stripping them away. Rolling with him in a tangle of arms and legs, she guided him inside. Frenzied, they pumped together, reaching a climax quickly. They fell back panting, stunned by the urgency of their lovemaking.

As her breath slowed, Rosella reached for her skirt, turning it over to search for the vial of musk oil she had hidden in a pocket. Finding it, she turned back to the still unmoving Lucien. Removing the cap, she poured a small amount of the liquid into the palm of her hand and, propped up on one elbow, began to rub it gently onto his chest. She rose to straddle him, massaging the warm oil in little circles that increased in size until the oil disappeared into his skin. Pouring a little onto each shoulder, she moistened her fingers in the puddles it created, spreading it over the muscles of his upper arms and kneading each area of skin until it glistened.

The sunlight that filtered through the tree above them faded as tiny raindrops fell, landing on Lucien's oiled skin, then separating as they formed jewel-like mounds. Rosella pulled him to his feet and toward the river where they splashed in up to their knees. Raising the vial above her head, Rosella poured the remaining liquid over herself, then reached down to gather handfuls of water, spreading it over their bodies until they shimmered.

She laughed aloud, throwing her head back, and said, "Oh, Lucien, I do love you so very, very much!"

"Then come with me, Rosella," he said quietly. "I am leaving tomorrow night. I've made reservations for two persons on the evening train to Calais. We will go from there to London and on to America in a few weeks." His voice was throaty with intensity.

Tears came to her eyes and she choked on the words that were hardly more than gibberish as she babbled of her love and how frightened she had been that he might leave her behind.

He brought up the inevitable. "What about Emile?"

"I don't know, Lucien. He will be very angry."

"Should I go with you to tell him? It would be the honorable thing to do after all," Lucien offered.

"No! No, Lucien, I will tell him. Or perhaps I will just leave when he is not around," Rosella mused.

"That would not be fair, Rosella. Emile has been my teacher and my friend, and has made it possible for me to be recognized as an artist of worth. I must say goodbye and thank him. It would be cowardly of me to sneak away with you," Lucien said, troubled by their predicament. They decided that Rosella would go home to pack her few belongings and tell Emile that she intended to leave him. Lucien would see him later.

Rosella approached the terrace with trepidation. She looked around for Emile, then called out, "Emile? Emile, are you here?"

Emile's tone projected his annoyance when he answered. "Of course I'm here! I've been working all afternoon and when I wanted a glass of iced tea to quench my thirst, where were you? Nowhere to be found!"

"I'm sorry, Emile. You've never cared where I was before. Why were you looking for me today?"

"You've always been underfoot before, but lately you seem to disappear quite often. Where were you and where have you been going so often lately?" he asked peevishly.

Rosella did not respond immediately. She sighed. This was not going to be easy after all. Emile appeared in the doorway, the paintbrush he was cleaning still in his hand. Frowning, he studied her face, his eyes narrowing.

"Come to think of it, you've been behaving strangely ever since the party for Lucien." He looked her up and down. "And you're dressed differently, more ladylike. You're even wearing underwear! What is it, Rosella?" Emile's eyebrows shot up. "It's another man, isn't it, Rosella? Isn't it?" he shouted.

Rosella began to cry. "Oh, Emile, I never knew, I mean I didn't mean to hurt you, it just happened."

"Who, Rosella? Who is it?" Emile was livid as he crossed the room to stand in front of her. Rosella shrank from him, edging sideways. His face contorted in rage.

"Please, Emile," she begged, "let me tell you. Don't be angry. We couldn't help it! He loves me, Emile, and he wants me to go away with him," she tried to explain.

"Do you really believe that this man loves you? That he doesn't want you only because you're so lively in his bed? That he doesn't delight in fondling those lovely breasts or in parting those delicious legs? He *loves* you? Who is this idiot, Rosella?" Emile sneered viciously.

"It's Lucien," she sobbed. "Lucien does love me! Oh please, Emile, we didn't mean for it to happen, it just did!"

"My student? You would leave me for a mere boy? And you believe that he is prepared to take care of you? How stupid can you be, Rosella?"

"He is not a mere boy, Emile, he is twenty five years old and he has sold another of his paintings. We are going to America. You don't love me, you're only angry because it never occurred to you that someone else might."

In a moment of insight, she said what made sense to him immediately. He paused, stunned by the realization that she was right. Staring at her briefly, he turned, his angry posture slipping away.

"You're right, Rosella," he said slowly. "I never thought about it at all, but even though I know you've had men before me, it didn't occur to me that anyone wanted you for anything other than your beautiful body. I don't know if that's all I wanted from you or not."

The only sound in the room was that of her weeping. The minutes went by, then he looked at her and with a perfunctory wave of his hand, said, "Go. Pack your things and go to him if that's what you want to do."

He sat without moving for more than an hour, failing to notice when she tiptoed out with her small cardboard suitcase. It was dark in the room when he finally realized he was alone. He rose and lit the lamps, then got a bottle of brandy from the cabinet, settling back into the one comfortable chair he owned. Why had it upset him so when she said she was leaving? He had assumed that it would be he who tired of her, and that he would make some other arrangement for her when he wanted to be rid of her. It certainly wasn't that he depended on her for anything. She wasn't much of a cook and like any other woman, she could be replaced in his bed.

Her lack of sophistication, her total lack of pretension, made her a wonderful model for his paintings and those of his students. There was an unspoken exchange between Rosella and anyone who captured her luscious body on canvas. It was something indefinable, a current that made her limbs come alive on a canvas as the artist felt, without touching, each curve, each muscle. Her spontaneity, her earthiness, made her unique.

Could it be that he felt more for her than physical desire and convenience? As the liquid in the bottle diminished, his mood altered to one of anger again. How dare she leave him? She was nothing. He went into the studio, searching for sketches, paintings of her, gazing at the colors in the garments she wore, the tilt of her head. Gathering them in the center of the room, he picked up a palette knife and began to slash them as though by destroying her image on the canvas, he could destroy the effects of her presence in his life.

As the night wore on, he began to think that she wasn't worth all this. He finished the bottle and fell into a deep, but short-lived sleep, waking to stagger to the cabinet for another bottle. Determined to rid himself of whatever feelings he might have for her, he continued to drink throughout the night, drowsing now and then as his brain numbed.

The sky was grey with the approaching dawn when he finished the second bottle of brandy. The sun rose, blinding him, which served to anger him further in his stupor. He dragged the slashed canvasses outside and piled them in a heap. Searching through his pockets for a match with which to start a fire he hoped would destroy all memory of her, he raged when he found none. He rummaged through the tangled brush around the house for dry sticks to rub together. In frustration, he rubbed them frantically, but in vain, adding to his demented fury when not a spark came forth.

Images distorted and branches seemed to reach out, snatching at him with their claws, thwarting his effort to make his way back to the house. Nearly insane from alcohol, rage and the intensity of the morning sun, he managed at last to start the fire that consumed the wood frames on the canvasses and made a grotesque show of the pigments on them. Laughing maniacally, he opened a third bottle of brandy and sat on the terrace gleefully watching the flames. He spent the remainder of the day drinking and dozing.

By sunset, Emile was between the intense awareness and total oblivion that sometimes results from emotional upheaval combined with the use of intoxicants. He realized that he did love her. The thought of losing her caused the seeds of fury to grow, beginning in the pit of his stomach and creeping up through his throat until it was released in a howl. He must destroy the man who would take her from him, he thought, and got out the gun he'd hidden under a pile of seldom-used brushes.

He'd bought the six-shot Irish pepperbox hand arm because of its distinctive ivory handle, carved in the shape of a beagle's head that reminded him of a dog he'd had in his youth. Its small barrel made it easy to conceal and he stumbled off in search of Lucien.

A frenzied stop at Lucien's apartment building yielded the information that Lucien had left with a young lady for the train station. Emile hurried through the streets, his mind fuzzy, with no particular plan in mind other than to stop them. He staggered through the terminal, finding the track on which the train for Calais was already steaming, ready for departure. Passengers were boarding the cars as Emile pushed his way through the crowd until he caught sight of Rosella's brightly colored skirt. He tried to call out, but the sound stuck in his throat. Summoning all his energy, he screeched, "ROSELLA!"

Rosella was just ahead of Lucien and had nearly reached the car in which they were to ride. Hearing her name, she turned and was stunned to see Emile plunging toward them. Neither she nor Lucien moved as the drunken Emile wove his way through the crowd. Suddenly she caught sight of the gun in his hand and her eyes widened in fear. Dropping the cardboard suitcase she carried, she ran toward Emile, screaming, "No! No, Emile!"

Emile, surprised by Rosella's sudden move in his direction, squeezed the trigger inadvertently, then again and again, unable to stop himself. Rosella fell to the ground, the colors in her skirt blending with the bright red blood that covered her blouse. Lucien had nearly reached her when another of Emile's bullets felled him. Clutching his chest, he crawled the last few feet to where Rosella lay. Her eyes fluttered and she grasped the hand that he held out to her.

"Lucien...no, no...I'm sorry, so sorry," she cried weakly. Her head fell, twisted strangely toward him and she whispered one last word, "Paul..."

CHAPTER TWENTY NINE

arah's hand was still outstretched toward Lucien as she left Rosella's lifeless body. She gasped as she saw Paul Winslow's tattered form rise from the body of Lucien and then another hand took the one she held out. Emile's image faded and she found herself staring into John's anguished eyes. The three of them hung suspended in time as Paul reached out to the woman he had loved through many lifetimes and the friend with whom he had shared her so long ago. Then he was gone.

Sarah and John tumbled gently from nineteenth century Paris to the room they had left together near San Francisco in 1972. Their eyes met and locked as they hovered briefly above the bed, then slid back into the bodies that awaited them. Neither of them spoke, each wondering if the other had really been along on this astounding journey into the past.

John was first to break the silence. "Oh, dear God, I don't believe it. Tell me it was a dream. Tell me I wasn't Emile."

Sarah felt a burning sensation in her chest and touched it carefully, searching for the hole left by Emile's bullet. "If you remember his name, then it wasn't a dream because I was there, too," she said.

"Rosella. You were Rosella and Paul was Lucien. It's incomprehensible to me that what I was so sure was fantasy on your part could really have happened, but if we went back together this time, then the others must have happened as well. If they aren't dreams, then what are they? My god, I killed both of you! But I loved you even then. How could I have done such a thing?" John's distress was apparent as he tried to comprehend what to him was completely incomprehensible.

Sarah sighed. "Now you understand why Paul has been such an obsession. Why I couldn't let him go even though I've never met him in this life. I didn't know anything about Emile before tonight, nor Rosella until last night. But it doesn't seem too surprising, does it? I've read that people tend to come back in groups, especially if they have something to work out. But since I've run the gamut from disbelief to acceptance to panic over the whole thing, it never occurred to me that anyone else might be part of it. I just assumed it was between Paul and me alone."

Recalling Rosella's love for Lucien, Sarah thought suddenly of the lovemaking beside the river. She trembled, remembering her utter abandon, the passion she had felt at his touch, Paul's touch. Then she stiffened, wondering how much John could know of it. If he had gone with her to this former existence, had he seen all of it or only his part in it?

As though he'd read her mind, he said softly, "No, I didn't see you with him, but I do remember Emile's terrible visions throughout the night he spent in a drunken stupor. It was unbearable for him and is not something I want to dwell on now. I have to think only that you loved Lucien, or rather, Rosella loved Lucien."

Sarah giggled a little hysterically, thinking of Rosella's voluptuous figure and complete lack of inhibition. Could the Sarah of today really have been that kind of woman? Could she and John have the kind of relationship they both wanted, now that they knew of the intimacy she had shared with Paul?

Again, he sensed her thoughts. "Don't you see, Sarah? Those were entirely different people. I'm *not* Emile now and you're not Rosella anymore. I've been given a chance to make it up to you. Emile treated you badly, even ended your life, but *John* can make amends for that by loving you here and now, in this life. You must have known somewhere deep inside that the story couldn't end in tragedy. When you were desperate, you turned to me!"

She lifted her head to gaze into his eyes and saw the tenderness, the sincerity in them. How like him, she thought, to see opportunity where I saw only despair. Could he be right? Please God, let him be right. Let me find solace in his arms. She leaned against him, nestling in the arms that promised safety. He held her tenderly, his cheek against her hair, his lips leaving tiny kisses among the tangled strands. Content just to be together, they succumbed to fatigue and slept.

Sarah was first to wake. She stayed very still, clinging to the sense of well being that was such a welcome change. Lifting her head just a little, she was able to see his face, the face that had become so dear to her, promising a future unencumbered by memories of the past. But would they be able to forget or would it always be between them? He stirred and opened his eyes, smiling contentedly. His arms tightened around her and she raised her mouth to his.

Kissing her lightly at first, treasuring her, his kisses soon turned ardent. She responded tentatively, then gave in to the longing that was spiced with passion, reveling in the stability that was the essence of this man. She welcomed the touch of his hands as he caressed her, and knew with certainty that she loved him. She told him so.

They stayed near each other throughout the day, touching frequently – a hand, an arm, a shoulder, their intimacy becoming more comfortable with each passing hour. Their passion began to thrive and Sarah drifted into a serenity she had not felt for many months. This was a relationship that she could count on, trust.

They went out to dinner, strolling down the street hand in hand as they approached the entrance to a small Italian restaurant. The interior was dim, with chubby little candles on each table that created playful shadows on the faces of other diners, lending an air of romance to the ambiance. John ordered champagne, then reached into a pocket to take out a small box.

"I've been carrying this around for months," he admitted. "I saw it in the window of an estate jewelry shop and heard it calling out your name." He laughed aloud at the thought. "Who knows, maybe you *have* worn it before! But it made me think of your eyes." He opened the box and held it out to her, revealing a large diamond ring with slightly smaller emeralds on either side. "Will you marry me, Sarah Fremont?"

She took the ring and put it on her finger. "It's perfect, and it would be an honor, John St. James. I'll treasure both the ring and you for the rest of my life." His eyes twinkled and she laughed with him, finishing the sentence by saying, "this life anyway!"

The champagne arrived and they toasted the future together. Sarah felt that her worlds were coming together at last. One thing still troubled her, however, and she had to bring it up.

"John, there's something we haven't talked about. Your interpretation of our past together seems so plausible that it's easy to accept and I'd really rather do just that than to disrupt this wonderful euphoria. But my experiences with Paul haven't been only in the 'dreams' or whatever they are of previous lives together. I've seen him and been with him as we are now, Paul and Sarah. I've touched him. Remember when I told you about having seen him disappearing into the light that I knew was death? I called out to him and he turned back toward me just before I woke up. That seems to mean that he didn't die and if he isn't dead, what happens if he comes back someday?"

John leaned back in his chair. "I can't answer that, Sarah. He was my best friend in college, and part of me says, yes, I want desperately for him to come home, but another part of me says, no, even if he did come back, he might be so damaged that he'd no longer be the man I knew. And the possibility of losing you to him is something I can't think about. Life does have a way of working out and I guess we'll just have to cope with that if it happens. Besides which, the times you've seen him may have been a one-way trip. He may have no knowledge of them. And if your connection with him is one that is meant to go on, perhaps it was meant to be in a future lifetime rather than this one. If he loves you, he'd want you to be happy, and he'd want the same for me. Let me try, Sarah. Be happy with me."

It made sense and wanting to believe him, she pushed any remaining doubts as far into the recesses of her mind as possible, hoping she'd never be faced with making that choice. Her burden had been lifted and her future was bright once again.

"Is it too soon to talk about plans for the future?" John asked.

She smiled. "What did you have in mind?"

"How would you like to take over the position of Vice President of my company in charge of marketing and promotion? And how soon can you do it?"

She laughed. "You mean you've actually thought about that?"

"I've thought of almost nothing else since I met you, Sarah. I knew I wanted you near me and with your talent, what better way to keep you as close as possible?"

He went on to tell her more of the developments that had come about in the family owned hotel group that he headed. Expansion continued as he acquired properties in London and on the Italian Riviera. Negotiations had stalled temporarily on the New York property he hoped to acquire, but he intended to restore an element of progress during a stopover there on his return trip to Paris. What had begun with one small inn nearly a hundred years earlier was now a sizeable and very profitable company.

"As head of the company, I earn a very healthy salary, and I'm also paid rather handsome consulting fees on occasion by other firms that want to benefit from my experience. In short, I am a rather wealthy man. Though you would never *have* to work, Sarah, I wouldn't expect you to give up your career to be a good little wife. You have a wonderful quality about you that enables you to relate very well with people and to know without being told what will make them happy.

"What I propose is that you assume a position of Vice President in the company in charge of promotion and marketing. You will have complete freedom to travel as you choose, the where-with-all to do it first class, and we will have each other to love and cherish. At least I will cherish every moment with you by my side. If I wasn't absolutely certain of my love for you and that you would be happy with me, I would not be suggesting any of this."

"I don't know what to say, John. You make it sound like a fairytale life, but I do have commitments here and people I love." Her eyes clouded, remembering the recent loss of one of those people. "I wish Merrie had lived to know about us, John. She'd have been so pleased. Did I tell you that she had a copy of the photograph of you and Paul made for me? It's in a silver frame and was gift-wrapped. Pete gave it to me the night Merrie died."

"Maybe it would help Pete to know that we're going to be married.

I want to see him anyway and pay my respects. I've been selfish today, wanting to keep you all to myself for a little while before the world is pounding on the door again."

"No more selfish than I am, John. Since Merrie went into the hospital, I've neglected my office and my work, and then I was so overwhelmed with grief and the thought that I was losing my mind when Rosella appeared that I wanted nothing more than to hide away in the shelter of your arms."

The balance of John's visit to San Francisco seemed to fly by as they shared their happiness with Pete and then with Julie Schaefer. Pete had grasped Sarah's hand, holding it tightly, smiling and nodding, but saying nothing. She had exchanged looks with John, both of them suspecting that Pete's silence was caused by the lump in his throat.

Julie had hugged them both gleefully and a stop at the hotel to see Van Carducci had brought about champagne toasts in the lounge. Sarah was touched by Van's concern when John told her later that her former boss had taken him aside to tell him that she was the finest girl in the world and he was the luckiest man in the world if she loved him.

Over the weekend, they picnicked in Golden Gate Park, wandered through the DeYoung Museum, and lunched on the terrace of the Alta Mira Hotel in Sausalito. Mesmerized by the view of the Bay, the City and the Tiburon Peninsula, they failed to notice the chill in the air as they held hands while the always discreet staff of the restaurant looked on in amusement.

Then Sarah stood again in the corridor that led to the airline gate through which John was to depart. She watched as he disappeared down the ramp, turning to wave one last time before he vanished into the jumbo jet that would take him away. It seemed as though they had been together for a lifetime and yet as though it had been only yesterday that she stood in the same place watching the planes that were landing.

As the plane backed away from the gate, she turned and walked back through the terminal. Seeing someone off on a plane is such a lonely thing to do, she thought. One minute you're busy with luggage and finding the gate, then one last kiss and suddenly you're by yourself, surrounded by strangers. Waiting at the curb for a chance to cross to the parking lot, she considered all the things that had to be done before she and John were married. She'd have to tell Michael Davidson that she was resigning her position; she'd have to decide what should be shipped and what should be disposed of from her furnishings; she's have to pack, and they would have to find a place to live in Paris.

Paris! It was suddenly overwhelming. She caught her breath as the enormity of the changes she was planning swept over her. It had seemed so romantic and glamorous while John was there beside her, but the reality of the responsibilities involved was something else entirely!

It was dark by the time she got home. She let herself in through the back door, switching on the kitchen light absentmindedly, then stood leaning against the counter, thinking of everything and nothing. The light from the kitchen fell through the opening above the sink and into the dining room, its brightness filling one room, reaching out to the other and fading into shadowy depths. A reflection of my life, she thought. One part shining radiantly, the other slipping away into the anonymity of the darkness. Everything had seemed so easy while John was there. She had fallen into a comfortable mold, feeling protected and cherished as their relationship was nurtured. But she could not glide into what lay ahead as effortlessly as she seemed to glide into the past. Then she laughed at herself and said aloud, "What a ravenous appetite for self-destruction I seem to have!"

CHAPTER THIRTY

The sun was shining brightly outside, but the room in which Pete Winslow sat was dark and gloomy. It had been days since he'd opened the drapes and longer than that since he'd opened a window. In fact, the whole house was a mess. When he was hungry, he opened a can or pulled something out of the freezer, leaving the empty containers lying on the kitchen counter, the dishes in the sink or wherever he sat to eat. The cupboards and refrigerator were empty except for a few things that had long since lost their original color and were more or less unidentifiable.

Pete knew he should get cleaned up and get out to buy groceries, but he couldn't seem to find the energy, and worse, he didn't care. Without Merrie, his life had lost all meaning.

What is wrong with the world, he pondered. He remembered the days when people were patriotic, when Memorial Day was more than a day at the beach. This year, Memorial Day had come and gone and the Fourth of July was nearly upon them. The news from Vietnam was worse every day and American troops were leaving rapidly as President Nixon announced further withdrawals. It seemed the United States might be losing the war and Pete just didn't understand anymore.

The doorbell rang. Ignoring it, he leaned back in the chair and closed his eyes. After a few moments it rang again, then continued to ring insistently until Pete could no longer ignore it.

"Go away," he shouted in the direction of the door. The response from whoever stood outside was to lean on the bell, causing it to ring continuously. Grumbling, Pete went to the door and pulled it open, intending to curse the inconsiderate nitwit on the other side. He stopped, his mouth agape, when he saw Julia Schaefer and Sarah Fremont standing on the stoop.

"You're going to let us in, Pete," Julie said brusquely, brushing past him. She stopped in shock as she took in the state of the living room. "My God, Pete, this place is a pigsty!"

"Why haven't you answered the phone, Pete? We've both been calling you and you can't have been out of the house that much," Sarah said. "From the looks of this place, you've spent weeks creating the mess." The two women stood in the center of the room, the urge to begin cleaning up the mess immediately threatening to overshadow their concern for Pete himself.

He was defensive. "So it's a little messy," he grumbled. "What difference does it make anyway? No one sees it but me."

"We're seeing it, Pete," Sarah commented. "How could you let things go this way?"

"You wouldn't be seeing it if you hadn't barged in here," Pete retorted. "It isn't as though you'd been invited."

Julie and Sarah noticed Pete's disheveled appearance at the same time and their attention was diverted back to him. Sarah went to him, putting her arms around him sympathetically. The man, strong, in command, accustomed to an orderly life, had been broken. Her friend, someone she loved as though he really was her father, was hurting as badly as it was possible to hurt.

"Pete, let us help," she pleaded. "Don't shut us out."

He began to cry. The tears that fell from his eyes became heart-rending sobs as his shoulders began to shake. He broke away from Sarah and turned his back on them. They resisted the urge to reach out to him, knowing that he needed the release, but would conceal his agony in their presence if he could, a reaction born of a lifetime of self-control. Julie went into the kitchen where she cleared enough of the mess to make a pot of coffee while Sarah sat quietly on the sofa, waiting for Pete to get some of the misery out of his system before offering any further comment.

It was several minutes before he was able to speak. "What am I going to do?" he asked plaintively. "I can't face life without Merrie. When I was young, I was so proud of my uniform and all I wanted was to be the best damn officer in the United States Army. Then I met Merrie and she was the gentlest, most beautiful thing I'd ever laid eyes on. When Sheila was born, I thought my heart would burst, she was so beautiful, almost as beautiful as her mother. So tiny and so perfect, with her mother's eyes and hair so light and soft that it looked like cotton candy.

"Then Paul came along," he continued, "and I asked God why I'd been so blessed. The three of them were my whole world and everything I did from then on, I did to make them proud of me." He choked as his voice broke. "Now they're all gone. What did I do wrong? Why has God taken away everything I loved?"

Neither Julie nor Sarah spoke, letting Pete release the emotions that were threatening to destroy him. He went on, "Little Sheila. She was always a rebel, but she was so adorable that we let her get away with almost anything. Should I have been stricter with her?" he asked rhetorically. "How did she make such a mess of her life? I should have paid more attention to her, I guess, but she was so fragile that I was afraid to touch her for fear she'd break or something. Does she resent me so much that she'd bring that man here? A man just the opposite of me, a man who reviles everything I stand for, everything I believe in? Where did I fail her?

"And Paul. My son. He listened to me. I could talk to him like I couldn't talk to Sheila. I just didn't know what to say to a little girl, so I left her to Merrie. But Paul! He respected me. He wanted to learn from me. He was really smarter than I was and he went ten steps beyond what I knew when it came to those automobile engines. He was just out of high school when the first passenger jets came around. From then on, all he wanted to do was fly. And them some total stranger halfway around the world fired a gun that blew him out of the sky.

"I kept up the pretense for Merrie, but I can't believe that Paul is still living," Pete said, his shoulders heaving again. "Oh God," he cried, "why Paul? Why that superb human being? The finest son any man could ask to have!"

It was more than Sarah could bear. "Pete," she cried out, "I'm sure that Paul is still alive!" She didn't notice Julie's shocked expression and went on, "I can't tell you how I know, but I'm sure in my heart that he's alive. And I think he's escaped, Pete!" She stopped, feeling both Pete and Julie staring at her.

"Please," she begged, "don't look at me that way. I'm not crazy, really I'm not. I can't explain it, it's something I know as surely as I know that the two of you are sitting here!" She put her hand to her forehead, squeezing her eyes shut, visions of Paul turning back from death swimming before her.

"You can't give up, Pete. Keep fighting for Paul. Do it for Merrie," she finished miserably.

No one said anything for some time. Sarah knew that Julie thought she'd put all the dreams behind her when she agreed to marry John and was startled to hear her speak as though they were still part of her reality. It had been over a year since the letter from Jack and there had been no further indication that he was still alive. Little Sandy was now three years old and had never seen her father. Would she ever see him? Would Julie ever be sure that Jack felt about her and their daughter the way Pete feels about Merrie and his children?

Sarah was miserably unhappy. She had blurted out what she felt in her heart was true, but couldn't tell them why she was so sure. She was, in their minds, an outsider to their pain. She was not truly a family member, much as they cared for her. If Pete gave up, there was nothing she could do but sit at card tables getting signatures on petitions, labeled a 'concerned citizen,' though she knew that her relationship with Paul was one that transcended time.

Pete broke the silence. "I'm touched that you care so deeply, Sarah," he said, "but I don't think I can continue to be a part of the league without Merrie. I can't even imagine an existence without Merrie and I'm not sure I *want* an existence without Merrie. I don't say that to get sympathy, it's just the way it is."

"We understand, Pete," Julie replied. "Maybe we'd all feel better if we got to work and cleaned up this place. Merrie would be ashamed of you." She rose to begin picking up the clutter that was everywhere. Relieved that she would not be asked to support her assertion that Paul was alive, Sarah went to the kitchen to clear away the dishes that had accumulated on the counters.

Julie didn't speak as they drove back to her apartment. Sarah had left her car there and the two of them had gone to Pete's together. Turning off the engine, Julie urged Sarah to come in for awhile. "We haven't had a good chat for a long time," she said.

Sarah knew that her friend was curious about her outburst at Pete's house. Julie made iced tea and they settled into the cushions of the sofa, each wondering how to begin the conversation.

"I wonder if Pete is really going to be all right," Sarah said tentatively. "I think he knows that he can't go on forever without caring about the house and maybe we motivated him a little by telling him how ashamed Merrie would be of him for letting things go like that."

"I'm sure it helps to have friends who care about you. I can certainly vouch for that," Julie replied. "If I hadn't had you and Merrie on my side last year, I'd never have made it. My parents still don't know why I did what I did. I think they're afraid to ask because they really don't want to know."

"How are they? Have you been up there or have they been down to see you?" Sarah asked, postponing the discussion she knew Julie really wanted to have.

"I took Sandy up there last weekend and left her there to spend some time with them. I stayed overnight, but that's about all I can take at one time. I catch Daddy looking at me sometimes, like he'd like to talk to me, but I guess he's like Pete and doesn't know where to begin with a female child. Of course, my mother can't see beyond her image of what she thinks I *should* be."

"How did you turn out to be so level headed and so terrific?" Sarah wanted to know.

"Thanks for the kind words, but I wasn't always so terrific. I thought I was pretty special when I was in college. I had to have more dates than anyone else, with all of the most popular guys. It wasn't until I began to realize that most of them wanted to be seen with me for the same reasons I wanted to be seen with them that I started thinking there must be something more to life. And then Jack was the one who proved that there was. Did I ever tell you about the little gifts we gave each other just before he left for Vietnam?"

She rose and went to the bookshelf where she retrieved a small volume of Robert Burns' poetry, opening it to the page where a single rose was pressed. She handed the book to Sarah and reached for her purse, pulling out the torn photo she kept with her at all times.

"I gave him a lighter inscribed with 'From each danger keep him free' on one side and 'Send me safe my somebody' on the other side. He left that rose on the seat of the car along with the photo. He kept the half with me in it," she finished.

Sarah's eyes clouded as she read the poem in the book, then gazed at the inscription on the back of the photo: "All my love until we're together again."

"It says it all, doesn't it?" she murmured.

"Would I be assuming too much if I said I get the impression that you haven't been able to let go of your 'past' with Paul, all appearances to the contrary?"

"I thought I could do it, Julie. I really did. I'm truly happy with John, but when Pete was so terribly wretched, I couldn't help myself. I told you about the time I was trying to communicate with Paul and saw him heading toward the light. I *know* he turned back toward me when I screamed at him and I feel sure that meant he didn't die – at least not then." She paused, at a loss as to how to tell Julie that John had accompanied her on still another excursion into the past and that he now believed in what he, too, had considered only fantasies or dreams.

It seemed so absurd as she tried to think of the words to tell the story that she quickly decided that some things were better not said. It was enough that John had accepted the apparent phenomena of reliving past lives, and to tell Julie would be to leave her open to judgment and possible censure. If it weren't for her devotion to Pete, she was sure she could move ahead with John. The memories of Paul would remain in a corner of her heart, but the message seemed clear. She and John were destined to live out whatever karma remained from the lives of Emile and Rosella and resolving residual karma with Paul would have to wait for a future life.

The temptation to seek more information about previous lives was no longer as appealing as it once had been. It could only bring on greater pain in the remembering. The knowledge lusted after by the mind was balanced by the ability of the heart to protect itself from abuse. The photo of Paul that she'd seen in the newspaper so long ago had triggered hidden memories that needed to be acknowledged, even cherished, but then tucked away where they could do no harm to the reality of this life.

Only Julie and Pete remained of the people who had formed such a hopeful alliance so many months, now years ago. As the war in Vietnam dragged on, becoming more and more unpopular as opposition turned into defiance, even the most stalwart of their supporters were falling away. Sarah was torn between her own need to leave it all behind and her devotion to those who had become her extended family. Julie and Pete – both so alone and vulnerable. Could they carry on? Was there some avenue unexplored, something they hadn't thought to do that would bring about the resolution they sought? Letters to congressmen and senators, petitions sent to the Paris peace talks, the never-ending search for some tiny scrap of information that might lead to reunion with loved ones – was it all in vain? Would Merrie be alive if her hope had not turned to despair?

What more could Sarah do to reverse the direction in which their quest seemed to be headed? Was it her fault from the beginning? If she hadn't phoned the Winslow's in the first place and then spearheaded the kickoff dinner, things might have been different. On the other hand, if she had ignored the instinct that drew her so compulsively to Paul Winslow, she would not have met John and she had to believe that fate was on her side.

CHAPTER THIRTY ONE

The window behind Sarah's desk afforded her a marginal view of the Bay Bridge beyond a hodgepodge of buildings that huddled together in downtown San Francisco. She had turned away from the heap of paperwork on her desk to gaze out, if only for a moment.

Artwork for the prospective brochures leaned against furniture and walls and demographic profiles of Davidson clients had been merged and expanded. The project was nearly ready for final approval.

Sarah could hear Ellen's voice on the phone making airline reservations for her trip to Chicago on Sunday. The presentation she would make would be one of her last assignments as Director of Public Relations. She had already told Michael that she would be getting married, but had not yet given notice of her intention to leave the company. It had taken several weeks to make the decisions that had to be made regarding the disposition of her apartment and furnishings and prepare some kind of timeline for the future. It looked like she would be able to leave San Francisco in another month or two.

She had spent as much time as possible with Pete and Julie. The three of them had become regular companions, spending many of their evenings and most of their weekends together. Pete was beginning to respond more positively, but was often silent for long periods of time, lost in his memories.

Sarah was certain that, evidence to the contrary, Sheila loved Pete as much as he loved her. They were simply unable to communicate that love. She knew that she was probably the last person Sheila would care to see, but she intended to make an attempt to pave the way toward reconciliation while she was in Chicago.

It was early evening when Sarah's plane landed at O'Hare Airport and she hailed a taxi to take her to the Davidson Chicagoan. Checking in, she noticed how similar in atmosphere it was to the New York property. Homey in an elegant sort of way, the lobby walls were wood paneled and the guests appeared to be comfortably sophisticated as they sat conversing or passed through the area. There was an air of stability about the Chicagoan that inspired a sense of permanency. As she waited for the elevator, Sarah watched some of the guests, visualizing them on the tennis courts in San Diego or dining on the waterfront in San Francisco. The picture seemed fairly compatible and she was reassured the new brochures would be effective in establishing an identification with all four Davidson Hotels.

It was not yet dark so she decided to go for a short walk. The hotel was located in a mostly residential neighborhood, surrounded by old brownstones and a few small apartment buildings. She strolled down Astor Street toward Division and then back up Michigan Avenue, looking into windows as lights began to go on in homes along the way. She knew that Sheila lived a short distance north of the hotel. Sarah had no idea what she might say when she phoned the girl later, but she hoped something might come to her as she walked.

Stopping in the cozy lobby bar as she re-entered the hotel, she ordered a drink and sat considering her dilemma. She was afraid that Sheila might simply hang up on her if she didn't say just the right thing to begin the conversation. Or she might be angry and have more choice words with which to tell off the woman she considered a rival for her father's affections. Well, I have to try, she said to herself, no matter what Sheila says. Pete needs her.

It wasn't until after the fourth ring that she heard Sheila's voice say dully, "Hello?"

"Sheila? This is Sarah Fremont. Please don't hang up. I'd really like to talk to you."

"What do you want? You're not going to tell me that something's happened to my father, are you?"

"No, he's all right now, but he suffered a great deal after you left, Sheila. He wouldn't answer the phone and he didn't leave the house for weeks. Would it be all right if I came over to see you? Or would you meet me somewhere so that we could talk?"

"Are you in Chicago?"

"Yes," Sarah replied, "I'm at the Davidson Chicagoan for a few days on business. Please Sheila, it's important that I talk to you."

"Okay," Sheila sighed, "come on over if you must. I guess you have the address."

"Yes, I do. I'll be there in half an hour. Is that all right?"

"The sooner you get here, the sooner you'll go away," Sheila said waspishly and hung up.

Sarah changed quickly into slacks and a sweater and went down to get a taxi. The doorman helped her out as the taxi pulled up in front of Sheila's building and held the glass door open for her, inquiring politely whom she wished to see and if she was expected. She gave him Sheila's name and was directed to the apartment.

The woman who opened the door bore almost no resemblance to the glamorous person Sarah remembered. Sheila's hair was dirty and disheveled and she wore a raggedy terrycloth robe.

"Well, if it isn't Goody Twoshoes," she sneered. "Come to tell me what a rotten daughter I am, did you?"

"No, Sheila, I came because I believe that Pete needs you more than you know, but he's hurt and angry and probably doesn't have any more of an idea what to say to you than I do."

Sheila stared at her for a moment, then crossed the room to turn off the television set that was tuned to the shipwrecked passengers of the 'Minnow' on Gilligan's Island. "Want a drink?" she asked, waving one arm at the ice bucket and scotch bottle that sat on the coffee table within easy reach of the sofa.

Sarah hesitated only a moment, then decided Sheila would resent her even more if she refused to be sociable. She picked up a glass from the tray and made herself a drink, commenting, "I'm glad you drink scotch. I guess we have that in common at least."

Sheila stood at the window, her back to Sarah. "Do you really think Daddy needs me?" she asked wistfully.

"I'm sure he does, Sheila. I'm not sure, however, why you're so antagonistic toward me. What is it that I've done to aggravate you so much? You don't really believe that either Pete or Merrie cared more for me than they did for you, do you?" Taking a breath, Sarah decided to plunge in all the way. "Could it be that you think you haven't lived up to their expectations?"

Sheila's shoulders began to shake as she began to cry. "I've never been able to do anything right," she gulped. "I've made a mess of two marriages and now even Dave has dumped me. Daddy threw me out of the house, so nobody wants me! Why doesn't anybody like me?"

Sarah knew then that she'd been right about Sheila's craving for love and approval. "Dave dumped you? Why?"

"It seems that I don't fit in anywhere. I'm too rich and too traditional for Dave and too unconventional for Daddy. I guess I'm alone in the world." Her voice trailed off as she cried even harder.

"You're not alone in the world, Sheila. Pete is just as miserable as you are. He loved his family more than anything and he can't understand why his wife died, his son is missing in Vietnam, and his daughter has so little respect for him that she would bring a man to her mother's funeral who is the antithesis of everything he stands for, everything he believes to be of value. Why did you bring Dave, Sheila?"

"I thought he loved me," Sheila sobbed, "and I thought maybe he could explain to Daddy why there's all the opposition to the war and make him see that if the Americans got out of Vietnam and stopped killing people over there, that the Vietnamese would let the prisoners go and Paul would come home. I thought if I did something that helped get Paul home, he'd love me again," she finished, sinking dejectedly to the floor.

"Oh, Sheila," Sarah said, shaking her head. She rose and crossed to where Sheila lay in a miserable little heap. "Come on, get up and come over to the sofa." She helped the girl to her feet and stood holding her, comforting her.

Sheila pulled away, crying, "You're so perfect! You're the daughter

Daddy wished he had. You're beautiful and talented and you're smart and you have a career. How can I compete with all that?"

"You don't have to compete with anyone, Sheila! I can't help what I am, but *you* are Pete's daughter. He loves *you*! He just never knew what to say to you. He was a man in a man's world and you were the most beautiful fragile thing he'd ever seen. Don't you understand that? He was afraid you'd break if he got too close. You should have heard him telling that to Julie and me!"

She whimpered. "Why didn't he tell me? He was always gone and when he was home he spent all his time with Paul. Paul was the one he wanted to be with, the one who understood him. I was just some poor excuse for a child, a bit of fluff to be petted once in awhile and dismissed."

"No, Sheila, you're wrong. Pete loved you, still loves you. But he thought of himself as a clumsy oaf who might hurt you, so he trusted Merrie to take care of you. Don't you see?"

"I just thought that if I could bring Paul back to him somehow that he'd love me. I botched things up again, didn't I?" she said pathetically.

Things weren't going at all the way Sarah had expected them to go. The glamorous, sure-of-herself woman who had been in San Francisco had vanished, replaced by an unhappy little girl who was trying desperately to please the adult who meant the most to her, the one whose respect she yearned to have. That worldly image she projects is all a sham, Sarah thought. She's really terribly naïve and covers it with sarcasm.

"Sheila," she said tentatively, "tell me more about Dave. How did you meet him?"

"I was downtown shopping and ran into an anti-war demonstration on Michigan Avenue when I tried to get a taxi. Dave pulled me out of the way just as I was about to get trampled. We got to talking and he wasn't like anyone I'd ever known. He was so smart and knew so much more than I ever have," Sheila explained. She began to cry again and reached for her drink, taking several gulps.

"I take it he tried to educate you to his way of thinking. How long had this been going on before you brought him to San Francisco?" Sarah asked curiously.

"About six months, I guess," Sheila estimated. "At first I went to his apartment near the University and then he started coming up here for dinner and I thought he really loved me. I thought if I learned more, he'd respect me and maybe he'd mellow a little, and then we'd get married and I could help him get promotions. I'm good at entertaining, you know," she said hopefully.

Oh God, she's worse than I thought, Sarah said to herself. How could anyone be so innocent after the life she's led? No wonder Quinn Donnelly got tired of her!

"How long ago did you break up with Dave?" she inquired.

"Right after we came back from San Francisco. He said he thought I needed time to get over Mother's death and that he'd be busy with final exams for his students. I tried to tell him how much I needed him. I even went down to the bratskellar where he and his friends hang out. When he came in, he told me to go home where I belonged," Sheila related, the tears beginning to fall again.

"That must have been several weeks ago, Sheila," Sarah exclaimed. "You mean you've been sitting around this apartment ever since, feeling sorry for yourself?"

"You'd feel sorry for yourself, too, if you'd been thrown out of your parents' home and the man you loved had dumped you!" Sheila screeched. "What am I supposed to do? I don't have to work and I probably couldn't get a job anyway. Most of the friends I used to have were people Quinn knew and they stopped calling me when I got involved with Dave, and besides, they never really liked me anyway, just sort of tolerated me, so here I am with nobody."

"Why don't you come back to San Francisco with me, Sheila? You may not believe it right now, but I'm sure your dad loves you and needs you as much as you need him. Maybe if you sit down and talk to him, tell him how you feel and try to understand how he feels, you can work it out together. You're sitting here in Chicago drinking yourself to death and Pete is sitting in San Francisco wishing he was with Merrie. Please, Sheila, you need each other!"

"What if Daddy doesn't want me there? And I don't have any friends there, either. At least here I have my own apartment and I know my way around," Sheila argued. She's secretly hoping I'll coax her into it, Sarah thought.

"Julie and I will be your friends, especially if you'll try to meet us halfway. And you can always come back to Chicago anytime you like. Come on, give it a try. You can't be any worse off than you are now, can you?"

"You'd be my friend? Why?"

"Well, I'll be your friend for awhile anyway. I'll be leaving San Francisco soon to marry John St. James and move to Paris. So you see, I'm not a threat to you at all," Sarah explained.

"Married?"

"Yes, Sheila, married. You couldn't really believe that your father and I are anything but friends, could you? Or that he'd really have any interest in replacing you in his heart? I think you're your own worst enemy."

"You really think Daddy wants to see me?" Sheila asked pitifully.

"I'm sure of it," Sarah replied, inwardly praying that this was true. She left Pete's daughter making lists of what had to be done before she could leave for the West Coast and returned to the hotel. Even if it didn't work out for some reason, neither Pete nor Sheila could be much worse off than they already were. Or was she playing God? Maybe Sheila had been right all along and she really was a Goody Twoshoes, intent upon making the world right for its inhabitants and maybe botching it royally. Well, it was done now and she'd just have to see it through.

CHAPTER THIRTY TWO

Sarah dressed carefully for her appointment with Michael Davidson the next morning, choosing a tailored, dark suit. As the elevator descended to the second floor executive offices, she went over a few of the key phrases she meant to use in her presentation of the project that had come to mean a lot to her since it was probably the single most important contribution she'd made in her corporate capacity.

"Sarah!" Michael boomed as she entered the office, "It's a pleasure to see you again."

She assured him that it was as much a pleasure to be there and sat down in the chair toward which he directed her.

"I want to thank you again for being so kind to Maggie in New York," he began. "You made quite an impression and I'm grateful."

"Thank you," Sarah murmured.

"My daughter is somewhat headstrong, Sarah, though I can't imagine where she got it from! She may have told you about the unhappy attachment she had to a young man who was totally unsuitable. Her mother and I hoped that meeting a young woman as bright and successful as you are might help her recover from it."

"I found her to be very charming, Mr. Davidson, and very mature for her age," Sarah told him.

"Yes, well I guess parents always think of their offspring as being children, not adults, no matter how old they are. You'll be interested to know that she's met a fine young man with a promising career in the banking industry. They haven't set a date yet, but the marriage will be taking place. Speaking of marriage, how are your wedding plans coming along?'

"We haven't set a date yet, either, Mr. Davidson," she told him, "but we hope to be married in about six weeks or so."

"John St. James, I believe his name is? Fine reputation in the hotel business, but in Europe, right?"

"Yes, his family owns several small hotels in most of the major cities there. John also does consulting work in this country for companies that are impressed with the growth of the St. James operation since the war and since John took over leadership of the company."

"Does this mean that you'll be leaving us to live in Europe when you marry, Sarah?'

She hesitated. The moment had come to make that final commitment. Telling Michael Davidson of her departure would mean no turning back. She took a deep breath and said firmly, "Yes, it does. Much as I hate to leave my position with your hotels, that is one thing I meant to discuss with you today. I'll stay on until you find my replacement, of course, and I have obligations to close friends in the Bay area that are important to me as well, but my estimated time is, as I said, about six weeks."

"I know you were deeply affected by the death of your friend when we had the sales meeting in San Francisco. Has time helped to heal your grief?"

"Some, but I feel a little as though I'm deserting the cause that we've all worked so hard on. The group has disintegrated so drastically what with Merrie's death and the violence that surrounds the anti-war sentiment. Are you familiar with the issue of prisoners and missing in Vietnam?"

Michael frowned. It wasn't something he gave much thought to as a busy executive. "I know about the peace talks," he said, "and that negotiating seems to revolve around release of prisoners based upon withdrawal of American troops."

"Yes, but it goes beyond that. The North Vietnamese signed the

Geneva Convention accords that agreed to allow a neutral agency such as the Red Cross to inspect their prison camps, and also to allow the prisoners to receive and send mail, not to mention a full accounting of prisoners held. So far they haven't lived up to any of those conditions. The woman who died, Merrie, was the mother of a missing man and I've become very close to the family over the past couple of years. That's why I've had a hard time accepting her death and why I feel so committed to what's left of her family."

"Well I hope you can put things in perspective, Sarah. After all, your own marriage and your own family are the most important things." Michael Davidson was becoming clearly uncomfortable with the subject of Vietnam, a subject that had little relevance in his world, other than as a political issue to be digested with the rest of the evening news. His company was his family, his hotels his children, and his children were responsible for maintaining the family structure he'd created.

A perfunctory knock, followed immediately by the entrance of Allison Jennings and Buzz Craddock, saved him from further discussion of the matter. "I hope you don't mind if Buzz and Allison sit in on this meeting, Sarah. They'll be consulted on the project anyway and I value their opinions," he said, dismissing the possibility of any disagreement.

"Of course not. I've brought copies for just that reason."

A couple of days later, Sheila joined Sarah at the airport for the flight to San Francisco. They had decided that Sheila would stay at Sarah's apartment initially, approaching Pete gently rather than telling him in advance that Sheila was coming.

Sheila was extraordinarily quiet as she huddled in her seat next to the window. She was recalling the last flight she'd made to San Francisco with Dave Marshall beside her. Sarah pretended not to notice the sidelong glances, knowing that her feelings remained slightly ambivalent. In Sheila's mind, Sarah was still a goody-two-shoes, an impression probably confirmed in recent days. She wanted desperately to believe that Sarah was right and that her father really did love her in spite of her inadequacies, though she was still unsure of exactly what those might be. Her spirits alternately soared, then sank.

Sarah's car was in the parking lot at the San Francisco Davidson Hotel and the courtesy van picked them up in front of the baggage claim area. Sheila grew more nervous as they drove down the freeway, passing the area where the Winslow home was located. Sarah left her to unpack in the guestroom and went to the phone to call Pete.

"Hi, Sarah! Back from your trip to Chicago?" He said cheerfully in response to her voice.

"Just got home. Pete, could I stop by for a few minutes? I'd like to talk to you, but not on the phone."

"Sure, come on over. I was just about to fix the martinis anyway and I can't think of anyone I'd rather share one with than you!"

A few minutes later, she was ringing his doorbell. Pete embraced her warmly and ushered her into the living room where the pitcher was waiting. He had filled out a little and looked much healthier than he had when she and Julie had forced their way into his home.

"Something special on your mind?" he asked when they were comfortably settled in the living room.

"As a matter of fact, there is something important I want to talk to you about. I saw Sheila in Chicago, Pete. She's a very unhappy person. Dave Marshall dumped her right after they got back from here. She thinks nobody cares if she lives or dies. She says she's too rich and traditional for Dave and too unconventional for you."

Pete turned his head away, staring up at the ceiling for a moment before he said, "Poor little Sheila. She was so beautiful. She should have led a storybook life."

"Have you forgiven her yet?'

"I don't know. I think of her as she was before she married Bob Koslowsky, when she was a happy-go-lucky teenager, and my heart melts. Then I remember the things she said that day after the memorial service and I don't know if I can ever forgive her. If I thought she had changed or wanted to change, I'd give anything to hold her in my arms and make everything 'all better' as we used to say when one of the kids got hurt."

"She needs you, Pete, even more than you need her. Why don't you phone her?" Sarah suggested.

"You don't think she'd subject me to more bad temper and foul language?" Pete was skeptical. He hesitated, then said, "Oh, okay, I'll call her tonight."

Sarah smiled broadly. "Would you rather see her, Pete? I brought her back with me. She's at my house right now."

"The hell you say," Pete exclaimed. "Took quite a chance, didn't you? What if I'd refused to have anything to do with her?"

"I know you, Pete, and I can't believe that you'd turn your back on Sheila, especially when she's so miserable," Sarah said gently.

It took only a few minutes to go back and get Sheila, who was trembling as she approached the front door of her father's home. Dressed in a soft pink cashmere skirt and sweater, her hair loose around her face, she looked for all the world like the little girl her father remembered.

Pete had been watching for them and opened the door before they had a chance to ring the bell. He stood for a moment, taking in the sight of his child, vulnerable and afraid, and opened his arms to her. Sheila fell into them, crying, "Oh, Daddy, I'm so sorry!"

Sarah stayed back a few steps, waiting. Pete turned to lead Sheila into the house, nearly forgetting that Sarah was there. He motioned for her to follow them, but she shook her head, silently urging him to go on in with Sheila. Returning to her car, she said a tiny prayer to no one in particular, asking that everything work out well for them.

A heavy mist obscured most of the buildings in the compound that was hidden among the trees on a rugged mountain. Silent monks slid quietly through the dawn, moving as they had for centuries, indistinguishable from those who had gone before them to early morning worship. Summoned from their cells by the slow, mournful vibrations of the bronze temple bowls struck with padded mallets by an unseen hand, the saffron clad monks drifted into the sanctuary to begin their meditation.

Paul had grown accustomed to the sounds that had seemed so strange at first, often failing to take notice of them as they became a familiar part of his existence. He now wore the same type of robes as the monks, there being no other choice of apparel, and had taken to joining them in meditation. The stillness in the temple was reassuring, as was the simplicity of life within the compound.

Fever and delirium were still occasional companions and time had ceased to have meaning. During lucid periods, he sometimes tried to distinguish between what he thought were memories of people he'd known before his arrival at the monastery, and the fleeting impressions he was sure must be fantasies caused by the delirium. As visions swam before him, however, separating dreams from reality lost its importance.

The soulful cry of a hand carved woodwind instrument carried across the courtyard to where he sat in the sun. He was cold and that meant the fever was probably coming back. There didn't seem to be any way to avoid it and he had learned that it was best to lie down on the cot in his cell before the fire that burned relentlessly in his body rendered him incoherent. Blankets were left there at all times in anticipation of the relapses and the monks checked on him, spooning liquid into his mouth and sponging his head when it happened. They seemed to know without being told when illness overcame his ability to function.

He trudged slowly toward the line of doors across from the temple that led to individual eight- by ten-foot cells occupied by the residents of the monastery, entering the one on the end that had been assigned to him. The cot, one straight chair and a small table were its only furnishings. There was water in a pitcher on the table. He splashed a little on his face before lying down to await the onset of the chills and shaking that preceded temporary oblivion.

As he slipped into the void, he was suddenly surrounded by a cocoon of rich colors that undulated like waves on a gusty sea, billowing and plunging, tossed by an unseen zephyr. A hand appeared from behind a blaze of emerald cloth, the fingers reaching out, caressing the folds. A Junoesque leg kicked a golden beam of light toward an indigo moon. An enchanting mouth blew purple bubbles into a field of riotous blooms. The features merged and separated, floating just beyond his reach.

A train whistled, signaling imminent departure as steam rose from beneath its wheels, dissolving the panorama of color. A sharp sound startled the passengers boarding nearby cars and Paul felt himself falling. He clutched his chest, his arm extended toward the woman whose voice was calling to him from far away, "Lucien!"

He crawled the last few feet toward her, grasping her hand as her head fell, twisting unnaturally as blood stained her blouse and she whispered his name one last time, "Paul..."

He awoke bathed in sweat in his tiny cubicle, the fever broken. The room was stifling. He had to get outside for fresh air. Rising with difficulty, he staggered out, taking great gulps of cool air, then sank to the ground exhausted. He had no idea how long he'd been lying there when he regained consciousness. It was very dark, the candles used for light by the monks long since extinguished.

Paul picked himself up from the ground and walked slowly into the night. He had no destination in mind, only the desire to feel the cool breezes that ruffled his hair as he moved. Reaching the edge of the compound, he bumped into a tree, alarming small birds that snoozed in its branches. Their wings whirred above him as they took flight.

Flying, he thought. I remember flying. He looked from side to side, visualizing the wings of a plane. Stretching both arms out, he began to run. If only he could soar away into the clouds, he knew he'd remember who he was and where he belonged.

In the darkness, he failed to see the edge of the cliff and shouted in exaltation as he felt his feet leave the ground, sure in the madness of his mind that he was flying.

CHAPTER THIRTY THREE

The euphoria that resulted from bringing Pete and Sheila back together was brief. The threesome of Pete, Julie and Sarah, had now become a foursome as Sheila joined them on the less frequent petition drives and took over as hostess in her father's home.

Darkness fell before the workday had finished and winter fog greeted early risers in the morning. It was taking longer than anticipated for Sarah to wind up her affairs in San Francisco and make the move to Paris. Though she was surrounded by people who respected her at the office and by people who loved her in her personal life, she was lonely. She longed to be with John and yet was reluctant to leave the odd little family that had become such an important part of her life.

The Christmas season was approaching and though he admitted to some impatience, John had agreed that she should spend the holidays with her friends. The wedding was planned for early spring, with a honeymoon on the Mediterranean coast in April. She had begun packing some of the things that would be shipped ahead to France. On one dreary evening, she sat surrounded by piles of books, organizing them by category into boxes. Each volume housed old friends and she was unable to resist the urge to peruse the pages, visiting those who resided among them.

Picking up a small, leather bound book of the Rubaiyat, she ran her fingers over the gold script on the cover and opened it to the inscription on the flyleaf. 'To Bill, with all my love, Suzanne.' Given to her father by her mother, the little book must have been very old even then. There were passages marked with comments. At the bottom of a page midway through the book, Sarah read:

"We are no other than a moving row
Of Magic Shadow-shapes that come and go
Round with the Sun-illumined Lantern held
In midnight by the Master of the Show;

"But helpless Pieces of the Game He plays
Upon this Chequer-board of Nights and Days'
Hither and thither moves, and checks, and slays,
And one by one back in the Closet lays."

Turning ahead a few pages, she continued reading:
"Ah Love! Could you and I with Him conspire
To grasp this sorry Scheme of Things entire,
Would not we shatter it to bits and then
Re-mould it nearer to the Heart's Desire!"

Lines written more than a thousand years before and yet so appropriate for generations throughout eternity. We are only shadow shapes, helpless pieces, moved from place to place, and then laid to rest on a dusty shelf. And if we could, who among us would not take the opportunity to rearrange the playing field?

We delude ourselves into believing in our own importance and yet the time we spend incarnated is but a moment. Our rational minds know this and yet the passions that fuel the engines of our existence lead us blindly down inevitable pathways, thrashing all the way. How easy it should be to let life happen instead of orchestrating every episode into a medley of disorder.

Leaning back against the base of the sofa, Sarah paused to ponder. Her future was assured, exciting, but safe, free to soar if she chose, sure of shelter in the arms of a man whose love she did not doubt. Could she do it? Could she let life happen, leave the past behind? The answer had to be yes.

She rubbed the copper bracelet on her arm absentmindedly. Paul's face was already fading like the memory of a long ago prom night. Even the song she had come to think of as theirs failed to agitate her anymore. She hummed a little of it, then sang a few lines: "for this time it isn't fascination, or a dream that will fade and fall apart." No more dreams, no more fascination. She sighed, tucked the Rubaiyat into a box and picked up another volume, Kahlil Gibran's 'The Madman.'

"My friend, I am not what I seem. Seeming is
but a garment I wear – a care-woven garment that
protects me from thy questionings and thee from
my negligence."

Ah, yes. Are we ever what we seem to be? Reflecting, she thought, I used to be what I seemed. What you saw was what you got. But what was it that you got? The Sarah that used to be was just going through the motions – she did the right thing at the right time without much thought to alternatives. She had gone off to college, dated, partied a lot, learned a little, graduated and come to San Francisco to look for a job that would earn money and allow her to continue in much the same fashion in which she had lived life up to that point. And though she had never been unhappy in her job, she had continued to live the only lifestyle she knew, the lifestyle pre-approved for her. Until the night she saw Paul's picture in the paper. It was then that something deep inside began to gnaw its way out, leaving wounds that were hidden from view.

Words formed poetry in her head, her own poetry. If she wrote them down perhaps the wounds could be purged from her body, a catharsis begun. She wrote quickly as the words tumbled over each other, scurrying to join the others on the page.

"There are wounds that hide so far
Down inside that they cannot be shared.
There is a hole deep inside my being
Like a cave, where my wounds hide
To be alone.

"Did I know him in another life?
Do I see him now in this one?
Does he call my name?
But what name does he call?

"Do our paths cross more than once,
Or not at all?
I want to die to know him.
I want to live to love him.

"Is he speaking to me now?
I think he must, for the words
Come too quickly, unbidden,
To the page.

"Ah, he is gone, but not gone.
He lives in that cave that
Is my heart.
He cannot die, I cannot live…"

Sarah stared at the page for a few moments, then folded it carefully and put it between the pages of 'The Madman,' adding it to the box on the floor. The pile of cartons in the hall was getting higher each week. How had she accumulated so much stuff, she asked herself.

Turning to the large envelope that had come just a few days ago from John, she pulled out the photographs and floor plans of apartments he had looked at as possible homes for them. At first glance, they had seemed awfully large for just two people, but perhaps he knew her better than she knew herself. He had urged her to make a trip over to choose her favorite, but since she trusted his judgement, she had said she'd review the photos and plans and give him an opinion, leaving the final decision to him.

The one that appealed to her the most was in a large, square building that had a look of permanence. The rooms appeared to be spacious, with plenty of light and suited to her traditional taste. Spreading the pictures out on the table, she mentally placed her furnishings, books, and artwork in the ample spaces. The cabbage rose chintz sofa against that wall, the piano over here, the floral painting above the fireplace with the newly acquired statue of Kuan Yin on the mantle. It would be lovely. She smiled and let herself anticipate inhabiting her new home.

Christmas Day was pleasant, spent with Pete and Sheila, and then with Julie who came later following another tense day at her parents' home in Marin. Sheila was still eager to please Pete, but her jealousy had abated as she gained confidence and began to rejoice in the knowledge that her father really did care about her. She even accepted Sarah's offer to help in the kitchen and the two of them enjoyed a careful camaraderie to Pete's great pleasure.

Conversation had turned cautiously to the continuing peace talks in Paris. Henry Kissinger had announced in October that he believed peace was at hand, and the world watched hopefully as private meetings between Kissinger and North Vietnamese negotiator Le Duc Tho went on. Both sides accused the other of failure to keep promises and made changes in their demands, but the one consistency in U.S. requirements remained the return of prisoners of war prior to withdrawal of U.S. personnel.

With the announcement that bombing of the North would cease, the talks proceeded in earnest and a cease-fire was initiated by both sides on January 23rd. Four days later, the agreement was officially signed and final arrangements for an exchange of prisoners began.

Following the news eagerly, each member of Sarah's little family reacted differently. Pete's thoughts centered around the possibility that his son might turn up as a prisoner, but the joy he felt was dulled by the knowledge that it would come too late to save his beloved Merrie.

Sheila's feelings were mixed. Just as she was beginning to feel secure in her father's love, that security was threatened by the possible return of the son who had been the center of Pete's attention, the boy she had envied all her life. That she secretly, deep down inside, harbored a tiny hope that Paul's name would not appear on the list of prisoners to be returned made her physically ill with guilt.

She had lost so much time. In the mistaken belief that her association with Dave Marshall and his friends might do something to help end the war in Vietnam, she had given her heart to another man who ultimately rejected her. It seemed she was doomed to rejection, by her father, by two husbands, by a lover. Just when life seemed brighter than it ever had, she was threatened once again with rejection. She knew that these feelings were worse than unworthy, but try as she might, she was unable to stop the gnawing fear that made her stomach churn.

Julie made a tentative phone call to the casualty assistance officer assigned to her by the Marine Corps as an information liaison, but was told that though Jack was now officially listed as a prisoner of war, they did not have adequate knowledge to confirm that he would be coming home. She was urged to be patient a little longer and told that as soon as there was anything to report, they'd be in touch with her. She began to sleep with the television on in case of special bulletins. She raced to get the newspaper each morning and jumped every time the phone rang.

Sarah's moods were mercurial. One day she was exhilarated by the thought that Paul Winslow might soon be coming home, the next she was appalled at the thought, though for entirely different reasons than Sheila's. What if the previous lives she was so sure were realities, the out-of-body experiences of having been with him, were only her imagination? What if he did come home and had no interest in her? What about John? If Paul came home and *did* know her, would she choose him over John? If Paul came home and *didn't* know her, would John laugh at her? Even scorn her?

Then she recalled her conviction that Paul had escaped from the Vietnamese prison camp. If he was not being held, he couldn't be returned. And since the journey into the past of Rosella, Lucien and Emile with John, she'd felt in her heart that Paul no longer lived. Had he died when she committed her future to John, the man who had been Emile in that previous life? Was she responsible for his death? Was she being completely ridiculous, really losing her mind? At times she was convinced of it.

CHAPTER THIRTY FOUR

Julie stood beside the wall phone in her kitchen, her knees trembling. Her assistance officer had just told her that Jack's name had appeared on the lists received from the North Vietnamese as being held captive and that his return was anticipated through Clark Field in the Philippines to Travis Air Force Base in California. The officer was unable to give her details, but he suggested that she be prepared to head for Travis in the near future.

Now that the moment had arrived and seeing Jack again was nearly a reality, she was at a loss as to what to do next. Should she tell Sandy that her father would be coming home? The little girl didn't even know her father. She had seen pictures of him, wedding photos and some from the early days of their marriage, but Julie knew that Sandy thought of him as incidental to her life. Only four years old, Sandy was closer to her grandfather than any other adult male, though Julie had overheard her tell a little friend that her daddy was far away and couldn't come home. That explanation had seemed to satisfy the curiosity of a pre-schooler, but Julie had wondered at the time how long it would be before she might be asked for something more.

She decided to put off phoning her parents and dialed Sarah's number. She had to share the news with someone. Sarah was elated and said she'd leave the office at once, refusing to hear Julie's protest that it wasn't necessary.

"Julie," she said firmly, "what have we been doing for the past three years? This is the realization of our dreams, isn't it? If you haven't anything better to do, how about spending a little time talking about the good news for a change. I'll be there before you know it."

Thirty minutes later they were hugging each other joyfully, both talking at once, then laughing as they shared the moment. Sarah had considered bringing champagne, then decided against it when it occurred to her that Julie might not want to jinx the future by celebrating prematurely. Besides, they had begun a previous celebration with champagne – one that had ended so disastrously.

"Tell me!" she exclaimed. "Has Jack actually been released or has anyone, American that is, actually seen him?"

"Oh, Sarah, I don't know what to think. Captain Millikin, my casualty assistance officer, phoned and all he knew was that Jack's name is on the list of prisoners. He said everything was still very much up in the air, but that the first lists they'd been given showed that Jack was to be released."

"When will they know for sure what's happening?" Sarah asked.

"I guess it's probably something like it would be if the Americans had lists of Vietnamese names. They're so 'foreign' that it's hard to tell whether they're accurate or not and don't forget, we've had different stories and changes in demands all along," Julie replied, her frustration apparent.

"How do you feel about it? And have you told Sandy anything yet?'

"I don't know what to tell Sandy," Julie said thoughtfully. "To her, her father is only a photograph on the shelf. I don't want to raise her hopes too much until I'm sure. Captain Millikin said that the lists were due to be published in the newspapers either tonight or tomorrow, but that I shouldn't consider anything as gospel until it was confirmed by his office."

"Have you talked to Pete? Has he heard anything about Paul?" Sarah was torn between hope that Pete's news would be good and the conviction that Paul's name would not appear on the lists.

"I haven't talked to either Pete or Sheila since yesterday. Why don't we call them? I'm sure they'd want to know about Jack." She reached for the phone on her desk, dialing the number quickly. Sheila answered on the first ring.

"Hi, Sheila. It's Julie. Have you heard anything yet?"

"Dad's been on the phone to everyone he could think of to get information, but nobody seems to be able to tell us anything," Sheila replied. "Just a second, here he comes."

Pete's voice was harsh when he came on the line. "Hello?"

"Pete, it's Julie. Sheila tells me you haven't heard anything yet, but I have some news for you." She went on to tell him of the call from Captain Millikin.

Sarah crossed the room to a window and stood staring out, rubbing the bracelet on her arm that carried Paul Winslow's name. Strange thing about the bracelet, she thought. It's almost as though it's a little part of him somehow. She wondered if everyone who wore a POW/MIA bracelet felt the same way about the man whose name appeared on it. The promise to wear it until the man came home or was accounted for was about to be fulfilled for many who wore one. How many would not come home? How many would never be found?

Pete, of course, was overjoyed at the news that Julie's husband was listed as one of the men to come home soon and Julie herself had stories of happy times, full of promise, to relate as she and Sarah talked during the afternoon. The sound of a thud as the evening newspaper hit the steps outside startled them both. They froze for an instant, knowing that the pages of the paper might contain the first lists of American prisoners. They rose simultaneously and headed for the door.

"TREATY SIGNED, CEASE FIRE IN EFFECT"

Under photographs of U.S. Secretary of State William Rogers and Foreign Minister Nguyen Duy Trinh of North Vietnam signing the agreements, a smaller headline read, "First POW Names Released by Pentagon." Both women caught their breath in anticipation. Too impatient to wait, they spread the paper out on the floor, kneeling in front of it as they turned the pages to find the first of the lists. It was divided by branch of service, then alphabetically.

Sarah's eyes race down the Navy list searching for Paul's name as Julie scanned the list of Marines.

"Jack's name isn't here," she cried.

"Look under Navy, maybe it got mixed up," Sarah urged, running her finger down the Army list, then the Air Force list, finding nothing.

"No," Julie said, sitting back, "it just isn't on here anywhere."

Another column read, "Civilian Prisoners Alive, Dead Listed," and still another carried the heading, "Reds List 56 Who Died." Neither Jack Schaefer nor Paul Winslow were on any of the lists.

"There has to be a mistake somewhere," Julie said. "The papers must have been given lists that hadn't been checked," she surmised. Pursing her lips, she looked toward the phone, then got up and went to it. "I'm going to call Captain Millikin. He should know more by now."

The information was still vague and unsatisfactory. All that the Assistance Officer could say was that the list he had carried Jack's name on it. "Try to be patient just a little longer," he said sympathetically.

Phones began to buzz as other family members found the names of their loved ones on the list, but seemed unable to verify the information. Still unwilling to trust the Vietnamese and afraid to let themselves believe in the safe return of loved ones, families kept rejoicing to a minimum though their hearts were in danger of bursting from their chests as hope increased.

"The next person who tells me to be patient a little longer just might get a knife through the heart," Julie said.

The next few days were a blur of television reports, newspaper reports and conflicting phone calls, all endured through alternate moods of jubilance and despair. Defense Secretary Elliot Richardson predicted that the shaky cease-fire would evolve into a stable situation. Newsmen would be barred from the exchange of prisoners lest hostile statements or bitterness on the part of returnees endanger those left behind. POW organizations called the lists tragically small. Attacks by Viet Cong troops continued on small hamlets in the south.

Sarah spent some of her time with Julie and some with Pete and Sheila, but though they kept in touch by phone, the four of them were not together at any time. Pete didn't want to spoil Julie's happiness and was afraid that she might be inhibited by the fact that Paul's name had failed to appear on any of the lists, official or unofficial. Julie, on the other hand, was torn by her own doubts and hope for the safe return of both men.

In conversation, Julie expressed her concern that Jack might be desperately ill or injured or that he might be psychologically damaged by his experience as a prisoner. There were times when she didn't know whether to laugh or cry, to shout from the rooftop or hide from what might become a terrible truth.

Reporters began to call when Jack Schaefer's name finally appeared on one of the published lists. They were easier for Julie to deal with than her mother was.

Most of them were happy for her, in contrast to the dire predictions voiced by Mrs. Summerhill.

"Julia," she had said, "your father and I want you to know that we'll stand beside you if Jack is mentally incompetent or too badly deformed. You are too young to waste your life on a man who may be nothing more than a vegetable."

Doing her best to keep her voice level, Julie had responded, "You don't seem to understand, Mother, that Jack is the man I love more than life itself, the father of my beautiful child, your grandchild. I have no intention of abandoning him no matter what his physical or mental condition might be."

"Julia, dear," her mother had continued, "I'm sure that Jack will be given the best care by a veteran's hospital. And surely he'd want you to get on with your life if he comes home at all."

In recounting the conversation to Sarah, Julie had said, "I told her I couldn't discuss it with her, that she would never understand and that we would never agree, and that I thought it would be best if we didn't communicate for awhile. Then I hung up on her. How can anyone be so insensitive? *If* he comes home? She has no comprehension whatsoever of how I feel! She's more concerned that I might show up at one of her cocktail parties with a man who drools!"

"Forget her, Julie," Sarah advised. "Concentrate on how it will feel to have Jack hold you in his arms, how it will feel to hold him in your arms."

On Saturday, February 10th, the front page of the paper carried a picture of a red carpet being laid out at the airfield at Clark Air Force Base in the Philippines. The former prisoners of war would walk on it from the hospital planes to waiting ambulances, on their way to freedom. The hospital corridors at Clark had been decorated with posters by school children, welcoming the men home.

Communist propaganda continued, however, as Hanoi reported that there was 'Joy at the Hilton Hotel.' A press release quoted one American as having asked them to sympathize with him, indicating that once he was freed he would be required to say what the American government directed him to say, the implication being that he might be forced to falsely condemn his captors.

Finally, on Sunday, February 11th, the first planeload of prisoners arrived in the Philippines. Sarah spent the evening with Julie, watching the television coverage. One by one, the men stepped from the plane. As each appeared in the doorway from the cabin, Julie searched their faces, hoping to see Jack's. Sarah prayed silently that Paul might miraculously deplane, but didn't really expect that miracle.

CHAPTER THIRTY FIVE

ost of the first group to arrive were Air Force officers. Only forty-two were Navy men and a mere four were Marines. As the last of them deplaned, it was clear that neither Jack nor Paul was among them. Captain Millikin phoned to reassure Julie that she must try to remain patient – at which she strangled the receiver – that Jack would be coming soon.

The first Air Force C-141 transport carrying twenty of the prisoners from Clark to Travis Air Force Base in California was met by a crowd of 5,000 well wishers, many carrying welcoming signs. Tears streamed down the faces of most who watched as wives and mothers ran toward loved ones. Many of the men were carrying heart shaped boxes of candy, purchased during a shopping spree at Clark.

Welcoming ceremonies came to a temporary halt as an Air Force captain waved away a wheel chair and made his way slowly down the ramp from the plane and across the tarmac on crutches. Pausing in front of the two generals who waited to receive him, he tucked one crutch under his arm and saluted each of them individually before continuing on to the reception area. A young woman wearing a mini skirt hugged another serviceman, then presented him with the POW bracelet bearing his name that she had worn for several years.

Sarah rubbed the bracelet on her wrist in silence and thought again of how many names were on other bracelets and how many of those men would not be coming home. The joy she felt for those families who were being reunited mingled with the pain that made her heart heavy as she waited with Julie.

Sarah's last day at the office had finally arrived. There had been a great deal of juggling done to put another person in her place as Director of Public Relations. The project on which she'd been working, that of coordinating the image of the four Davidson Hotels, had been completed and new brochures were in place at each property. The first of the sales reports had been encouraging as clients from the individual hotels formed loyalties that extended to the others in the company. San Diego reported increased business from the East Coast and Chicago was hosting business meetings that were extensions of San Francisco business.

Michael Davidson had decided that the public relations operation should be moved to the corporate office since Sarah would be replaced by Allison Jennings, who was already there and had been working closely with him for years. The downtown San Francisco office was to be closed since it had been an experimental concept designed to bring the two West Coast hotels into closer contact with Chicago and New York, as well as to accommodate Sarah herself. Ellen would take care of last minute details before returning to Van Carducci's office on the Peninsula.

Since Sarah's attention had been focused on the returning POW's, any thought of a farewell celebration had been postponed until a time just prior to her departure for France. On this last day, she had decided to do some shopping at Union Square stores and walk a bit in the area. It might well be her last chance to stroll down the streets that were so familiar and she would be sorry to say goodbye.

There was s small Scottish shop a few blocks up Geary Street that she wanted to visit, hoping to pick up some fabric for a wool skirt. As she headed toward Van Ness, she paused often to window shop.

The mellow sounds of a piano and saxophone tuning up in

preparation for the evening's entertainment drew her to the entrance of a jazz club to listen. It was still too early for the nighttime crowd and only a few patrons sat at the bar in the dimly lit establishment. Impulsively, she went in and took a seat near one end of the bar.

She watched as the piano player spoke into a microphone, testing the sound system, and the percussionist adjusted dials on a console behind him. A third man carrying a saxophone crossed leisurely to the stage and sat down, his feet casually stretched out in front of him. He blew into the horn to clear it of obstruction, then absently played a few notes. Sarah listened as the notes wove their way through an introductory passage, then became a tune. She hummed along, then sang the words softly.

"When I fall in love, it will be forever, or I'll never fall in love." She smiled at the thought. It certainly did seem that she'd fallen in love forever. There could be many more lifetimes ahead with the same two men and there may have been many more in the past that she would not remember.

She was startled back to reality as she heard a voice say, "Sing louder!" Looking around, she discovered it was the man at the piano and he was talking to her. She stopped singing, embarrassed, then mouthed the word, "Me?"

"Come up and do it with the mike," he urged.

She protested, shaking her head, then slid off the barstool and made her way to the stage as the bartender and the few patrons encouraged her. Handing her the traveling microphone, the pianist adjusted the key to suit her voice. She began hesitantly.

As the words to the song came back to her, she thought what the hell and sang out, grinning at the applause that followed. A camaraderie developed as the group played one song after another for her to sing.

"Hey, you're okay!" exclaimed the drummer. She laughed, accepting their praise along with a complimentary drink when she returned to her seat at the bar.

The musicians began talking among themselves, discussing a tune that they wanted to rehearse before the evening sets. Explaining briefly that it was just something they were writing for their own enjoyment, the man at the piano picked up a triangle and struck it gently, slowly, like a call to worship in an ancient temple. The drummer joined in with single beats on the bass drum, alternating with the triangle. The stringed bass played a mournful accompaniment as the three instruments combined in what resembled a Buddhist chant.

Mesmerized, Sarah closed her eyes and began to sway from side to side. The music developed slowly, increasing in volume, rising to a crescendo as the drummer switched to bongos, joined by a flute. Gradually, the strange tune faded as the instruments ceased playing one by one until only the tinkle of the triangle was heard as it had been in the beginning.

As the melancholy music drew everyone into its spell, for one tiny moment there was no sound in the room. The stage was still in semi-darkness since the musicians were only rehearsing and not yet playing for the audience that would come later. Wisps of smoke from cigarettes skimmed the edges of the luminous glow from the one spotlight that shone on the small stage, creating shadows that undulated sensuously. Suspended for that instant, the room became a faraway temple and Sarah suddenly knew with absolute certainty that fate had drawn her to this place. It was intended to be final evidence that Paul Winslow no longer lived.

The sadness that filled her heart also served to liberate her spirit. She was free to put the suffering behind her and allow herself to anticipate joy and gladness once again. She could move forward without fear.

Sliding from the barstool, she waved farewell to the musicians, nodding her thanks as they called out invitations for her to return anytime to sing with them. The air outside was crisp and cold. She filled her lungs gratefully, eager to be on her way home.

CHAPTER THIRTY SIX

For the first time in her life, Sheila Donnelly was eager to bring in the morning newspaper. It was rare, however, that she got to the front door before her father did. The peace between them was strained as each scanned the headlines for the latest information about the uneasy truce in Vietnam. Pete had retreated into the private world in which he had lived for so long, analyzing the articles that appeared in an effort to sort out the discrepancies between what the media reported and what was to be gleaned between the lines.

Sheila found it difficult to concentrate on the intricacies that were reported in the negotiations. As the first phase of Operation Homecoming came to an end, she was startled to see a short article on Henry Kissinger's visit to Beijing following his departure from Saigon. Apparently, he had met with Chairman Mao as well as Chou En Lai in discussions that were not specific in nature. She wished that she could hear what Dave Marshall and his friends must be saying about the significance of such meetings. She also wished that she knew the proper questions to ask if she were to discuss it with her father, but was careful to say little, knowing that the wrong words could jeopardize her newly developed relationship with Pete. She longed for someone with whom she could develop a dialogue that would help her understand what was happening. She wondered if Sarah Fremont would help her and weighed the consequences of allowing her vulnerability to become apparent.

Another twenty prisoners were released as a gesture of good will on the part of the North Vietnamese and the American government asked the communists to free the next group as soon as possible. No one seemed to know exactly who would be on the next lists, as the Vietnamese were maddeningly indefinite. Sheila was further confused by the first news conference held by returned prisoners in which they claimed that Americans who had visited Hanoi had shamed the nation in the eyes of the enemy. She'd thought that the visit by an American actress and a general had been a gesture of goodwill, an effort to end the war. She began to think that perhaps her father was right after all and that Dave had been a misguided rebel.

In an effort to please Pete, Sheila pored over cookbooks, shopped for the requirements in recipes and spent hours in the kitchen preparing special menus. Pete's mind was not on food, however, and he failed to take note of Sheila's endeavors. On the third evening of such labor, Sheila was thoroughly disheartened by her father's lack of response.

"Don't you like chicken cacciatore, Daddy?" she asked timidly. "I've never made it before, but I think I followed the recipe pretty well."

"What?" Pete responded absentmindedly, "Oh, the chicken? It's fine, dear, just fine."

Sheila couldn't stop the tears. Pete looked at her distractedly, a vague smile on his face, then noticed the tears that were making little trails down her cheeks. "Sheila!" he exclaimed. "What's wrong?"

"I just wanted to please you, Daddy. I tried to fix dinners that you'd like, but I guess I can't do that right either," she snuffled.

"Your dinners have been wonderful, Sheila. Why would you think I didn't like them?" Pete was baffled.

"I've made so many mistakes and there's so many things I don't understand and I know you want Paul to come home, but I want to learn, Daddy. If you could just teach me to do what you want me to do, I'll try, really I'll try!" Sheila's breath was coming in little gasps between phrases as she begged her father to tell her what to do to earn his love.

"Oh Sheila," Pete said, his head sinking into his hands. "I've done it again, haven't I? I've been so preoccupied with the possibility that

Paul's name might be on a list somewhere that I've neglected you badly." Putting his napkin on the table beside his plate, he rose and went to her, pulling her to her feet and enveloping her in a bear hug.

She clung to him, sobbing. Pete experienced a momentary twinge of the old helplessness until he realized that it was up to him to find the right words to tell her how much she meant to him and beyond that, he must build a firm foundation for the relationship before it was too late. Temporarily abandoning the chicken cacciatore, he led her to the sofa and sat stroking her hair until the sobs had subsided.

He began to talk to her, telling her once again of his feelings of inadequacy as she grew up, but going on to admit that he knew now that he should have shared more of himself with her in recent weeks as hope began to glimmer for Paul's survival. He explained that his preoccupation with the effort to find out as much as he could from whatever sources he could would have been equally as intense if it had been Sheila who had been missing instead of her brother.

"It isn't that I love you any less than I love Paul. It's just that you're here safe with me and Paul isn't. If you were the one who was in danger, my efforts to find you might be even more frantic, Sheila. The thought of anyone harming my little girl would turn me into a crazy man," he said, shuddering involuntarily.

Sheila finally started to see things in a different light as it struck her that her father was telling her the truth. She had believed that it was her failure as a person that made her undeserving of Pete's love. Her attempts to please him had been unnecessary.

As they talked, they shared little memories of the days when Paul and Sheila were children, laughing at some, saddened by others. Pete came to understand that he still thought of Sheila as a little girl, incapable of adult emotions or understanding. He stared at her, seeing for the first time the beautiful woman she'd become. He saw, too, that her failures were honest ones, resulting from her desperate attempts to please him. The fault lay with him; the failures were as much his as hers. The patterns that had taken years to establish would not change overnight, but Pete resolved in that moment to do anything in his power to help his child believe in herself. Silently, he thanked God that he'd been given another chance.

He further resolved that he'd do his best to share his thoughts with Sheila. It was too late to do that with Merrie, but perhaps he could make up for it by building a happy relationship with their daughter. As for Sheila, she made up her mind that she'd try to learn from her father. She hadn't done very well on her own, after all. Maybe it was time to stop resisting the only truly positive influence in her life.

As the end of February approached, the mid-point in the time frame for removal of American troops from Vietnam in conjunction with the repatriation of American prisoners of war, the lists containing the names of the next group were anticipated. On February 26th everyone was shocked by the newspaper headline" "North Vietnam Halts Prisoner Release." The article that followed told that the expected lists had not been delivered and that there would be no prisoner release the next day. A vague claim had been made by the North Vietnamese that they were waiting for an exact time and number of men to be reported by Hanoi.

Crowds of local residents hurled rocks at North Vietnamese officers in Da Nang and Hue. On the 27th, a spokesman for the North Vietnamese delegation announced that there would be no further release of prisoners until three points had been honored.

The first point called for strict application of the cease-fire, the second required a simultaneous return of civilian and military prisoners, and a third demanded the guarantee of improved working conditions for the four-party Joint Military Commission. The reference to improved working conditions was followed by claims of harassment and lack of security, the inference being that the United States showed 'bad faith' and was only interested in getting prisoners back.

On the 28th, the United States pressed its demand for immediate release of prisoners and told the North Vietnamese that missile sites below the demilitarized zone must be dismantled or they would face whatever action Washington deemed appropriate, hinting that a resumption of force might be considered appropriate action. The Americans specified that the release of prisoners was an unconditional obligation and must be carried out at a rate no slower than that of U.S. troop withdrawal. Since over one half of the American forces had been withdrawn, the corresponding number of prisoners must be released.

For Julie Schaefer, each day seemed to be at least double its normal length as she awaited further word on her husband. Finally, on the first of March, Captain Millikin phoned to tell her that Jack's name was on the list of those scheduled to be released the following day. On Friday, the second of March, she and Sarah scanned the printed newspaper lists again. Fear and anxiety gave way to joy and exultation when they found his name among those who would be coming home.

Laughing and crying at the same time, they were making so much noise that they failed to notice little Sandy had wandered into the room.

"The champagne!" they cried in unison. They whirled to go to the kitchen, skipping a few steps before they saw Sandy in the archway to the hall, her small mouth quivering.

"Why are you crying, Mommy?" she inquired tremulously.

"Oh, Sandy," Julie exclaimed, "Mommy isn't crying because she's sad, she's crying because she's so happy!"

"Cry for happy?" Sandy asked, puzzled.

Julie scooped her up and whirled her around in circles, hugging her tightly until at last the startled little girl began to squirm.

"Daddy's coming home! He's really coming home," Julie told her, putting her down gently. Sandy stood staring at her mother, then went to the bookshelf where Jack's photo sat. She looked at the man in the picture, put her index finger to her chin in contemplation, then said, "I'd better draw a picture so I'll have a present for him when he gets here."

With that, she scampered back upstairs to her room, leaving Julie and Sarah dumbstruck. They looked at each other and burst into laughter again, heading for the kitchen to get the champagne.

Confusion continued in the second phase of Operation Homecoming as the North Vietnamese delayed another day for unknown reasons. On Saturday afternoon, Julie received another call from Captain Millikin with the news that the first planeload carrying thirty-nine POW's would arrive in the Philippines around one thirty in the morning, Pacific Standard time, four thirty in the afternoon at Clark.

"The whole group should be back in time for dinner," he joked.

Too excited to sleep, Julie stayed up to watch for the arrival on television. The coverage was not as extensive as it had been upon the arrival of the first Americans to be released, but Julie was sure that she did not see Jack among the group that descended from the plane in the order of their capture. At three o'clock in the morning, she was on the phone to Captain Millikin.

"I don't know why he wasn't on any of the planes," Captain Millikin said miserably. "His name is definitely on the list, but for some reason he wasn't released."

Julie fought the panic that was rising inside her as the officer promised to cal her as soon as he knew anything more. The urge to call Clark Air Force Base herself was almost too strong to resist, but she forced herself to wait. She tried to read, but was unable to concentrate and gave up in favor of pacing the floor. When the phone rang, she jumped even though she'd been willing it to ring for hours.

"Yes? Hello?" she said tersely.

"I have more information now, Julie," Captain Millikin said immediately. "It seems there was another man whose mother is seriously ill in a hospital and the Vietnamese substituted him for Jack. We don't know, of course, but we have every reason to believe that Captain Schaefer will be coming back with the next group."

"Did Jack volunteer to stay behind?" Julie asked.

"We have no way of knowing whether it was an arbitrary decision on the part of the Vietnamese or whether he volunteered," the captain told her.

"But he will be coming home with the next group?" Julie wanted reassurance.

"We have no reason to believe otherwise," her assistance officer said gently. "To repeat myself, try not to worry. I'll stay on it and get back to you as soon as I can."

CHAPTER THIRTY SEVEN

It was another ten days before the next group of prisoners was released. They went by with maddening slowness. The media was full of photos of joyful reunions and some of the early returnees began to hold press conferences. Though any discussion of their treatment was forbidden, all of those who spoke agreed that they would have refused to leave had their release been arranged by any of the anti-war groups.

"It would have been dishonorable," said one.

Julie tried to keep busy in an effort to keep her mind from imagining any number of scenarios. She visualized Jack being dragged from the line of prisoners waiting to board the plane to freedom. She saw him lying helpless on a prison bunk, unable to join the others as they were led from their cells.

She dusted and vacuumed her apartment until there wasn't a possibility of a dust bunny anywhere, then she polished silver, took books from the shelves and cleaned each one before putting them back. When there was nothing left for her to clean, she called Sarah.

"I may lose my mind before Jack gets home," she said desperately. "I don't want to leave home in case the phone rings, and I can't bear another minute of confinement!"

"I think Pete and Sheila may feel a little housebound, too," Sarah said thoughtfully. "Why don't I do some grocery shopping while you call them and we'll all have a picnic in your living room?"

Pete accepted the invitation gratefully after consulting with Sheila and it wasn't long before the four of them were gathered at Julie's. Pete didn't have the same fear of being away from the phone that Julie had, as there was little hope that Paul would be on any lists that might be forthcoming. And in his capacity as a retired military officer, he had exhausted all the sources of information available to him. He wanted to help Julie in some way, but knew it was not likely he would be given any information that she didn't already have.

Conversation was a little stilted at first, but Julie put the rest of them at ease by thanking them for being there and telling them that there wasn't much they could say that she hadn't already thought of anyway, so please feel they could speak freely. It was Sheila who made them all laugh by suggesting that she was getting pretty good in the kitchen and that if they'd like to talk about her, she'd be happy to disappear for awhile. The smile on her face and the twinkle in her eyes told them that she meant it in fun. It was her way of saying that she knew how badly she'd behaved in the past.

"If my old Army buddies could see me now, they'd never believe it! Three beautiful women – maybe we should alert the media." Pete said jokingly.

"What's the latest on the handsome Frenchman?" Sheila asked, looking at Sarah.

"He's a little impatient," Sarah admitted, "but he knows it won't be long. I've sent all the boxes on ahead and the furniture goes on the first of May. Then my ship leaves a few days later. I'm not sure what I'll do if all of this hasn't been resolved by then." She waved a hand vaguely in the air and they knew that she was referring to the returning prisoners.

"Are you happy, Sarah?" Pete asked affectionately.

Her eyes glistened as she answered. "I won't deny that I'm a little apprehensive about making such a major change in my life and I'm sure you all know how much I hate to leave you, but yes, I do love John and I am looking forward to being his wife."

"I should think you'd be flying rather than sailing," Sheila commented.

"I could have. But I'll have a lot of baggage that will be easier to take by ship and we decided that since I can't have all of you with me, we'd do without his family as well and get married in Ville Franche. The ship anchors just off shore from there and we plan to spend our honeymoon at a little inn nearby. Besides, I wanted to be alone for a few days to rest rather than be exhausted from traveling before the wedding."

"It sounds so romantic," Julie said dreamily. "Maybe Jack and I can do something like that and then come to visit you. When he's well enough to travel, of course."

"Didn't you hate to leave your job, Sarah?" Sheila inquired. "To somebody like me who's never had a really meaningful job, I'd think it would be hard to give up such a successful career."

"I'm not giving up my career, Sheila. Once we're settled in Paris, John wants me to work with him in his company, essentially doing pretty much the same thing I did here. He even wants to give me a title – Vice President!" She paused, then frowned slightly before continuing, "I do want to be here to see this through to the end, though. I know I'm not technically a family member, but I feel as though I am. I've felt an attachment to Paul from the first moment I saw his picture in the paper." She glanced at Julie.

"I think maybe Merrie and I felt the same way about you, Sarah," Pete said. "Perhaps that's why we thought of you as our 'other' daughter. We sensed something that associated you with Paul from the beginning. We never talked about it, but in retrospect, I know we both felt it."

"Would you think I was crazy if I told you that I think Paul and I have known each other in previous lives?" Sarah asked tentatively. She had no intention of telling the whole story, but felt that for some reason she wanted Pete to know how deeply she cared.

"Previous lives?" he asked in surprise. "I've never given that sort of thing any thought at all." He stopped speaking abruptly, frowning, then went on, "But you're a sensible girl and I suppose there's no proof that it couldn't have happened."

"I've never thought about that either," Sheila said, "but that would explain why you're so close to the family. I feel pretty silly about my jealousy now. I was so wrapped up in myself that I thought you were taking my place. Were you in love with Paul in another life?" Her eyes narrowed slightly and she looked closely at Sarah. "Are you in love with him now?"

"Sheila!" Pete exclaimed. "What a thing to say!"

"I don't mean to stir up any trouble, Daddy. I just seemed to sense it all of a sudden."

"It's all right, Pete," Sarah said. "She's right in a way."

"I wonder if we've all known the people in our lives in one lifetime after another," Julie mused. "That would explain why we're drawn to some people and why you sometimes have that feeling of 'déjà vu.' Maybe we *have* been here before, known people before."

"Do you think you may have known Jack before?" Sheila asked.

"I don't know," Julie replied. "I knew that Sarah felt that she's known Paul, but I have no idea whether I've had other lives. *This* one has been difficult enough lately."

"I guess if you'd heard anything more about Jack today, you'd have told us," Pete said, a little glad to change the subject.

"No further news. Captain Millikin has called each morning, but he hasn't anything new to report. We still don't know if the man they substituted for Jack was released earlier than they meant to release him or if Jack volunteered to let him go in his place or what. The next lists should be coming out soon."

"Those lists have certainly turned our lives inside out, haven't they?" Pete remarked.

"If there was some way of knowing for sure, it would be so much easier to bear," Julie said. "It's the not knowing, the waiting, the hoping that's tearing me apart."

They all nodded their heads in agreement. Later, after Pete and Sheila had left, Sarah indicated that she intended to spend the night with Julie so that she wouldn't be alone, unless for some reason she wanted to be alone. Dr. Summerhill had driven down to get Sandy earlier to spare Julie the pain of telling the little girl that her daddy might not be coming after all. He had tried to defend Julie's mother by saying that she only wanted the best for her daughter and for Julie to try not to be too hard on her.

"Why do you suppose she's so determined to be nasty about Jack?" Julie wondered. "He didn't go to Yale, but he did graduate from Annapolis and he *is* an officer in the United States Marine Corps. I think his major crime is that he's not a doctor like my father. She's so shallow," she finished ruefully.

"You have to remember that her generation grew up believing that a woman's place is behind her man," Sarah remarked. "It was okay to be educated, but their ultimate responsibility in life was to maintain a proper home for their husbands."

"No, their ultimate responsibility was to marry well in the first place! And then boss everybody around and make life generally miserable!" Julie said bitterly.

"Julie, try not to think about your mother. It just makes you unhappy and you have enough to worry about now without adding another problem."

"What would I do without you, Sarah? You've stood by me through so much. Both you and Merrie were there when I really needed somebody. I always thought that I was so strong, but that was because I'd been brought up to believe that I was somehow better than most people and therefore there wasn't anything I couldn't handle. But I've discovered a lot about myself in the past four years. I thought Jack and I were indestructible, that we were charmed by life. Then he was gone and if it hadn't been for you, I'd be dead now. I can't tell you how much you mean to me."

"You've been the closest friend I've ever had, Julie. I've had a lot of acquaintances, people who were there to play tennis with or who belonged to a club I did, or something, but I've never been close friends with another woman. And you've understood and not judged me through all this past life stuff, too. Actually, I've always preferred to be with men. I thought most women were shallow, but you and Merrie proved that theory to be wrong. It's funny, but even Sheila is showing promise. There was a time when I wouldn't have bothered with her at all. I've found a richness in life that I didn't know existed." Sarah raised her glass for a toast to friendship.

The next morning Captain Millikin phoned to say that the official lists for the next prisoner release had been presented to government representatives and that Jack's name did not appear on them. He was quick to add that they had every reason to believe that he might be coming anyway since his name had appeared on the previous list. Once again, the first plane carrying returnees was due to land at Clark Air Force Base at one o'clock in the morning Pacific Standard Time.

Again, Sarah stayed with Julie through the night. Another hundred and eight American servicemen deplaned, looking tired, but happy. Jack Schaefer was not among them. His wife broke down and sobbed. How could this be happening? Sarah tried to reassure her that there would still be another group coming at the end of the month, but she was losing hope as well.

"*Why* can't the American government or the Marine Corps or *somebody* do something?" Julie wailed. "This is supposed to be the greatest nation in the world and they can't even keep track of one man! They *know* he's alive and being held over there; why don't they *demand* that he be released?"

"I suppose they don't want to jeopardize the return of the men still there, Julie. I'm sure they'll make strong protests when they're sure they won't endanger the other men," Sarah said far more positively than she really felt.

"What if they're too late?" Julie whispered.

"You can't think that, Julie. You can't let go of hope."

On March 27th, it was announced that the impasses had been broken and that all captives were due out by Thursday. The communists had agreed to give in to American demands that prisoners being held in Laos would be added to the group remaining, and one hundred forty eight men would be freed. The final exchange would take place over a period of four days, coinciding with withdrawal of the last American troops from Vietnam.

On Thursday, headlines read: "U.S. Ends War Role in Vietnam Today." There were only sixty-seven prisoners left. Operation Homecoming was nearly complete.

Julie Schaefer sat in stunned silence as Captain Millikin broke down while telling her by phone that Jack had not been on the last planeload into Clark. He had not slept in four days as he made persistent contacts in an effort to ascertain Captain Schaefer's whereabouts and safety and could not believe that he had failed.

By Saturday, March 31st, the newspaper headlines revealed that livestock prices had risen nine percent in the past month, and the lead article told that President Nixon was being criticized for his failure to set price controls until it was too late. There was almost nothing on the returning Americans.

On Sunday, April 1st, actress Jane Fonda called former prisoners hypocrites and liars, saying that history would judge them severely. She continued by saying that the condition of the returning prisoners should speak for itself as proof that they had not been tortured and that one of the only ways that the United States could redeem itself for what it had done there was not to hail the pilots as heroes.

Three days later the joint military team scheduled to track down Americans missing in Vietnam held its first meeting, but the North Vietnamese said they would not be ready to get down to business until their delegation chief arrived from Hanoi. Another three days after that, a brigadier general said that his torturers probably could have forced him to shoot his own mother. Realizing that he was not as tough as he'd thought may have been the hardest thing for him to accept.

The student organization that began support for the prisoners in 1969 reported that five million POW bracelets had been distributed and that in 1972 alone, nineteen million brochures and fourteen million bumper stickers had been distributed. A San Diego based group launched a campaign to remind the American public that at least 1,300 servicemen were still listed as missing in action. California Governor Ronald Reagan served chicken, roast beef and champagne to twenty-six former POW's.

On Sunday, April 22nd, a newspaper editorial began its second paragraph with "Our prisoners are home..." The same day, columnist William F. Buckley reported that when questioned by former POW's, the American general who had accompanied Jane Fonda to Vietnam said that everything he did, he did in the cause of peace.

In May, President Nixon invited five hundred eighty-seven former prisoners and their wives to dinner at the White House. The United States reclassified two hundred MIA's to 'killed in action.' Dead.

Julie Schaefer wondered if she should plan a memorial service for her husband. Pete Winslow rejected the idea. Sarah had postponed her voyage to the south of France and wondered how she could possibly leave at all. Sheila Donnelly said nothing.

CHAPTER THIRTY EIGHT

Grief would have been easier to bear. There was no hero home from the war to cherish and nurture and there was no body to bury. The dream had been shattered. As long as there was hope, there was purpose, even a lamentable purpose such as theirs. There had been reason to pull together, to *be* together. Now they were alone with their sorrow, the nobility of the cause lost to them. They wanted to rejoice with those who had seen the return of loved ones, but were unable to celebrate as they wondered where to go from here.

They had no idea what to say to each other and so avoided the necessity of trying by pretending a busy-ness that did not really exist. Julie decided to look for a job and enrolled Sandy in a nursery school, explaining as briefly as she could that Daddy had been delayed in coming home again. Since Sandy was accustomed to that explanation, she accepted it and put away the picture she'd drawn, saving it for the time when it might be needed.

Sheila decided to go back to school. There was a junior college nearby that offered a variety of classes, so she began with some entry-level courses in history and literature. She did her best to be a cheerful companion to Pete, planning outings to the theatre or an occasional lecture at the college. Pete accompanied her without complaint, but she knew that he was aching and hollow inside. Sarah made plans to leave for France, but her heart was heavy and though she tried to sound enthusiastic when she spoke with John on the phone, it was difficult. In the last days of Operation Homecoming, she had felt necessary and useful to her friends, but now had nothing to keep her busy. The furniture had been shipped; she had given up her apartment and now occupied a room at the Davidson Hotel where she'd been employed when it all started. Julie had offered to share her home, but Sarah knew that being together would be a strain on both of them.

On the night before she was to leave for New York, the four of them got together for a farewell dinner that was pleasant, but the underlying sorrow was cause for making it an early evening. Sarah waved goodbye amid promises that they would remember each other and keep in touch.

As she turned out the light and settled back against the pillows on the bed, she recalled the swan that had carried her with Paul to a castle in the sky. They had been so happy in their eagerness to tumble among the flowers that surrounded the castle, blithely passing by the rooms inside. Turning onto her side, she hugged a pillow and drifted into a drowsy reflection of that magnificent journey.

The white swan appeared, poised to carry her through the night to the mansion that housed reminders of days long gone. She slipped onto his feathery back, stroking his slender neck and they soared upward. How peaceful, how safe it was as they ascended slowly and she watched the lights of the cities below growing smaller before they plunged into the fleecy whiteness of a cloud and the castle appeared ahead.

The mammoth bird settled gently to the ground beside the entrance and she slid from his back. As she tugged open the heavy door, she glanced back to see that the swan had settled down on the ground and tucked his head under a wing, prepared to wait while she explored the chambers within.

Entering the grand foyer, Sarah looked around at the closed doors that led from it. She approached the nearest one and opened it cautiously, stepping into the room. She was transported immediately to the seventeenth century world of Ikkyu and Yoshiko, but this time as an observer rather than a participant. She watched as they ate their evening meal in silence and tranquility. Glancing around, she was startled to see the stone statue of Kuan Yin, the goddess of mercy that she had so recently purchased in Los Angeles. So that was why she'd been so drawn to it! It represented a time when she and Paul had been happy together, a compassionate tie to the past. She hovered quietly for a time, then left to seek out the treasures she might find elsewhere.

The next door led to Marguerite's cozy salon. Tonio was seated at the piano, lost in the melody he was creating and Sarah knew that he and Marguerite had many years of happiness together in that life. Another period of time when her spirit had been joyous and secure with the man who was her soulmate. It occurred to her that the piano that Sarah Fremont loved had also figured importantly in the lives of Tonio and Marguerite.

Moving on, she found the room that led her into the world of Emile, Lucien and Rosella. Startled to see Emile alone in a sparsely furnished room, she crept in apprehensively. He was standing before an easel, paint brush in hand, working furiously on a canvas she recognized instantly. It was the painting that hung above her fireplace, a jumble of flowers in shades of red that inspired a variety of emotions.

As she watched, she noticed the tears that slid down his cheeks and heard him whispering, "Rosella, Rosella, Rosella," over and over again. There were bars on the window of the tiny room and she understood that Emile had lived out the balance of his life in an institution, mourning the love he had lost. All animosity evaporated as she accepted John's devotion to her in their present incarnation without reservation.

Returning to the foyer, she gazed at the wide staircase leading to more doors above. She paused, considering whether or not she wanted to go up and perhaps find further evidence of other incarnations. Deciding that she had seen and remembered all that was necessary for her to continue her life as Sarah Fremont, she left the castle to mount the waiting swan for the return trip to the San Francisco peninsula.

As she left the splendid bird, she wondered if she'd ever again feel his downy feathers or soar through the night on his soft back. Probably not. His mission is complete. She slept soundly, waking refreshed and happy the following morning, eager to be on her way to John St. James.

The following week she stood at the rail of the luxury liner, watching the wake created as the ship moved slowly on its course toward the south of France. The weather was mild and a full moon shone on the water in a silvery streak a little to her right, lighting up the otherwise dark sea.

She was finally on her way. Pete, Julie and Sheila had surprised her at the San Francisco airport, hoping to make her departure a joyous one. Though the last goodbye had been tearful, they were happy tears, full of good wishes. Then her Aunt Charlotte had been at the dock in New York to see her off, armed with mountains of confetti and a basket of presents that included everything from books to read on the ship to filmy lingerie for her honeymoon. Memories of recent weeks had already begun to fade as her spirits rose in anticipation.

One last task remained. The worn copper bracelet with Paul's name inscribed on it was a constant reminder of the past and she had decided it was best to dispose of it. It couldn't be put away in a drawer - she'd always know it was there and be tempted to reminisce. To throw it in the trash would be unthinkable. The solution had come to her as the ship moved across the Atlantic Ocean. She would toss it into the Mediterranean Sea, a final burial.

She'd spent most of the day alone, avoiding other passengers. Standing by the rail, she moved the bracelet up and down her arm. It was dented along one side and discolored from the years of wear, never having been off her wrist. Had it really been years, she wondered.

Closing her eyes, she pressed her eyelids tightly to her cheeks. Paul's image appeared in her mind and she pulled the photograph of him with John beside the old Chevy from her purse. His deep blue eyes, the slow smile, his dark blonde, unruly hair – the honey-colored jungle cat. She smiled at the picture, recalling the passion she had shared with both men.

Watching the waves from the stern of the ship, she felt her chest tighten as she thought back to the day when she first saw the article in the paper about Paul's disappearance in Vietnam. She began to hum softly, "the night is like a lovely tune…" The song made her feel his presence even now, as though he were close enough to touch. Strains of a Schubert concerto wafted from the ship's main lounge and she turned from the rail to listen.

The concerto made her think of the lovely and fragile Merrie, whose inner strength sustained her until, like the fragrance in a perfume bottle, it finally ran out. Sarah's eyes grew moist, remembering how they had giggled over the lemons in their refrigerators – only the insides remained, the peels having been stripped away for Pete Winslow martinis.

Dear, sweet Pete, who kept his feelings bottled up inside for so long that it had been almost impossible to share them with his daughter. But he was more than just trying now and it seemed to be working for both of them. Sheila had learned to watch and listen before she jumped into a situation and made errors in judgement that caused unnecessary suffering. She was softer now, quieter, and seeing Pete's face beam as he looked at her was more than enough reward for Sarah's efforts to bring them together again. Seeing Sheila at the airport, she'd thought how much she was beginning to resemble Merrie.

Her friends. Julie's face had changed as well, but due to the inner misery she would carry for years to come rather than the serenity that Sheila had finally found. Julie's smile was brittle and forced and though she did her best to hide the anguish that tormented her, it was evident. While Pete had had no concrete reason to believe that his son was alive, Julie knew that Jack Schaefer had been left behind during Operation Homecoming. That certainty gnawed at her every day of her life and there was very little she could do to alleviate the pain.

Sarah stared at the photograph she held. What if Paul had come home? Would he have known her? Would he look like he did when that picture was taken or would he be irrevocably changed by his confinement in a Vietnamese prison camp? What had happened to him after her dream of seeing him retreating into the light? How had he died? Would they find each other again in another lifetime and finally live out their destiny together?

She straightened. She had accepted the fact that they were not to be together in this lifetime and now she must stop thinking about him. She must let him go if she were to find happiness with John. Paul would remain in that corner of her heart, the cave that existed so far down inside. Merrie would be there, too. Would the day ever come when she could get through a whole day without thinking of them?

It was growing chilly, the breeze whipping her skirt around her and the hour was growing late. It was well after midnight. The sounds of music and partying from the ship's bars had begun to diminish, but she wasn't quite ready yet. She walked up one deck to the casino and ordered a bottle of white wine with a glass to take back to her post by the rail.

As she returned, she heard the sounds of a crew party coming from below. Their music was getting louder as the night wore on into morning, while the more subdued sounds from the upper decks faded. Sarah sipped the wine and thought what a beautiful night it was, one she knew she'd remember always. The sadness that hovered in her heart began to slip away, replaced by a feeling of serenity.

She looked up and noted the appearance of a few white clouds in the sky, rising from a misty sea into peaks that reminded her of the fog shrouded mountains of Japan so long ago, and of Ikkyu, her courageous samurai. She closed her eyes and let her imagination recall the simple little house where Yoshiko had prepared tea for her lover. She could almost feel his arms around her as they lay on the soft futons where they had spent so many joyous nights. Flicking her tongue over her lips at the memory of feathery kisses, she shuddered with pleasure.

She opened her eyes slowly, the quiet lapping of the sea against the ship comforting. She wrapped her arms around herself as the breeze caused her to shiver. Suddenly she was once again in Marguerite's cozy parlor overlooking the cobbled streets of Milano, the sound of Tonio's music as his fingers flew over the keys on the piano filling the room.

Her fingers stroked her throat as the remembrance filled her with warmth. How could she have been so frightened by those experiences at first? Her heart skipped a beat as the wineglass fell from her hand, landing on the deck with a sound not unlike that of a bullet being fired from a gun. She picked it up, grateful that it had not broken, and refilled it from the nearly empty bottle. Her hand shook slightly and she took several deep breaths to calm her rapidly beating heart. The recollection of that moment before she fell to the ground as Emile's bullet pierced her chest made her gasp.

It was still hard to believe that John St. James, the gentle and understanding man she intended to marry, could have been the volatile Emile in that life nearly a hundred years earlier. The image of Lucien approaching the house she had shared with Emile swam before Sarah's eyes. Lucien had been so like Paul, she realized. His graceful stride, the sad, liquid eyes that reflected the same sensuality that exuded from Paul's deep blue ones. It occurred to her that perhaps it was because Lucien's life had ended so abruptly at nearly the same age that Paul would be, that he had come back with much the same physical appearance. Had fate interfered in that life and this life? Made him look the same so she would be sure to recognize him?

Suddenly impatient with herself, she murmured aloud, "Oh stop all this rehashing and get on with it!" So many lives altered by what was not even considered a real war. How little she had known of what was to come; how naïve she'd been to believe that she could somehow bring about a happy ending; how futile was the effort to 'keep the home fires burning.'

It had seemed so noble and been so useless in the end. No, that was not strictly true. They had helped effect the return of many American servicemen, so it hadn't been in vain. Sarah had been standing at the rail near the stern of the ship for hours. It was time to say goodbye to the past and look forward to the future.

John St. James paced impatiently on the dock at Ville Franche. The boatman he'd hired to take him out to the ship that carried Sarah toward southern France seemed to be taking forever to ready the boat. He was grumbling audibly at being roused from his bed in the middle of the night, but the money the well-dressed man had offered for the journey made his greedy eyes gleam.

The ship was still several hours from the Mediterranean village, moving at a snail's pace so that it would arrive at dawn. John was eager to see his bride. He had made arrangements for the marriage ceremony to take place late that afternoon in the tiny stone chapel on the hill overlooking the sea. He had also arranged for them to spend two weeks alone in a romantic little inn that had bougainvillea climbing its exterior walls, covering them with colorful blossoms. Then they would go on to Monaco where they'd spend a few days in the glittering world of the Hotel de Paris and the famous casino across the street prior to their return to Paris. They would reside in a suite at the St. James Hotel until their apartment was ready to occupy.

Finally the boatman motioned to John that he could board, and they would begin the journey out to sea. He climbed aboard, rubbing his hands together in anticipation. He'd be with his beloved Sarah in a matter of hours.

The boat was an old one, used mostly for taking tourists on short fishing expeditions or sightseeing. The deck showed signs of wear, but it was clean and apparently seaworthy. Its lack of speed threatened to drive John a little mad as he decided he might well be able to swim to the ship faster than this boat was going. He contained his agitation as best he could, however, and stared into the night, trying to penetrate the darkness for some sign that he was nearing his destination.

The boatman radioed the ship to advise the captain of their approach, requesting a ladder to take on a passenger. It was nearly three hours before the gleaming white ship came into view and a ship's officer radioed back that they had the boat in sight.

John climbed the ladder from the small boat to the deck of the cruise ship, oblivious to any possible danger. He explained to the officer who greeted him why he was there and appreciated the understanding grin that he received as he finished the story. Checking the passenger list, the officer directed him to Sarah Fremont's cabin and John hurried off.

Sarah removed the bracelet from her wrist and stood holding it, rubbing the name and date inscribed on it as though perhaps some last minute revelation might be forthcoming. The moonlight remained and the sea was patient, waiting to claim what belonged to it. She kissed the bracelet softly, said, "Goodbye, Paul," and threw it in an arc into the shaft of moonlight. It vanished almost immediately from view.

She drained the wineglass and threw it into the water, then put the cork into the almost empty bottle and consigned it to the sea as well. As she turned from the rail, a warm gentle breeze wrapped itself around her shoulders, then drifted back to sea. She lifted her head to listen as a voice called out to her.

She couldn't make out the words at first, then was sure she heard someone call out, "Marguerite!" It seemed to be coming from somewhere off to her right. She hurried toward the sound. As she followed it, the voice moved farther away, but she heard it again, "Marguerite!"

"Tonio?" she called out. "Tonio, where are you?" Then from the other side of the ship another voice called out, "Yoshiko!"

She whirled again, running toward the sound. Peering into the darkness that enveloped that side of the ship, she was sure she saw the colorful robes of a samurai disappearing into the horizon.

"Ikkyu? Is that you? Oh please, Ikkyu, answer me!" The only sound she heard in response to her plea was the tinkling of a temple bell far off in the distance.

Behind her, Sarah felt rather than heard the presence of someone else. Spinning around, she searched the shadows on the deck for a sign of someone and was startled to hear a gentle voice much closer, no more than an arm's length away.

"Rosella, don't be afraid. Come with me, Rosella," the voice commanded. She reached out, sure that it was Lucien. She stumbled and nearly fell as she bumped into a deck chair. Regaining her balance, she went on until she was once again at the rail above the sparkling moonlight. Suddenly, she heard several voices calling to her from somewhere beyond the moonlight.

"Marguerite!"

"Yoshiko!"

"Rosella!"

"Yes, yes, I'm coming," Sarah cried, too anxious to find the source of the voices to be afraid. She put one foot up on the lowest rail, catching her heel against the edge. She hardly noticed as her shoe fell into the water below.

John had searched nearly everywhere on the ship for Sarah. The last of the gamblers had left the casino and a chain-link gate barred entry to it. Only a few insomniacs had occupied the tiny piano bar and he had begun a systematic search of the outside decks, starting from the top. He had just rounded the large, fin-shaped smokestack when he caught sight of a movement in the stern on the deck below.

"Sarah?" he called out, but she didn't hear him. He stopped in shock when he realized that she was climbing the rail.

"Sarah!" he shouted.

She heard only the cacophony of voices that called to her. As she threw one leg over the rail, she heard Paul Winslow and saw his face in the moonlight.

"Paul!" she cried out to him. "I knew you were there somewhere, Paul! I knew I'd find you again."

"Marguerite, hurry!"

"Yoshiko, where are you?"

"Rosella, I need you!"

The last voice she heard as she slipped over the rail and into the dark water below was an agonized scream.

"Sarah! Sarah, no!"

EPILOGUE – 1979

The sky was blue with clean white fluffy clouds.

"Hard to believe it was grey and raining all day yesterday," Julia Schaefer said. "It should be grey today. How can the trees be so green, so full of life and promise, when Jack is so dead?'

Her attention returned to the flag draped coffin and she had a sudden wild urge to rush to it, tear it open and make sure that it was really Jack. But she knew that all she'd find inside was bones. The only proof they'd given her was Jack's I.D. tags, and the torn photograph that had once been of the two of them together. The silver cigarette lighter inscribed, "From each danger keep him free and send me safe my Somebody' had vanished, of course.

She held the book of Robert Burns' poetry in her hand. Inside was the rose that had been pressed there nearly eleven years before, and the photograph, taped together again, the two halves reunited. She wondered how the picture had survived at all and resisted the urge to believe that it was all a horrible mistake and the body in the coffin was not Jack at all. Even after all these years, a tiny corner of her heart wanted to believe that there would be another planeload of Americans coming home, and this time Jack would be on it.

He'd be thin, but his arms would close around her and all the lonely years would be a terrible dream. She sighed, knowing it wouldn't happen and that she had to accept his death. The government scientists had told her there was no doubt that it was Jack. They had compared dental charts and bone structure, they said. She wondered just how many bones they had to work with.

Realizing that the chaplain in his full dress uniform was standing in front of her, Julie reached out to accept the neatly folded flag. Her daughter, Sandy, crumpled visibly at the sight. Sandy was nearly eleven years old now and would never know her father.

Pete Winslow's arm went around Julie and she turned to smile at him. He had aged significantly. Sarah Fremont death had been a blow that nearly crushed him. They had all been shocked at the news that she had fallen overboard on the eve of her wedding to John St. James. John had made use of every resource he could manipulate, but Sarah's body had never been found.

Sheila Donnelly had gone back to Chicago briefly to sell her condominium there and pack her things in preparation for a permanent move to San Francisco. Always more of a city girl, Sheila now lived in a Russian Hill apartment and was dating, of all things, a doctor. Julie smiled ruefully at the irony. Her mother would have given anything to see Julie married to a successful doctor. Sheila and Pete had grown very close over the past six years and Sheila had definitely become a younger image of Merrie.

People were beginning to drift quietly away from the gravesite, some stopping to grasp Julie's hand or her arm in mute understanding. Taking the faded rose from the book, Julie placed it gently on the coffin and turned to walk away. She had mixed emotions. The indecision and the waiting was over. The hope was gone, but now she must look forward, make plans further ahead than the next month if she chose to do so.

I can move to another town, get a new job, become a *person* again, she thought. Not just a POW wife, a part of the whole. She felt a little guilty, remembering the hope they had all felt even when it seemed hopeless. The companionship and closeness, the shared anger and frustration of the wives, mothers, fathers, brothers and sisters, the security of being together in silent comfort, had ended.

The world might expand for Julie Schaefer, but along with broadening horizons would come a new kind of loneliness.

THE END
SEND ME SAFE MY SOMEBODY

AUTHOR'S NOTE

While the characters and the story in Send Me Safe My Somebody are entirely a product of the author's imagination, the bonding of the families of Americans missing or captured in Vietnam was very real, as was the return of the American prisoners of war. The efforts to obtain an accounting of the estimated 2,500 men who remained missing continued for many years after the final withdrawal of American personnel from Saigon in 1975, and for some it continues to this day. The status of all of the men who did not come home was eventually changed from MIA (missing in action) to KIA (killed in action) by the U. S. government.

A U. S. Senate committee, headed by Senator John Kerry and Senator Bob Smith, visited Vietnam in the late 1970's and concluded that there were no Americans left alive and being held against their will in Vietnam.

Novelist Geri Bennett began writing for publication when she was invited to provide a case study to be used in a marketing textbook at the University of Hawaii. After time off for a career in hotel management, she published a book based upon the diaries of the men who served aboard six American submarines in the Pacific during WWII. She is currently working on two more novels. Though she considers San Francisco her home, she currently resides in Tennessee.

DRINKING SAKE ALL ALONE
By Geri Bennett

"No blossoms and no moon,
And he is drinking sake all alone."
Matsuo Basho
1644 – 1694

Sunao Tokumura, descendent of an old and honorable samurai family, has risen to the powerful post of Vice Minister in the Japanese Ministry of International Trade and Industry. Unable to forget the tears of shame shed by his father as Japan surrendered in 1945, Tokumura has vowed vengeance against America.

Together with aging billionaire industrialist, Satoshi Yoshida, he has devised a scheme to bring about the economic destruction of the country they both loathe. Yoshida's hatred stems from his conviction and subsequent imprisonment as a war criminal because of his outspoken support for America's enemies. His money and influence extend from the dark corners inhabited by the yakusa (Japanese mafia) to a former president of the United States, and he has discovered a secret that makes it possible for him to blackmail the current president.

Raised in sheltered comfort, Maggie Davidson Stuart was unable to defy her father's objections to her Japanese suitor and married Charles Stuart, the young banker considered to be of proper background. When her father dies suddenly and Charles leaves her for his male lover, Maggie assumes leadership of the prestigious Davidson Hotel Group, the family owned company.

Stan Mitsunari, rejected as unsuitable by Maggie's parents, has returned to his homeland bitter and angry. Now editor of Nihon Kenzai, the Japanese financial newspaper, Stan becomes an unsuspecting pawn in the plot.

As the story develops, America is thrown into chaos by labor strikes, a treasury bond boycott, the sabotaging of an innovative computer storage system, and the American version of Japanese yakusa. Will the evil plot be discovered in time to save the country? Will Stan Mitsunari be able to stop the madness? Will his knowledge lead him back to Maggie?

WATCH FOR <u>DRINKING SAKE ALL ALONE</u>

SCHEDULED TO BE RELEASED IN LATE SUMMER 2011